# "You're Sending Out a Member of the Tri-Galactic Intelligence Service to Catch a Bloody Poisoner?"

"You should be delighted, Mr. Jones. For once you have an assignment that a child could handle. No danger. No messy counter-espionage. Just an ordinary garden-variety poisoner. You will have luxurious quarters, your every wish granted, and you should be back here in about ten weeks, give or take a week or two. Why are you bitching? Perhaps you cannot bear to be separated from your charming Tzana Kai even so briefly?"

Coyote snorted into his beard, and the Fish smiled.

"Is it an ego problem then, Mr. Jones?" he cooed. "Perhaps you feel that an agent of your stature should not have to stoop to dealing with such a minute problem? . . . Look on it as a kind of vacation, like a summer by the sea, all expenses paid."

Coyote left as abruptly as he could, leaving the Fish snickering at his deck. He could have turned the assignment down, of course; since it was not a matter of intergalactic security he was not obligated to take it.

But he had a reason. He had never, not once in his entire life, seen a subjugated woman.

Curiosity took Coyote lots of places.

# SUZETTE HADEN ELGIN

# COMMUNIPATH WORLDS

PUBLISHED BY POCKET BOOKS·NEW YORK

Another *Original* publication of POCKET BOOKS

POCKET BOOKS, a Simon & Schuster division of
GULF & WESTERN CORPORATION
1230 Avenue of the Americas, New York, N.Y. 10020

# BOOK I

## The Communipaths

# CHAPTER ONE

I AM TESSA, and this is Gentle Thursday. Usually on Gentle Thursday there is so much to do that I have no time for writing; but today is very different because this morning they came and took Anne-Charlotte's baby away. I am sorry they took the baby, because I loved it very much. And of course with Anne-Charlotte so unhappy no one can do anything but sit and try to bear it.

Patrick suggested that since I am younger and thus am less affected by Anne-Charlotte it would be a good thing if I would try to write it all out—how it happened, I mean—and then perhaps we could all read it over, what I wrote, and see if there was anything we could do. (I'm sure there isn't; the laws are very definite about babies like Anne-Charlotte's.) But Patrick thought it would be good for me, and so he tried to give me a strong motivation to keep at it. He doesn't need to do that anymore, not since I've turned ten, but it seems to be a habit he can't break.

At any rate, I'm going to try to write it all down, just as it happened, simply to please Patrick. And I must do it quickly, since I've only the Log with its little bits and scraps and notes to remind me, and Anne-Charlotte is very rapidly ruining the way I remember it with swords and flames and a sort of fan that folds and unfolds with a great slow dignity—and a lot of black, a great deal of black. Soon, if I'm not careful, between what she is doing and the attempts of the others to make her forget, I won't be able to remember it clearly enough to write about it.

I don't have much range yet, and that helps. I've come as far from the livingdomes as I'm allowed to go, and picked out a really big Anais cactus with a red parasol bloom that's big enough around to shade me perfectly, and I'm sitting here on the arm of the cactus with my feet propped up. It's far away enough that not much gets through except all that black from Anne-Charlotte, and that's only likely to make me go to sleep. Fortunately the Anais cactus is prickery to sit on, and that will keep me awake.

I loved that funny baby, I really did. I loved it as much as anyone. But I don't suppose that's the place to start, is it? The place to start would be to tell about us.

There are twenty-one of us now, a good number to be, with seven of us children, and we all live together at Chrysanthemum Bridge. We are Maklunites, and of course everyone knows about Maklunites, so I don't guess I have to explain about *that*. Or do I? Patrick said I was to pretend I was writing this for someone very far away, perhaps as far away as Saturn with its glowing rings (that's how Patrick put it), and I suppose it is possible that there might be someone on Saturn who does not know about Maklunites. On the other hand I don't want to be boring. . . . Let me see. What I must do, I guess, is put just enough about things like Maklunites and our names and what we eat and so on, and then scatter it along through the whole thing so there's never an awful lot in a clump. Then no one—this someone I am writing for, I mean—then this someone will not be tempted to skip around. I think I can manage to do that well enough.

Maklunites began on Earth, a very long time ago; I don't know just how long. And we weren't very popular there, of course, and so we moved, as far as we could go. And as more was learned about traveling through space we moved farther and farther, and now there are a lot of us through the galaxies. My group lives on the third of the Extreme Moons, the one called 34.922.107 on the star maps. That's an awkward name, "thirty-four-point-nine-two-two-point-one-oh-seven," when you want to tell somebody where you live, and so the people who came here first renamed it Iris.

They weren't Maklunites, those first people, but they were loving people,—a Mr. and Mrs. Alhafi Fez, from

New-York-Complex. Mrs. Fez was very fond of flowers and the flowers of Earth (for one thing ours can move around, and they sing, and I know the flowers of Earth don't do either of those things). It's a good thing the flower Mrs. Fez liked the most was an iris, I think. Imagine, if it had been one of those outlandish things I've read about in Patrick's big Panglish dictionary— just imagine living on a planet called Sweet Pea, or Bachelor's Button! Iris is bad enough, Patrick says, and he thinks this flower bit can be carried too far, particularly since it's become a tradition and all of the eleven settlements of Iris have names that are for flowers in one way or another. Patrick says it's getting sickening, and he thinks we ought to rename Chrysanthemum Bridge for a fish, or something, and he's probably right. I don't think it will happen though, because names just sort of grow on you, and our cluster has always been called Chrysanthemum Bridge.

Our livingdomes are beautiful, I think. Of course I've never been any farther than the next settlement and I haven't had much chance to compare it with anything, but I've seen a lot of pictures and threedies and I've never seen any reason to think the less of Chrysanthemum Bridge. In the very center is the ashram, with our altar, and I will tell more about that later. Then around that is our common room, like a ring, with our made-mantras painted over the doors so that they will be always before our eyes. (This is the first one: TO BE SELFISH IS TO DO HARM, AND TO DO HARM IS FORBIDDEN. This is the second one: THE VISIBLE MANIFESTATION OF LOVE IS RADIANCE. This is the third one: WHAT IS NOT LOVINGKINDNESS IS NOT PERMITTED HERE. This is the fourth one: THERE IS NO STERNER DISCIPLINE THAN JOY.)

When Anne-Charlotte had her baby they say she lay beneath the second made-mantra and never ceased to smile. And now they have taken the baby away, what will she do? The baby's father died before it was born, and Anne-Charlotte had promised him that she would save it, but surely she must have known she could not. When they came for it, sending four Fedrobots for just one little baby girl, eleven months old, Anne-Charlotte tried to kill it. I heard her, even though they tried to keep me away, and she was screaming that she would kill the baby before she would let them take it to the hell they had reserved for it. She lifted the baby high into the air to dash it against the wall. But Patrick went very swiftly and he took the baby before she could hurt it, and he handed it to the tall man who came with the Fedrobots, and they were gone while I was still hearing what Anne-Charlotte had screamed.

But I was telling about Chrysanthemum Bridge. At eight points around the common room there are doors, and leading from each door is a livingdome like the big central common roomdome. It's all made from the pale yellow clay of Iris, and from the air it looks like a flower with eight petals. Patrick says that's only an accident, because if it were intentional it would be horribly "cute," but it happens to be the most practical way to build a Maklunite cluster. There are people living in seven of our eight domes, and someday, if all of the children marry, we may have to add a second ring of living-domes around the outside. Then again, we might all move away, though I can't imagine living anywhere else myself.

They wanted Anne-Charlotte's baby to man a Com-munipath station on the Bucket. They were very stern with her about it. "That baby is a very valuable and delicate piece of property," they said, as if a human being could be property! Patrick's woman put her hands over my ears when the Fedrobot said that, but then she laughed at herself and took her hands away. How am I to learn if she does things like that? And so I heard it all. They have charged Anne-Charlotte with high trea-son against humankind, because it is a very grave crime to have a baby alone like she did and not allow it to be registered, particularly since she knew that it would have a high Factor Q.

I don't really understand about Factor Q. I should, but I can't seem to make myself be interested in what they tell me about biology and life science and all the rest of it. I'm sure it would be good for me if I paid more attention, and perhaps I will resolve to do that soon. But not yet, because I am too busy, and because there are too many other things to learn.

But I know roughly how it goes, the Factor Q thing. Every baby, through all the three known galaxies, must be registered at its birth and given a blood test by the nearest government medical computer or inspector, whichever is closest. All those babies who have a potential for above-normal telepathic development show Factor Q in their blood at birth, and they are always taken from their parents immediately and put in the Tri-Galactic Federation Creche on Mars. (I think it used to be on Earth, but Earth is used only for agriculture now, and all the government offices are on other planets.)

Anne-Charlotte knew her baby would have Factor Q, because both she and Drijn, its father, had been raised in the Creche themselves and had had very high Q ratings. Neither of them was released from candidacy for the Communipath network until they were eleven, and that is very late. They decided, she and the baby's father, that they would not register the baby, that they would hide it and keep it, and in a way I understand that, but it is a grave crime. If one woman is allowed to keep her baby, then how can any woman be asked to give hers up? I can see that.

I can also see how, when Anne-Charlotte had only the baby to remind her of her man, and he had died, she did not want to let them have the baby. The law about the Bucket is a cruel law; if it did not have to exist, everyone in the Three Galaxies would rejoice, Patrick says.

You see, because of the work they do the Communipaths that man the Bucket live only to the age of eighteen, very rarely to nineteen, and from the time they take over the stations at twelve until they die they are never allowed to leave their quarters. I am told that they live in incredible luxury, that they may have anything that they want merely for the asking, but what is that to them? If they were ever allowed to leave they would not return to their stations, and that is why they must be prisoners. And they all must die, in spite of everything that the doctors can do they always die, and so they must be prisoners. It is so terrible, and so sad.

Ian is our teacher, and he told us all about the Bucket. He says that long ago, on Earth, before there ever was a rocket or even a flier or a landcar, before the times we learn about in Small History, people fought fires with what was called a Bucket Brigade. They would form a line outside a burning building, from where they got their water up to the building itself, and they would pass buckets of water along the line and send the empty ones back to be filled. They had no hoses, no sprays, and no quicker way to move the water. And that is why the Communipath Network is called the Bucket, you see, after those bucket brigades. The stations are lined up across the Three Galaxies and the Communipaths pass information along from station to station, just like the buckets of water. We have no other way to do it, no other way to move messages across space, and so we condemn the Communipaths to death. Deliberately, knowing exactly what we are doing.

I am so glad I have no Factor Q in my blood! I have as much psibility as any normal human child, and with the usual training (plus the Maklunite training, which is much better, of course) I will be taught to use what I have. Already I am able to receive messages within a single room, if they are no more than three or four semantic units in length, and Ian says that that is very good indeed for a ten year old. I cannot send anything at all yet, of course (except, Patrick says, if I was in real danger, and then I could probably send a good loud yell for help, he says), but with more training and practice I will be able to keep from disgracing myself.

Of the twenty-one in our Maklunite cluster there are seven from the Creche, and that is a lot, because the Factor Q babies are rare. I think that is one reason that our group is so far out from the Galactic Service, and if they were closer it would be hard for them to get out of it.

As it is, Tomaso has to. I like him very much. He has a big deep voice and a curly black beard almost halfway down his chest and he is always laughing. But he has to be a Forest Ranger here on Iris because his Q rating is so high and because he comes from a family of high ratings and they watched him very closely. (I have never seen a forest, by the way, but when I am older I will be taken on a trip to see one, and a waterfall, too. A waterfall is something I would really like to see.) But forest or not, Tomaso must be a Galactic Forest Ranger, and the government will not release him from the Service.

Patrick laughs about it. He says, "After all, Tomaso, you are paid eighty credits a month just to baby-sit some cactuses and a herd of peripatetic flowers—and eighty credits buys all our seed and enough left over to put fuel in the flier. Why do you complain?"

The trouble with Anne-Charlotte's baby was that it had so much psibility. It was like hiding a bolt of lightning to try to hide that baby. Why, when it was no more than two months old, if it wanted something to eat all of us would scream at Anne-Charlotte to hurry, because the baby made our heads hurt so badly.

"And what are you going to do with it as it gets bigger, my lady?" Patrick asked Anne-Charlotte often and often. "Any day now the Communipaths will be getting all these pretty little baby thoughts about HUNGRY HUNGRY HUNGRY HURT HURT HURT just like we do. How are you going to hide it?"

Anne-Charlotte is lovely. She has black hair in two long braids almost to her hips and her skin is the color of the Tsai bushes after the rain (and in case you never saw a Tsai bush that's a sort of pale golden brown with a shine to it). Her eyes are big and black and she has a good wide mouth that used to be always smiling until the baby's father died. When she thinks, there is a sort of flicker all about her; and I could watch her move and listen to her talk and never be tired of it.

She knew what Patrick meant, about the baby, and so she took to carrying the baby with her everywhere she went, in a little net bag. No one paid any attention to that, since all of the Maklunite women carry their babies that way most of the time anyhow. But it was good for Anne-Charlotte because she could grab the baby quick when it wanted anything and stop it from putting out all those headache-making signals.

But naturally the baby was beginning to be much too big to carry all the time. We watched it every minute, because we knew that if it wandered away and a stranger got close to it and began to hear it projecting they would know it should be in the Creche. Anne-Charlotte carried it as much as possible, and it slept in her bed curled up in her arms, and we set up a schedule during the day so that it was never alone.

Even so, something must have been getting through. It has to have been that way or they would not have come and taken the baby away. Somewhere on the Bucket one of the Communipaths heard it, poor little thing, and knew the signal wasn't anything that was supposed to be loose in the air. No signal of that strength should be anywhere but in the Creche, and since the Creche is totally shielded at all times, whoever heard the baby knew at once that something was wrong.

You know what I think, though? I think only a monster would turn in a little baby to the government. None of the Communipaths are Maklunites, of course. A Maklunite would have been glad that the little baby had escaped the Creche. A Maklunite would have carefully kept the secret of one little telepathic baby somewhere out near the Extreme Moons.

I am going to find it very hard not to hate that Communipath who told the Galactic Service about Anne-Charlotte's baby. I am going to find it very hard not to hate the four Fedrobots that came to take the baby (though that's silly, since they are like our coffeepot, or the computer that Ian uses for teaching, and hating them is a big waste of time). And most of all I am going to find it very hard not to hate—even though hating is a bad thing—I am going to find it very hard not to hate the one human man who came and took the baby from Patrick's arms.

They called him Coyote Jones, and he did not look at all like a bad man. He was big, bigger even than Patrick, bigger even than Ian, who is the biggest in our group. He had long red hair and a red beard and I could have loved him. But I hate him. I will remember him, and someday I will take something away from him, something that he loves. Just wait and see if I don't. (And when Patrick reads that, is he ever going to be angry with me! It is bad enough for me to feel that way in any case, but on Gentle Thursday it is inexcusable.)

I expect what I had best do is go back to the living-domes and ask permission to spend the rest of this day in the ashram, because I am foul and black and dreadful inside. I thought that the writing it down might help, but it hasn't; it's only made it worse. How *could* they come and take Anne-Charlotte's baby away like that, when it is big enough to know what is happening to it, when it has heard its own mother say that it would be better dead than going with them!

I think I am going to be very, very sick.

# CHAPTER TWO

COYOTE JONES handed the baby over to the director of the Infant Ward of the Tri-Galactic Federation Creche. He wished them luck with it. All he had gotten from it was a blinding headache that had very nearly forced him to turn the child over to the Fed-robots for delivery to the Creche. Only a grim determination not to be humiliated in what was already an exceptionally nasty task had kept him from doing so, and he had marched into the Creche with his teeth gritted, his stomach churning, and black lines streaking across his field of vision like jet fireworks.

"Here," he said bitterly, "here's your bloody contraband child. And never, do you hear me, never are you to involve me in such a piece of piracy, rape, and carnage as this was again! Do you understand me, Director?"

"Citizen Jones," the director snapped. "I was not the person responsible for assigning you to the task of claiming this child. I will thank you to keep both your mouth and your mind to yourself."

Coyote Jones was not much good at receiving, being able to do little more than get broad amorphous messages of distress or pleasure, but he was a mass projective telepath and his wrath was a fearsome weapon. Between the effects of the baby's totally unblocked rage and terror, and the more controlled but stronger fury of Coyote Jones, the director was hard put to it to maintain her equilibrium. She was being forced to use every bit of control and skill at blocking that she had (which was considerable, or she would not have been in charge of a ward of the Creche) and the effort of maintaining it at peak for such a length of time was exhausting her.

Coyote Jones looked at her with contempt, projected a large and regal male image of spitting—with a superbly wide trajectory—projected a second image of washing his hands, and walked out, leaving the whole thing to be dealt with by the Fedrobots. They were lucky; they were completely impervious to telepathy, having been built that way deliberately, with chemical rather than electrical circuits to make it certain.

If he had known for one moment when he got the assignment that it was an eleven-month-old baby girl that he was intended to pick up, he would have flatly refused. It was one thing to take a baby that had never seen its parents and transfer it at once to the Creche; it never knew anything else, had no life to compare with the one it had in the government facilities. But this baby was a different matter entirely. It knew its mother; it was accustomed to her arms. Worst of all it was a Maklunite baby, which meant it had been surrounded from birth with the tenderest and most intensive love that existed in the Three Galaxies. It had lived slung on its mother's back, or carried on the shoulder of someone of its Maklunite cluster-group, from its first moments of life. It had known the closest association with other humans that it was possible to know—and now it was supposed to be happy in the laboratory atmosphere that was the Creche!

He knew perfectly well, though, that they hadn't deliberately refrained from telling him his quarry was a baby. They had not known it any more than he had. All there had been to go on was the information from the Communipaths that there had to be a telepath of incredible strength at large somewhere and untrained, because there was static on the Bucket. No one had known that it was a baby—not that it would have made any difference if they had. The problems would have been exactly the same.

Static on the Bucket was very dangerous. Under normal circumstances—which meant ALL circumstances, up to now—every human being in the Three Galaxies who was capable of projection of a strength that could cause disruption of the Bucket was in effect a prisoner of the government and under its literally constant surveillance. All of those with such strength were known to one another; they shared the same purpose, and most important they were trained not to interfere with one another so that information could move without obstacle. When the static had begun coming through during the past spring they had been baffled and alarmed. At first they thought one of their own number was playing a practical joke. In order to rule out that possibility, the Communipath Department had had to put the stable of Communipaths under total sedation and then revive them one at a time, and still the very first one they waked up had reported the static.

Then a freighter coming in from the Sirius Gap had tried to send a Mayday message when fire broke out in its hold, and the entire message had been scrambled with a powerful image of a golden fish. The fish and the fire, the fish and the freighter, all had been confused to such an extent in transmission that the rescue teams had arrived too late to save the freighter. And it had not mattered greatly except in financial terms, because all freighters were on automatic pilot. But what about the next time, when it was a passenger liner with four hundred people aboard?

The rogue telepath (and Coyote made a face, thinking of the tiny girl they had hung that title on) had to be found at once, found and put under government training. Whoever it was, he had to learn to control his projection, had to learn not to interfere with the vital communication of the Three Galaxies, had to learn not to simply blast out into space with every thought indiscriminately. The Department had naturally assumed that the person responsible was a full-grown adult human, someone in whom in some freakish way a telepathic ability had developed to a greater extent than had been estimated at its birth. There had never been a known mistake in the blood test that identified Factor Q, but there could always be a first time. They had thought that perhaps this was the result of such an error, and everyone, whatever their hypothesis, had assumed that it was an adult, because the concept of untrained projection of such strength from a child was simply not within the realms of known possibility.

Various unpleasant things had been contemplated when he was given the assignment. He had been called in by Tzana Kai, ostensibly head of the Tri-Galactic Translations Bureau, Inc., handily located on an artificial asteroid near the central point of the middle galaxy. Tzana was a double agent in the ancient tradition, and she never sugarcoated anything. She had given him a list of possible nasty projects that might be involved.

"It may well be," she had said, "that this rogue telepath will not be willing to submit to government training and control."

He had nodded. He wouldn't have been willing either.

"You know it is only possible for the government to control the Communipaths as it does because they are conditioned from birth to martyrdom for the sake of mankind. This person, whoever he is, has no such conditioning, and he has tremendous power. He has it within his hands to totally wreck the communications system of the galaxy and reduce us to the state we were in before the Bucket was developed, with every message taking years, decades, even centuries to arrive."

"And if he knows this and isn't willing to become a pet?"

"You will do your best to simply render him unconscious and bring him back here for surgery. In such a situation we would not dare allow him even one instant's consciousness before the surgery, you realize."

Surgery. That meant severing all the known telepathic pathways, with the interesting side effect that it left the subject of the surgery little better than a vegetable. Charming.

"And if I can't, as you put it, render him unconscious?"

"You will have to kill him."

Tzana was a good deal tougher and harder than he was, and he hoped he never was able to match her in either quality. But he had agreed to the assignment, since it was obviously a question of the life of this one man versus the lives of all the thousands of people who might die in various accidents caused by Bucket static. It was extremely, overpoweringly obvious.

A baby, though, was most definitely not a part of the package he had thought he was buying.

And what kind of a baby could do what this baby had done? He wasn't sure he enjoyed contemplating the idea at all. A superbaby?

He had an interesting memory of the effect upon him of the baby's mother's projection of utter agony. It had been like going down for the third time into a black and slimy swamp, but not being granted the privilege of death. The swamp had been full, teeming, swarming with creatures like obscene snakes. . . . He shuddered, remembering. If the baby could do anything like that, it was not going to be sunshiny fun and games at the Creche.

Which was perhaps a good thought. Perhaps the baby would be more trouble than it was worth and they would have to release it. And then he remembered that that could only happen with suitable alteration to the baby's brain, alteration that would leave it a happy idiot, harmless and useless, for the rest of its life.

His flier was hovering off the landing port of Tzana's asteroid, and through a fog of irritation he requested permission to land. The landing crane reached out, hooked him abruptly but neatly, cut the power to his engines, and deposited the little car efficiently on the front Terrace of Tri-Galactic Translations, Inc. A bell rang announcing his arrival, the door opened of itself, a melodious voice in the walls said, "Welcome, Citizen Jones," and Coyote's rage increased. He detested all things automatic. In his cover, which was as a traveling folk singer, he played an antique nonautomatic twentieth-century guitar. His flier had no automatic pilot except the emergency unit required by law. And next year, definitely, he was going to move to the outmost of the Extreme Moons, maybe beyond them—if there was something beyond them.

"Tzana!" he bellowed. "Where the bloody hell are you?"

She stepped out from behind a pillar of inflated plastic and stared at him with raised brows, so he stared back, up and down. She was good to look at, in spite of her age; a woman constructed along simple but satisfactory lines and well-maintained. He happened to know that she had corn-yellow hair that clung about her head in a neat shining cap, and that that well-formed head fit neatly into his hand when he wanted her to hold still while he laid her properly. She had a tendency to rush things. At the moment, however, all he could see was her face, peering out of a hooded silver tunic, a little in advance of current fashion but very becoming. Her excellent legs were in silver tights and sandals, and she looked what she was—efficient and capable—and also what she was not—chilly and uptight.

"Your cover is showing, Tzana," he said. "I can't even find your butt in that thing you've got on."

She sent various rapid images at him, all of them uncomplimentary, but all he got was a succession of purple blobs with black spots.

"You're wasting it, Tzana," he said.

"Not at all. It makes me feel better."

"Are you mad?"

"The way you came in here shouting and carrying on? This is a place of business, you know. What if I had had a client of fine sensibilities, Citizen Jones?"

He began to tell her what she could do with her clients of whatever sensibility, and he intended to make quite a project of the telling, but she interrupted him before he could get more than half started.

"Wait a minute, Coyote," she said gently. "You are really upset. What was it? Did you have to kill the rogue after all?"

She stared at him, waiting, and he let her have it all, not caring just how much it might hurt. He saw her eyes widen with shock and pain as she got it.

"Oh, dear heaven, Coyote," she said at last. "I am so sorry. I should have gone myself, but we never thought of it being a child."

"It was a little girl, less than a year old, and weighing about as much as a kitten. Thank God we spent five weeks of the trip back in hibernation, Tzana, because the last few hours after revival were hell. It didn't cling to me, you know. It was scared and mad and it just stood straight up in my lap and stared at me and hated me and gave me splitting headaches."

"Why do you keep saying 'it'? What was the baby's name?"

"It was Maklunite. They don't name their kids, Tzana, because they feel it is an invasion of freedom. They let the kids pick their own names when they get old enough."

"Maklunite . . . that means carried by the mother everywhere she goes, from birth, doesn't it?"

"That's right. And all the rest of it."

"I begin to see. Coyote, come in here and sit down and let's have something to drink."

He followed her through the door, and the anteroom deflated behind them, folded itself neatly into a bundle, rolled up into its pod, and was still. The room they were in was large and cool, and a houserobot appeared immediately with two long tall drinks called Birds of Paradise. Their usual effect was to convince the drinker that he, too, was a bird of paradise, and could fly. Coyote took his eagerly. He could do with feeling like a Bird of Paradise because at the moment "buzzard" was the only bird he could quite see himself resembling.

# CHAPTER THREE

WHERE Anne-Charlotte walked there were thickets of the Anais cactus, from little ones only a few inches high to the giants towering fifty feet in the air. They weren't really cactus, of course, they were far more like a tree; but they *looked* like cactus, and most of them were spined like cactus, and the settlers out from Earth had named them cactus before they knew any better. In the eastern sector of the planet, where the climate was warm all year round, the colonists built their houses high up in the giant cactuses on broad platforms, but here the giants were empty except for the spreading red parasols of their flowers. All the land around Chrysanthemum Bridge was still wilderness, covered with the cactus thickets and a low cover of aromatic brush. The mobile flowers roamed here freely, apparently having learned that no trappers were allowed on Maklunite lands.

She had the thickets all to herself. She had made her way up over the red bluffs behind the livingdomes and followed the trail out into the wilderness. The members of her group rarely came out here. Not that there was anything to fear, particulary for Anne-Charlotte, for no venomous thing was able to harm her and there were no large animals on Iris. But the wilderness area was slow traveling; it took hours to get here and hours to return, and there was so much work to do in the cluster that there was rarely time for anyone to go so far.

She would not be able to return to the livingdomes that night and would have to sleep out in the open. But she didn't mind that at all, for she had plans for the night and solitude was an essential factor if they were to be successful.

Patrick was following her, she knew, because she felt the gentle touch of his mind from time to time. Always she rejected him fiercely, but she made no effort to cause him pain or difficulty. If he had really wanted to interfere with her he would have come by flier. The fact that he, too, was on foot was sufficient evidence that he simply wished to stay near her and see that she did no foolish thing.

Anne-Charlotte was not concerned about Patrick catching her. He could never keep up with her on foot, because among her psi abilities was a skill of skimming the ground lightly, never quite leaving it, never quite touching it, almost a kind of low flight, an effortless movement that carried her at easily three times the speed an ordinary human being could produce. Patrick could never reach her in time to stop her from anything she chose to do, and she was sure he knew that.

Why, then, she wondered, was he following her at all? It was unusual. No Maklunite interfered with another one, even if his purpose—which was unlikely—was to take his own life. Only if all his cluster-group had agreed that he was not capable of being responsible for his own actions would any steps be taken to limit his freedom. She knew that no such agreement had been reached by her group, because she would have been told if it had, and she would not have been allowed to leave. Very gently she would have been accompanied everywhere, probably by Ian and Freya, who together constituted their strongest pair, psychically as well as physically. Someone else would have taken over Ian's work in the cornfields, another woman would have been sent to do whatever task had been set Freya for that day, and she, Anne-Charlotte, would have found herself under at least attempted control.

She was by no means sure that it was really possible for them to control her, unless all of the other six psis in the cluster joined against her. Perhaps not even then. She felt her strength like a fountain, playing within her, growing always, and she intended to encourage that strength. Soon, she was sure, she and the baby together would be more than strong enough for what she intended to do, though she never would have been able to accomplish it by herself. She wondered what the officials at the Creche would have done if they had known that her baby found the so-called "impenetrable" psychic shield around the Creche as easy to slip through as a piece of cheesecloth, and she hugged herself in delight at its power. Always she felt it, its thoughts completely unformed, little more than pictures, but so strong and so sure, finding her as easily as if it had still lain curled against her hip instead of in its narrow bed almost three full galaxies away.

It was beginning to get late now. Above her the other ten of the Extreme Moons were rising, balancing their ring so that they seemed flung out in an oval of silver spheres from where she stood. The wind was coming up, too, to greet them, and soon the sand would be gusting in miniature whirlwinds in the open spaces. She would have to go into a thicket, out of the wind, before very long.

Behind her Patrick was puzzled. He dared not touch her often, for if he did she would put up all her shields against him and he would lose her totally. If he continued, as he had been, merely sending an occasional light touch her way, he felt reasonably certain that even in her present state she would tolerate it, because she loved him. But what was she up to? He wondered if Drijn, had he lived, would have known what to do with her now—perhaps so, but he doubted it. She was growing, changing, and soon she would be so far beyond them they would not be able to follow her at all. He could not understand how she could possess such psi strength and power and have escaped the Bucket! And when they asked her, she only laughed and said that she was being taught by an expert. Who? He shook his head hopelessly.

All that day after the baby had been taken away the whole cluster had stayed within the domes, except for the younger children. They had gone into the common room and seated themselves together on the floor, all their hands touching, so that they could amplify even the feeble psiblity of those of them who were not Factor Q's, and they had ridden out the storm of agony that Anne-Charlotte had loosed on them. It had been a terrifying ordeal. It had even reached out to the child Tessa

where she sat writing and brought her back to the livingdome in terror at the blackness within herself, since
being a child she had not realized that it was not she
herself but Anne-Charlotte who was creating all that
evil. It had been worse than anything they had known,
worse than the storm when her man had died, but nowhere in its content, nowhere in the thought-winds that
she had sent screaming through the cluster, nowhere had
there been an indication that she planned to harm herself in any way or that she was not in control of her
actions.

It was customary in Maklunite clusters for each Thursday, Gentle Thursday, to be spent by the entire cluster-
group in an attempt to make some tangible dent in
the misery that many lived in throughout the Three Galaxies. All other work, all activities performed for the
cluster itself, were suspended on that day in favor of
work done for others who needed help, of whatever kind.
Anne-Charlotte had canceled that particular Gentle
Thursday for them, however. They had had no choice
but to bear what she did to them, and ordinarily such
selfishness would have brought down the full weight of
their disapproval upon her.

It was not that Anne-Charlotte could not have avoided
what she did. She could have done so easily. She was by
far the strongest single psi in the cluster. She could have
shielded them against the worst of her pain if she had
chosen to do so. In her agony, though, she simply had
not cared about them, and though they would have preferred her otherwise, still they had understood. No one
had reproached her. And through the weeks that followed, while the baby had lain in hibernation on the
government ship that took it to the Creche, they had
been gentle with her. She had seemed calm, more calm
than they had expected her to be.

And now today, the third day after the baby's return
to normal animation, she had suddenly taken off by herself at dawn without a word to anyone. Why?

It was, of course, possible that all she wanted was a
chance to be by herself. Out here she was beyond the
reach of all their thoughts, since only the two of them,
her and himself, had a telepathic range of more than a
few miles. Because the Maklunites lived in such close

communion it did at times happen that one of them felt an overpowering lust for total solitude, and at such times a Maklunite would go out from his group, beyond their sight and their range, and remain there alone until he felt once more ready for group life. If that was Anne-Charlotte's intention he would leave her at once and no one of their cluster would presume to go near her until she returned to them of her own volition. It certainly was possible that that was the case; she had had a very difficult time since Drijn died. First his death, and then the birth of the baby, and then the tension trying to hide it. . . . It had been bad for her. And she had lain with no man since Drijn had grown sick, though all of them had offered willingly; even Tomaso, who tended to be reluctant to go to anyone but his woman Naomi, had seen the need growing in her and asked her to let him help her, and still she had refused. It had all been bad for her.

And yet, nothing in her mind made him even half sure that it was simply a need to be away from their constant closeness that had brought her out here. He decided to stay with her a while yet and see what happened.

Anne-Charlotte had found an ideal spot for her activity. Here a single giant cactus loomed forty feet high, and around it had grown a sort of family of smaller ones, so that their combined flowers made a great circle of roofed shade. The cacti were so thick and so close together, ringing about their central pillar, that she was completely isolated. If a real sandstorm should come up this night the bubble-tent she had brought in her net bag would be ample protection for her in this strong circle. It made a natural ashram, and only the altar was lacking.

She looked about her until she found a flat stone, whorled in gold and green spirals like all the rocks of the wilderness, and she considered it carefully. It was not really heavy, it could not have weighed more than fifty pounds, and the distance from the spot where it lay and the base of the giant central cactus was only a hundred yards.

She laid down her net bag, closed her eyes tightly, and drew all the strands of her mind into a single golden knot back of her eyes. Holding her breath, she set an image of the base of the cactus pillar upon that knot. She brought her full strength to bear upon it until she was able to leave it, confident that it would remain.

The stone was next. Carefully, slowly, because this was more difficult, she created in her mind the image of the stone, ignoring the baby's distant pleasure in the colors, seeing with intensity each whorl, each fold of green into the gold matrix, making it as real as her hand or her foot.

Now, to place the stone at the base of the cactus, it would only be necessary to bring the two images together . . .

With Anne-Charlotte's horrified scream, slashing on and on into the air, Patrick's mind was torn by two images. The first was of a falling cactus, smashed by the impact of fifty pounds of stone slamming into it on a trajectory toward the great central one. The second image was of Anne-Charlotte's baby, torn and bleeding from the cactus spines as she slammed into them like the stone had done.

Anne-Charlotte stared at the smashed cactus, knowing now that Patrick would be upon her as fast as he could reach her. She had not intended for one instant to let him guess what it was she intended to do, but she had overestimated her strength and skill, and when she had failed to teleport the stone high enough for it to clear the ring of cacti the thought of a similar failure with the baby had thrown her off her guard. And that had been foolish. After all, when she teleported her baby out of the Creche it would be vastly different, because the baby would be helping her, and it was far stronger than she was. Damn!

It would take Patrick a while to get to her, but there was no point in fleeing. He would only get the flier and follow her, and he would bring all the other psis along to help him find her. She was strongest, but not strong enough to escape the six of them on foot when they were flying. Her only hope now was to convince them that she was right to do what she did, and then perhaps they would all help her.

She had been a fool to give herself away so easily, and she was disgusted. If she had only been more careful Patrick would soon have left her and returned to the cluster and she would have been free to do as she chose.

She had meant to fast, first of all, so that her mind would be clear and her body free of all impurity. She had meant to practice the skill of teleportation, something she rarely had occasion to do and was by no means good at, beginning with very small objects and working gradually to larger ones, beginning with small distances and increasing them a little at a time. But in her folly and her overconfidence she had destroyed all chance of such a program, unless the rest of the cluster was willing to help her and would agree to her plan.

She knew the baby would help. She could feel it, always rocking gently inside her mind, clinging to her psi-presence as it had clung to her body when she had had it near her. The tiny feelers of its thoughts were not very clear, they were mixed with a strange freight of terror and hatred and frustration, but all of them were so strong, so incredibly strong.

Anne-Charlotte knew what that had to mean. It meant her baby was something very different, something new, something special. Even the strongest of the Communipaths, although ordinary distances were irrelevant to them, could not pass stellar distance alone. That was why it took eleven stations, carefully spaced, to span three galaxies. And this one little baby, all alone and untrained, was tossing its thoughts across the full expanse of the known universe as easily as it would throw a handful of sand in play.

She was confident that she would be able to reach it and make it understand what was needed for it to come to her again. The baby would provide the strength and she would provide the knowledge, if not at the first try then very soon, and the Creche would unknowingly help her, too, because they would be training the baby there.

Remembering the Creche, she laughed softly. What puny beings she and her fellow prisoners had been compared to this baby that was held there now! She would have given a great deal if she could have been there, if she could have seen how the directors and their doctors and their experts—and most of all, their psicompu-ters—reacted when faced with the baby that she and Drijn had brought into this world!

She closed her eyes and leaned back against the cactus to wait, resigned for the moment to her failure. It was only a temporary delay, she was sure of that. She would convince them all, they would help her, they *must* help her. And if they would not agree willingly, she was sure there were other things that she and the baby could do, together, that would convince them.

# CHAPTER FOUR

TODAY HAS BEEN a day to try to remember. You would not think it, to look at the entry in the Log, though! It has only the day's date, and then it says, "On this day the woman Ledyce was considered for Choosing and was rejected by us. It was felt by all of us that she would be only a source of trouble at Chrysanthemum Bridge and that at this time our difficulties with Anne-Charlotte make it impossible for us to attempt to heal her of the characteristics that caused us to reject her. She went away very disappointed and we regret it that we caused her sorrow. Both Patrick and Anne-Charlotte were absent from the Choosing Meeting, but both have affirmed our decision since their return.

It would look to an outsider reading our Log as if Patrick and Anne-Charlotte had perhaps merely gone to the next settlement to borrow something or out to work in the fields. But of course an outsider would not know how rare it is to have a Maklunite absent from a Choosing. I wanted to add something to the Log to make the real excitement of the day clear, but I was firmly put down by everyone else and told to write it all down myself as usual if I wanted every detail recorded.

That's easy to say, of course; it's not so easy to do. I guess I will just say that this happened and then this happened and then this happened, until I come to the end of the happenings. There are a lot of times when I wish I were like the other kids and interested in something that did not take so much time. This writing things takes hours and hours, and Patrick will not let me take one of the recorders and just dictate it instead of writing it down. He's very strict about that. "You will not value what you do if it is so easy for you, Tessa," he says to me. "It must come hard so that you will take great care, so that each word will matter to you as you set it down." He is right, of course, and so here I am putting down one letter at a time, hour after hour. I also wish that he would be wrong just once in a while.

Anyhow, the woman Ledyce arrived just after dawn this morning. She wore a Choosing garment, but she had not made it herself, even I could tell that. You could see the machine stitches. It was a long full shift, falling almost to her feet, with full sleeves and a hood, made of scarlet syntholinen, and sewn instead of just extruded, so that it would look more like a handmade garment. Except that no handmade garment ever had stitches of such regular irregularity. It had a wide border of herons embroidered in silver and gold. I liked the garment very much, and I will remember that border of herons for a long time, but I think we all knew at once when we saw that it had been made for her by machines that she was not for us. Still, she had a right to the Choosing Meeting, and I could feel Patrick's stern admonition in my mind. "She is not to be prejudged—there may be many reasons for her coming in such a garment."

I couldn't imagine what the reasons could be, though. After all, if she had many duties and her hours were just too full to allow her to make her own Choosing dress she could have simply come to us naked. Many Maklunite candidates do just that, and there is no prejudice against it. You have two choices, you see. Either you prepare a garment, as beautiful as your own hands can make it, as proof of your desire to be a thing of beauty and industry in the cluster you want to Choose and be Chosen by, or you come with only your body, because you feel that nothing you could prepare could be as beautiful as that which you were given at your birth. You make a beautiful garment for the Choosing to do honor to the cluster you want to join, to show that the occasion is as important to you as it ought to be, since it can mean your whole life from that day on. Or you make none, and celebrate your body for its own loveliness. There are things to be said for each course, and if the day should come when I want to join another cluster

instead of stay here—which I can't imagine my doing,
but if it should—then I don't know which of the two
things I would do. It would take a lot of thinking to decide.

What the woman Ledyce had done, however, was
something else entirely. She had purchased a garment to
make herself beautiful. None of her own time had gone
into its preparation, it had no more meaning for her
than something she would have worn to a party or to
any social gathering. It was chosen to feed her own vanity, not to give pleasure to our eyes.

We all heard Patrick, just at the edge of the wilderness, as we began the Choosing. I still have trouble recognizing some of the mindvoices of the others when they
are beyond a very short distance, but Patrick I can always recognize. It's very odd, how you can only hear
the voice from the throat, but the voice of the mind has
a certain look to it and a certain taste, and I am told
that there are some people who have mindvoices that
bear with them a perfume as well, although I have never
known one. Patrick was much too far away for me to be
able to understand the details of what he was telling the
others who are better at psi, and I was terribly
frustrated, but I could not ask aloud what he was saying.
Sally heard me wanting to and the instructions she gave
me about what such a demonstration of bad manners
would get me made my whole mind sting. Later, though,
she told me that he had said that all of his attention was
going to be needed to follow Anne-Charlotte and
that they were simply to go ahead and make their decision without either him or Anne-Charlotte to help.

We were all in the ashram wearing our best in honor
of the occasion, and I was feeling almost pretty, although
I'm not at all. I had a new tunic to wear, and Mark had
made me a new necklace of the beautiful beads he carves
from the seeds of our trek-apples. Each bead was carved
differently, each in a wonderful curving and rippling
pattern that made me think of folded flowers or the
threedies I have seen of the oceans of Earth. Mark can
make more beautiful things than almost any one of us,
and he is only thirteen. When he is a grown man, he is
going to do great things and we all have such hopes for
him. (And I am not supposed to be writing about how I

looked, but about what happened—whatever is the matter with me today?)

Ian and Freya went to the woman Ledyce, and welcomed her, holding her close and giving her a cup of our own wine that we make from the juice of the cactus. Then they led her to the place of honor in the center of the room and had her sit down, and then the Choosing Meeting began.

"Do you prefer ordinary speech, Ledyce-who-comes-to-us-for-Choosing, or do you wish mindspeech?" Ian asked her first.

"Ordinary speech," she said at once, "so that all may understand."

I was glad of that, since I would not have been able to follow as well if it had been mindspeech.

"And why do you come to Chrysanthemum Bridge?" asked Freya.

The woman bit her lip, and we could see that she was nervous, but no one is allowed to interfere at a Choosing. The one who comes to be Chosen must manage alone, by whatever arts he has at his command, to convince the cluster that it should Choose him. So we all waited until Ledyce mastered her trembling and began to speak.

"I have been rejected by three clusters," she said sadly. "At each I have been found wanting and sent away. I have lost confidence in my own reasons."

"Perhaps then," said Ian, "you should accept the judgment of the others and find some other solution for your lifespending."

"No!"

"Why not?"

"I must and will be a Maklunite; it is the only thing that I have ever wanted to do with my life."

"Explain to us, then, why you feel that way."

"I want to be of use," she said, so softly we could hardly hear her. "I want to help."

"That is a good reason," said Ian, "because the galaxies have great need of people with that desire. But there are many other ways of accomplishing it. Why do you come to us?"

Ledyce shook her head and began to cry.

My heart ached for her, but I knew it was no use. If she could not even tell us why she was here, it meant probably that she really did not know why, and that she was simply seeking help. Perhaps she would be potentially someone who we could all love and who could love us, perhaps she would be valuable to the cluster somewhere, but at this time we could not possibly take her even on probation, we all knew that. Anne-Charlotte and Ledyce both? The very thought was horrifying.

"Please," she said at last, while we stood grieving for her. "I am strong and healthy, and I work hard. I know three of the Ancient Tongues and I can dance and sing and play all of the new instruments. I would be good for all of you, I know I would. Chrysanthemum Bridge is beautiful now, but I would make it more beautiful still. All of your men would find my body a pleasant place to be. I know how to make perfumes and bake bread, I have skills of carving and weaving . . ."

It went on for quite a while, and I kept feeling more and more miserable. What if at my own Choosing time I should act like this poor woman? None of the things she was saying was an answer to the question that had been asked. We had to know why she wanted to choose us, not just why she thought we should Choose her.

When she was quiet at last, Ian tried one more time.

"We must know," he said, "why you wish to Choose us. Until we know that I am afraid that it does not matter what skills you have, though all the things you have told us would be pleasant and useful. Why have you come to us? We must know that, Ledyce."

She stood there without saying a word, her head drooping.

"Ledyce," said Freya, "if you cannot put your thoughts into words, would you agree to open your mind to us? Perhaps we could then understand what you cannot say."

The woman shook her head firmly.

"No," she said. "No, I will not allow that."

"This cluster is very close," said Freya. "We are as much one person as we are twenty-one. If you could not share your mind with us you would be unhappy here, because you would be left out of so many things."

"Then you reject me, too?"

Her voice was dead, flat and empty of hope, and I wanted so much to go put my arms around her and tell her that of course she could stay. I felt Sally's forbidding like a bar across my chest and stood where I was, but I didn't want to obey her. Poor, poor Ledyce, to be rejected four times!

"We have trouble here now, among our own," said Ian gently. "If it were not like that perhaps we would try to take you in for a little while, perhaps we would be able to help you overcome the fear you have of mindsharing. But not now, not at this time. All of our strength is going to be needed in the next few months to deal with all the problems we already have. I am so sorry, Ledyce."

She went away without making any fuss or quarreling about our decision, and we were left feeling that we had hurt someone who had been hurt too many times before. It was only the second Choosing I had ever been to, and the first one—when Gdal and Jonathan had come to us —had been such a time of joy. We had taken a three-day holiday then to celebrate their coming, and I still remember how happy we were, even if I *was* only five then. I had been looking forward to this, looking forward to having a new mind to know, a new voice to hear, someone else to love and to love me, and to have it end like this made me heartsick.

We all went to change, then, without talking, most of us staying naked because it was so warm except for the ones who had to go work among the cactus. You could not go naked in the Anais fields, not unless you enjoyed being continually stuck with pins; and so Naomi had worked out for us a garment much like the Choosing garment, that covered you all over but was loose everywhere so that you could move to work. There isn't anything you can do, of course, to actually cultivate the cactus, they just grow on their own, but you do have to keep the weeds out from between them, and Maklunites do not use any sort of chemicals to kill the weeds. We pull them up, one at a time. And many of the vegetables that are native to Iris grow best when they are planted in among the cactus, and of course they *do* need tending.

All that day long we worked quietly, saddened by the morning. And the fact that Patrick and Anne-Charlotte were still away didn't do anything to help. It was so miserable that in midafternoon Ian called us all into the domes for music and a togethering. We were sitting and singing the old ballads, listening with great pleasure to Jonathan, who knows all the old space songs, when they finally came back.

Freya heard them first and told the rest of us. I couldn't hear them for a long time, but most of the grown-ups did, and of course Mark did, because he is a Factor Q and has been trained far more than the rest of us.

"They are all right," Sally said. "At least we know they are all right."

"But Anne-Charlotte's mind—"

They switched to mindspeech then, showing each other things, and I sat there, frustrated, getting a word now and then, and fuming, wishing they would hurry up and get within my range. I've just got to get more practice, and that's all there is to it, I've got to spend less time writing and a lot more time working with Mark or some of the other kids. It's horrible to know that a whole conversation is going on around your head and not be able to share it except for little tags and pieces. Mark was grinning at me, so I knew that he knew perfectly well how fussed I was, and then he stopped grinning and looked completely shocked and I knew that whatever I was missing was something dreadful.

Usually the grown-ups are not so inconsiderate of us; usually they do not use just mindspeech when we are together in a group, any more than they would speak in an ancient tongue or pass one another private notes. I knew it had to be something dreadful that had made them forget their manners so completely.

"Tessa?"

"Yes, Mark," I mindspoke silently, thinking the words as carefully and as clearly as I could. I knew he wouldn't really get them because I couldn't send properly and he was trying to listen to all the other conversations going on while he dealt with me; but he would be able to interpret my thought as a semantic unit for agreement.

"I'll tell you what it is as well as I can. If I am going too fast you'll have to stop me."

"All right," I thought again.

"Patrick and Anne-Charlotte were up in the wilderness, out beyond the bluffs, and there was some kind of accident. I don't really understand, except that no one is hurt, and it had something to do with the baby."

"But the baby isn't here!" I thought, forgetting he would get only something like a noise of distress.

"I *told* you I didn't understand," he thought crossly. "I'm doing the best I can." And then he went on, scolding.

"You are going to have a terrible mindvoice! It hurts my head to listen to you, even now when you can't *say* anything!"

I didn't try to answer, because I knew it was true. I had been told often enough. It's just that I get excited and I forget about being gentle and about being careful, and I guess what I do is about the equivalent of screaming in somebody's ears, and not very clear or interesting screaming at that.

"I want to listen now," Mark thought at me. "You be quiet and you should hear them pretty soon; they're not far away now."

I strained as hard as I could, and made my head hurt doing it, but I couldn't hear a thing except the quick flashing that was the grown-ups. They don't think in words like I do, they just think in big pieces that everyone understands at once in the same way, and Ian says that I may be able to talk that way too one day. (And then again I may not; normal psibility is usually pretty much restricted to words, and normal is all I am, and I might as well resign myself to it.)

Finally, when I had begun to think they would never get there, I felt them, just at the outside edge of my range, and then I heard them coming in the door, and it hit me all at once.

Dimly, I heard Patrick shouting, "Stop that, Anne-Charlotte! Stop that at once! Look what you are doing to the children!" But I couldn't really pay any attention to what he was saying, I was drowning in something black and sticky, and there were screaming things whipping round my head like the sandstorms, and someone was pushing me, pushing me down, down, down into the black and the black was screaming and had little sticky hands with claws—and that is all I remember, because I fainted.

When I woke up I was lying out in the grass where they had carried me, and someone had put my necklace of carved beads into my hand. Patrick was sitting beside me, looking patient and tired and loving, and he smiled when he saw that I was awake.

"That was pretty silly of me," I said. (And it was. I'm pretty big to be knocked over that way by Anne-Charlotte's dramatics, especially since I've had a chance to hear them all before.)

"I don't think so," he said. "Anne-Charolotte is very strong, and she is getting stronger all the time."

"There's something the matter with her, isn't there?"

He didn't answer me for a long time. I could hear the love-thinking in his mind, and I knew how sad he must be.

"Yes," he said finally. "There's something very, very wrong with Anne-Charlotte. It's a sickness that is almost gone from the Galaxies, the Light be praised, and I never thought to see it in my lifetime."

"What is it called, Patrick?"

"Insanity, sweet. Madness."

"Oh. Oh, yes. I've heard of that. In the books."

"Well, I suppose that's what it must be. In one way, though, it may be a blessing."

I was shocked.

"How could that be, Patrick?" I asked.

"Because we may be able to save her life, Tessa. If she was mad when she had the baby and tried to hide it, they cannot accuse her of treason."

"I see! But what would they do with her then?"

He shook his head. "I wish I knew the answer to that, Tessa, but I don't. I have to find out."

"And then we have to have a meeting."

"That's right."

He stood up, then, and dropped a cactus blossom onto my chest.

"You lie there a minute," he said, "and then when you feel better come on inside. We've put our private mind-storm to sleep for a while."

And I guess that's the end of the things that happened. At least for today.

# CHAPTER FIVE

FILE 374.10.b, Segment 1114
TOPIC:  Q Factor Aberrations
FROM:   Nysse Falconer, Directress  Infant Ward,
        Communipath Creche  GALCENTRAL,
        STATION 11

TO:     Communipath Control Committee  Galactic
        Council  GALCENTRAL, STATION 14

DATE:   Mayfourth 3018

1.  The subject of this report is the present charge of
the infant ward of the Communipath Creche, daughter of
the Q Factor Aberrant Anne-Charlotte (member of the
Maklunite Cluster called Chrysanthemum Bridge, on the
Planet 34.922.107—colloquial name Iris.) This infant
is as yet unnamed, in accordance with Maklunite custom,
for which see the Maklunite Texts, Vol. 2, Sec. 13, Paragraph 4, and will be subsequently referred to in this report as Subject Infant.

2.  Reference is made to the history of Q Factor Aberrant
Anne-Charlotte, Communipath Creche Report File 374.
10.a, Segment 391, from which we quote as follows:

> We find Anne-Charolotte, subject of this report, to
> be mildly aberrant in that (1) she has consistently
> refused to respond normally to those portions of
> Creche training intended to induce the fondness for
> luxury which is so significant to the later tolerance
> of Communipath status, and (2) she has consist-

ently resisted indoctrination in the Romeo-Juliet Myth Syndrome, also requisite for such tolerance. Such abberant tendencies, while not in any way dangerous to subject or to society, do make subject unfit for Communipath function, and inasmuch as subject's Q Factor, though high, is not of any such extraordinary highness as to justify an attempt at psychosurgery to correct the aberration, it is therefore recommended that subject be released from the Communipath Creche on her own recognizance after suitable indoctrination erasure.

We further quote as follows:

Subject Anne-Charlotte on Decembersixth 3008 was reported to this agency by the teachers at Galschool 840 (Special Wing) to be consistently untrainable and untractable as a productive member of Standard Culture society. It was recommended to this agency that the subject be released in the custody of the nearest Maklunite Cluster in accordance with her own wish; psychoprobe indicates that despite a certain rebellious profile she is correct in her own estimate that the life of a Maklunite would be the most appropriate for her. She was therefore released from Galschool 840 on Decembertwentieth 3008 to the Maklunite Cluster Sunfish.

Subsequent reports on Aberrant Anne-Charlotte indicated maximally satisfactory adjustment, as would be expected in view of the high probability factor in her case. No further entries are in the subject's file with the exception of the normal reference to her voluntary transfer to the Maklunite Cluster Chrysanthemum Bridge upon her forming a sexual relationship with Q Factor Aberrant Drijn. (See Communipath Creche Report File 374.10.a, Segment 382.)

NOTE: It is perhaps at this point that a certain laxness could be attributed to Communipath Control; however (see Wergenhoff, Vol. 9, Chap. 3; also Xthpa, Vol. 2, Chap. 4; also Standard, Vol. 11, Chap. 2, Chap. 9) experience in sexual alliances between Q Factor Aberrants has not previously been observed to lead to aberrancy in the offspring of such alliances, since the aberrant factors do not appear to be inherited to any significant extent. END OF NOTE.

3. Reference is made to the history of Q Factor Aberrant Drijn, Communipath Creche Report File 374.10.a, Segment 382. (See also note above.) We quote as follows:

> We find Drijn, subject of this report, to be mildly aberrant in that he shows abnormal resistance to indoctrination in the Esprit-de-Corps Myth Syndrome requisite to satisfactory adjustment to future Communipath status. Subject Drijn is abnormally individualistic and independent. It is further noted that subject is of frail health and probably could not stand up physically under the strain of Communipath duty to even the unfortunate limited extent that is normally expected. It is therefore recommended, despite the very high Q Factor subject possesses, that he be released from the Communipath Creche on his own recognizance after suitable indoctrination erasure.

Further reports on Aberrant Drijn record his release from Galschool 3722 (Special) to the Maklunite Cluster Chrysanthemum Bridge, his subsequent sexual alliance with Q Factor Aberrant Anne-Charlotte (see above) and his death in 3016 at that Cluster.

4. No reference is made to birth records of the Infant Subject of this report inasmuch as said birth was illegal and unregistered. However, information available from those of the Maklunite Cluster Chrysanthemum Bridge who were present at the infant's birth give its birth date as Aprilninth, 3017. The subject is at this time, then, twelve months, three weeks, four days, of age, and has been confined in the Infant Ward at Galcentral, Station 11, since Aprilfourth of this year. Charges of high treason against humankind (See Forthright, Vol. 23, p. 809; also see Galactic Statute 11,313.26-a.ii) have been brought against Infant Subject's mother with reference to the illegal and unregistered birth. (For discussion of these charges and their legal proceedings see Galcentral File 19348, Segment 11.)

5. Reference is made to the report of the PsiComputer on Subject Infant, from which we quote as follows:

> Subject Infant has been given the usual battery of

examinations by computer and results have been correlated to produce its psi-profile. Results are the following:

| | |
|---|---|
| Q FACTOR | 99 |
| TELEPATHY (PROJECTION) | 81 |
| TELEPATHY (RECEIVING) | 83 |
| RANGE LIMIT | No known limit |
| DURATION LIMIT | No known limit |
| TELEKINESIS | 78 |
| RANGE LIMIT | No known limit |
| DURATION LIMIT | No known limit |
| GENERALIZED PSIBILITIES | 99 |

It should be noted that there are a number of complicating factors in this report from the computer. First, the percentile figures are, as is customary with a subject of this age, intended to represent potential and not actual performance. It is of course most difficult to measure actual performance with an infant who cannot as yet speak, whose attention span is necessarily limited, and so on. (For a discussion of techniques for psi-testing in infants see Neona, *PSI-Testing in Infants:* see also Galcenter Bulletin 11,286.) We should like to suggest caution in the interpretation of these projected percentile limits, since it appears that they are so far beyond the norm (on the usual scale of 100 maximum) that it is difficult to take them seriously. On the other hand, the psicomputers are not given to fantasy or error. We suggest that judgment on these projected figures be reserved, in view of the normal projection profile for the Q Factor child. An average profile is cited for purposes of comparison, as follows:

| | |
|---|---|
| Q FACTOR | 36 |
| TELEPATHY (PROJECTION) | 43 |
| TELEPATHY (RECEIVING) | 57 |
| RANGE LIMIT | one-fourth galactic dimension |
| DURATION LIMIT | three hours |
| TELEKINESIS | 13 |
| RANGE LIMIT | 30 meters |
| DURATION LIMIT | 2 minutes 13 seconds |
| GENERALIZED PSIBILITIES | 40 |

It should be noted that the above profile is considered high normal and would indicate an infant who would probably prove capable of Communipath function. A comparison with the putative profile for the Infant Subject of this report will show the basis for the caution urged. It is, in fact, not really possible to determine just what such scores as are alleged for Subject Infant would mean. There is no question, of course, but that special and close attention must be given Infant Subject, and that all the facilities of the Creche must be brought to bear upon her training.

6.    Reference is made to the report on the behavior of Subject Infant submitted by Wardmistress Jane Partridge, as follows:

> This child appears to be absolutely intractable. It will not respond to normal stimulus and the impression that is received by the teachers is one of deliberate willful refusal to participate in normal infant activities of the creche. Subject Infant ignores any and all stimuli presented to it, refuses to acknowledge sensory notice of music, light, color, presence of other children, and so on. However, a complete physical examination indicates that Subject Infant has normal sensory perception. We would be inclined to say—as a result of simple exasperation—that this is a very NAUGHTY child; however, in view of the fact that there is no data whatever available with regard to the traumatic effects of separating a Factor Q infant from its parents so long after birth, naughtiness and willfulness simply cannot be seriously attributed to this child. It is recommended that every conceivable scientific effort be made to minimize trauma in this case; in particular, vigilant supervision of personnel is indicated to assure that they do not allow fatigue or exasperation to cause them to misinterpret Subject Infant's behavior.

Reference is made to the fact that the longest known interval for separation of a Factor Q child from its parents is a matter of some twenty-seven minutes, this previous occasion having been due to a premature birth occurring to parents on an asteroid where there was no Galactic Inspector Medical Computer, necessitating dispatch of one by relay rocket. The normal interval between birth of the baby and separation is about two minutes, and current research indicates that within the next few years a method of determining presence of Factor Q while infant is still unborn may make even that brief interval briefer.

7.  It is noted for the record that all recommendations made by personnel and computers with regard to this Subject Infant will be scrupulously followed. It is also noted that the government finds the entire circumstances of this situation repugnant and feels that an example should be made of the Infant Subject's mother, Factor Q Aberrant Anne-Charlotte, in order to prevent any such situation from arising in the future. It is felt that punishment of the utmost severity consistent with the principles of humane treatment of criminals and aberrants should be administered to the woman despite the very natural tendency to sympathize, since any other course might well lead to an attempt by other mothers of Factor Q babies to follow her example.

NOTE: Synthesis of all data in this file by Central Computer indicates that actual repetition of this situation is unlikely by a factor of $10^{13}$ to 1 odds, which is reassuring. Nonetheless, all precautions must be taken, since the odds against it happening once were also of astronomical magnitude. END OF NOTE.

END OF REPORT

PS: Buzzy, this poor little baby is absolutely pitiful; she'd break your heart. She just lies there and stares straight ahead with those huge brown eyes and wants her mother. This whole thing stinks.

Nysse

# CHAPTER SIX

"ANNE-CHARLOTTE," said Patrick, "we are prepared to listen to what you have to say. I warn you, though, that if you try again to perform as you did yesterday, we will put you to sleep again. We will not tolerate any more obscenity before these children."

Anne-Charlotte laughed softly, hugging her knees to her chest and letting her eyes close for a moment to hide the confidence in them.

"Are you sure," she asked, triumph smothered in her voice, "are you sure that you *can* overpower me?"

"All of us together? Of course we can."

She shook her head. "Don't be sure, Patrick," she said. "I advise you not to be so sure, not to be sure at all. I advise you to go very slow. You remember what I did with that big boulder out in the wilderness, Patrick?"

She turned her head and swept them all with her eyes. "Did he tell all of you what I did?"

"He says," answered Naomi, "that you lifted a boulder weighing fifty pounds or more and flung it through the air into a cactus a hundred yards away, and did it with such force that you smashed the catcus to a pulp."

"And that I did it by telekinesis alone!" Anne-Charlotte exulted. "You all know that?"

"We know that, Anne-Charlotte," said Ian. "Why insist on it so? Telekinesis is not so rare as all that."

"Really? Could you do what I did?"

He didn't answer her, and and she laughed again. "Of course you couldn't! You have more psibility than anyone in the cluster except for Patrick and me, and you would be hard put to it to move a slice of bread from the plate to your fingertips! You don't know anything about it!"

"And so? What does that mean to us?"

"It means that you should be careful, all of you! How do you know I will not do to you just what I did with that stone?"

There was a silence in the room, then—it fairly rang with the silence—because all of them knew, with a sick certainty, that there was that possibility. They could not believe it, would not believe it, but they didn't really know. Not one of them could have moved that stone. And the silence was doubly oppressive, because they dared not use mindspeech either. Their minds were as open to Anne-Charlotte as their faces and none of them believed for an instant in his ability to shield his thoughts against her, not with the strength she had.

"Are you going to talk to us, Anne-Charlotte," Patrick asked at last, "or are you just going to threaten us? If that's all you intend then none of us is willing to stay. There is work that needs to be done, a great deal of work, and if we wanted to take time for something else this is not how we would choose to spend it. Make up your mind. Anne-Charlotte—either speak to us reasonably or we will end this meeting now and go on to other things.

She looked around at them, setting her glance on each of them in turn as they sat in a circle around the walls of the common room. "I don't really need a meeting," she said, talking almost to herself. "If I choose I can force you to hear anything I have to say, whether you like it or not, whether you are working in the fields or at the looms or in the schoolroom or out in the desert. Don't you know that?"

"Choose that, then," said Patrick abruptly, standing up. "At least while we listen we can get some work done."

"Sit down, Patrick," she said at once. "Sit down and listen. I have no desire to make everyone angry with me."

"Then you must at least make a pretense of consideration."

She looked at him carefully, the light that shimmered about her coming and going with the violence of her thought, and they all held their breaths. That she was mad they did not doubt; there could be no question of that. For a Maklunite to threaten violence to a member of his own cluster was the depth of madness; had she done nothing else at all, that would have adequately demonstrated her condition. But what sort of madness was this —in a mind such as hers? What were they to do with her?

"You are to help me," she snapped. "That's what you are to do with me! I am of your own cluster, we are of one mind, you must help me!"

"Give us a chance to do so, then," said Tomaso gently. "Explain what it is that you want to do."

She drew a deep breath and let it out slowly, and then she said it all at once.

"I want to teleport my baby out of the Creche."

Across the room Sally's hands came up and covered her face; the gasps of the other women were almost simultaneous. Only Patrick was unmoved by the announcement, since he had had his shock the day before.

"Say that again, Anne-Charlotte," said Johan, and they all turned in surprise. Johan was very quiet; he almost never spoke, and his psibility was little better than the children's. He spent his time doing something none of them understood with a complicated set of equations and a stack of old books; and even Valya, the woman who lived with him, knew most of what she knew about him because his mind was always open to her. He was upset, or he would not have spoken.

"I said," Anne-Charlotte repeated, "that I want to teleport my baby out of the Creche. Out of the Creche and back here to me. I think that's clear enough."

"Anne-Charlotte," Sally cried, "that baby is not *your* baby! It does not belong to you!"

"And I suppose you do not call Patrick 'your' man?" Anne-Charlotte snapped. "I suppose Tomaso does not call Naomi 'his' woman?"

"Anne-Charlotte," said Patrick, his voice very stern and cold, "you are a Maklunite. You have been with us since you were a young girl. You know very well that this is nothing more than a manner of speaking, a way of naming. To say 'my' woman, 'my' man, is only a way of saying 'the person I prefer to be with above all others.' It does not and cannot mean possession!"

"I don't care," Anne-Charlotte bristled. "I don't care at all. The baby is part of me."

"As all of us are part of you."

"It's not the same thing."

"But the baby is needed, Anne-Charlotte, it is needed

for the very existence of humanity. Very, very few of all the billions born throughout the Three Galaxies are able to do the task that it will do. You must not try to prevent that."

"You hate me, all of you!" Anne-Charlotte cried.

"Nonsense," said Tomaso. "We love you. We love you with all our hearts."

"But you aren't letting me explain!"

"Explain then. Tell us."

"Let me use mindspeech only!"

"No." Patrick shook his head, seconded by the others. "That would not be fair to the children."

"Why must I be fair to the children? What concern is it of theirs?" she demanded. "It is too slow, too clumsy, to have to put in all the words. Why not write letters? Why not carve out words in stone? It's just as bad!"

Patrick sighed. "Anne-Charlotte," he said slowly, "I will say to you once again, and for the last time, that you will either observe the rules of this cluster, as they are observed by the rest of us—in which case we will listen to you, and you will explain in a manner that is intelligible to the youngest and the least of us—or else we will close this meeting and go about our business and we will hear what you force upon us if we must, but we will not be favorably disposed to consider what you ask of us."

He looked about him, anxious for the children, knowing from the expressions on their faces that Anne-Charlotte was filling their heads with her usual inventory of lights and noises and frightening shapes. They had to learn to deal with it, of course, because she was one of their own; but it was bad for them, and the rest would have to work to undo the harm she did.

"Well, Anne-Charlotte?" he asked. "What do you intend to do?"

"Abide by the rules, since you insist."

"Go ahead, then. We're listening."

"Very well. I say that my case is not the usual one. I say that my baby is not like the other babies at the Creche. She has been with me since her birth, she is not going to be able to accept the martyr conditioning at the Creche. It will not work with her. She is different, she is an exception, and she must not be kept from me. She is unhappy away from me, she is suffering, and I suffer with her! Can't you understand that? Don't you realize, can't you understand for just one moment what it is like for me to feel her suffering, to know what she endures hungering for me, and be separated from her?"

"How can you be sure, Anne-Charlotte, that the baby is unhappy? How can you know? The Creche is shielded."

"Not for my baby," said Anne-Charlotte proudly. "Their bloody shield doesn't work any more than if I laid a handkerchief over my head it would keep you from hearing me think!"

"Anne-Charlotte," said Patrick in the wondering silence that followed, "I believe that what you say is true. But if it is, then it is even more important that the baby be in the Creche where it can be trained."

"Why? For the Light's sake, give me one good reason?"

He told her, then, what Coyote Jones had told him when he came to take the baby, about the freighter that had been lost because of the baby's interference with the Communipath network.

"Don't you see, Anne-Charlotte," he said, "that the baby, if left to just grow up here with us, is a danger to all the people who depend on the Bucket, not only just as an inconvenience to communication but because it threatens their very lives? That can't be allowed, Anne-Charlotte."

She watched him wildly, standing now, her hands rising slowly from her sides, her whole body quivering and flickering with the energy echo from her thoughts.

"And," Patrick went on, "we will have no choice except to advise the authorities at the Creche at once of the fact that the shield does not work where your child is concerned. It can only be pure good luck that there have been no other accidents if the baby is still able to project as if there were no shield there. And you, Anne-Charlotte, instead of plotting to do evil, must try to reach the baby and make it understand that it must *not* send its thoughts so far. You, or someone else if you are unwilling, will have to make it understand, young though it is, that it literally has the power to cause people's deaths."

"There is something else," Tomaso broke in.

"Yes, Tomaso?"

"There is the matter of the charges against Anne-Charlotte. She does not seem to understand her present position."

"We have all forgotten that in the confusion," Patrick agreed. "Damn and damn and double damn! Don't you see, Anne-Charlotte, that even if we approved of what you choose to do, even if we were willing to help you do it, it would do you not one bit of good? My poor darling, you are charged with high treason and it is only a matter of time until they send the Fedrobots to take you back to Galactic Center for trial. If you have the baby with you then they will only take it back to the Creche again and that will mean two separations from you instead of just one, and all that horror to be repeated once more. You must see that!"

"Patrick?"

The small voice from the tiny girl who sat at Sally's feet stopped him in the middle of his speech. "What is it, child?" he asked.

"I want to know something."

"Yes?"

"I want to know what will happen to Anne-Charlotte if the Fedrobots come. I want to know what they will *do* to Anne-Charlotte."

Patrick hesitated, but Anne-Charlotte did not. She turned to the little girl, Patrick's smallest daughter, and very clearly she explained.

"What happens to someone charged with high treason against humankind, Patricia? It's quite simple. The brain of the traitor is severed from the body, completely, and it is placed in nutrient tanks where it is kept alive until such time as it is needed by humankind."

"Give her an example," Ian directed.

"The brain of Marcus Strake," said Anne-Charlotte, "who tried to create a market for a drug he had invented by adding it to the water supply of a planet. His brain was maintained in nutrient solutions for almost forty years. Then it was wired in directly into the controls of the explorer ship *Nightwind* that was used to locate the habitable planets of the Third Galaxy. It served in that capacity for eleven expeditions before it finally went mad and died, and then the name of Marcus Strake was considered to have been cleared by its service."

"And the body?" the child insisted, staring at her with big eyes.

"The body is burned," said Anne-Charlotte brutally.

"With fire?"

"With high energy blasts."

"Like when someone dies," said Patricia, her voice trembling.

"Yes! Like when someone dies, exactly."

Patricia forgot then about the decorum of the meeting and ran to her father, crying bitterly that she did not want that done to Anne-Charlotte, that they must do something to stop it; and Patrick did not scold her nor would he allow Sally to take her from him. Holding her close and stroking her fine yellow hair, he spoke to all of them.

"The child is not alone," he said. "None of us wants to see that happen to Anne-Charlotte. None of us feels that what she has done is in the same class as attempting to make drug addicts of a whole planet. But I do not think we need to worry about it, because there is no question of her being convicted. I think," he said, his voice breaking, "I think we are all able to see, without the need for any doctor's help, that Anne-Charlotte is completely, totally insane. The mad are not held responsible for their crimes."

And as he said that, without one word or one sound, Anne-Charlotte disappeared.

# CHAPTER SEVEN

THE SUN from the high windows in Tzana's room fell through a great prism the size of a fist that hung from the ceiling, split into a sevenfold glory and turned Tzana into a creature of rainbow. Beside her Coyote lay contented, tracing the brilliant stripes along her thighs and the soft curve of her belly, up along the tilted breasts and back down again. She lay quiet under his touch, watching him through half-closed eyes.

"Tzana?"

"Yes, love?"

"Do you know, it's very nice to see you like this."

"Replete, you mean? Like the ancient Bordencow?"

"No. Quiet, I mean. Quiet, relaxed, loving. None of the efficient superspy about you at the moment at all."

She smiled at him, reached out one hand and stroked his cheek, and sent him image after image of soft warm shapes in scarlet.

"I'm sorry I don't understand everything you're sending," he said gently. "I really am sorry about that."

"I don't mind," she said. "Why should I?"

"I don't know. Isn't it something like talking to someone who's almost deaf?

She didn't answer, and he nudged her with one sturdy toe. "Come on, Tzana," he said. "I've been told before. Very much, they tell me, like mouthing words at someone who can't hear you, just like I said. Very frustrating, apparently."

"We have other ways of communicating," she said, chuckling, "and I find them totally *un*frustrating."

Coyote laughed and began to concentrate carefully on

the patterns of his stroking, watching the changes in her mouth and the nipples of her breasts. She was a good woman to bed, satisfyingly hungry, free of any remnant of the inhibitions that still marked some women, especially those who lived near Old Earth. Despite the fact that her psibility was so far beyond his, they had enjoyed one another through some dozen of the past years, whenever their work chanced to throw them together. He would miss her, he knew, if he did not see her at least once or twice a year, and to a certain extent that amazed him, since he ordinarily would not have noticed if the people he knew had disappeared from the face of the earth. And she respected his privacy totally, never entering his mind unless he asked her to do so, never pressing him for anything. . . .

He smiled, thinking of her eminent satisfactoriness as a woman. She deserved the best he had to give, and the best was precisely what she was about to get.

He gathered her toward him, settling her expertly against his side, and bent to her mouth, feeling the quickness of her breath against his face—and from the com-system in the curve of the room across from them there came the high series of triplet tones, A,C,E, over and over; the same quick minor triad that meant top priority government call.

Her feet hit the floor with the second sounding of the A, and before he could finish cursing she had punched the RECEIVE button and the voice of their mutual superior informed them crisply that they were wanted. At once. Immediately, if not much, much sooner.

"Cover?" asked Tzana, and Coyote noted with distaste that her voice was almost completely back to normal.

"Coyote—I presume you are able to reach him, Miss Kai?"

"I'm able," she snapped. "As you know perfectly damn well, you officious bastard."

"Shame on you, Miss Kai," said the voice. "A little more respect, please."

She ignored it and repeated, "What cover, please?"

"Coyote Jones is expected to give a concert—antique Twentieth Century Ballads—for the vice-president of the Tri-Galactic Federation, and a group of twelve guests, at the Marsgovernment House. You, Tzana, are needed as translator for a group of aliens—wiggly things they are, too—from beyond the Sirius Gap, here to observe methods at the Creche. Actually, we will need you both at a meeting at once. Or sooner. Make it fast."

"How fast?"

Coyote went to the comsystem in one lunge, grabbed Tzana across the flank and pinned her securely against him, and bellowed at the voice.

"We can't possibly make it for at least three hours, and more likely four, because—"

"On the contrary," the voice cut in, "this is an emergency, a Federation rocket is at this moment on Tzana's landing port, and I will expect you within the hour."

The system went dead, the man's usual way of dealing with obstreperous agents, and Coyote knew from long experience that calling back would produce only a series of charming, patient, useless secretary-robots. If he was lucky he might get a human being, but there would be little or no difference between her and the robots.

"BEM dung," he observed, flatly. "Piles of odorous BEM dung. Piles and piles of—"

"Coyote," she chided, "you are only wasting your time."

"Time with you is never wasted, love."

"You are a dear and a darling and a gallant blessing to have about the house," she said, slipping out of his grip and heading for the bath, "but it's no use. You know that perfectly well. If there were any chance of our ignoring him we'd both be in some other profession."

"Like folk singing? Or running a translation bureau?"

"Yes. Like one of those."

Coyote reached up and slapped the prism, shattering the rainbow into thousands of scraps and patches that went scuttling and skipping across the floor in frantic clusters. There would be another time, no doubt, if they were both lucky, but he was not pleased. Not that his pleasure was relevant in any way.

"Hurry up," he shouted after her. "We wouldn't want to keep a government rocket waiting, at xty-ump credits per three minutes, now would we?"

Tzana chuckled, came out of the bath at a run, and pulled over her head a spectacular little piece of yellow synthowool that was made up mostly of empty spaces, a pair of yellow tights, and working slippers, little clear plastic things slotted for magnets for use in low-gravity situations. She smoothed her hair with both hands, smiled, and was ready to go, and there he stood still naked in the middle of her floor, watching her with great satisfaction. If there was anything he could not abide it was a woman who took forever to get herself dressed and groomed, and Tzana was the absolute antithesis of that.

"Forty-five seconds flat!" he said appreciatively. "That has got to be some sort of a record."

"Forty-three," she said. "And now I have to wait for you."

"Nope," said Coyote. "I'm ready."

"You call that ready?"

"Hell, yes! I'm not primping for that old bastard and his crew of lobotomied robots and yes-men. I'm ready as is."

"Naked?"

"Naked?" he mimicked, in a piping falsetto. "With your not inconsiderable equipment hanging out? Whatever will we do? La, what *will* the neighbors say?"

"Coyote," Tzana said patiently, "we are going to Mars, remember? Government Central. Big muckymucks. Protocol and high class twaddle. All sorts of—"

"BEM dung. All sorts of BEM dung. I'm going to give a concert, as I recall, and I always give concerts in my skinny-skin-skin."

"I don't believe it."

"Sometimes I wear a sort of loincloth."

"I don't believe you, man."

"Unless I'm on a planet with very low temperatures and no central heating."

"You really mean it?"

"Mean it. Yes. I do."

Tzana sighed and pressed the stud that released the little yellow dress.

"Hey," Coyote protested, "must you do that?"

"Certainly. If you're going naked, so am I."

"Then I'll dress," said Coyote promptly. "Not that I don't know when I've been had, lady, because I do, and don't expect it to work every time. But I can't possibly listen to Old Whatshisface if you're standing beside me with *your* equipment hanging out. I'd keep patting and fondling. I'd find my mind wandering. I'd be unable to keep track of Whoozis's conversation. I'd lay you right there on the table. Here."

He reached into the black guitar case that lay against the wall, pulled out a black caftan with a hood, popped it over his head, added sandals, and watched her restore her dress.

"Good enough," he said. "Let's go."

They went out through the Bureau, deflating everything behind them except the living quarters of the rest of the staff and the reception room, and boarded the rocket, with Coyote humming at the top of his lungs an antique ballad he knew Old Whatshisface particularly despised.

"What is that tune?" Tzana asked, settling herself beside him.

"This one?"

"That one. What the bloody is it?"

"Don't you like it?"

"It's awful. It's incredibly awful."

"It's really old, lady! 1953, I think. Thing called 'Harbor Lights.' Our friend the Fish really hates it."

"I don't blame him! *Yechh.*"

"Isn't it though?"

"And that's why you're practicing?"

"Exactly! That's why. He *really* hates it."

Coyote leaned back, closed his eyes, and really put his heart into it.

# CHAPTER EIGHT

HERE I AM, up in this cactus again. It's getting to be some kind of a tradition, this cactus, and me writing in it. Yesterday I heard Mark tell two of the little kids to "stay out of Tessa's cactus." I'm not sure that's a good thing, even if he didn't mean it. That is, I'm not sure I like what it indicates about me.

Once, long ago, Patrick says, there was a great philosopher who could only think if he could see a certain tree from his window as he worked; and when the city where he lived was going to cut down all the other trees around they left that one because he explained that he needed it. That was nice of them, of course, but I certainly wouldn't want that to happen to me, because I want to be able to work no matter where I am. I think tomorrow I will definitely go and work on a rock or something, instead of coming here.

It's very peaceful now, quiet and peaceful and beautiful. From where I sit I can see Freya working in the salad beds with Dan and Nathan, and Ian has Tomaso's three boys and my little sister Patricia down by the well practicing the skit they are putting on in honor of Patrick's birthday. I wrote it, so I'm not required to be in it, and that leaves me extra free time today, and unless Sally catches me and makes me come back to help her with the breadbaking I will be able to write for a couple of hours! I feel a little bit guilty, because Sally is tired from yesterday, and baking bread for twenty people is a big job. But I don't feel guilty enough to make me go back and help her. Patrick says this is a good quality in a writer —he calls it "protective insulation"—but he says I am to keep a careful eye on it and if it starts approaching selfishness I will be forbidden to write at all until I have learned to do my share again.

That would be awful, I think. I think if I were forbidden to write I would die like something that had been shut up and stepped on. (And of course that means I must be *very* sure it's not selfishness.)

In fact, now that I have started on this train of thought, there is just no question about it, I will have to go back and help Sally instead of writing. A conscience is a very uncomfortable thing indeed to have, and I wish it were in the depths of space. Here I go!

Now I have only perhaps half an hour left before dinner, and I will have to rush through this, but at least my conscience is happy. Sally and I made enough bread for a whole week, I'm sure, if not enough for a month, and I thought she would never be satisfied that it was enough. She is a hard-working woman and I don't know what we would do without her at Chrysanthemum Bridge, and I sincerely hope I don't grow up to be like her just because she's my mother. I'll fight my heredity!

What I was just beginning to say was that it was so very peaceful here for the first time in weeks. The reason it's peaceful is sad, though; it's peaceful because we have Anne-Charlotte under complete sedation, and so there's not a single really ugly thought in the air for a change. I do love Anne-Charlotte, we all do, but we were just all worn out with her constant messing up our heads. I know what it was like for me; I can't even imagine what it must have been like for the others, who have Factor Q. Having her completely asleep is like having a weight lifted from off my head, and I'm a little giddy, I guess, with the ease of it.

I wouldn't have thought what Anne-Charlotte did was possible. I know about telekinesis, of course, and at least in theory I know about teleporting, because Maklunites are trained in all known forms of psi from birth. I know they teach teleporting in the Creche, too, and even without training some humans can use it. But I have never seen anyone teleport his body more than just in simple levitation exercises, a matter of a few feet. Even the sort of skimming along the ground that Anne-Charlotte has always done was nothing more than a fancying up of levitation. We used to try to copy her, all of us kids did, and we found out very fast that it wasn't so awful hard to make a couple of little leaps, but to keep it up over and over like Anne-Charlotte does is a terribly rare thing. None of the rest of us can do it, and Tomaso says he's only known one other person in his whole life who could.

But the day we had the meeting Anne-Charlotte did even more than that! She was very angry with us because we would not do what she wanted us to do, even though she must know that it is terribly wrong for her to plan to steal her baby from the Creche. We could not do that, or help her hide it if she was able to do it, especially after Patrick explained to us how the baby is an actual danger to people living in the Galaxies.

And then she was very angry because Patrick said that she had that mind sickness that he calls insanity. She was so angry, and so beautiful. And one minute she was standing there, wearing only her beads and sort of pulsing and glowing, with anger just pouring from her so that I was really almost afraid of her, and then suddenly she was gone! We didn't see her move, it happened so fast; she just disappeared like something that had never been. Patricia screamed and Patrick began to curse, which I don't think I've ever heard him do before, and everyone first stood like they'd been hit on the head and then we all ran at once for the doors and windows.

Outside our livingdomes the country is flat for the space of our fields, and then it begins to slant up, just very easily, and soon it turns into low hills with thick groves of the Anais cactus. Out at the edge of the distance you can see from the domes the hills turn into high red bluffs that rise up out of the ground all of a sudden, and then on top of them is the wilderness where the cactus are so thick you can get lost in them. The first bluff at the edge of the hills is called Troublesome, after some mountain on Earth when people still lived there. At least that's what Ian tells us in the history talk-classes, though he couldn't show us where it might have been on the maps. He says it may well have been just a story mountain, something out of a myth or a fairy tale, but that there are old songs that tell of a mountain named Troublesome.

We were all looking out of different windows and doors when Freya called out, "There she is, Patrick! Come look —oh, please hurry!" And we all ran, just in time to see a

tiny figure standing on top of Troublesome before it disappeared into the wilderness.

Freya just dropped to the floor then and began to cry.
I'd never seen her cry before and it made me cry. Then
Ian went over and put his arms around her and rocked
her gently and soothed her, and Sally came and made all
the children go outside. Freya is the oldest of our women
except for Naomi and she has always mothered Anne-
Charlotte, as much as anyone *could* mother someone wild
like Anne-Charlotte is. And Sally told us it was just as if
Freya was losing a beloved child, except really almost
worse than death to have Anne-Charlotte lost and sick
and frantic like that.

Then when Freya was calm again we had another
meeting. With all the meetings and discussion nothing was
getting done, and it's a wonder all our crops aren't ruined,
but there was no way to get around it. There had to be a
meeting for us to discuss declaring Anne-Charlotte not
able to decide things for herself. This was a serious step
to take, because Maklunites do not interfere with one
another. I don't understand, myself, what it could be like
to live under any other sort of arrangement, and Ian says
I am very lucky indeed to be able to say that. He tells us
that there were thousands of years back in the beginnings
of human history when the great majority of people
lived their entire lives, from birth to death, without ever
knowing what it could be like to be free to decide *anything*
for themselves, and that that is why we are so extremely
careful now in our clusters to preserve freedom for one
another.

Patrick and Ian explained to us all at the meeting, then,
that Anne-Charlotte is like a small baby now; she cannot
be trusted to care for herself or even to know what she
really wants to do. And so we must do all her deciding for
her from now on.

"We are all responsible for her," Patrick said, "down to
the youngest of you children, because she is one of our
own and she is so completely lost and alone. And she is
much worse than a child in one way, because she is capable of doing great harm and not capable of discriminating
between what is right and what is wrong. She is like a fire
that has gone out of control, and we must see to it that
she does no more damage, to herself or to others."

Sally asked Patrick what he thought should be done,

and for a little while I thought he had no answer, because he just stood there and said nothing.

After a while Tomaso came over and touched him on the shoulder, and Patrick sort of jumped as if he had been asleep. And Tomaso spoke to him in such a gentle voice, like someone speaking to a person who is sick or hurt. So *funny*, to hear anyone speak to Patrick like that! Patrick has always been our tower of strength, all my life long.

Tomaso said, "Patrick, you must let someone else help you with this. You've been too close to Anne-Charlotte all along and you've worn youself out with the whole terrible mess. Let it go, let us take it all over for you. Go and rest!"

But Patrick shook his head. "No," he said. "No, I can't."

"But you love her entirely too much to be able to think properly," Tomaso said.

"That's just it," said Patrick, and he explained that it was precisely because he had loved Anne-Charlotte so much that he had to take his full share of the deciding and the action where she was concerned.

"I think I must have let her go on her own way too long," he said sadly. "Perhaps I loved her too much. I think if I had loved her less, if she had been less dear to me, less close, I might have taken action against her months ago."

"You mustn't blame yourself," Freya said. "I did exactly the same thing. I've known her from the very first, and I knew always that she was wild and in many ways in need of control, and yet I always spoiled her. She was so lovely, and so very free, and I loved to watch her. Patrick, we've all done just what you did."

"That's no excuse for me," he said, "because I knew. I knew before any of you did, from the day that they came and took away the baby. When she raised it over her head to smash it against the wall, my friends, she wasn't just being dramatic. I saw her eyes, and she would indeed have killed that child rather than give it up if I hadn't moved as fast as I did and taken it from her. I knew then that her mind was ruined, completely ruined, and I should have called this meeting then, at once."

He shrugged his shoulders, and went on, "But that's all pretty irrelevant now. The question is what action should be taken. You all agree that she is completely mad and must not be allowed her freedom?"

We all nodded and raised our hands in the sign for agreement, the formal sign that we use only when it really matters, and Patrick looked all round the circle to be sure it was a matter on which we were united.

"Then," he said, "it will be entered in the Log that as of today the laws of freedom are suspended where Anne-Charlotte is concerned. And I think what we must do is go after her in the flyer. Freya and Ian and Valya and Jonathan and I together should be able to handle her, unless she is completely beyond all control. Tomaso, will you stay here? Someone with a good range must stay here so that we can contact the cluster if we need to."

It was a cruel thing they were going to have to do, he explained to us, because obviously they could not just go pick up Anne-Charlotte as they could have done with any of the rest of us. Not when she could teleport herself for miles at a time.

"We will have to exhaust her," he said. "All we can do is use our collective psi to anticipate the direction of each jump she makes so that we don't lose her completely, and simply run her down at each one, keep her making jumps until she drops with exhaustion, and then we can land and bring her home. Under complete sedation."

"Patrick, does it have to be like that?" Sally asked. "It sounds like the way animals are hunted . . . driven till they drop like that!"

"What else would you suggest, darlin'?" he asked her.

"Is there no other way?"

"I really don't think so, Sally."

"We don't dare do anything else," Freya said. "We don't know how strong she is, we don't know what her limits are or even if she has any, in practical terms. It's even possible that she will be able to bring down the flyer like she would bring down a bird with a stone. I don't think we can afford the luxury of mercy any more."

They told us that if she were to come back to the cluster we children were to make ourselves as scarce as we possibly could. Not that they thought she would hurt us, none of us could believe that she would, but they said we couldn't really know and that we must take no chances.

"And you must not hate her," Patrick said in a sick voice. "Her poor mind is sick, it is ruined, just remember that. She does not know what she is doing, and you must not hate her."

As if any of us could have hated Anne-Charlotte! Why, before they took her baby away it was always Anne-Charlotte who took us on trips into the Anais cactus, and she would tell us stories there. She knew better stories than any of the other grown-ups, and she knew more and better songs. And once she took me into her bed and held me all the whole night long when I was frightened of a storm, and not once that night did she call me a silly baby or laugh at me. I love Anne-Charlotte, and I wish someone could make her well.

She is asleep now. It took them almost fourteen hours to reach the end of her strength. They say she made no attempt to harm the flier or any of them, but just kept leaping, miles at a time, with the jumps getting shorter and shorter, until at the end she could only move a few feet at a time. And they had to sit in the flier above her, watching, until she actually dropped unconscious in the sand below them, bruising her poor head on the side of a rock, and then they went down and gave her a sedative that would keep her out, and they brought her back.

Ian carried her into the ashram at last and laid her on a pallet under the made-mantra that was her favorite, where she had lain when her baby was born. I watched him lay her down and cover her with her own blanket, and she looked small and thin and young, and so tired. There was no glow about her then at all, almost no life, because they had lowered all her life processes as much as they dared with the sleeping drug.

I asked to sleep there beside her, but they wouldn't let me. Patrick said no, I must leave her to whatever healing Valya might be able to do. Valya is a powerful healing-woman, fully trained in psimedicine. We ourselves rarely need her, because Maklunites are almost never sick; but out here on the edge of the Galaxies where there are so few doctors Valya is kept very busy, and she is often away for days at a time. Patrick said that she must be able to be alone with Anne-Charlotte and free to concentrate only on Anne-Charlotte, and that if I were to stay my mind would interfere with that concentration, and of course I can understand that. I am sorry, though, that I could not have stayed, because I worry now when I cannot see her. I know it's silly, because obviously she cannot teleport with her body filled with that drug, but seeing her disappear once has somehow made me feel that she may not be there unless I can see her with my own eyes.

Valya has been with her ever since they brought her back, except for a short while during the night when her man Johan went and made her sleep a bit and took the watch in her place.

It's peaceful, like I said. Everyone has gone in from the fields and there's a low wind rising, and twenty feet from me there is a mobile flower, about as high as my knee and a pale lavender color, doing a solemn little dance in the breeze all by itself in a circle. So peaceful, and so mournful, and so quiet.

Whatever is going to happen next?

# CHAPTER NINE

I KNOW who I am. No one else knows. But I do know who I am. I am not BABY. A woman comes. A woman comes and she calls me BABY and she says to me HELLO BABY. She brings things. She puts me in a bed and all around me there are colors. I like colors. I like the fish that swim there. But I am not BABY.

There is a box that comes, too. Anne-Charlotte says the box is called COMPUTER. That is its NAME. I like colors. I like fish. I like names. The computer calls me BABY too, but that is not my name. I am not BABY. I am SUSANNAH now. I am SUSANNAH.

There is a golden light on the wall now. It will change when the song changes. The song will change because I am going to make it change. I know how to make the songbox go the other way. There are little wheels inside the songbox and it is far away. It is clear far away where the woman is. The woman who does not know my name. And she has a button to push to make the songbox change so that the color will change. But she is too slow. I like to see the color change. I am tired of the gold. I want to see red now, red on my wall and on my floor and across my bed. There are people talking in the air. They are talking about me. They call me BABY. They do not know that I am not BABY. They do not know that I am SUSANNAH.

There. There, now. Now the light is red. In a minute I will make it blue. Far out in the dark there are silver things moving, but I know now that I must not bother them. I know because the computer told me and because a man came and told me. The silver things could fall out of the air if I wanted to look at them, but I must not do that. I must not touch them and I must be careful of them. The people who talk in the air can be hurt, too . . . they are busy, and I must not bother them. I must not make pictures for them and I must not talk to them. I don't like all the MUST NOTS.

Now the light is blue and the woman is coming. She will say to me BABY YOU MUST LET THE MUSI-COLORS ALONE. PLEASE BABY. Why should I let them alone? There is no one who will fall or be hurt if I play with them. If she will stop calling me BABY then maybe I will do what she says.

Anne-Charlotte is not talking to me tonight and I am afraid. Why isn't she talking to me? I know her mind-voice. It is like the brown sand they put in my fruit. CINNAMON. That is the name of the brown stuff. It would be very nice if my mouth could make all the names that my head knows, but I cannot make it work. I can change the colors though. I can change the songbox and change the colors. I can say the name CINNAMON. I will be able to say SUSANNAH, too, if I try. I will try it now. SUSANNAH. Why isn't my mother talking to me tonight?

Nothing is wrong with my mother, though. I know that. If something happened to her I would know about it. I would know and I would start to bother and bother and bother everyone until they helped my mother. I would make the silver things fall down and I would scream at the people who talk in the air and make ter-rible pictures for them.

But Anne-Charlotte is just sleeping. She is sleeping, but somehow she has turned off her mindvoice. How can that be?

The woman is here now. If I could make the words I would ask her how that can be. She is touching me. I could make her hand burn where she touched me but I won't do that because she is good to me. But I don't want her to call me BABY. I am not BABY. I am SUSAN-NAH.

Now the light is green. The woman has turned off the songbox but it is easy to turn it back on. If I do not get too sleepy I will keep changing the colors all night long. Now it is orange. I cannot say its name but I know the look it has.

I want to hear Anne Charlotte's mindvoice. . . . I am afraid without it.

Now the color is blue again.

I am not going to go to sleep.

I am going to stay awake all night and wait for my mother to talk to me.

I am not going to go to sleep.

I am SUSANNAH and I am not going to go to sleep.

I am not . . .

I . . .

# CHAPTER TEN

"WE WISH to thank you for coming so promptly," said the tall man in the brown tunic; and the other men, dressed like him in the official worktunics of the Tri-Galactic Intelligence Service, nodded their agreement. "It was good of you," said the man in brown.

He was called the Fish, because the legend was that he had never shown signs of having human blood in his veins, not once in all his years of service. The men around him had similar code names, and those who knew them well could use those, or they could use the TGIS numbers marked on the shoulders of the tunics.

No one *wanted* to be a TGIS man; it was a service filled by lottery from among the most capable, both male and female, human and alien, each year. Once chosen, an agent served ten years. Often it happened that by the end of that time his awareness of how badly he was needed kept him in the service past the end of the obligatory term. All of the men in this room were on voluntary, some of them had seen thirty years. For the Fish, it was the thirty-fourth.

"You are not at all welcome," said Tzana crisply. "I have just finished two nasty assignments for you, Coyote has just completed one of the nastiest you've ever given anyone, and besides that we are tired, both of us. We both need a long rest."

"My heart bleeds," observed the Fish.

"We are sorry, despite his attitude," said another of the men. "This is important, or we would not have called on you again so soon."

"It's always important, according to you," said Tzana.

"Please be quick with it and let us get this over with. We were interrupted at a most inopportune moment."

The Fish smiled and opened his mouth, but Coyote beat him to it.

"We know," he said. "Your heart, it bleeds."

"What is it this time?" Tzana insisted. "Drug smugglers? A broken robot gone berserk in a cafeteria? The khadilh of Abba lost his favorite pet? A mutant insisting on his civil rights? What incredibly urgent matter demands our attention that could not have been handled by one of your other agents just as well?"

"Miss Kai, you are positively vitriolic," snapped the Fish. "Kindly control your venom."

"Damned if I will," Tzana said. "Get on with it."

"It's this Rogue Telepath business again."

"What?" Coyote stood up and shouted at the old man. "I told you by god when I got rid of that poor little baby—that poor little so-called rogue telepath that I could have held on the palm of my hand—I told you I'd have nothing more to do with it. I'm not kidnapping any more babies from their mothers, not if you order me at laser point, is that clear?"

"My, my, such youthful exuberance," murmured the Fish. "It's not that at all."

"No, no, Citizen Jones," said a man on their left, known as the Ruby because he was a brilliant ruby color from head (if it was a head) to foot (if it was a foot).

"What, then?"

The Ruby smiled. "It's the child's mother we need now, my friend."

"The mother?" Tzana was amazed. "Haven't we done enough to her already?"

"You forget, Citizen Kai," said the Ruby. "The woman is a criminal, charged with the gravest crime known to mankind."

"Those charges were meant seriously?"

"The Light be patient, Miss Kai," said the Fish harshly. "That's not the sort of charge that's made as a joke!"

"Yes, indeed," came the agreement from around the table.

"Why did you think they weren't serious?" asked the Fish. "High treason against humanity is not ordinarily seen as a pecadillo."

"Well," said Coyote slowly, "I agree that the woman

broke a law. A very important law, basic to the survival
of all of us. Okay? I grant you that. However, it seems to
me that there were very special circumstances involved
here."

"Such as?"

"Such as the fact that she was known to be a Factor Q
Aberrant. Such as the fact that she had spent the full limit
of years in training in the Creche before the government
finally decided to let her go, and no one really knows
how much that hurts the mind, even if we do erase the
training by psychosweep. Such as the fact that she was
only twenty-two years old when the baby was born and
had undergone severe psychic shock only a few months
before when the baby's father died. And, most important
of all, such as the fact that I think she's suffered enough
already."

The Fish made a noise of derision.

"I am inclined to agree with Coyote," said Tzana.

"You are always inclined to agree with Coyote, Miss
Kai," said the Fish. "I don't consider that relevant."

Tzana glared at him. Pigheaded old bastard, with his
affected ancient terms of address and his stupid slavish
devotion to minutiae of the rules and his utter disregard
for the human heart. Perhaps this would be her lucky
day. Perhaps he would die horribly before her eyes.

The Fish glared back at her, very much alive.

"There are courts, after all," said another man mildly.
"There are courts and judges and all the rest of it. If there
are extenuating circumstances the woman will be par-
doned or her sentence made lighter. It is not up to us to
do that."

"It *is* up to us to see that she is brought back to civilization to stand trial," said the Fish. "That's what we
want you two to do."

"Why us?" demanded Coyote. "Why not a couple of
Fedrobots? You've got lots."

"Because," said the Fish, "for all we know she would
melt them both into puddles of plastic and make herself
a raincoat out of the puddles. That's why you."

"Oh, crap," said Tzana digustedly. "What are you
talking about, or have you at last gone senile?"

"Well, let me tell you a thing or two," said the Fish,
"and perhaps you will find it less 'crap,' as you so very
elegantly put it. We have had a long and detailed com-

munication from that bank of freakish fanatics in the outback—"

"Maklunites are not freakish fanatics," objected Coyote.

"Nonsense, of course they are. Living like Stone Age savages in conditions more appropriate for the year 2018 than 3018. No hygiene. Food cooked by hand. No morals. Ugh. Please do not spout froth at me."

"Look, my fishy friend—"

"I will *not* 'look' and there's no point in your insisting. In this day and age only fanatics, and totally demented fanatics at that, could conceivably live as do the Maklunites. They have a philosophy of life which would do credit to a child of three and is a disgrace thereafter. They are idiotic, backward, sloppy, cravenly sentimental fanatics, and if it were up to me they would certainly not continue to escape three-fourths of the duties of a galactic citizen because of the so-called precepts of their so-called religion. Don't talk to me about the Maklunites! Nonetheless, we have had a communication from them. A long and flowery and archaic communication, but, I am happy to say, comprehensible."

"Pray do tell us," Tzana said through her teeth, sending soothing messages at Coyote as hard as she could. If he were to punch the Fish in the mouth that worthy might very well die just as she had wished, but Coyote would be taken away and shut up and she had no desire to see that happen. In view of the fact that Coyote, being a mass projective telepath, could have rendered every man in the room unconscious with one thought, it was funny that she had to worry about his fists, but that was how he was. She could see the muscles twitching in his hands.

"I intend to," said the Fish. "It seems that this woman has gone quite berserk, threatening to teleport her child out of the Creche and all sorts of other nonsense. Although I do not think that this is within the realm of possibility, much less probability, the Maklunites inform me that they have seen her teleport a fifty-pound boulder through the air over a distance of several hundred feet. They also inform me that they have seen her teleport her own body for as much as fifteen or twenty miles, instantly and repeatedly. They inform me that they have no idea what the limits of her psibility may be, but they strongly advise caution in dealing with her."

"But that would mean they are betraying her!" exclaimed Coyote. "I find that hard to believe. Maklunites don't betray their own people."

"They don't have betrayal in mind," said the Ruby. "The communication demands that we drop all charges against her on the grounds that she is totally and completely insane and is therefore not responsible for her acts. The detailed list of things that she has done is given not as betrayal but as support for their contention that she is mad."

"I see," said Coyote. "I see what they are doing."

"I see, too," snapped the Fish. "And I don't intend to let them get away with it, my young friend."

"I am not your friend," said Coyote. "Thank God."

"God who?"

"Take your pick, you old humbug. Astarte. Jehovah. Icthy 12. I don't care. Thank anybody. Just so you don't count me in among your friends."

"What do you plan to do?" Tzana asked.

"I want the woman brought back."

"Even if she's mad?"

"Nonsense. Madness has been unknown in the Three Galaxies since the 2080's. Nonsense."

"Not completely unknown," observed a quiet man from the end of the table. "Eleven cases reported since then."

"Eleven cases in thirty years? Not very impressive," said the Fish. "I want her brought back here. We have psychcomputers. They will be given full access to her."

"Oh, really? How are you going to manage that?" demanded Tzana. "You know perfectly well that the moment she was allowed to be awake enough for them to examine her, if what the people at Chrysanthemum Bridge say about her is true, she would just teleport herself or the psychcomputer halfway to hell. How do you propose to examine her?"

"We'll find a way."

"How are they dealing with her now? At Chrysanthemum Bridge, I mean?" asked Coyote. "Aren't they in danger?"

"The woman is under total sedation."

"And that's how we are to bring her back?"

"You are quite correct."

"In that case, you don't need us. Send a Fedrobot."

"Unfortunately," said the Ruby, "we can't do that. The Maklunites refuse to turn her over to anyone but a human being. We do not wish to create an intergalactic riot by taking her from them by force."

"Ah," said Tzana. "I begin to see."

"Perspicacious of you, Miss Kai."

"We are to bring her back quietly, without upsetting any Maklunites, because despite your opinion of them, they make up a very respectable proportion of the total population of the Three Galaxies. We are to bring her back under total sedation . . . what, then? How do you plan to try her?"

Coyote cut her off short. "They don't plan to try her at all, Tzana! Don't you see? They couldn't possibly. They wouldn't dare wake her to stand trial, she'd dissolve the lot of them. They'll bring her back here, pass sentence, take her poor muddled mind and put it in nutrients for some pet project, all very quietly, without any fuss, all without ever waking her up again."

The Fish sighed loudly.

"Don't I just wish we could get away with that," he said. "If only we could get away with that, Mr. Jones, we wouldn't have any problems. Unfortunately, we can't do it that way. In spite of the fact that she and her brat literally endanger the entire world, the law is going to insist on protecting *them* from *us*. We have to wake her for the actual trial. We can keep her as heavily sedated as we dare, but we have to wake her, in the formal sense of the word. And that is going to be very dangerous indeed."

Coyote whistled long and slow.

"Perhaps they're exaggerating?" he ventured.

"Maklunites don't exaggerate," said the Ruby. "Whatever one's opinion of the sect, and I must say I find them rather charming and appealing, they are certainly truthful. If they say this young woman can send herself bouncing about like a rocket, then she can. And if she can do that, I, for one, would not care to have to guess what else she might be able to do."

"She glows, by the way," said Coyote. "How about that, for a beginning?"

"Glows? What do you mean, glows?" said the Fish. "Nobody glows."

"This chick does."

"Chick? Mr. Jones—"

"Chick. Archaic twentieth-century term for a woman. Very common in a particular type of hard rock song. I happen to like the term. And this one, this chick, glows. Like a candle."

"What's the plan?" asked Tzana. "Why aren't you just ordering her killed, which would be the obvious move?"

"For the simple reason that we don't dare. Number One, there are too many Maklunites. Number Two, we don't have any idea what the damned baby might do if we did."

"Oh, I see!" laughed Tzana. "Baby has talents like her mother, eh? The joke seems to be on you!"

"It happens, however," said the Fish grimly, "that at the moment we have physical custody of the baby, and we don't *think* it can teleport itself. So long as we have her baby, we think the woman will be careful what she destroys. We hope so. It's a chance we have to take, at least at the time of the actual trial. But not before."

"I don't want anything to do with it," said Coyote.

The Fish curled his thin lip. "I don't give one thin damn, Mr. High-and-mighty Jones, whether you want anything to do with it or not. I chose you because I knew you were soft in the head. If you won't do it and Miss Kai here won't do it I'll send somebody nastier. You seem to have a soft spot for this grubby band of nomadic noodniks. Who would you suggest that I send in your place? How about our mutual friend, Trik-thi-gridj, the one that looks like a giant eggplant? He's at liberty right now, and he's not noted for his sensitive feelings. Shall I send him? He might do the little hellcat good."

"He'd probably throw her out the porthole in one-inch cubes."

"Possibly. Then he'd have solved at least part of my problem."

"Coyote?"

Coyote Jones turned his head and looked at Tzana. They traded pictures for a while, with Tzana's head ringing at the stuff he was pitching her; but she was stubborn and he knew she was right, and he gave in at last.

"All right," he said. "Give us six Fedrobots and the fastest ship you've got, and we'll go get her."

"Why six Fedrobots?" demanded the Fish. "You don't need even one."

"I do it my way or I don't do it," said Coyote. "I want

this to look official. I don't want the people at Chrysanthe-mum Bridge worrying that it's some kind of underhand operation."

"All right. Six Fedrobots."

"We'll leave right away," said Tzana and she stood up. "Come on, Coyote. It smells bad in here."

The two of them stalked out, followed by an agitated servomechanism that wanted them to hold still for sanitiz-ing. In the hall, Coyote carefully dumped the contents of his belt-pocket over it and left it clucking miser-ably to itself and trying to deal with a wad of assorted, sticky leftover lunch.

"BEM dung," Coyote said. "Just BEM dung."

# CHAPTER ELEVEN

FILE 374.10.b, Segment 1116

TOPIC: Q Factor Aberrations

FROM: Al-havania Jo, Directress Women's Ward,
Fed-hospital GALCENTRAL, STATION 30

TO: Communipath Control Committee—Galactic
Council GALCENTRAL, STATION 14

DATE: Julythird 3018

1. The subject of this report is the Q Factor Aberrant
Anne-Charlotte, member of the Maklunite Cluster called
Chrysanthemum Bridge, on Planet 34.922.107 (colloquial
name, Iris).

2. Reference is made to previous reports with regard
to this Q Factor Aberrant, specifically to the report of
Mayfourth 3018, this file, Segment 1114, from the Directress of the Infant Ward of the Communipath Creche.

3. Aberrant Anne-Charlotte has been in our care for
the past three days. Details of her arrival are formally as
follows:

On Julyfirst 3018 subject was brought to Fed-
hospital as a passenger in hibernation on Galactic
Rocket #813. Subject arrived in the custody of Citizen Tzana Kai, head of Tri-Galactic Translations

Bureau, Inc., and agent of TGIS. Presumably such custody was authorized by appropriate government agencies, although this writer finds the position of chief translator strangely inadequate for the task of transporting a seriously ill woman through space. However, the papers carried by Citizen Tzana Kai were all in order and no challenge to her custody was issued by this office. Subject arrived in poor condition, extremely thin; severe prostration was diagnosed and the recommendation was made that sedation be discontinued immediately in the interest of subject's health. This recommendation was refused by the Chief Medical Officer of this hospital, as was an identical recommendation made the following day when subject's life processes appeared to be approaching a dangerous low. Subject is still under total deep sedation.

4.   At this time this writer wishes to register a formal protest against the continued deep sedation of this subject; there appears to be no reason why such sedation should continue in the face of the poor physical condition of the patient. Reference is made to the statutes of this galaxy, specifically Galactic Statute 1,314, which guarantees persons charged with crimes—of whatever magnitude—the same medical care that is guaranteed every other citizen of the Three Galaxies.

5.   Instructions issued to this writer were to maintain deep sedation and perpetual care for the subject until such time as she can be brought to trial. Instructions will be carried out as given, under formal protest. (See Item #4, above.)

6.   It is requested that formal investigation into the unorthodox nature of the treatment and handling of this Q Factor Aberrant be initiated at once by the appropriate agency at GALCENTRAL.

7.   Copies of this report have been forwarded to the following:
GALCENTRAL, STATION 3 (Department of Human Relations); GALCENTRAL, STATION 6 (Department

of Justice); GALCENTRAL STATION 41 (Department of Health)

END OF REPORT

PS: Buzzy, just what the hell is going on around here? Are they trying to kill my patient, or am I just getting foolish in my old age? Somebody had better do something very double damned quick or there isn't going to be anybody alive to stand trial for the heinous crime of wanting to keep her own baby. This whole thing smells to high heaven.

Jo

# CHAPTER TWELVE

FROM:   Citizen Coyote Jones Coordinates 11/353
        Postbox 19,333   PJlanet 13.22.4

TO:     Office of the Director TRI-GALACTIC IN-
        TELLIGENCE SERVICE GALCENTRAL,
        STATION 5

DATE:   Julyfifteenth 3018

You are hereby advised of my formal resignation from
the Tri-Galactic Intelligence Service as of this date 3018.
It is my considered opinion that the TGIS is an archaic,
outdated, superfluous, ill-founded, busybody organization
dedicated to making unfortunate situations worse, and I
can no longer find it in me to be a part of its operations.
                                            Finally,
                                            Coyote Jones

FROM:   Office of the Director TRI-GALACTIC IN-
        TELLIGENCE SERVICE GALCENTRAL
        STATION 5
TO:     Citizen Coyote Jones Coordinates 11/353
        Postbox 19,933 Planet 13.22.4
DATE:   Julyseventeenth 3018

You are hereby advised that your resignation of Julyfifteenth 3018 is not accepted by the TGIS. Your services are sorely needed by this agency and your opinions
are not considered relevant. Your status is unchanged
and your cooperation appreciated.
                                            Immovably,
                                            The Fish

PS: Don't be an adolescent idiot, Mr. Jones. Next you'll be telling us you've been converted to that Maklunite claptrap and you're joining a cluster out by the Extreme Moons.

FROM:    Citizen Coyote Jones Coordinates 11/353
         Postbox 19,333 Planet 13.22.4
TO:      Office of the Director TRI-GALACTIC IN-
         TELLIGENCE SERVICE GALCENTRAL,
         STATION 5
DATE:    Julynineteenth 3018

You are hereby advised that the main body of your let-ter of Julyseventeenth is being ignored as irrelevant and of no conceivable interest to this writer. However, the suggestion made by you in the postscript to said letter is accepted with gratitude and enthusiasm.

Delightedly,<br>
Coyote Jones

PS: Don't try to pull any strong-arm tactics on me, Fishface. This whole double agent bit is against my RELIGION!

# CHAPTER THIRTEEN

FIRST OF ALL, where was she? Her last memory was of dropping to the sand in the wilderness on Iris, not just too tired to teleport again, but too tired even to stand and shout her hatred and rage at the merciless members of Chrysanthemum Bridge who had tracked her across the wilderness hour after hour after interminable hour. The sand had been cool on her face and hands . . . and she remembered nothing after that. Where was she now?

"Now" included a room with square walls, square flat ceiling, neat right-angle divisions marking off the meeting of wall with floor, nice neat square window—opaque —nice neat square door. Over the door was a nice square clock with neat black numbers and a sweeping red second hand. And she lay in a nice square white plastic bed. Only two places in the Three Galaxies could she have found such sterile precision, and the Four-Corner Fundamentalists wouldn't have allowed the red second hand on the clock. Therefore, "now" had to be somewhere in Galcentral.

She was quite sure she was being watched, although there was no one in the room and no object immediately identifiable as a monitor screen. This was obviously some sort of medical facility, and all medical facilities were monitored twenty-four hours a day. She lay very still, waiting to recover from whatever had been given her, and tried to remain calm enough not to attract immediate attention.

She was so weak. Not a weakness that would come from the ordinary effect of the state of hibernation that would have been necessary for her travel here. How long had she been asleep?

She tried to lift her head from the pillow, and found that even that simple action was beyond her strength. It must have been a very long time indeed since she had been put to sleep.

She ran over carefully what she knew about the medical installations at Galcentral, and her knowledge was pretty extensive. As a Factor Q Aberrant she had had a chance to see quite a bit of the Tri-Galactic government's medical facilities. And the style of this place gave it away at once. It was antique, almost museum quality. The furnishings were not even of one piece with the floor and walls, although they had been plastisprayed to create that illusion; where the light struck them at a certain angle you could see the outlines of legs and bases under the spray. Think. . . .

Mars. Only on Mars would such archaisms still exist. Only in the vast facilities of the great Galcentral stations, where the government had established its central seat when there had been only one galaxy to administer instead of three. And where in that huge complex would such makeshift operations as plastispraying of hospital furnishings be allowed? It could only be a Federal hospital, and an immense and ancient one. And if that was true, no matter which one it was, she was very near the Communipath Creche, and very near her baby.

Immediately she knew she had made a mistake, because a small bell rang beside her head and a medrobot appeared in the doorway, followed at once by a human being in an official medical tunic.

The human smiled at her.

"We are glad to see you awake," he said. "You must be extremely tired of sleeping."

He ha, she thought, and tried to smile; she had no intention of causing these people to be more wary of her than they were already.

"How long?" she asked, her voice so hoarse she scarcely recognized it as her own.

"How long have you been here?"

"Yes. How long?"

"About three weeks."

"Three weeks!"

The medrobot came soundlessly but with incredible

speed from the door to her bedside. There was a blur
of silver and before she could move or speak to protest
she felt the chill that meant a drug-spray had touched
her arm. Apparently any sign whatsoever of emotion was
likely to cause them to put her out again completely. She
was going to have to be very cunning.

In the depths of her mind she felt the baby's pleasure
at having her near once more. How could they have left
it alone for three weeks? What had they told it that had
kept it—of course. The baby would have been under
sedation, too, all this long time. They could not conceivably have controlled it in any other way.

She questioned it, gently, carefully, the familiar sensation of mindspeech, like flying through cool currents
of mist, proving to her delight that whatever the weakness of her body her mind was not in such dreadful
shape. As she had thought, the baby had no memory of
having been cut off from her for weeks, it seemed to believe that it had had trouble reaching her only through
part of one afternoon. She hushed it, noticing that it had
named itself Susannah, and agreed that that was good,
very good. HUSH NOW, SUSANNAH. Obediently, the
baby curled its thoughts with hers and was still.

Already she could feel the effect of the drug that they
had given her. Her lips were numb, her eyelids were heavy.
But what could be the point? Why wake her at all, if they
were so afraid of her reactions?

"Why," she asked through leaden lips, "are you waking me up? If this can be called waking me!"

"Your trial is today, Anne-Charlotte," said the man in
the tunic pleasantly. "You can't be tried in your sleep, I'm
afraid."

"Are you medical or police?"

"Both, Anne-Charlotte. Medical police."

"I see."

She was exhausted already, after so few words. She
lay limp in the bed, so conscious of the slow rise and fall
of her chest, of how sharply etched her bones were, of
what an effort it was not to go to sleep again. The medrobot apparently noticed it, too, because another chill
touched her arm, and in a minute or two she felt more
awake. She smiled, thinking of the complicated set of
drugs and antidotes that must be having to be balanced in
the poor little computer's innards.

The medical policeman—or police medical man, whatever he was—was joined by another, and they whispered together, watching her, until a third came, bearing a tray. Anne-Charlotte was amazed. Either she was incredibly important or all the power had failed in Galcentral! It had been a thousand years since human beings had been served trays in hospitals by other human beings. In fact, the newer hospitals simply inserted the sick person in a plastic pod, which proceeded to feed him, minister to him, evacuate his wastes, take his temperature and pulse on a round-the-clock basis. The pods would, if an actual emergency were to arise—which was unlikely, since they were directed by a very sophisticated central computer that was capable of dealing with almost anything—summon the single human doctor who stood by for just such occasions. They could deliver babies, perform surgery, set broken bones, change diapers, entertain a cross sick child. Even death could be handled skillfully by the medical pods. Yet here stood a crisp white live lady with a crisp square white tray. Anne-Charlotte was impressed.

"We'd like you to try to eat something, dear," said the lady with the tray.

Anne-Charlotte was wise enough to know that food was probably her primary need at that moment. She managed her best good-little-girl smile.

"Gladly," she said. "I'm hungry."

"How nice! Here you go, then!"

The bed rose, propping her up and extending an arm for the tray, and swung it across in front of her. Music began to play, then stopped abruptly at some signal from the medical computer that she was about to lose her temper. She ate, as much as she could, docilely; somewhere they had found a Maklunite to prepare the food, and the Light be praised; it was nothing like the mess of plastics and additives that usually passed for nourishment in Galcentral stations.

All three humans stood quietly watching her until she was through, and then the tray disappeared into a slot in the wall. She waited for them to make their move, whatever it was, too exhausted by the effort of eating to even ask.

"Anne-Charlotte?"

"Yes."

"How do you feel?"

"How would *you* feel," she whispered, "after—what must it be—seven, eight weeks, perhaps longer, of total sedation?"

"I would feel very ill. Very weak and very ill."

"Well, then. I feel very weak and ill."

The man came over and stood beside her.

"I wish we hadn't had to keep you like that," he said gently. "It was only because we had no other way to handle you, you must realize that."

"I do," she said. "You couldn't possibly have kept me here any other way. You couldn't even have brought me here any other way."

"So we are told," he said. "It is a measure of our inadequacy that we have had to be so cruel."

"And I am weak enough now that you can be sure that I will cooperate?"

"No. Oh, no. We are sure of nothing where you are concerned. I am not even sure that you will not kill me in the next few seconds."

"Then why am I awake? It seems very risky!"

"Because many thousands of years of judicial tradition stand behind your right to a trial."

"How do you know I won't escape?"

He looked at her for a moment, then reached down and lifted one of her wrists a few feet above the bed. When he released it her arm dropped like a dead thing.

"We cannot be sure," he said. "But you see that we have done what we could."

"And you have my baby," she said bitterly.

"We would not harm your child, Anne-Charlotte."

"You have had it under total sedation for weeks," she said. "You don't consider that 'harm'?"

"How did you know that?"

She didn't answer, and in a moment he nodded his head. "Ah, I see," he said. "Of course you would know. Yes, of course you would know. Is the baby relatively happy?"

"As happy as is possible, under the circumstances."

"We are not proud of having done that to the child, you know," he said. "On the other hand, do you know what your baby would have done if we had *not* sedated it?"

"Wrecked this galaxy," said Anne-Charlotte. "And probably the two galaxies beyond as well!"

"And you are proud of that!" exclaimed the man. "You

glory in it, don't you?" He shook his head and stepped back from her bed. "You are proud that it could kill millions of people, proud——"

"You waste your breath," she said swiftly. "I have no sympathy for this society after what it has done to me. Of course I am proud of my child's ability to destroy such rottenness."

The medrobot clicked and another chill struck her arm. Anne-Charlotte laughed.

"This poor machine is going to be sicker than I am," she observed. "What sort of program have you fed it?"

They didn't answer, and she went on, "It wouldn't be fast enough to kill me. Do you know that?"

"In one hour," said the police person, ignoring her question, "we will come to take you to the courtroom."

"In one hour!"

"Yes, exactly that."

"But you will have to carry me into the courtroom!"

"We dare not have you any stronger than you are," he said. "Believe me, we hate that. You must try to understand. Morally, it is repellent to all of us. The idea that you should stand trial for your life when you cannot so much as move your head without help is morally and ethically an abomination, an obscenity. On the other hand, we dare not risk the havoc you would so willingly loose on the Federation if you were able."

She spat the words at him between her teeth. "Perhaps I am still able!"

"Perhaps," he admitted. "We can only guess. We have done what we had to do."

"You are beasts."

"No," he said. "We are trapped by a situation that is unique and for which no precedent exists."

"My baby," she said, "my baby and I, we will destroy you all. Every last wicked foul one of you, we will destroy you and all that you have done. I promise you that."

"Anne-Charlotte," he said softly, "please, what exactly have we done? Could you explain to me?"

"Explain! When you take babies from their parents and train them to be abominations, teach them to be mental monsters that could not live outside their luxurious prisons, deform their minds until they are willing slaves of a task that will see them die of total exhaustion before they are eighteen! Why should I explain?"

"What you say is true, in a sense," he mused. "And yet, what else could we do? Don't you realize that without the Communipaths to transmit information the outer galaxies could not even have been settled? We would be suffocating in our own filth, trapped on the inner planets, with no hope but the eventual extinction of our race . . ."

He looked down at her, his eyes dark with sorrow, and spoke gently.

"Anne-Charlotte," he said, "you are a very sick young woman. We have made you what you are, I suppose, and deserve your hatred. Still I wish we could help you in some way."

"I only wish I could hurt you," she hissed, "and I will! I will!"

He reached down and touched her wrist, his fingers warm and strong on her cold skin.

"Try to rest," he said. "You have about an hour."

"You're going away?"

"Yes. I'll only upset you more if I stay."

"Tell me," she insisted, holding him by force of will, "do you believe in reincarnation?"

"Of course," he laughed. "Doesn't everyone? Do I believe in the sky? Do I believe in my five fingers?"

"Then, tell me," she said, "what does a Communipath become after reincarnation? Is he a Communipath again, and again, and again, age after age, because you condemn him to a life of such total depravity that his soul can never grow, never learn?"

He turned his back on her.

"Try to rest," he said, and was gone.

She lay watching the door he had gone out through, trying to calm the reaction of her body to her own helpless rage. She knew where she was now, she had seen the marking on her tray. This was Galcentral Station 30, Fedhospital, the Women's Ward. The Creche was Station 11. That meant that the distance between her and Susannah could not be more than a handful of miles, perhaps ten miles at the most. These stations were built straight up, not out.

She closed her eyes, going over in her mind the map she had so carefully memorized when first she considered her plan to get the baby back again. There was Station 30, and in its row all the other 30's. Next to it, across a mall, were the 20's. Beyond them, the numbers from 10 to 19. The second of those, Station 11, was the Creche, and it should be in an almost directly straight line from here. . . .

She was incredibly weak, much weaker than even she knew. The force of her desperate attempt to teleport herself across two malls to Station 11 was just sufficient to throw her against the side of a freighter coming in at the Galcentral Food Warehouse, Station 20. There was no smallest scrap of her body to create problems for anyone.

The baby was still very young and not capable of any quick decisions or action. They had time, just barely, to reach it with their drugs before it realized what had happened.

# CHAPTER FOURTEEN

TZANA KAI's translation bureau functioned smoothly and without any hitch, ordinarily. Her staff was very good at taking the product of a computer, which would simply substitute rough morpheme equivalents in bundles, with various feature and intonation markings attached, and turning these chunks of raw language into suitable vehicles for communication. Most of the work they did was, of course, literary output, since the computer's own product was usually sufficient for ordinary business purposes. And then there was a certain minor leftover portion of their business which was made up of diplomatic assignments and vanity stuff. Gentlemen wishing to propose marriage to ladies of alien tongue, scientists asked to present papers at conferences where a majority of the delegates would not know Panglish, that sort of thing. And poetry—always and forever poetry.

These days Tzana Kai was glad she had a good staff, because she had little heart for any of the work. Ordinarily she rather enjoyed it, and despised the intelligence work for which it was presumably the subordinate camouflage. But the superlatively nasty problems that had piled up over the little Maklunite baby seemed to have mushroomed into a Medusa-like monster that she could not get off her mind. She worried about the baby; she mourned over the grim death of its mother. She could not stop puzzling over the problem of what could have been done instead of what *had* been done, and on top of that, she missed Coyote Jones.

This was stupid and she despised herself for it. And she couldn't quite decide what it meant. She had seen the doctors, who had prescribed the immediate and obvious antidote.

"Another lover, and at once," the doctor had said. "If the fixation seems to be persistent, perhaps a group arrangement, something very different from just a man-woman encounter."

"Nonsense."

"I beg your pardon, Citizen Kai?"

"I've had eleven since Coyote," she told him crossly, "in all shapes, sizes and combinations. All kinds. All skillful. All charming."

He had cocked his head and stared at her for a full five minutes, while she pigheadedly stared back and refused to be intimidated.

Finally, he had nodded as if something had clicked in the back of his head, and spoken to her soothingly.

"You're not suffering from the Romeo-Juliet Syndrome," he said, "if that's what's worrying you."

"The Light have patience," she said, "that's the very last thing that would occur to me! I have a nice normal head, thank you."

"That's just what I said," he agreed.

"Then how come I can't get the thought of Coyote Jones off my mind?"

The doctor smiled at her.

"Dear Citizen Kai," he asked her slowly, "did it ever enter your mind that you just pure and simply are happier when you have him around to keep you company?"

"That's not the Romeo-Juliet Syndrome?"

"Certainly not. With R-J you suffer from the notion, a curious and sick one, that *only* in the presence of Citizen X can you bear to continue living. That is an illness, Citizen, a condition requiring hospitalization, treatment, therapy. What you are feeling is just normal human fondness. You like the man, the two of you work well together, you enjoy his company and you like to go to bed with him, and now that he's gone you miss him. Why should that worry you?"

"Because I've never felt this way before, that's why! He's always been 'gone,' as you put it. I rarely saw him more than once a year, ever—that's why I can't understand the way I keep moping about him."

The doctor had leaned over and patted her hand reassuringly.

"Ah, but this time he's gone for good," he pointed out. "Psychologically, that's a different matter. A very different matter indeed."

She had sat there for a moment, just a little bit stunned, as much by her own stupidity in not having figured it out for herself as by what he had said.

Finally she had stood up and thanked him, and still in a half-daze, she had taken a taxi-flier back to the Bureau. Of course, that was it, she had been an idiot not to see it—it was the fact that this time Coyote was gone for good! Of course, there was the outside possibility that she might run into him somewhere, years from now, but it wasn't likely.

She hoped he was happy, wherever he was.

When the Fish had called her from Mars to tell her what Coyote had done, she had been overjoyed.

"You realize what the idiot's gone and done?" he asked her.

"What? Shot you, I hope."

"Nothing so simple."

"Well, what, then?"

"He's become a Maklunite, Miss Kai. That's what."

"But that's very clever of him!"

"Clever? How so?"

"Because then you have to accept his resignation after all."

There had been a long and disapproving silence from the Fish.

"You knew he had resigned?" he asked finally.

"Sure. He sent me a carbon."

"And your refusal—you've seen that, too?"

"Yes, indeed."

"Most unethical," the Fish said. "Most unethical."

"You can't make a Maklunite do undercover work," she laughed, "because it's against their religion. Good for Coyote, I say!"

"Good for Coyote, eh? We need him, Miss Kai. How many mass projective telepaths do you suppose there *are* in the Three Galaxies, Miss Kai?"

"Not many."

"Eleven," he said flatly. "Eleven of them to do what it would take at least two or three hundred to do properly. Perhaps you'd like us to go back to controlling riots with Mace and tear gas, Miss Kai?"

"Look," she said, "I've got a lot of work to do. I'm sorry, on a general basis, that you don't have enough people to do all your dirty jobs. But on a personal basis, I'm glad Coyote got away from you."

"Oh, I'm not so sure he got away!"

"If he's a Maklunite you can't—"

"I know the law, Miss Kai," the old man had cut in. "I know it very well. And before he can be officially a Maklunite, he has to be accepted by a cluster. He's tried one, and been turned down."

"Oh, dear."

"Hmph. Oh, dear, you say. I hope they all turn him down. Do him a lot of good. Maklunite! Why not an Ethical Chocolatist? Why not a Reformed Traditional Atheist? Why not a Forfending Fundamentalist? Why not, for that matter, a Five-Square Krishnakon?"

She had hung up as quickly as she decently could and gone straight to her comsystem to request data on the Maklunites. What she found had made her a little dubious about Coyote's prospects. He had to be "Chosen"—and she didn't know just what that meant; but it apparently had to be based on unanimous acceptance from the group.

Of course it would have been simple, theoretically, for Coyote to have mass projected just that sort of unanimous acceptance and assured his Choosing. But she knew him. He wouldn't do that.

Now she sat at her desk, staring at, but not seeing, a new glossary of Sirian technical infixes that had come in that morning's mail. She could not manage to get interested in the intricacies of internal structure of the Sirian scientific word. She punched her comsystem remote input button and called the Galcentral number.

"Yes?"

"You're the Fish's secretary?" she asked briskly.

"I am secretary to Citizen Wythllewyn," said the voice in tones of ice.

"You'd better not let the old bastard hear you call him 'citizen' instead of 'mister,' if you intend to keep your post," said Tzana.

There was a silence, and then the voice spoke again.

"May I help you—whoever you are?"

"This is Tzana Kai. I want to talk to old whatshisname."

"He isn't in."

"Then perhaps you could supply me with the information that I need."

"Perhaps. If it is not confidential."

"I want to know the present whereabouts of another agent."

"Name, please."

"Coyote Jones."

"One moment, please."

Tzana sat and fumed. If there was anything she despised it was these top secret com-numbers, where you could not see who you were talking to. She could imagine the person on the other end, though! Whoever it was, its hair was pink-and-green-striped, the current In thing, and it was excessively thin, and it sprayed its perfect body instead of wearing clothes, and it chewed synthetic marijuana. All of that was predictable. She hoped it had piles.

"Citizen Kai?"

"I'm still here," she said.

"I'm a little bit hesitant to give you this information."

"If you don't give it to me," said Tzana pleasantly, "I will come get it. And a considerable quantity of your pink and green hair. Or are you bald?"

"Really!"

"Give," said Tzana. "I mean it, now. I am a fearless and redoubtable secret agent, and I eat little girls for breakfast. You know what my security rating is and I'm not asking for rocket coordinates. Tell me about Coyote and make it swift."

The voice that came back at her was so chilly it made her giggle. She really did wish she could see the girl.

"Coyote Jones," said the voice. "That was the person in question?"

"That's the one, dearie."

"According to our last reports Citizen Jones has been accepted on probationary basis by a Maklunite cluster called Faw-Griver."

"Called *what?*"

"They are religious fanatics," said the voice smugly. "You can't expect the names to make sense, Citizen."

"Spell it."

"F-O-G-R-I-"

"Oh, Fog River! You were saying Faw Griver, you know."

"As I was saying—"

"Yes, do go on."

"As I was saying, this cluster, Faw Griver, has accepted him on a probationary basis."

"What does that mean, pray tell?"

"I'm sure I wouldn't know."

"I'm sure you would, missy, because I'm sure the Fish made it his business to find out and it will be in the file. Give."

"According to the file it means he won't make it. I'll read it to you. 'These people have taken him on trial for three months but have great doubts, they say, because they think he's too much an individualist to adapt to group living no matter how sincere. Ha! If they knew he was only joining them to get out of doing his duty to his government they'd think less of his so-called sincerity. We should have him back in six weeks.' That's all it says."

"In the Fish's handwriting?"

"Yes, Citizen Kai. Exactly."

"And where is Fog River?"

"Let me see. Planet 27.108.333, it says here."

"Colloquial name?"

"C-A-L-F-I-N-N-A. Calfinna?"

"Mean anything to you?"

"No, but with that number it's quite a ways from here."

"Thank you."

Tzana hung up. Well, at least she knew where he was. She could have looked up the coordinates in the Tri-Galactic Atlas, but she didn't think she wanted to. It was very far away, and so was Coyote, and she hoped to heaven he managed to adapt to the Maklunite way of living if that was what he wanted. And if he did manage it, then there could be nothing more between them. Not that there was any rule against it, but just because he would be too busy, always, and too far away.

She squared her shoulders and went out into the reception office to talk to a fat Dravidian lady who wanted an acceptance speech of an award made to her for her roses. In eleven languages, she wanted it.

# CHAPTER FIFTEEN

ANNE-CHARLOTTE is dead.

I write that down, but I find it very hard to make myself believe it, even when I'm looking right at it. She was so much *more* alive than so many other people, if that makes any sense. . . . I guess it probably doesn't, though. And she *is* dead. That is a true thing. My not believing it won't change it any.

Maklunites do not mourn their dead. We know that death is only a beginning and is an occasion for rejoicing, not for sorrow. But usually those of us who die die in the ashram, with all of the cluster around them, and it is a time for great loving and celebration. When one of us dies as Anne-Charlotte did, that's so awfully different—they say there was nothing left of her at all, not so much as a scrap of flesh, just a mark of blood and slime on the side of the freighter. She was destroyed as if she had never been. And that is awful, because she was alone, and probably she had time to be afraid and to hurt, if only for a second, and none of us was there with her to comfort her.

But Patrick says we must not grieve. He says it is the greatest good fortune that could have come to Anne-Charlotte—not that she died as she did, of course he doesn't mean *that*—but that she died before anything else could happen to her. He says that nothing that was suffering as Anne-Charlotte suffered should be allowed to live, any more than we would let a hurt animal that could not be mended lie and drag out its dying. And he says that the disease of her mind is so rare now that probably no doctors could have been found that would have known how to help her; and even if they had been able to cure her completely, it would only have meant that she would have had to stand trial for high treason.

He is right, of course. Patrick is always right. There is no way that Anne-Charlotte could have survived without horror. It is better like this. My mind knows that. Unfortunately my heart doesn't and so I requested permission for an Aloning, away from the cluster, and they said yes, and here I am, almost all the way to the bluffs, with my bubble-tent and my writing things. And no food, because I want to really think.

Of course I know perfectly well that it's just pretend, my being alone. It's not as if I were a grown-up. I'm sure Patrick knows every move I make and every thought I think, and although my psibility is not much it is certainly good enough that I can tell they've sent Mark to camp out on the other side of that gully over there just in case I break my leg or go berserk. But at least I can't *see* any of them, or hear them, and the pretend aloneness will have to do.

There is a great goodness that has come out of all this awful time, you see. I am proud to be able to sit here and write about it, and I wish Anne-Charlotte could have been alive to hear of it.

It's her baby, the baby that has named itself Susannah. The doctors at the Creche have written to Patrick and told him that the baby seems to be completely free of Anne-Charlotte's illness and that it seems to be able to understand that her death was an accident and not something it must tear the universe apart over. And wonder of wonders, the doctors say that for Susannah the work of manning a station on the Bucket will be just an ordinary day's work, like any other day's work. There is no reason to believe that she will have to die any younger than she would have if she had stayed here with us. She does not even need the other stations on the Bucket, apparently; she can just pass information across three galaxies as if there were no space there at all.

Just think what that is going to mean! They say that if there is one like her there are probably others, or will be soon, and in any case, now that they know the psibility to such a degree of power is possible they will find out how to make it *certain* that there are more like her. I don't understand it and I don't even care, but it is a matter of eugenics and genetics and a few more "-ics" I can't remember the names of. It doesn't matter what it is, really, the important thing is that it means an end of the Communipaths like they are now, slaves and prisoners of all the rest of us!

Patrick says that no one had ever dreamed that the sort of psibility Susannah has was within the limits of possibility. They had never even considered that a human being might be able to do a tenth of what she can do, and do it easily and happily as well. He says that now they know, the technology and the money and all the rest of it certainly exists to put an end to the Communipath obscenity forever and ever and ever.

They won't be able to do it overnight, and probably not in a year, and certainly if they find a way to do it quickly (which they probably will, because the computers will help) it's not possible to make these new kinds of human beings grow up to an age where they can serve as Communipaths. It's not going to be possible to make them grow up any faster than any other human being does. That means that a few more Communipaths, maybe quite a few more, will have to die, before they can be replaced by the new kind of people. But at least the end is in sight!

I think I am feeling better already. Writing this down has done me a great deal of good, I think. In fact, I don't think I want to fast at all, or even be alone, and instead I am going to see if I can't join Mark over there on the other side of the gully and just he and I can be alone together. And then later I'll write some more about all this, okay?

# BOOK II

## Furthest

# CHAPTER ONE

"A secret is like a small child; the more you do for it, the more of a nuisance it becomes. Before you take upon yourself such a burden, consider well— the chances are that unless you take elaborate pains to conceal something it will never be noticed."

(from the Devotional Book of Tham O'Kent)

HE HAD TO sit very still. The slitherboat was not an easy craft to manage, and the beginner was likely to end up in the water almost at once, with no hope of ever getting on the bloody thing again. So far as Coyote knew, of course, he was the only beginner.

That was a bit hard for him to understand. But then almost everything on this planet was hard for him to understand.

He had put in a lot of time preparing for this night, and had gained himself a reputation as a harmless idiot offworlder who actually found it amusing to putter around at night in a slitherboat. The idea had been that when he got to doing something more than just putter, nobody would pay any attention to him, and he sincerely hoped that would turn out to be an idea with an accurate base.

He had stopped using the miniature paddle and was letting the current carry him, seemingly aimlessly, knowing he could count on it to head him in the right direction eventually, and he was digging the view around him while he drifted.

It was spectacular, you had to give it that. By day there was nothing to see out here, and the land spread out in all directions, the same dull gray color, unrelieved by tree or grass or any mark except the bluffs and spurs that loomed up here and there. If you could call it land, that is, because strictly speaking there wasn't much land there. It was a sort of rock net, somehow holding together the millions of flowing streams that were the real stuff of the planet. Sometimes there would be a strip of the gray rock as much as ten feet wide, but not often; the streams were everywhere, twisting and winding, honeycombing the rock so that the actual surface was almost entirely water. The streams themselves were gray, too, because they ran through the gray rock, and none of them more than two feet, perhaps in rare cases three feet, in width. By day it was all gray, as far as you could see, and one of the ugliest sights in the universe, to Coyote's way of thinking.

At night, though, it was different. It was different and beautiful and splendid, because that same gray water bore in it a small creature invisible to the naked eye, but fluorescent, and multicolored, and in the dark the rainbows flowed everywhere in a glory that Coyote knew he was never going to be able to describe to anyone who had not acutally seen it.

There was not an inch of the water that did not teem with the spangled life, not an inch that did not dance and pulse with red and green and gold and a deep soft blue. The little geysers that went unnoticed in the daylight, not very high and not very impressive, were incredible in the dark, throwing fountains of color like flung fireworks into the air. They went off all around him, apparently random, although he knew there must be a pattern to them. And the streams poured magnificently stippled and pied down the sides of the bluffs and the pillars of rock, leaping from face to face and throwing bridges of brilliant color across the sky.

Coyote could not imagine tiring of it. He could have sat and watched it all the night long. But he sat there all alone. On any other planet of the Three Galaxies such a display would have been crowded with people, its magnificence would have drawn eager watchers not only from the planet itself but from all the planets of the Tri-Galactic Federation. Not here. In the course of more than twenty nights that he had spent out on these . . . What could you call them? Deserts? Could there be a

desert of water? . . . these whatevertheywere, he had
seen another living being only once, moving purpose-
fully on a slitherboat and not even looking at the
rampant beauty around him.

He had asked RK, the boy who worked for him, why
no one ever went out to watch the water at night, and
had received a blank look of incomprehension. "Watch
the water? Why should anyone want to do that?" RK
had said flatly.

Perhaps these people were color-blind. Perhaps familiarity bred contempt, even in the face of all this. But
if familiarity was the problem it seemed that the children
and younger people, to whom all this display would be
more new, would come out at night to enjoy the view.
And they didn't. No one came, except himself, all alone
on the cursed bare flat sliver that they were pleased to
call a boat.

As first he had continually fallen off, since there was
nothing to hold on to and not even a ridge to give
you purchase. The slitherboat was a lot like a surfboard,
except that when you fell off you didn't go into open
surf but smashed against the rock walls of a stream not
much wider than you were. And every time he fell off
he had had to climb out and race madly along the web of
rocks until the slitherboat reached an abrupt turn that
would slow it down enough to let him grab it. At such
times he had been delighted to find himself alone, since
he would have been a hilarious spectacle for anyone
watching.

"Do your people ever fall off the slitherboats?" he had
asked RK, and gotten that same strange look. "Why
would anyone fall off a slitherboat?" the boy had asked,
as Coyote would have asked, "Why would anyone forget to alternate left and right legs as they walked?" Such
a question could only mean that everyone rode the
slitherboats from infancy, that they were as much an
automatic part of bodily motion as walking or running,
but if that was the case, when did they ride them?
Where did the children go to learn? He had never seen
anyone riding one, except that one lone man, and he
had never seen groups of kids going off to practice together. When and where did it happen? Or was the
"obvious" explanation entirely wrong to begin with?

There was a faint chime in the air beside his head

then, and he gritted his teeth and tried not to move, since that was the proper way to handle the situation. But he couldn't stand it; when he felt the little feet on his shoulders, and the tiny hands gripping, he gave in as he always did and started trying to brush them off. And of course the instant he did that the two that had been on him became twenty, or a hundred, and the air around him was alive with the soft sound of a multitude of incredibly small high bells.

Coyote shuddered, cursing himself for drawing the crowd with his thrashing around, knowing that if it happened again he would do exactly the same thing.

The jeebies were a lot like bats, except that they were bigger, standing perhaps a foot high and having a wingspread of better than three feet. And they were completely transparent, which was certainly different. In the daylight you could sometimes see them, faintly, against the background of gray; but at night they were as invisible as the air, and they came out of nowhere, each one making the tiny chiming sound that functioned like the squeaking and screaming of bats but was definitely a hell of a lot more attractive. And the jeebies, unlike bats, were friendly—so damned friendly.

RD had told him over and over. "If you just hold perfectly still, Citizen Jones, if you just don't move at all, one or two of a flock will come and check you out and decide you're boring and move on. They just like to pat you a little and find out what you are like, and they can only do that by touching you, you know? Because they're blind."

"Don't move at all, huh," Coyote had repeated after him. "Sure. Something that feels like a little man a foot tall climbs all over you patting your cheek and rubbing your back and making tinkling noises the whole time, and you just don't move."

"Well," RK had said reasonably, "if you don't move they will go away. And if you start moving they will get excited and call the rest of the flock. So not moving is best."

RK was absolutely right. Not moving was best, and it was stupid to move, since the little beasties were completely harmless. But he had done it, and now he had a flock following him, clustering on his head and should-ders, crawling down his back and over his arms and legs, chiming and patting and rubbing.

And he was just going to have to put up with them all, he knew that from experience. It would be a long time before they got tired of investigating him and took off for whatever it was they came from. Grimly he took his paddle from its loop on his back and began to make what he hoped were inconspicuous adjustments in the course he was taking, reminding himself that no matter how incredibly much activity was going on around a man who had drawn a flock of jeebies it was all invisible. Nobody knew but him.

He had no idea, of course, just how closely he was being watched. Or for that matter if he was being watched at all. It would have been easy to assume that he was just out here in magnificent isolation, no one aware of him in any way, since that was the way things looked. But he knew better than to jump to any such conclusion. For all he knew a giant radar somewhere was tracking his every movement. For all he knew a group of men sat hunched over a screen watching everything he did as if he were a threedy program being played for their benefit. He didn't know. Certainly these people should be capable of an advanced technology; on the other hand, since they never left the planet and almost no offworlders ever came in, it was possible that they were retarded in technological development or simply did not consider such an application of it worth their time. In the six weeks he had been on Furthest he had seen no sign, none, of any sort of surveillance equipment. But the chances were very good that if he had seen it he would not have recognized it for what it was, so he was completely in the dark.

He was operating on the hypothesis that he had been watched, probably very closely, when he first began these night jaunts, and that someone somewhere probably still checked on him from time to time, but that by now they—whoever they might be—had accepted him as a harmless nut glomming their scenery and not requiring any great amount of attention. If he was right, and that was by no means sure—and if he could refrain from doing anything unusual that would attract attention (and since he had no idea what *would* attract attention, that wasn't very sure either), and if it didn't just happen to be time for a regular monitoring check on his activities, he might just come out of this all right.

He sure as hell had to do something. Six weeks, and he hadn't learned one thing. And his license to remain on this world had an eighteen-month limit that might turn into eighteen hours on him any time.

He had gone quite a distance now. The little boats were like twigs on the water and the currents strong, and two hours would take you a very respectable number of miles. You'd have to hike back, of course, since those currents weren't going to obligingly turn themselves around for you, and the paddles were no use against the force of the water, but at least one half of any given journey would be pretty rapid.

Off to his left he saw what he was looking for. Now he would really have to be careful, and to his relief the jeebies were beginning to tire of him. He could do without their distraction now.

He turned the slitherboat, not directly toward the black bulk he was aiming for, but on a meandering course calculated to get him to it without giving away his purpose. He wanted to allow plenty of time for a police-copter to appear and warn him off, or whatever it was that might be likely to happen to a trespassing outworlder, before he actually found himself beyond the point of no return on this excursion.

The looming black was now perhaps five hundred yards away, and except for the light from the fluorescent water he would not have been able to see it at all. It had no lights, no markings, nothing to warn anyone off. He supposed it must have the regulation aviation beacon on top, but it couldn't be seen from the ground in any case.

He was very close now, almost upon it, and nothing had happened yet. He wondered what the penalty might be for breaking into a forbidden city, and decided he didn't want to know. The time for worrying about that was long since past.

He had found the fork made by four streams that he used as a marker. There was a low rock spur on his right, and he reached out for it, using it to brake his motion, and he pulled the boat hard against the rock. It made a scraping noise, but he could always tell the city fathers, if they came running out to investigate, that

he had fallen off. Or that he had had to take a leak. Or
that he was lost. He stepped off, or more properly
wriggled off, the slitherboat, and lashed it to the rock
with an elastic loop.

Now came the tricky part.

Strictly speaking, what he was about to do was probably suicidal. This citydome was forbidden to him, he
had been told so kindly but firmly. He was allowed to
move freely within the city where he worked, there was
a small town on the other side of the planet that he was
free to visit, and there was a single village, rather near
the city, that he had been told he might enter. Except
for that, everything was forbidden—including this dome
that covered a city called T'a Klith. But he had found a
way in. He hoped.

There was a fissure on this side of the dome, one of
the countless streams of water, and it flowed under the
edge. Now presumably all he had to do was slip into
that stream, wearing his diving gear, and swim right
under the dome wall into T'a Klith. Presumably.

There were a lot of other things that might happen.
The stream might narrow to six inches and he would get
stuck, unable to go either forward or back, and he knew
what would happen after that. There might be an electric
grid beneath the dome, set to trap just such critters as
himself, that would fry him when he touched it. There
might be great motors, or exhaust fans, or disposal
chutes, any of which he would swim blithely into without finding out in time that they were there. There might
be a welcoming committee at the other end with unpleas-
sant implements reserved for nosy offworlders who
broke trespass laws.

Those were just some of the things that might happen. He could think of worse. And then there was the
possibility that was prompting this whole venture, i.e.,
that he would be able to make it down the stream and
into the city, pop his head up unobserved for a quick
look, and get out with a whole skin and whatever information he could gather in the minute he would dare allow
himself. It wasn't really likely that that was what would
happen, since there was something very fairytale about
the concept of a city that was at the same time forbidden
and unguarded, but he was going to buy the fairytale for

the moment. He really had no choice. He had to have something to report pretty soon or even *his* ordinarily resilient conscience was going to start bothering him.

He explored the water carefully with one hand, trying not to touch the sides of the walls, on the offhand chance that by not touching the rock he would fail to activate any alarms or traps. It seemed to be a wide enough channel, maybe two feet across as it went under the dome.

He checked the straps on his airpack, pulled the waterhood over his head, and snapped it to his wetsuit. RK had laughed at him for insisting on the cumbersome wetsuit, but had cheerfully accepted his explanation that he would get pneumonia if he kept falling into the water in his ordinary clothes.

Now. He waited for one last moment. Now was the time. Now was the time for the flyer to blast out of the air and order him up against the wall. Now was the time for a lawrobot to appear and shoot a hole through him. Now was the time for the giant loudspeaker to open up and order him away. Or something.

Nothing happened. A jeebie chimed, somewhere off to his right. Except for that all was silence and color and silence. Apparently nothing was going to happen to keep him from having to go through with this. He shrugged, and snapped the last snap on his gear.

Under the edge of the dome the water was colder than outside, but it wasn't uncomfortable. The current rushed him through the blackness, the channel narrowing not at all, the total dark unbroken. It was completely and unendingly weird, and he resolutely refused to think. Whatever it was that was going to happen, it would happen, and he would deal with it as best he could. For the moment he would just float. Period.

And then, about the time he had begun to think in spite of himself, he was out, past the other side of the dome, and he barely managed to catch a spur on the rock wall and keep himself from being swept right out beyond the edge into the city.

Very carefully he edged to the rim, clinging to the wall of the stream, and exposed just his eyes. Then he put his whole head out and took a long, long look, turning from side to side, unable to believe it. And finally he went back the way he had come, unlashed the slither-boat, and headed for home, numb.

There had been nothing there. Nothing at all. Just the great dome, fully big enough to cover the city of three hundred thousand people it was supposed to house, and the bare expanse of rock and water, and that's all there was of T'a Klith.

Now why in the name of all the swirling attendants of the Holy Light would anyone build a citydome over nothing at all, name it as a city, claim three hundred thousand citizens for it, and forbid people to enter?

Coyote was mournful. Things just weren't going very well, and a lot of people were going to be very unhappy with him, and the magnificence all around him had lost its glory and gone tawdry garish port-city vice strip. He kept his head down and ignored it, and when a jeebie lit on his shoulder he didn't even move.

# CHAPTER TWO

"Twinkle, twinkle, little star,
what a ball of gas you are . . ."

(from an old nursery rhyme)

WHEN THE Fish called him in to give him the assignment on Furthest, Coyote went in with his customary reluctance. He could not remember a single occasion when the Fish had called for him that he had not managed to make the comsystem ring at the single most inappropriate moment possible, generally when Coyote had just managed after a great deal of effort to make some beautiful woman absolutely ready to be absolutely happy. Then the comsystem would ring, with that blatant triad that meant an official—hence, not ignorable—call. He didn't know exactly how the Fish managed to time things so perfectly, but no doubt this was one of the spinoff benefits of being head of the Tri-Galactic Intelligence Service.

He had stared at the Fish and the Fish had stared back, until Coyote had gotten tired of the game and said abruptly, "Oh, shit, man, come on—what did you call me in for?"

"Shit, Mr. Jones?"

"Archaic. Twenty-fourth century term for human excrement."

"I see. It *is* amazing how much really useful information one can learn by specializing in ancient folkmusic."

Coyote ignored him. The profession of folkmusician

was as good a cover as could be had these days, and the Fish knew it as well as he did.

"For what, your Porscineness, did you call me in?"

"You were busy?"

"I was busy."

The Fish smiled at him, and Coyote seethed.

"I'll count to ten," he told the Fish. "One. Two. Three—"

"All right, all right. I need somebody to go to Furthest, Mr. Jones."

"To go to where?"

"Furthest."

"Where the bald-headed hell is Furthest? And is it?"

"Is it what?"

"Furthest."

The Fish made a small sound of indignation. "Look here, Mr. Jones," he snorted, "is Earth Earth? Is Mars Mars? Is Alpha Centauri—"

"I don't mean that," said Coyote, shaking his head. "Furthest is a word, not just a name. Antique variant for 'farthest.' "

"Really? I didn't know that."

"No charge," said Coyote. "And is it?"

"Farthest? Yes, it is. It surely is. Let me show you."

The Fish pushed the button activating the great map on the wall beside them. It took the whole wall, and at that it was on not only a small scale but a distorted one. Vast areas of empty space had simply been deleted and replaced with small black dots indicating VAST DE-LETED EMPTY AREA. If it hadn't been for that convenient mechanism, it would have taken half a dozen walls to put the map up.

The Fish pushed the pointer stud and a bright green light came on, out in the upper right-hand corner.

"See that?" he said.

"That's Furthest?"

"That's right."

Coyote whistled. "I didn't know there was anything out there."

"Furthest is."

"That's beyond the Extreme Moons."

"Right."

"Well," said Coyote, "I'm impressed."

"No charge," murmured the Fish, and Coyote smiled.

"So what am I supposed to do?" he asked.

"Go live there."

"How long?"

"However long it takes, up to the eighteen-month maximum they'll let us have, and believe me it took an unholy amount of pressure to get them to give us eighteen *days*. They don't like offworlders out there."

"Live there."

"Right."

"What's it like?"

The Fish shrugged. "I don't know. Want to see the threedies?"

"If you would be so kind."

The map on the wall flicked out and immediately the wall clouded slightly, cleared, and disappeared. In its place was a street, curving off into the distance, flanked by houses. The houses were all precisely three stories high and very narrow. Each had a central door with two windows on each side on the first floor, five windows on the second floor, and the third floor had no windows at all. The houses all seemed to be connected by a sort of pipe or tube that ran from the third story of each one to the house next to it. All were built of an unprepossessing gray stone.

"What *is* that?"

"That's K'ith Vaad, capital of Furthest."

"Ugly."

"Of an ugliness seldom seen," the Fish agreed. "Sort of an ugly-specialist's ugly."

Coyote glanced at him, instantly suspicious. If the Fish was making jokes—sodden jokes, but jokes—there was something nasty about this assignment.

"Okay," he said. "What else?"

The street disappeared and was replaced by a vast unending expanse of gray rock, like lava wastes, broken by small creeks and humps of the rock.

"Mmmmm."

"Exactly."

"And what else?"

"That's all."

"That's all!" Coyote sat up straight and glared. "Come on, I don't believe it. How could that be all? Where are the tourist threedies?"

"No tourists."

"You're kidding."

"No, Mr. Jones, I'm not. No tourists are allowed on Furthest. You get on with a permit, on official business only, and you get off almost as fast as you get on. And they're damned choosy about what they consider official business. Those two slides are all we've got."

"Incredible."

"I agree with you."

"Well, what do you know about it? There must be some facts."

"Surely. Planet Furthest, dimension such and such, settled in the year 2083 by an Amerindian, a Europer, and two idiots from a Jupiter colony, plus a handful of unspecified other colonists. A very small handful. They were some kind of extremist cult, fleeing what they claimed was religious persecution."

"In 2083? Moonspittle."

"No, apparently that was still possible."

"Amazing. Go on."

"Climate is temperate, no dangerous wildlife or plants. No industry. No export except a plant called 'hwal' that's used as a base for perfume, and two or three rather esoteric musical instruments made of a kind of fiberglass. Almost no imports . . . coffee and sugar, I think. Government is paternal oligarchy, religion listed as something called the Holy Way. People are human, naturally, since they started out human and have been completely isolated ever since. Must be very inbred by now, however."

"What else?"

"That's about it. Some eyewash about ideals, a picture of a building, just trivia. That's all we've got."

Coyote sighed. "Well, I'm afraid I don't see it. Here's this godforsaken planet at the end of nowhere, completely anti-social, bothering nobody—"

"They're bothering somebody, Mr. Jones. They're bothering the Tri-Galactic Council."

"Ah, now we're getting to the point."

"Yes. You see, a . . . dear heaven. Mr. Jones, I have a problem."

"Tell me."

"What does one call these people, Mr. Jones? Furthestanians? Furthestites? There's always 'citizens of

Furthest' but that's awfully awkward for extended discussions. Just a minute."

He punched his intercom and the secretary machine, this year's absolutely newest and fanciest Amanuensis Mark IV model, gave out an attentive soft tone.

"Please check for correct spelling and pronunciation," said the Fish, "for the citizens of the planet called 'Furthest.' "

"Yes, sir," said the Amanuensis, and Coyote blinked.

"Yes, sir?" he marveled.

"Damn right," said the Fish.

"Now, how did you get a robot programmed to say 'yes, sir' instead of 'yes, citizen'?"

"Custom-made. It will say 'yes, most gracious master' if I want it to."

Coyote chuckled and the Amanuensis gave out with its tone again.

"Furthesters," it said with an intonation of the most dulcet competence. "F-U-R-T-H-E-S-T-E-R-S, Furthesters."

"Very good," said the Fish. "Fine."

"Thank you, sir," said the Amanuensis. "Will that be all, sir?"

"That's all," said the Fish, and the light went out on the Amanuensis, leaving behind in Coyote's mind an image of quivering eager pleasure. The thing looked as if you ought to pet it and scratch it behind its ears.

"I don't like your secretary," observed Coyote. "It's sickening."

"Irrelevant," said the Fish.

"You were saying?"

"Yes. I was saying that the Furthesters were annoying the Tri-Galactic Council. You know how, Mr. Jones? I'll tell you how. The next person to hold the office of President of the Tri-Galactic Council will be the delegate from Furthest."

"Who is he?"

"Let me see, I've got it written down here . . . oh, yes. One Bressthen Hkwylle'e. I have no idea if I'm saying that right. The Panglish for Bressthen is Andrew, no equivalent listed for Hkwylle'e."

"Never heard of him."

"Well, why should you have? With 20,393 delegate worlds how could you possibly know any individual delegate, unless he's done something that's made him known? But the situation with Furthest is a little special."

"Tell me about it."

"In the first place, it's only been three years since Furthest finally consented to join the Federation, which means the delegate has had very little experience. Not only that, he belongs to a religious group which damn near keeps him in total isolation. He's got seven hours of obligatory ritual meditation a day. He's got three hours of obligatory ritual isolations, and I don't remember what else. He's not allowed to leave Mars Central, and so far as anyone knows he's never been seen anywhere except in his quarters and at meetings of the Council."

"He doesn't sound to me like a very good bet for President."

The Fish shrugged his shoulders. "Bureaucracy, Mr. Jones. The Presidential succession goes in alphabetical order, and Furthest is next on the list, never mind how unlikely the result may be. Bressthen Hkwylle'e takes office twenty-four months from next Thursday."

"All right," Coyote said, "I can see that this might not be the ideal situation. But I'm damned if I see what my role is supposed to be. Were you suggesting, for example, that I use mass projective telepathy and convince the Three Galaxies that 'F' comes last in the alphabet?"

"Be serious, Mr. Jones."

"Then explain."

Coyote walked over to the wall behind the Fish's desk and pushed the button to make it transparent. He stared out for a moment at the sea of green trees one hundred and thirteen floors below and silently thanked the deities that kept him from having to spend his days in one of these rabbit warrens. It was better than it used to be on Mars Central, he supposed; at least there were trees now. But who would want to be cooped up all the time in block after block of identical two-hundred-story office buildings? Yecch.

"It causes a problem."

"Why? Is he some kind of lunatic?"

"That's the problem. We don't know. We don't know anything about him. We don't know what kind of lunatic a Furthester lunatic would be."

"What does the psychological profile show?"

"At Computer-Central, you mean?"

"Sure. What does it show?"

He went back and sat down across from the Fish.

"That's the problem, too. It shows nothing."

"You mean to tell me there's no psychological pro-file—"

"Wait a minute, Mr. Jones," interrupted the Fish. "I mean no such thing. By law there *has* to be a psychological profile, one male, one female, for the citizens of any people within the Three Galaxies. But that profile is made up by the psychcomputers on the basis of data fed them by those same citizens, and that's what was done in this case. And in this case there's something wrong."

"How bad?"

"We don't know. The routine measure is always the same. Every time a new President is two years in the offing there's a routine check. We have the Presidency about as nearly safe-guarded as is possible, but nonetheless it is a position of great power. It has to be. The President of the Tri-Galactic Council is the *only* person with full access to the Central Computers, for example. There are checks on him, but still he has full access. He is the only person with instant access to all of the other delegates. He is the only person with authority to act should there be—"

"I understand all that," said Coyote. "Of course he's powerful. How could an official over better than twenty thousand worlds be anything else? I'm not an idiot."

"Well, then. The routine check is to look up all existing information on the upcoming President, his people, his homeworld, and so on, and submit it to the computers for review. When we did this for Furthest we came up with some disturbing information."

"What?"

"*Everything* is average. Everything without exception. There is no smallest deviation from the mythical norm in even one statistic, in the data we have. The psych profile for a Furthester citizen is the ideal Mr. Human Being and his wife, Mrs. Human Being. It's too average. The computer says it can't be genuine."

"Maybe out of all the worlds there are it was bound to happen that there would be one average one."

"The computers say no. They say it's too perfect. There are very impressive and convincing figures about the odds against it. There just can't be any such Perfect Average World in this universe, Mr. Jones. Therefore, something is wrong. Therefore, something is being covered up. Therefore, something has got to be done, and well before the succession comes around. We've got to be able to judge the new President. We have to be able to make an accurate estimate of his behavior. If the things he is doing constitute abnormal behavior for a Furthester, if they mean that he is under strain or pressure, we have to know that. We have to know what the signs would be of a Furthester about to crack under a burden he could not bear. The safety of those twenty thousand worlds you mentioned depends on our having that information."

"And I'm supposed to get it?"

"That's right, Mr. Jones. Like I told you, they don't like offworlders. We had to exert every bit of pressure this office can muster, which is considerable, to get you permission to go there, let alone to stay eighteen months, and they may get sorry and retract it any time. Therefore, you are to assume while you're there that you have twenty-four hours to do the job. Just keep assuming it."

"Oh, lovely," Coyote muttered.

"And guess what?"

Guess what? The Fish was being arch, and that tore it. Coyote quickly considered alternatives.

"The women are all eight inches tall," he said.

"Not quite," chuckled the Fish, "but knowing your appetites I think you should know one thing. Of all those many thousands of planets there are only five left, in all the Three Galaxies, where sexual prudery still exists. Furthest is one of those five."

"Prudery?"

"Look it up," laughed the Fish. "In your dictionary of archaic terms."

Then he stopped laughing and went on, "You were the best possible agent available for this job. In the first place you're not especially sociable yourself, which makes you a good choice for an anti-social planet. In the second place, you're our most experienced man in exotic planet sorts of things. And in the third, and most important place, you are the strongest mass projective telepath we have. If anybody can convince the Furthesters that he is innocent, well-meaning, one hundred percent pure, you can. All you have to do is just put out clouds of psi good will, Mr. Jones, full strength."

"That's all I have to do, huh."

"Right. And find out what they're hiding. Convince them to let you in on their little secret. Fast. Without offending anybody."

"When do I leave?"

"Immediately. Top priority, federal rocket, warp drive, suspended animation for top speed. It's a long way out there."

Coyote stood up and turned to leave, grabbing the envelope of instructions that the Fish was holding out to him, and he headed for the door. Two steps from it he thought of something and looked back.

"Oh, by the way . . ." he said.

"Yes, Mr. Jones?"

"What's my cover? Traveling minstrel again?"

"Not this time. This time will be different."

"Different how?"

The Fish laughed again. He was a positive comedian today.

"This time, Mr. Jones," said the Fish with glee, "you are going to stay put. You are going to be the proprietor of a MESH. And how do you like *that?*"

# CHAPTER THREE

"Mary had a little rocket,
  tried to put it in her pocket,
  met a telepath who told her,
  'A pocket's not a rocket-holder.'

Lucky, lucky little Mary!
if she'd met an Ordinary,
she never would have thrown it
      from her—
*that* trip would have been a bummer!"

(old nursery rhyme)

HE WALKED into the building they had rented for him, still suffering from a severe case of time/place disorientation and a stomachache. He knew nothing at all about the warp drive that made it possible for ships to get around the Three Galaxies in less than a couple of lifetimes, but he knew that the process never did him any good, and the longer he had to spend at it the worse he felt when it was over. And this trip had been the longest there was . . . there wasn't anyplace farther than Furthest.

He still was unable to shake off the effect the warp drive always had on him, that curious feeling of being separated, of shuffling along behind himself pointing and snickering, chuckling at his foolish bellwether body, and longing for the integration that would gradually deliver him from the acute consciousness of self.

How far away was he from the center of the First Galaxy? The figures didn't mean anything to him. His head persisted in telling him that he was now located in the far upper right-hand corner of a wall in an office building on Mars Central.

The building was perfect, and he loved it, both of him, the body that went in first and the spirit that followed. It stood on a street just off the main drag of K'ith Vaad, and it was just like all the other structures he had seen in the threedies, three stories of gray stone, tall and narrow and forbidding. But inside was something else entirely.

All the inner walls had been taken out, except those around a kitchen and bath on the first floor and two small bedrooms on the second. The stone floors and walls stretched away all around him, smooth with the patina that comes of centuries of walking feet, and the sun streamed in through the high windows and blazed across the floors. Dust motes swam in the paths of light and danced about him; by waving an arm he could raise them in swarms and swirls of mad whirling, and Coyote was purely crazy about the place.

He had never seen a building like this, not outside a historical threedy, in his entire life. No one had, if he was living now. There were plastibubble houses that inflated as you entered their doors and deflated behind you and rolled themselves up as you left. There were the circular clusters of earthen domes that made up the dwellings of the Maklunites, spread like petals around the central ashram dome. There were the monstrous upended pillars of indestructable plastics that served for every architectural purpose in the inner planets. There were the houses of extruded foam and plastics that any citizen could have issued to him by the government upon reaching the age of seventeen and that made up the vast majority of private dwellings throughout the Galaxies.

But these buildings of Furthest carried him instantly back to the remote edges of history, to the days that had seen man first move out toward the stars, at incredible cost and only by virtue of brutally ignoring the misery that remained on the home planet. Such buildings as these of Furthest had disappeared from most of the known universe before the 25th century except for exhibits in museums— and now he stood inside one, and it was his dwelling-place for eighteen months. If he was careful, that is.

The first step was to get a helper of some kind, someone who could act as liaison between him and the people of Furthest, someone that he could ask questions and that could keep him from making stupid cultural mistakes. He didn't want to leave the building to take care of this at all; he would have preferred to spend the day just learning to be part of it. But such a course of action wouldn't do one thing to further his mission here.

He set down his flightbag on the floor, noting with pleasure that no servomechanism came rushing out to pick it up and carry it off. To test the thing further he scrabbled through his pockets and found a piece of disposable fiber that had been part of his ticket for Furthest and ostentatiously dropped it on the floor, too, whistling an incredibly ancient song about a sweet chariot swinging low.

To his great delight, it stayed there right where he had placed it. He would be able to get things dirty if he wanted to, and to clean them up himself, a privilege hard to come by outside the austere clusters of the Maklunites. Things were looking up. (Although he had looked up "sexual prudery" and found it less than an encouraging prospect.)

Reluctantly he went out into the street and headed for the center of town, where there was a public outlet to the planet's information computers, and inserted his credit disc, still whistling.

The outlet bonged loudly, a red light flashed on, and across the screen in brilliant purple letters he read IT IS NOTED THAT YOU ARE AN OFFWORLDER. PLEASE STAND BY WHILE YOUR AUTHORIZATION IS CHECKED. He waited, amused, while it satisfied itself as to his credentials, and then the standby notice went off and was replaced by an equally purple WELCOME TO FURTHEST. YOUR QUESTION PLEASE.

He noted that there was an oldstyle manual keyboard, capable he hoped of handling Panglish, since his command of Furthest speech was very new and raw feeling, and proceeded to punch out his request.

I WISH TO HIRE A HELPER FROM THIS CITY. HOW DO I GO ABOUT IT?

A HELPER? A HELPER TO DO WHAT?

I AM HERE TO ESTABLISH A MESH. I NEED SOMEONE TO DO SMALL ROUTINE TASKS AND ACT AS LIASON MAN FOR ME. IS THERE ANY SORT OF EMPLOYMENT CLEARINGHOUSE I MIGHT GO TO?

The computer supplied him with an address, ejected

his credit disc, and returned to rest status, and he went to the clearinghouse. There was a certain amount of difficulty there, because no one in the place had any idea what a MESH might be.

"You're joking," he had protested. "You can't possibly not know what a MESH is. Everybody knows what a MESH is."

"You're mistaken, Citizen," said a chilly lady at a desk. "We don't know, not any of us."

Coyote looked around him, a bit bewildered. He had been warned, to a certain extent, as to what to expect of these people. In a tri-galactic universe where the vast majority of the populace either went nude or settled for some sort of tunic or loincloth, these people garbed themselves like royalty from antiquity. They wore full-length garments of synthovelvet, with long flowing sleeves, high collars, elaborate ruffs, skirts fully yards around, like a costume ball. It was one thing to be told of this, and another thing to see it. He felt more disoriented than ever; his eyes were taking it in, but somewhere behind his body there was this discorporate entity making snickering noises about not believing it for a minute.

And on every one of their heads sat an article of clothing, or ornament, that looked like nothing so much as a pair of formal earmuffs; it was a broad band, elaborately decorated, that went across the top of the head and down the sides, and that was attached to an equally elaborate sort of puffed covering over each ear. Whew . . .

"Mmmm . . ." he said, playing for time. "Perhaps I could explain."

"I think you had better," snapped the chilly lady. "We certainly cannot allow one of our citizens to take part in something the nature of which is entirely unknown to us. Is it dangerous?"

"A MESH?" Coyote laughed. "No, of course not. Not unless you're one of those persons who only wants to see other people by appointment. It's just a sort of service center, a place where people can be together, love one another, do things, see things, hear things, learn things."

"Like a school?"

"No . . . more like a coffeehouse, more like a cafe."

"A restaurant, then."

"No."

Coyote shook his head, and reached into his pockets.

"Here," he said, "could I use your threedy projector? I've got some slides of MESHES from all over the Three Galaxies. I could show them to you."

The chilly lady's face froze over irrevocably. "It is not allowed," she said.

"What's not allowed?"

"Threedies. Threedies are illegal on Furthest."

Well, thanks a helluva lot for telling me that back at Mars Central, he thought first, and then he realized he was being unfair. Of course the staff of TGIS had not thought to find out whether threedies were legal on Furthest. Who ever heard of a planet where you were not allowed to watch threedies? He couldn't even imagine such a thing.

"Never?" he asked in amazement. "You've never seen a threedy?" And instantly he was aware that he had made a wrong move, that he sounded like an offworlder being critical of the backward planet. Definitely not a wise remark he had made.

He knew only one way to handle a situation like this. He began talking, softly, prattling facts about the institution called a MESH. And while he talked he projected just one message, at full power and without pause, and that message was A MESH IS A GOOD THING—FURTHEST NEEDS ONE. It was made easier by the face that he actually believed the stuff he was putting out.

"People can come and eat at a MESH, you see," he said. "Usually there is a pretty full menu, foods from all over the Galaxies, exotic drinks, things like that. And there is entertainment, usually lots of threedies, but not here, of course. And music. Theater. I'm a folksinger and guitarist myself, I specialize in antique instruments and songs, and I'll be performing very often."

A MESH IS A GOOD GOOD THING.

FURTHEST NEEDS ONE.

"And you can buy things there, too," he went on. "Local people, artists and sculptors, artisans, craftsmen, can exhibit their goods for sale. There would be an import counter, a place to buy offworld things. And MFs . . . a MESH always stocks everything that can be stocked in the way of MFs."

There had been a murmur from the chilly lady, who was beginning to warm up under the steady pressure from Coyote's mind.

"MF?" she asked, almost gently. "What is an MF?"

By the Light, were they still using *books* out here in this back of beyond? He couldn't believe it.

"Microfilms," he said carefully. "MFs. Microfilms."

"Oh, yes," the lady nodded. "I see. Of course we have microfilms . . . we're not savages."

He was beginning to wonder about that, but he noted that she wore an MF viewer as a pendant on a chain about her neck, like a fashionable woman anywhere, so apparently it was not so bad as it seemed.

"And you can learn things there," he said, after a moment to remember where he had left off. "If you only have one or two outlets to the Edcomputers in your own home, you can go with a group of friends and use the group outlets at the MESH and take courses together."

A MESH IS A GOOD THING.

FURTHEST NEEDS ONE.

A MESH IS A GOOD GOOD THING.

FURTHEST NEEDS ONE.

"It's a place for being together," he crooned, "for being together and being friends with one another."

Careful, he thought . . . remember, this is a prudery planet.

"Just being friends," he said. "All happy together, all learning, hearing, seeing, enjoying. It's sort of a community nexus."

A MESH IS A GOOD GOOD THING.

FURTHEST NEEDS ONE.

The chilly lady smiled at him.

"You know," she said, "a MESH sounds to me like a very good thing. I believe Furthest needs one."

Two men, incredibly gowned and draped and capped, came forward and shook his hand warmly, and he relaxed the projection just a little. He didn't want to make them suspicious, and there was no data in the Central Computers about the psibilities of the Furthesters, except that those abilities were "average."

"Could you help me, then?" he nudged them, gently. "I really do need someone to work with me. Someone young, preferably, and energetic. Able to run errands for me. Someone who knows his way about."

There was a good deal of bustle, and punching of buttons on comsystems, and shuffling through files, and then they told him they had just the person. A boy, about fifteen, of a very good family, and intelligent. He did not need to work but had just completed his schooling and was still too young to go on to advanced work, but was bored with sitting around doing nothing.

"That sounds exactly right," said Coyote. "Can you send me to him?"

"We'll get him for you now, Citizen Jones," they said. "Sit down, please, and be comfortable—it will take only a minute or two."

They were right, too; in five minutes flat the boy appeared before him, ill at ease but obviously bright and alert. He had the coppery skin and dark brown hair of all his people, the huge eyes of a brown almost black, the long straight nose that came from the forehead seemingly in an unbroken plane, and if you got used to the strangeness no doubt he was a handsome specimen.

They introduced him and told Coyote his name.

"May I see that written down?" Coyote asked.

"Surely." They wrote it down for him. Arh Qu'e.

He couldn't say it properly, in spite of the drilling he'd had in the exaggerated aspiration of the language, and he gave up the attempt at once. There was nothing like a small strategic failure to win people over.

"I can't say it," he said frankly. "But I'll compromise. The name sounds like the Panglish sequence R-K. May I call you that—may I call you RK?"

The boy frowned slightly, and then smiled.

"Certainly," he said in flawless Panglish. "RK is fine with me."

"Good enough, then," Coyote said. "Now, can you come with me at once? The job will require that you live at the MESH, you know—I suppose they explained that to you."

RK nodded. "I can't come with you," he said, "because I have things I must do for my parents before I leave for any length of time. But if you will give me the address I can be there this evening by nine o'clock."

Coyote nodded and wrote down the address for him. He was pleased. It was only the first day and he was making good progress. The headquarters for the MESH was satisfactory, he had found a helper that ought to be perfect, no doubt his personal baggage had been delivered from the port by now. He could go back to the house, unpack, have a leisurely dinner somewhere, and still have an

hour or two to himself to enjoy the sensation of being surrounded with something out of the dark past before RK
came. He could tramp up and down the stone stairs and
listen to the echoes of his steps—there were no echoes in
plastic buildings.

He thanked them at the clearinghouse, offered his
credit disc in payment and was waved away. No, no. It
was a public service he was doing. A MESH was a good
thing and Furthest needed one, and they wouldn't think
of charging him anything.

Coyote went away feeling almost ashamed. It was one
thing to use his psibilities against sophisticated people. In
that case—the usual one—his only advantage was in
sheer quantity. Whereas most human beings had the ability to send simple messages of three or four semantic units
in length and receive the same, and talented experts could
communicate far more freely and completely with their
minds than people ever had with tongues alone, he was
almost totally mind-deaf. A really powerful telepath could
manage to get through to him with vague sensations, sorts
of blobs of color and impressions of emotions, warnings
of danger, all that kind of thing. But that was the total
extent of it. He got all the feelings, but he could not get
content at all, any more than a physically deaf person
could hear music in the old days before deafness became
a curable disorder.

But he could certainly put *out* the messages. Mass projective telepaths were rare, and he was the rarest. He
could control a crowd of two thousand people at a mile's
distance, and he could do that without even getting out of
breath. And ammunition of that sort seemed a bit heavy
for use against one chilly lady and two nondescript
middle-aged gentlemen in fancy dress.

To get rid of his feeling of guilt he very carefully visualized the clearinghouse as he walked away, and projected
a message back at his three victims while he moved along.

YOU ARE VERY GOOD GOOD PEOPLE.

FURTHEST NEEDS MORE PEOPLE LIKE YOU.

EVERYONE LOVES AND ADMIRES YOU BECAUSE YOU ARE
VERY

GOOD

PEOPLE.

He felt a lot better then.

# CHAPTER FOUR

"Death is only a new becoming."

(from the Devotional Book of Tham O'Kent)

THERE WAS MAIL for him the next morning, and he sat himself down on the flight of stairs to the second floor, bathed in the brilliant light from the windows, and went methodically through it.

There was a garish chartreuse folder ostensibly from a company that called itself "Impact MFs Inc." A coy citizen from some outlying world peeked at him from behind a giant fan of microfilm. "Huge discounts! Saleday is Everyday at Impact MFs Inc.! Buy here, buy˙ here, see hear, see here." When opened the folder began to hum in a seductive female voice and gave off a powerful odor of roses.

Coyote frowned at the thing suspiciously. No legitimate firm in this day and age would produce such a monstrosity. He turned it over and over, ignoring the sexy humming, and found what he had expected—a tiny fish hidden in a curly capital "I." It was from the Fish, and was a demand for an immediate report.

He dropped it gleefully down the stairs, planning to drop lots more stuff on top of it and make a regular pile of trash at the bottom of the steps, and went on to the next item.

There were half a dozen legitimate brochures offering for sale the sort of goods that were sold in MESHes, which indicated that TGIS had done an appropriate amount of advance publicity for him while he was on the way here.

There was an ad for an assortment of mobile flowers from the Extreme Moons, all colors, hybrids with double flowers, and all of them singers. That would be worth keeping. And a price list for MFs, the real thing this time.

There was a note from an old friend, Tzana Kai, ostensible head of a translation bureau but really TGIS like him, wishing him success in his new venture.

And, finally, there was a small brown mailpouch, bearing a six-months-past postmark and the comsystem code number of the Maklunite cluster at Highmountain.

Coyote opened it carefully, wondering what could have prompted an extravagance like the mailing of an old-fashioned parcel instead of a telebounce facsimile. It would have had to be something very important indeed, because the Maklunite clusters had little money to spend and a thousand ways to spend that little.

The letter began: "To Coyote Jones, beloved of all of us at Highmountain. Last night our teacher and friend, Tham O'Kent, left us. It was his wish that the Change take place in our ashram, and that we all be with him; he left us without pain or any sign of fear. We shall miss him greatly."

Coyote stopped and looked up from the letter, afraid that he would cry and very much aware that Tham O'Kent would have laughed at such a reaction. It was only another evidence of how far away he was from the Maklunite Way that he could not look upon death as simply a change instead of as the end of things.

"Tham O'Kent had a message for you," the letter went on. "He asked that we tell you that it was one of the sorrows of his life that all the good will and work that both of you put into your time with us was not enough to make it possible for you to remain. He asked that we tell you that it was not your fault, any more than it was his, but that there are people who are not ready for our Way. He said that perhaps you are kept back because you are needed as you are. And he sent his love, as teacher and as friend.

"You know that it is our custom to keep all things in common, and that when one of us comes to the time of Changing, all those things that he has by him at that time continue to be held by all. However, it was Tham O'Kent's request that his devotional book be sent to you, and we are happy to do so. Use it in wisdom and in love.

"We all think of you and love you. Tessa sends you greetings from Chysanthemum Bridge. Return to us when you will."

Coyote put the letter down gently and picked up the book. He was having a certain amount of trouble seeing it, but he would have known it anywhere, by touch alone. He held it tightly and fought the tears that threatened to make a fool of him, and then he saw RK standing quietly in front of him.

"You are troubled, Citizen," he said gravely. "Is there any way that I can help you?"

"I've lost a friend, RK," said Coyote past the lump in his throat. "I've lost a friend and I'm having trouble accepting that fact with regretful serenity, as I am expected to do."

"Lost him, Citizen?"

"He is dead," said Coyote harshly. "The Maklunites would say that he is only Changed, but I say he is dead, and the world is a worse place for his absence."

RK sat down beside him on the steps and regarded him gravely.

"Is it all right to talk?" he asked.

"Oh, yes," said Coyote. "Yes. It might even help."

"I was wondering," said the boy. "What are they?"

"What are what?"

"What you were saying, Citizen, Maklunites?"

"You don't know what Maklunites are?"

"No. Are they people?"

"They're a religion, friend."

"I've never heard of them."

Coyote was amazed. "How can that be, RK? Do you read the news MFs, watch the newscasts? They're the third most numerous religion in the Three Galaxies; only Ethical Humanism and Judaism have more people '

The boy shrugged. "Perhaps I have just not paid careful attention, Citizen. What sort of a religion are they, these Maklunites?"

"A very gentle one. They live together, sharing everything; they love each other deeply. There is no closer being-together in all the Three Galaxies than that practiced by the Maklunites."

RK was frowning. "They are communists, then," he said severely. "Is that right?"

"Not communists," said Coyote. "Lovers."

RK looked shocked, and Coyote hastily amended his remark.

"Lovers of one another," he said, "in the highest sense."

"We are taught by our elders," said RK, "that communal living is a deadly sin, and that it was meant that each man should live with his family and protect them and love them only."

"You have every right to your beliefs," said Coyote reasonably. "They are held by many peoples, you know; for example, that is one of the doctrines of early Judaism."

RK looked at him, a long measuring glance, and clasped his hands behind his back.

"Are you a Maklunite, Citizen Jones?"

"No," said Coyote. "I tried to be, though. More than I ever wanted anything else in all my life, I wanted to be a Maklunite. I tried so hard, and many fine people tried to help me, but I was not able to do it. It's one of those people who is dead."

"I'm sorry."

"Yes . . . well, there's no help for it. Does it frighten you to find yourself sitting beside a sinner?"

He was half joking, but RK took him seriously, and appeared to be struggling with the problem.

"You don't *look* like a sinner," he said finally. "It makes it difficult to answer your question."

"How would a sinner look?" Coyote asked in amazement. "Is there a special appearance for sinners?"

"Yes, there is," said RK calmly. "They look miserable. Completely and totally miserable."

Coyote whistled.

"RK," he asked suddenly. "Do you really believe that?"

"It is not possible," the boy said with the steady tones of unshakable conviction, "for a sinner to be happy."

"The Maklunites are happy," said Coyote. "They are the happiest people I know."

"I can't accept that," said RK. "If they live as you say, they cannot possibly be happy."

This, Coyote could see, was not going to get them anywhere. The boy was spouting some sort of cant doctrine, and it sounded like a dangerous one and one of which he should be disabused. On the other hand, Coyote could not afford to make an enemy of his only human link with the Furthesters just for the sake of a religious or philosophical argument.

"Well," he said, standing up, "this is an interesting discussion, but we'll never get anything done this way, will we? Let me put up my mail and we'll get started."

RK seemed relieved to have the subject changed, and he went to work willingly enough. Coyote took the Devotional Book and laid it away carefully in his room, taking time to look for a few seconds at the well-used pages carefully filled with Tham O'Kent's meticulous writing, and then he went to join the boy. They had a great deal of work to do.

"From Coyote Jones, with love to all of you at Highmountain:

"I received your letter yesterday morning, with the book enclosed, and I thank you with all my heart. This is the first moment I have had free to write to you.

"I know that there are many of you there at Highmountain for whom the teachings in Tham's devotional book were of great importance, and you must have had a feeling of sadness at seeing the book leave your cluster instead of taking its place upon the shelves in your ashram. I am touched and honored, both at the tenderness of the sacrifice and at having the book for my own. (I can hear you laughing at that phrase, 'for my own,' but I suppose it will surprise none of you, knowing me as you do, and it is the most natural for me.) I will treasure the book until the time comes that I can pass it on to someone else, and I thank you again. If at any time you should have need of it, you have only to send me a message and I will return it to you.

"As you probably know, I am now operating a MESH on the planet called Furthest; I find the job very normal-seeming, but the planet is strange. My MESH opened for the first time last night, and I would like to tell you about it, except that I'm not very good at expressing myself. Perhaps if I just tell you about one of the ladies— and I use that term deliberately—you will be better able to imagine the rest.

"Try to imagine a young woman, very tall and thin,

with skin the color of pale copper. She is wearing a gown that covers every inch of her from the top of her throat to her feet, and you can see nothing of her but her head and her hands. The gown she wears is of heavy synthetic velvet and is vertically striped in alternate dark and light green. The collar is as high as it could be without choking her and the sleeves come down in points over the backs of her hands almost to her fingers. The skirts of her gown are fully a yard around and sweep the floor when she moves. Around the collar, the border of the sleeves, and the hem of her dress, there are three rows of heavy golden braid. She must be wearing something on her feet, but they are hidden by the gown, so I don't know what it could be. Her long brown hair is caught at the back of her throat by a loop of the golden braid that trims her gown. She wears no cosmetics of any kind, unless I simply am unable to detect them because of the skill with which she has applied them. Over the top of her head there is a band an inch wide, of the striped synthovelvet, going down the sides of her head and attached to what look like velvet earmuffs, heavily trimmed with pearls and gold lace, over her ears. (If you aren't familiar with earmuffs, they are a kind of round covering for the ears, attached to a band over the head, and worn to protect the wearer against severe cold. It doesn't ever get very cold here.)

"Now multiply this lady by fifty, pair her off with men who are just as incredibly dressed, except that they wear full trousers instead of skirts, caught tight at the ankles, and you will have some idea of the appearance of my opening night audience. There were no children present, not even one, but when I have seen them, they were dressed like their elders.

"Usually, you know, the opening night of a MESH is a very festive occasion. Everyone knows that it is a place for all the people in the area and there is always a lot of sharing, a lot of helping, and people come in to the opening warm and loving and ready to know one another. Not here, let me tell you. These people not only do not know how to act in a MESH, they've never even heard of such a place. Apparently their government has carefully censored such information, along with a great deal of other information, although there couldn't be any formal official policy against MESHes or they wouldn't have allowed one to be opened here. At any rate, the people came in hesitant and half-afraid, and in spite of everything I could do they stayed that way, wandering around in twos and threes, touching things as if they had poison spines on them.

"I let that go on as long as I dared, hoping it would get better of itself (which it didn't) and then I called them into the central area and sang to them. And that was the strangest thing of all. You know that I have almost no ability to receive the thoughts of others; like a twentieth-century primitive I get only blurry images and emotions instead of the clear information that normal people receive. But I have never faced opacity such as this before. There were perhaps a hundred people there, and they were like a hundred small squares of flat blackness, or black flatness. Just nothing. Emptiness. Total closedness. I wasn't getting messages of dislike or fear, there was just nothing there at all, and that's not normal. It was as if every single person in the Mesh was under orders to maintain an automatic and total psychic block at all times.

"I can't imagine what could have caused a whole people to be like that. It couldn't be accidental, they would have had to be systematically trained. It must be some part of their prudery code, something that is a part of 'good manners' for them, some part of their training for public behavior. Surely they can't be like that always, even when they are at home with their families.

"I don't mind admitting that I was awfully uncomfortable, and I wasn't sure exactly what to do about the whole thing. I decided that the best place to start was with the idea of building up confidence in their minds. So along with the music last night they got a constant full-strength mental dose of TRUST ME, I AM A GOOD MAN AND I AM ONLY HERE TO HELP YOU. I kept that up for two solid hours, until my whole head felt like a bruise, and it still aches, but I hope it did some good. I could sense no change in them (although it would have to be a pretty damn radical change, of course, before I *would* sense it). But when they began to leave they all came up and spoke to me in a friendly enough manner, so I suppose I should be satisfied with the results for the time being.

"They appeared to be completely mystified by the music I sang and played, but that's nothing unusual. People ordinarily are mystified by the new and strange, and apparently these people have never been exposed to any sort of antique music. They did seem interested and I think that that interest will draw them back here so that I can try to reach them more effectively. I can at least hope so.

"I thank you again for the gift of Tham's devotional book, and I send you my warmest wishes and my love, from Furthest . . .

Coyote Jones"

# CHAPTER FIVE

"The idea that telepathy was in some way a freak-ish, non-human—or even worse, superhuman—ability disappeared only slowly during the twenty-first century. Difficult as it is for us to imagine such a situation now, it was at one time the accepted practice to ridicule and to discourage any and all attempts to use telepathy or any of the normal human psibilities."

(from *A Brief History of the Human Race,*
by Dr. Evelyn Margaret O'Brien, Ph.d.)

RK WAS UNEASY and strange the next day, to such an amazing degree that Coyote began to worry. They were stocking MFs in the dispensers and checking them against the inventory strips, a simple job that should have been a matter of thirty minutes time. But RK was so distracted and half there that three times in the first quarter of an hour he agreed to an MF title that Coyote called out when he should have noted it as an error. By the time they should have been through, the inventory was hopelessly mixed up, and Coyote gave it up and called a halt.

"Look here," he said, "yesterday I was the one who was upset, and you did your best to cheer me up. Now this morning I would have to be an idiot not to know that *you* are troubled, and we're not getting anything done. I think it might be better for the business if we took a break and tried to fix your problem."

The boy flushed, and Coyote felt the curious sensation

that meant a blocked mind was opening, a sort of slippery sensation behind the eyes, as if something had broken the surface of some hidden water, and then it was gone. He sat down beside RK and waited, not wanting to push him. He could have done some mental pushing, of course, but he hesitated to do that. It was almost always safe to operate mentally with large crowds, because the facts about mass telepathic manipulation had been carefully suppressed, and in fact a number of articles had been written recently doubting the very existence of any such technique. And to be absolutely accurate, the existence of a skill held by only thirteen persons in three galaxies almost constituted non-existence. But if he were to attempt to project to an individual, at such close quarters, he ran the risk of having that individual become alarmed at the strength of the projection, and that kind of alarm would inevitably lead to trouble. He wouldn't risk it unless it appeared really necessary, and settled for holding in his mind a vague sort of reassurance concept, reasonably sure that the boy would not spot it as projected.

"Citizen Jones."

"Yes, RK?"

"I do have a problem, you know that? I've got a really awful problem."

"Maybe I can help you, if you'll let me."

RK stared at him gravely. "You would, wouldn't you? I know you would. The only thing is . . . I feel like I ought to be able to trust you, but I have always been taught—"

"That offworlders cannot be trusted."

RK nodded.

"Well," said Coyote reasonably, "you'll have to decide that for yourself. Are you telepathic? You could check my thoughts for evidence of evil intent, RK; I'd be perfectly willing to let you."

The boy went white, and Coyote knew he'd goofed. Apparently he'd touched some taboo area.

"What is it now, RK?" he asked. "Have I offended you?"

"You asked if I was telepathic."

"So?"

"Of course I'm not telepathic! Why would you—why do you ask me that? What made you think of that question?"

"RK, you're really frightened—why?"

"I'm not frightened."

"I don't believe you. You're shaking."

"RK," said Coyote patiently, "I'm sorry if discussions about psibility are taboo for your people. I know your police use telepathy, and I didn't realize it was a subject that one doesn't discuss. It was just an error of manners, and I won't mention it again. But so far as your problem is concerned, you are going to have to decide for yourself, like I tried to say before, whether you can trust me or not. If you can't trust me, then nothing I say to you is worth anything anyway. If I'm not trustworthy I can sit here all day and swear I am, and it won't mean anything."

RK dropped his face into his hands and moaned in sheer misery, and Coyote began to feel genuinely concerned. Apparently it was not just a minor problem.

"Try to trust me," he coaxed. "Try—you should know that you can."

*You should know,* he thought, *because you were here last night all evening long while I was putting out that trust-me stuff.*

RK drew a long shuddering breath and raised his head.

"I'll have to trust you," he said simply. "There's no other way. Only I'm going to have to ask you to trust me, too."

"Of course."

"I'm going to ask you to do me a favor, but just on trust. With almost no explanation. If you won't do it that way, then I'm up against it."

"Try me."

RK went and stared out of the front window onto the street, and Coyote waited. He had found waiting one of his most useful talents over the years. He only wished the Fish had just a little scrap of that particular talent, however; his report about the empty citydome had brought down a flock of URGENT notices on him from Mars Central, as if the inner secrets of a totally anti-social people could be brought into the light by shouting and shoving. He was waiting, and would continue to wait as long as he dared.

"Citizen Jones," said RK from the window, "it's not for myself that I am asking the favor. It's for my sister."

"Your sister? I didn't know you had one, young man."

"I do, though," said RK. "'I don't really know her well, because she has almost never lived with our family. I've only been with her during visits my parents and I made to her school, and very few of those are allowed. But she has always written to me, and she gave me my first *ak'ith*."

"Ak'ith?"

"It is a sort of knife," RK said. "It's more a decorative thing than a useful one, but it's important to a boy among our people."

"I see. Then you and your sister are close?"

RK hesitated. "I don't understand."

"You are fond of one another, I mean."

"I think so. As much as is possible when you see each other so rarely."

"And what is this sister of yours like, RK?"

"She's very brilliant," said the boy slowly, "and very beautiful—and she's been sentenced to Erasure."

Coyote dropped the stack of MFs he had been holding and bent to pick them up, with a long slow whistle. Erasure! That was the second most severe penalty in all the Three Galaxies, surgery by psycho-probe that erased the personality and all memories and left the victim in a state of literally prenatal blankness. It was exceedingly rare, being used only for those criminals who appeared to be totally beyond all hope of rehabilitation by any other means.

"What has she done, RK? That's not exactly a mild sentence."

"That's what I can't tell you."

"I see."

RK whirled to face Coyote, his face twisted with desperation and rage.

"I can tell you just one thing," he blurted. "Her crime was one of religion. That's all that I can say."

Coyote had the feeling he was really in over his head now. How could there be any religious crime on a planet whose religion was almost nonexistent? There was a church in each city, according to those so-average statistics, and Coyote had seen one, only a few blocks away from the MESH. But in spite of the apparent religious excess of the Furthester delegate, according to the material in his briefing papers the religion called the Holy Path was nothing more than a very watered down brand of Ethical Humanism. It was based on such inflammatory doctrines as "be good to your parents," don't tell lies, it's not nice," "do your share of the work that must be done," that kind of thing. There was a church service of sorts, called Tenth Day Observance, to which everyone was expected to go, and a Years-End Festival that seemed to be connected to the religion. But it was nothing more than a code of ethics and propriety—how could it be possible for someone to rebel against anything so vague and permissive, to the extent of incurring Erasure for it? It didn't make any sense; it was another empty citydome.

"Will you help me?"

RK was staring fixedly at him, his face a mixture of pleading and defiance, his hands clenched in fists at his sides.

"Will you, Citizen?" he repeated.

Coyote thought rapidly. Would he dare risk such a thing when the safety of three galaxies depended upon his being allowed to remain on this planet until he could learn what he needed to know?

"What would you want me to do, RK?" he asked as casually as he could. "I'm afraid you'll have to tell me that, at least."

"Of course," said the boy. "All I need is a place for my sister to stay, a place to hide her. That's all. You don't even need to see her. There is a little room on the third floor—"

"But RK, the third floor is padlocked and barred. I wasn't able to get permission to even go up there, for some reason which I haven't been able to determine."

"That's because you are an offworlder. I can go up there any time, and my sister would be safe there. Could I bring her, Citizen? She is only nineteen, my sister, and Erasure is . . . is horrible."

"RK?"

"Yes, Citizen Jones?"

"Is she guilty?"

"My sister?"

"Of course, your sister! It's your sister we're discussing, isn't it? Is she guilty of the crime she's charged with?"

"Yes."

"She is guilty. And do you think the sentence is too severe?"

RK swallowed, but he faced Coyote steadily, and Coyote liked him for that.

"No, I think the sentence is fair."

"Then why do you want to hide her?"

"Because," said RK, "she is my sister. I know she is guilty. She admits it; she glories in it. I know that what she has done is foul and vile and despicable and that Erasure is what she deserves. Nonetheless, she is my sister, and I love her; I will not let them do that to her if I can help it."

He turned his back then and all the pride seemed to go out of him like air from a pricked balloon.

"I talk such a good line," he said bitterly, "but that's all it is, just talk. I will be honest with you, Citizen— there is nothing that I myself can do. It is only you—if you will help me hide her, she has a chance. No member of my people would do it."

"Not even your parents, RK?"

"My parents! To my parents, my sister is dead. She does not even exist. They are like stone, both of them. And besides, they would not dare. They are being watched, of course, and if my sister were to disappear with their help they would be convicted along with her. It is only you who could help, because you are offworld —our laws do not apply to you in this case."

"If I should be caught—what then?"

"My sister and I would be taken away, and Erasure would be the penalty. You would simply be asked to leave; it would be obvious to everyone that you had simply acted in ignorance of our customs and our laws."

"I would be asked to leave." Coyote shook his head. "That would not be good, RK," he said. "I've spent all my life savings to start this business—I would be a pauper, destitute, with nowhere to go, no money to begin again." *Not to mention,* as he could not mention, *that he would have failed in his mission, and that there would not be even a prayer that the officials of Furthest would allow another offworlder to violate their precious planet after such an experience.*

"You're going to say no," said RK exhaustedly. "And I don't blame you."

"You must understand—"

RK cut him off. "Wait," he said. "Do this one thing for me. Let me bring my sister here to meet you, only that. Certainly, even if we were caught here, that could cause you no trouble. No one would dream that you had known she was an escaped criminal. Would you do that? And don't tell me your decision until you have had a chance to speak to her yourself?"

Coyote considered the matter carefully. He was reasonably sure the boy's assessment of the situation was accurate. If the police were to come and Coyote were to claim that he had had no knowledge of the girl's guilt, he would be believed. He could convince a few policemen easily, especially since he was an offworlder and would be considered inferior and stupid and liable to make mistakes in any event. He could surely afford to do that much, just as evidence to RK of his good will. But he had another question first.

"RK," he said carefully, "is it taboo to discuss telepathy? I mean, if I don't ask personal questions, can I talk about it in the abstract sense?"

He looked at the boy and nodded. "I see, you just don't like the topic at all, under any circumstances. All right, then. I'll try to be careful of the phrasing of my question."

"Thank you, Citizen."

"What I want to know is this—I know your police are trained telepaths. If I were to agree to your sister staying here, what is to prevent the police from learning about it in that way—and learning that I knew all about the whole thing, by the way?"

"How could they do that?"

"Wouldn't they make a routine search, house by house, something like that?"

"A—a mental search? Is that what you're suggesting?"

"Is that so horrendous a suggestion?"

"Citizen Jones," said RK, white with indignation, "we are not barbarians here, just because we are far from the center of things. No member of our police force would search a mind without a warrant granting him specific permission to do so. No policeman may go around probing houses at random; he must have the permission of a judge, and it is not at all easy to get. Such violations of privacy are taken very seriously by my people."

"I see. A warrant would be needed first."

"Certainly. And a petition for warrant requires firm, unmistakable evidence that there are grounds to suspect a crime. And a judge is very hesitant about granting such a warrant, because if the probe reveals that the suspect is *not* guilty, the government is liable for a huge penalty, payable to the wronged person on grounds of invasion of privacy."

"I understand. And there would be no reason for anyone to apply for such a warrant for this place."

"None at all, Citizen. The government is of the opinion that I do not even know of my sister's crime—it's supposed to be a state secret. Only a handful of people know, and all have been sworn to secrecy. I am supposed to believe that my sister is on a holiday."

"And after Erasure?"

"I would probably not be told . . . they would tell me that she had had an accident and her body destroyed beyond recognition, something like that. Unless they decide to make an example of her— But all that is irrelevant, Citizen. Because she escaped and I do know."

"Yes. Yes, well, that's all clear, RK."

"Will you meet her, then?"

"Yes, I will," said Coyote. What the hell. He was anxious to find out what a religious criminal, sentenced to Erasure, and only nineteen years old, might look like. Perhaps he would be able to get more of the details from the girl, and there was certainly nothing about this that sounded average. It should be the sort of details he needed.

"Can you bring her here for dinner?" he asked RK. "A late dinner, of course. After the MESH has closed for the night."

"A midnight supper . . . Yes, I can do that."

"Good enough, then. We'll consider it settled."

"You are very kind, Citizen. I'm grateful."

"I haven't agreed to anything yet, RK."

The boy smiled.

"Wait until you have talked to my sister," he said. "We will see, then."

"Oh?" Coyote's eyebrows went up. "It's like that, is it?"

RK just kept on smiling.

"All right, then," said Coyote, "I'll wait and see. And now, could you perhaps do *me* a favor?"

"Anything!"

"Could we perhaps get these MFs stocked in the dispensers before time for lunch?"

RK turned red, and struck an embarrassed fist against his thigh.

"I am not much help to you, Citizen," he said apologetically.

"You're going to be," Coyote assured him. "Don't you worry, young man, you're going to be a great *deal* of help."

He handed the boy a stack of MFs.

"Here," he said. "We've lost so much time that I'm going to have to go do the blasted market detail myself. You'll have to catalog these on your own. Can you handle that?"

"Certainly I can."

"Then do it," said Coyote. "And be careful, will you?"

# CHAPTER SIX

"Matthew Jessup loved a woman
a highborn Thrail from Astra Three;
through the sky he heard her call him,
'Starship Captain, rescue me!'

"He followed her because she called him,
always off the starboard side,
naked she ran on before him,
softly, mournfully, she cried.

"Ware, beware, ye starship captains!
Ware, beware!
Ware the witches back of Saturn
combin' out their scarlet hair,
sing ware, beware!"

(from an old ballad)

So THIS was the criminal sister.

Coyote tried to take her in without obvious staring,
gave that up as an unlikely task and stared. Yes indeed.
He could see now what RK had meant by the "you just
wait" routine.

Unfortunately, it wasn't going to work. He knew enough
about these people to realize that what confronted him
was probably the absolute quintessence of Furthester
beauty, supposed to drive him mad enough with lust
(worship? . . . terror? . . . what was beauty supposed to
inspire in a man on this antiquated old chunk of rock?),
mad enough with something or other, anyway to jeop-
ardize his entire mission just to be near the source.

But he didn't find her beautiful. Intellectually, he could make a note: ONE FURTHESTER WOMAN, RAVING BEAUTY PER HER PLANET STANDARDS. Emotionally, though, esthetically, she could not even touch him.

She stood a good five feet eleven inches tall, nothing of her showed except her hands and face and hair, and she looked mean enough to eat nails. The line from her forehead to the tip of her nose was a clean swoop, the skin was flawless burnished copper, and the lips were formed by a master, long and curled and strong, no doubt covering sharp perfect little white teeth like a vixen's. Her cheekbones set shadows against her skin, and her eyebrows were a permanent hauteur. If it had not been for the dark brown color of her hair and eyes, and the extreme tilt up of the eyes toward the brows at their outside tip, she could have stepped off the wall of an Egyptian tomb. He bet she could ignore three flocks of jeebies before breakfast every morning.

He could see her as splendid, as magnificent, as handsome, as striking, but not as beautiful. And most definitely, he could not see her as woman. There was no softness here, no roundness, no warmth, and he would as soon have had a pillar of marble in his bed as this sister of RK's.

She smiled at him, the long lips curling in a heartbreaking perfection of curve, and spoke in a voice that was far too deep and knowing for nineteen.

"You needn't tell me, Citizen," she said, mockery dancing in the great brown eyes, "because it's written across your forehead in letters of an extraordinary clearness— *Sweet Saints, what a forbidding landscape!*"

Coyote went as far toward blushing as it was possible for him to do, and instantly regretted it, because she chuckled deep in her throat at his unease; apparently he was as transparent to her as a pane of glass.

"I hope I have not offended you, Citizen—uh, Citizenness," he said. Along with the rest of their archaic customs, the Furthesters still retained the distinction of sex by address. He thought. He hoped. He was confused enough to be not at all sure.

"Certainly not," she said smoothly. "I have seen pictures of your women, and although I can't see what interest they would hold for a man I do see that our women would not strike you as beautiful."

In such a situation even a TGIS agent falls back upon the strategic resource of courtly prevarication; Coyote all but bowed and swept the floor with his plumed hat. "I beg to differ with you," he said, "you are very beautiful indeed."

"And you are a liar," she said promptly. "I am beautiful to you like a . . . like a scenic wonder. Not like a woman."

"Very well, then. But I remind you that this is the result of my unfortunate offworld tastes, and not some lack in yourself."

She laughed again and stood there watching him with dancing eyes while RK tried to tell him her name.

"I can't say that," he said at once. "Spell it for me."

"My sister is called Kh'llwythenna Be'essahred Q'ue."

"Impossible. It sounds like a cross between Ancient Celtic and Luna Pidgin. I can't manage it, I'm afraid."

"Try!" she said.

"Absolutely not." He shook his head firmly. "I'll give you no further excuse to laugh at me, my girl. RK, will you say that for me one more time?"

RK repeated it, and Coyote nodded.

"There's a 'Bess' in there someplace," he said, "and Bess it will have to be. Or, of course, Citizenness Q'ue. That's the best I can do."

" 'Bess . . .' " She tried it out, considering it, her head tilted to listen. "That's quite good enough, Citizen," she said.

"Come along then, Bess," he said, "and you, too, RK, and let's have something to eat. I'm beginning to feel very exposed standing here."

"Here" was the stairway to the third floor. From the way that RK had produced her after the last guest had left the MESH, Coyote was quite certain that she must have been up there all that day, even while he and the boy were talking about her coming to stay. But he preferred to act ignorant of that fact.

He led the way into the central room of the MESH, where the stage was. It had no windows and several doors led out of it, so it seemed safest to him if someone should by some freak come to the front door seeking him. He had set a table there and prepared an excellent dinner, which the plates were keeping warm for them, and a good Betelgeuse wine stood waiting.

RK seated his sister, and Coyote poured the wine, and
they lifted their glasses in a friendly salute. Coyote
hoped he looked more pleasant than he felt; it was her
fault, she had put that image in his head, and now no
matter how he tried he could not shake from his mind the
idea that he was dining with a Scenic Wonder. It was
grotesque, and funny, and absolutely unshakable, and
he knew he was not going to be able to be serious.

Bess cut a neat bite of her kthor steak, blew on it gently
to cool it, much to his additional amusement, and then
spoke to him in that amazing voice.

"My brother has asked you to grant me sanctuary,
then?" she asked, and he nodded.

"He has that."

"Have you decided?"

"Well," Coyote said, hesitatingly, "you understand
that it is not simply a matter of being gallant to a lady. I
would not think of saying no to him, except for my situation."

"Yes?"

"Ahem. Bess, my dear Bess, my lovely Scenic Wonder,
you must understand that I am not a wealthy man. All
my savings have gone into this venture, every penny—"

Bess stabbed her steak and cut him off, all with the
same gesture.

"Citizen Jones," she said, fixing him with eyes as cool
and knowing as some ancient crone, the eyes looking out
of that strong young body ((at least he assumed there
must be a body under all the trappings), "Citizen Jones,
it is all very well for you to tell my brother fairy stories.
He is young, after all, and you have no reason to value his
discretion. But I ask you not to insult me with such nonsense, because I am neither blind nor a fool."

"I don't know what you mean," he said, very much
afraid that he did know what she meant, and she proved
him right.

"Citizen," she said, "no one, no one at all, would come
all the way out to the very backtail planet of the Third
Galaxy, and set up a MESH with his last penny, for the
simple and single purpose of setting up a MESH to make
money at it. You can't possibly expect me to believe
that."

"Bess—"

"Not only that," she went on, "but my government

would not have allowed it for a moment, if it were only that. Do you see any other offworld businessmen in K'ith Vaad, Citizen? Have you noticed any signs saying 'Welcome to Furthest' and begging you to invest your funds? My government has a vested interest in the ignorance of its people, and a MESH represents a threatening factor of great strength."

"But—"

"Do spare me, Citizen," she continued, charging right over him, "or I *shall* be insulted; after all, for you to find my body of an unaccustomed and unbeguiling cragginess is predictable, but that you should find my mind wanting is absurd."

"What am I to say?" he floundered. "What do you want me to say to you. . . . I would like to convince you. . . ."

"You'll not convince me if you keep at it all night, which I'm not likely to allow, but I don't intend to keep embarrassing you. It's rude of me. Shall we return to the discussion of your finances, and this time I'll pretend to believe you?"

Coyote sighed, and refilled his glass.

"You know," he said, "I was reluctant at first to believe in such a thing as a nineteen-year-old girl who could have committed a crime that merited a sentence of Erasure. But having met you, I find myself convinced. The only thing that amazes me now is that the crime was religious—I would expect murder, at the very least."

Bess chuckled. "That shows where lies will get you, Citizen. I'm not a nineteen-year-old girl; RK only said that to play on your sympathy, foolish boy that he is. I'm a hale and withered twenty-three, my friend, and of those twenty-three I've spent a total of four years and seven months in solitary confinement for one thing or another. That tends to be aging. And the crime is not religious."

"Oh? Is it murder after all?"

RK, who had not said one word through all this exchange but had sat doggedly eating his food and looking miserable, stood up suddenly and struck the table with his fist.

"I forbid you, my sister!" he shouted. "You may mock and laugh and make a fool of us all, but I forbid you to speak your blasphemies in my presence—have you no shame at all?"

"Benighted moons," said Bess mildly. "I'm sorry, Ahr, Citizen, you must allow me to correct myself."

"Please do."

"The crime with which I am charged is defined by our government as religious, since religion is the mechanism by which we are controlled. That I do not agree with them, and consider it something else entirely, upsets my brother to an extent that amazes me. But he is quite right, in the sense that what I have done is technically looked upon as a violation of religious law by the elders and by the judge and by the rest of the creaking antiques who run this poor planet."

"I warn you," said RK viciously, "that if you continue I will not remain at this table."

"Then she will stop," said Coyote, and was rewarded at once by an almost imperceptible nod from Bess. "Sit down, RK, and eat your dinner in peace. We worked hard tonight."

The boy sat down slowly, the flush draining from his face, and took a long drink from his glass.

"Now, tell me, Citizen Jones," said Bess, with a flagrantly fake decorousness that very nearly caused Coyote to blow the whole thing by laughing at her, "how does our frontier life here compare with the sophisticated existence of the First Galaxy? You must find us dreadfully primitive."

"No," said Coyote, managing seriousness by staring at the wall above her head, "I really haven't had a chance to learn enough about your people or your way of life to make any kind of judgment. There are a lot of things that seem strange to me, but then that is true when I go to any planet farther out than Mars Central."

"You travel a lot, then?" said Bess demurely. "Perhaps that's why you find yourself so poor now . . . perhaps you should not have squandered all your worldly goods dashing about the Galaxies."

Coyote was ashamed of himself. He'd walked into that one like a junior diplomat at a tea-party, and this damned woman never missed a trick. Perhaps it was her beauty that RK had relied on to soften him up, and the beauty didn't impress him, but her mind impressed the hell out of him, and the boy just might turn out to be right with his "wait till you meet my sister" after all. The idea of throwing Bess to the government wolves and seeing that spectacular mind wiped cleaner than the newest babe's was beginning to really cause him pain.

"You're right," he said. "I shouldn't have. If I'd been more careful no doubt I'd be a rich man at this moment. More wine?"

"Thank you, Citizen," she said, extending her glass to him. "Have you always been wealthy—until now, that is?"

"No, not at all. As a matter of fact, two years ago I owned nothing whatever except a few personal keepsakes, and even those were locked away from me."

"Oh? Were you in prison, too?"

Pleased to see evidence of genuine interest, Coyote told her of his attempt to join the Maklunites and his ignominious failure.

"But why couldn't you have had your personal things, the ones you mentioned?" she asked.

"Because I missed them," he said. "As soon as I was able to say that I no longer missed them they would have been given back to me. It was not a punishment, Bess, just a part of learning communal living."

"They live in each other's pockets, then," she said.

"I suppose that's accurate, although they would say they live in each other's hearts."

"I would despise that," she said fiercely.

"I'm sure you would." Coyote laughed. "It's a pleasure to meet someone who'd be even worse at it than I was!"

"And this cult is really numerous? I find it hard to believe."

"If by cult you mean 'a small exotic group of religious crackpots or something of that kind, I'm afraid the word won't fit, Bess. I told RK already, the Maklunites are outnumbered only by the Ethical Humanists and the Jews."

"Hmmm. I find the whole idea of communal living repulsive. How can they manage with no privacy, no personal belongings, even their thoughts shared!"

To Coyote's surprise she shuddered violently, and he chalked one point up for himself. Apparently there were areas where it was possible for the rough and ready lady to be shaken up a bit.

"Oh, yes," he said, relishing her discomfort. "That's certainly an excellent description."

"But aren't there continual fights—don't people become half mad, cooped up together like that?"

"Well, I did," Coyote admitted, "but the majority don't. If they did, they would be told that they had to leave, just as I was. Of course there are very often novices, what are called 'Learners,' in the Maklunite clusters, and they do have trouble. They find it difficult and hard at first, even when they are very sincere in their desire to follow the Maklunite Way. Especially they find it hard to get over the clinging to 'things,' you know. They don't like to go to the closets and find that a garment they had wanted to wear has already been put on by someone else."

"And the novices are not a source of continual conflict?"

"Some conflict," Coyote said. "But they are necessary. It would be difficult for a completely settled cluster to avoid becoming smug and complacent if there were not Learners present to stir the surface up a little."

"I see. And marriages? How, in such intense communication, does a couple ever manage to build any sort of life?"

Coyote hesitated for a moment; he wasn't sure just how far he dared go at this point.

"Well," he said finally, "that isn't really a problem. Since the Maklunites do not believe in marriage."

"That's awful," said RK abruptly. "I really don't feel that you should speak in that way in front of a woman, Citizen."

"I am interested," said Bess. "Restrain your chivalrous impulses on my behalf, RK, they are superfluous. I wish to know—if the Maklunites do not, as you say, 'believe' in marriage, why don't they?"

"Because it is their conviction that the entire institution of marriage is based upon the idea of a human being as property, and they find that concept obscene."

Would she ask the obvious next question? He wondered. He had yet to hear the naughty word "sex" or any circumlocution for it even mentioned upon this planet. Perhaps she would ask what arrangements the Maklunites made for "you-know-what"?

"Well, the Maklunites' loss is our gain," she said instead, and he smiled to himself. Platitudes for emergencies, even from a hardened criminal.

"Thank you, Bess," he said, not sure the remark was appropriate but sure it would do as a filler, and then, abruptly, before he could change his mind, he committed himself.

"Bess, you'll stay here for the time being at least," he said. "I'm not going to promise anything; you obviously understand why I will not and cannot. But until I see some reason to be more concerned about this matter, I want you to stay here. RK seems to feel we can keep you safe."

"Thank you, Citizen!" said RK fervently. "I won't forget your kindness, nor will my sister, I swear that!"

"It's not kindness," said Coyote. "It's stupidity and old age. And I'll thank you not to remind me of it, since I'm sure to regret it eventually."

"I don't think so," said the boy. "I will do everything I can to see that you don't regret it, ever."

"There's *nothing* that you can do, Ahr," said Bess quietly. "If I am found I am found, that's all."

"I can see to it that Citizen Jones is not involved," said the boy firmly. "Somehow, I will see to that."

Coyote reached out and touched RK's hand gently. "Look," he said, "I know the risk I'm taking, and I take it with full responsibility for myself. I think I could play dumb if someone finds us, and I promise you I won't try to be a hero if that happens. I can't, because I have obligations that supersede any such abstract action. And I may change my mind tomorrow and throw Bess out. But for now, for tonight, we'll try it and see."

He thought for a moment that RK was going to really embarrass him. The people of Furthest were so cold and unemotional and grim that the sight of genuine tears in the boy's eyes gave him the feeling that he was witnessing some monstrous display of emotion, and anything more would have been too much. But RK's good manners saved them both. He stood up and excused himself politely; he was tired, he said, and there was much to be done in the morning. He would see his sister up to the third floor, where she would be safe and comfortable, and then he was going to bed.

They went off and left Coyote sitting over the fragments of the dinner, wondering how long it would be before he began to regret his soft heart. He could just hear the Fish. But on the other hand, what else could he do? He couldn't let a fugitive girl be taken away for Erasure for a religious crime—and what the hell could she have done, anyway, missed Tenth Day Observance?

He shook his head and gave it up. Nothing made any sense, but then nothing had yet. He wasn't surprised.

# CHAPTER SEVEN

"Since the only real function of officials is to serve
as repositories for mail—a sort of 'X Marks The
Spot' function—we have no such creatures within
our clusters. We have found that there is nothing at
all that an official can do that cannot be done by a
mailbox with equal skill."

(from the Devotional Book of Tham O'Kent)

FILE 803.09a, Segment 2
TOPIC: The planet Furthest
FROM: Citizen Coyote Jones
TO: Office of the Director
TRI-GALACTIC INTELLIGENCE SERVICE
GALCENTRAL, STATION 5
DATE: AUGUSTSEVENTH 3022

1. Last night, Augustsixth, it was my very unusual
good luck to be invited to spend an entire evening in
the home of a Furthester family. My helper here, the
boy Arh Qu'e, somehow managed to persuade his parents to have me as their guest. As you are well aware,
the Furthesters are extremely antagonistic to offworlders,
and I was conscious throughout the evening that the two
Qu'es were having to make an intense effort not to show
their resentment of my presence in their home. Under
ordinary circumstances I would certainly have made a
point of leaving as rapidly as possible. However, in this
case I realized that the opportunity should be made much
of, and I simply ignored the strain.

2. The home of the Qu'es is like those I saw in the threedy in your office; i.e., it is made of stone, three stories in height, bisected by a corridor and staircase, with a central door flanked by windows front and back. The furnishings were of interest to me, since any clue to what a Furthester considers to be "comfort" should be of some use in the establishment of a valid personality profile. (And by the way, is anyone there aware of the fact that there exists on Furthest nothing even remotely approaching a "catalog," either in the old-fashioned sense or in the contemporary form, through which a purchaser might look before selecting clothing or household items? I find this rather mysterious.) At any rate, the majority of the furnishings appear to consist of blocks of this same stone, or rather of a stone that looks much the same but is extremely light and porous. I would assume that the stone used for furnishings is that surface layer which is continually worn by the water of this planet. There were tables, shelves, some primitive-appearing stoves. Rugs and curtains are all of the heavy synthovelvet which is so popular with these people. The effect is like the effect of their clothing, a sort of forbidding magnificence.

3. There was one item of furniture which I found of interest, as it did not entirely fit the pattern displayed by the rest. The chairs used by the family were beautiful objects, giving the appearance of having been carved from a single piece of wood, and that a rich dark wood of a high soft luster. The chairs are rounded rather than angular, and are obviously intended to be curled up in, although no one did so in my presence. I inquired as to their manufacture and was told that each chair is made of a single nut from a tree, and that these nuts are imported from one of the Extreme Moons, where they can be found growing to a length of fifteen feet and some ten feet in diameter. (I can't imagine what size the *trees* must be, but nothing about the Extreme Moons surprises me any more.) It should be noted that this is the *only* offworld item other than foodstuffs that I have seen since I arrived here, excepting of course those items I have myself brought in to stock the MESH. I was not told which of the Moons was the source of these nuts, and in view of the incredible reticence of the Furthesters I did not think it advisable to press the matter. I would suggest

that someone at GALCENTRAL look into this, since the traders who deal with the Furthesters to supply the nuts might well have information that would be valuable to us.

4. The third floor of the Qu'e home was a genuine surprise to me. You will recall that my major impression —TOTAL impression, I should say—has been of austerity, cold magnificence, and so on. Even the luscious velvets and silks these people wear are in dark, somber colors and patterns. I was therefore surprised when taken up to the third floor of the building after our evening meal. In fact I was surprised to be taken up there at all, since I have not been able to obtain permission to go to tne third floor of the building in which our MESH is located. The third floor appears from the street to be a sort of attic—that is, the roof is peaked and there is only one small, very high window. This is quite false, however, as the whole area is open to the sky, and it is really a sort of garden. It should be remembered that I have seen *no* plants on his planet, although of course there have to be some somewhere, and I am told by my helper that food is grown in hydroponic stations. I have never seen even a blade of grass, the surface of Furthest being literally as bare as ancient Luna. You can well imagine my surprise, then, to find myself in a magnificent garden, three stories up. Samples of some of the plants (primarily leaves and stems, since I had to take them without being seen, and scrappy bits of leaves and stems at that) are enclosed with this report; your analysis will show, I believe, that they are without exception water plants.

5. Discreet questioning on my part established as fact that the third floors of all the Furthester houses are, like this one, a sort of water garden. Water flows throughout the city, from a main aqueduct, through pipes that flow from house to house at the third floor level. The water enters at one corner of the wall, drops over waterfalls constructed by these people, flows in patterns across the floor (in channels and pools, of course), and is then driven out the other side by small pumps and into the next house. Photographs are enclosed; I was forced to use extreme caution in obtaining them, even with the microcameras, and it may be that they are not of good

quality. They should nonetheless give you some idea of the situation.

6. This artificial stream that flows from house to house is used by the Furthesters not only for decoration but as a means of communication. Messages are inserted in small plastic vials, the name of the person for whom they are intended clearly showing through the plastic, and then they are dropped into the water to be taken out by the addressee when they make their way around the city to the proper spot. I observed some half dozen such vials go by during the hour that we spent in the garden. When I asked how one could be sure that a message would not be taken out by someone other than the person it was intended for I got that standard politely shocked response. Apparently no one, under any circumstances, would consider doing anything so uncouth as looking at someone else's mail. It is at any rate reassuring to me to discover that they do *send* one another mail.

7. I do not feel that I have necessarily obtained any information of great value with regard to these people (although the computers may react to the data far differently than I do.) I continue to have the constant feeling that I am attending some elaborate theatrical being performed, with impatience, for my benefit. On the other hand I see no *evidence* for any such conclusion—it remains intuitive. It is simply that everything is so formal, so precise, so perfect—it is difficult to believe that real life could go on that way for any group of human beings for any length of time. We shall see.

8. With reference to my previous report, FILE 803.09.a, Segment 1, and your reply to same: it is not possible at this time for me to make any attempt to investigate any other of the alleged citydomes on this planet. The others are all at a considerable distance from K'ith Vaad, and my traveling to them by any means other than slitherboat would cause an incredible flap, since I am forbidden to do anything of the kind. Since I am expected to be at the MESH seven nights a week, there is no segment of time available when I could plausibly make such a journey by slitherboat as would be involved in further exploration of this kind. It is my personal opinion that even one such empty dome is suf-

ficient cause for alarm; let us not compound our problems by finding that all the rest are empty, too.

9.   I will continue as indicated. I am aware, as you have pointed out, that time is passing by and only eighteen months were originally allotted to me. It is not necessary for you to remind me with such regularity of the deadline which hangs over me, and if you continue to do so I will return to GALCENTRAL and allow you to carry on here personally. I am sure you would find it quite pleasant, since you prefer machines to women in any event.

END OF REPORT

PS: In case it isn't clear, you old fart, get off my back or I won't do your stupid job.

# CHAPTER EIGHT

"madness became her—
she wore her follies in her hair;
she was so lovely
none of us would have had her cured;
and when she took a slender silver knife
    and set to killing
we knew ourselves, one and all,
    for murderers."

(from "The Nine Hundred Fables for
Autumn Afternoons," by Christopher Ganges)

WELL. Another night, another dose of hell?
He lay there rigid in bed, his hands in fists at his sides, his muscles tense and knotted, feeling as if he lay in fire and wishing he did, determined to get through this night as he had gotten through the interminable succession of other ones.

There were things to think about, after all, things to pass the hours by and get him through to morning again. He could think, for example, of all the slow and subtle and exquisite ways that he could make the Fish pay for sending him here. Unfortunately, he was not a violent man, and that gave him very little pleasure, although he felt that he might easily *become* a violent man if things went on the way they had to date.

Let's see. If torturing the Fish was out, he could always torture himself. He could review his present situation and reckon up all his failures, for example.

There was all the time he'd been here, now. All the

days and nights and weeks he'd been the happy but slightly stupid little shopkeeper from outer space, introducing the locals to the delights of that intergalactic social institution, the MESH. And where had it gotten him? It had gotten him bored and miserable, there was that. But gain? He knew little more than he had the first day.

The cold Furthesters came and went in his MESH, listened politely to his songs, and perhaps they listened with pleasure, since many of them came back time after time, but if they felt pleasure they showed no sign of it. They never used the MF stations to the edcomputers. They rarely bought anything from the shelves. They behaved exactly as if the MESH had been a museum; they strolled through looking with well-mannered interest at the exhibits, stopped for a song or some refreshment, then strolled out, unaffected. He had had no luck at setting up some sort of nucleus for community life at the MESH, some nexus of Furthester interaction which he could observe and learn from. Chalk up *Failure One.*

What else?

He thrashed in the bed. Unlike his bed back at the asteroid he called home, it did not adapt itself pliably to his movements. Furthester through and through, it lay there under him unyielding and let him bruise himself flopping around on it.

What else? He had learned nothing about these people. He had been ignoring the constant stream of demands from the Fish for reports, because he had nothing to report. There had been no repetitions of the visit to RK's parent's home. Apparently the boy had been able to persuade them only to the single token visit and that had been their absolute limit. He had attempted to talk, to get into conversations, to learn, but every trial was met with the same bland, unyielding, unresponding refusal to communicate. He rarely saw a living human being except for RK and the museum-strollers; and when he did see one, if he was seen first he was passed by hastily with head turned, as if he did not exist. Getting chatty with totally determined no-chatters was an exercise in futility. Chalk up *Failure Two.*

He had thought to probe more deeply into these people by growing close to RK, or perhaps to Bess, since he could not reach any of the others. But Bess kept to her rooms on the third floor—or did she live in a tent up there, since there *were* no rooms?—and RK maintained a continual shield of closed reserve, just as the rest of his people did. Coyote could have forced past that shield, of course, but if he had done so the boy would have known him at once for what he was, and that would have been sure to lead to expulsion from this planet, perhaps a very premature expulsion with no hope of return and no way to repair the damage. Chalk up *Failure Three*.

So he was a failure. So what? So where was the guilt he was supposed to be feeling? The population of three galaxies depended upon him and him alone to succeed in determining what a Furthester was made of, and all he could think of was his own misery. Never mind the fact that the fate of three galaxies might well rest on his shoulders. Never mind the fact that a madman might be president of the Tri-Galactic Council the next time around because he, Coyote Jones, had not been able to concentrate on his assignment sufficiently to finish it. Never damn mind. . . .

It was impossible. Here he was, in the midst of Victorian England Transplanted, him, Coyote Jones, who had happily made happy as many as four women in a single night. Here he was, surrounded by swathed creatures who exposed their hands and their heads, no more, and who might not have bodies at all but were perhaps single columns of aluminum and fiberglass for all that he could determine from being around them.

He had been so long now without a woman that he could think of nothing else with any clarity. About the thought of a woman, on the other hand, there was an overpoweringly brutal clarity that was driving him mad.

Not once, not since the first time when he had lain at the age of thirteen with an elderly but infinitely experienced professional on Mars Central, not once in all those years had he been so long without a woman, nor half so long, for that matter. It was unbelievable that he could still think at all, much less think coherently. He was maimed, tormented, destroyed, a poor blind creature in a state of advanced rut, and the hell with them. The hell with the populations of the Three Galaxies, and the hell with the Tri-Galactic Council. That was how he was, and if they didn't like it they should have sent a robot.

It had been funny, for a while. He had made lame

jokes to himself about it. He had always enjoyed such an abundance of women that he had informed himself it was only fair to give someone else a chance. He had decided it was only justice that he should now go wanting. He had even taken the antisex pills they had sent with him, in spite of their disgustingly cute name—ANTI-TUME, who'd thought of it? He should be castrated. He'd taken them for weeks, in spite of the fact that if he took enough of them to really do anything about his constant tumescence they made him throw up and suffer from violent diarrhea, and unless he took enough of them to incapacitate him they had no effect on him at all.

He'd been a good sport, he had. But now it was becoming decidedly unfunny. He wasn't having any more. He ached all over, his body felt like a vast boil, he was a great deal too old and set in his ways to take up masturbation, and the idea that he was duty-bound to stay here and spend months more in this condition was too much. He couldn't do it.

It did no good to lecture himself about his damn duty. It did no good to tell himself that he was being immature. It did no good at all.

He groaned and turned over onto his back for the thousandth miserable time, his whole mind one seething turmoil of thought of warm receiving female flesh, breasts and thighs and vaginas and all the rest of it, and wondered how it could be that the terrible pressure of his hunger did not simply bring the building down around him, and felt certain, knew for certain, that he wasn't going to be able to bear it this time.

And then a bell rang, like a gong, somewhere, and the words came fast upon its tone. . . .

HUSH . . . LET ME HELP YOU.

Help me?

He had time for only that one thought, and then the sprays of gold began behind his eyes, curling and uncurling, forming intricate dancing patterns that swooped toward him up to the last impossible instant before they burned him alive, grew and grew into roses of tender gold blooming into fountains, and then burst into trailing golden dust, chiming as they broke.

It was suddenly green, the green of the sea, full of the luminous rainbow color of the waters of Furthest, streaming before him into a distance that turned a corner and

was somehow behind him turning it again as he faced it
still, into a distance he could not measure, and he was the
rainbows, all of him went rapidly blue and gold and
green and flashed again into the fountains of scarlet
through which he flew, a great garlanded bird that melted
once more into a golden rose and floated down into the
sea.

There was a roaring . . . wind, was it? And words, he
knew there were words, but he could not understand
them, it was a miracle, a thing of wonder that he got one
or two here or there because he never had before, always
before he had thought that he was completely deaf to
mind-projected words, and what could this be that was
cutting through his ancient inability and healing it so?
There was a roaring, and water and mingled words, bits
of reassurance, promises that it would be all right, it would
be beautiful beyond description, and he believed it all
eagerly as a child.

He was high above a canyon that flickered, purple, the
color of sun-drugged love under cedars. Something caught
him, there was a sensation of knots being untied behind
his eyes, and on some high irresistible wind he streamed
out and up and out over the canyon, borne by and born in
the singing wind, with the flickering beneath him first
water, then canyon, then the deserts of an unknown
world, then the canyon again, then a field of scarlet vines
through which he looped and dived and grew and knew he
could never fall again. . . .

He was not sure just where and when it was that he
first screamed, or if he screamed aloud. Somewhere when
the . . . what? . . . slipped into his mind and took up being
the lovely things with him, and he became aware that in
his mind there were tendrils with which to twine and
twine and curl gently, intricately, in a dreaming dance of
love . . . but who was it? And what was it?

The ecstasy, coming after deprivation, washed over
him in a tide, left him drenched with the juices of his
own need, thinking that surely this was the end, that
no higher pitch of joy could be reached without his dying
of it. And just as he was sure of it he would be caught
up again, held and wound round, part of a pattern that
he only glimpsed before it ceased to be and was another,
a slipping into crevices deliciously where only thought had
been before, a burst of cinnamon and orange and wine

upon his sight, a feeling of small chords sounding smelling of pale yellow and white, a glimpse of hands pressing him, stroking him, tendrils winding him, until he knew he was going to come one more impossible time. . . .

I CAN'T BEAR IT.

NOT ANY MORE. . . . He thought finally, broken with joy and fullness, and at once there were ferns, cool green ferns, where he lay warm, unable to even imagine what hunger might be again, and then it was over.

It was over, and he lay staring up into the black darkness of his own room, where the ceiling clock told him it was three o'clock, and his whole bed was torn apart as if he had been caught in a hurricane and blown through it, soaked and salty and reeking with semen and sweat, and what—what in the name of all the saints and gods had that been?

He thought first that he would get up. Then he was afraid that he could not. And then it became clear to him that what he really felt, beyond amazement, was whole and renewed, and incredibly good, good beyond memory. He jumped out of the bed naked and wet like he was and went out of his room toward RK's. Whatever that had been, that incredible thing, it had been something of this world, something that RK would know about and that he, Coyote, was going to have to know about. He went into RK's room and shook him until he sat up blinking with sleep and stared at Coyote.

"What is it, Citizen Jones?" he mumbled.

Coyote grinned at him. "You see me?" he said. "You see the condition I'm in?" And then he remembered and turned on the light. "See me?" he repeated, "do you see? You see before you a man who's just been laid—pardon the shocking expression, O Furthester, but it's true and exact—a man who's just been laid by a legion of angels or a battalion of devils, he doesn't know which."

"You have been dreaming, Citizen," said RK in a careful voice, fully awake now.

"Oh, no! I am not sure I could survive whatever that was twice, but I assure you I didn't sleep through it the first time, and I wouldn't trade it for ten years of my life. RK, do you know what it was? Do you? Can you tell me?"

The boy spoke slowly. "I don't think I understand you, Citizen. I'm sorry."

Coyote started trying to explain, realized there were

no words that would handle it, and then saw, unmistakably, that he was being had. RK was white and sick and shaking, and if he were genuinely bewildered he had nothing to be disturbed about.

"You know perfectly well what I mean," Coyote accused him. "Now tell me!"

RK shook his head and turned his back, burrowing stubbornly into the depths of his bed.

"You had a dream," he muttered, yawning elaborately. "Why do you come bothering me with your dreams, Citizen?"

Coyote pulled the boy around to face him and gripped his shoulders fiercely.

"Don't lie to me, RK," he breathed. "Tell me what that was!"

"No! It is forbidden!"

"Forbidden? Nonsense! Tell me!"

RK shook his head again, stubborn and grim and white-lipped, and Coyote laughed. He was exultant with his relief, and the glory of what he had just known, and a feeling of being new forever. He had no time or patience left for stubborn boys who lived in cultural straitjackets. He forgot all about ethics, he forgot the danger of frightening this single tenuous link he had with the people of Furthester, and he gathered his mind like a whip around the single command TELL and lashed it all at RK at once.

RK could no more have withstood that than he could have chosen not to breathe. He fell back against his pillow like one struck brutally, as indeed he had been, and the words poured from his lips.

"It was my sister," he said, tears streaming down his cheeks. "Curse you for an outworld dog, you are just as the Elders say that you are, a dog, a filthy animal . . ."

Coyote ignored the outpouring of bitter words, and shook the boy gently, once again.

"RK," he pleaded, "what do you mean—it was your sister? You mean it was Bess?"

"Yes! Yes, it was Bess, curse her, too, curse her . . ."

He moaned it over and over, and pity touched Coyote even in the midst of his happiness, and he took his hands away from him.

"How could it have been Bess, RK?" he asked. "Tell me."

"She's a mindwife," RK cried, a cry of pure despair,

"she's a mindwife, perhaps the greatest one that there has ever been in all the history of my people! And I should have killed her long ago!"

"RK," said Coyote gently, "what is a mindwife? Can you tell me? I won't force you, don't be afraid—just let me know, can you tell me?"

"You know what a mindwife is," the boy hissed, "you just lay with one! Have you forgotten already?"

"No . . . that's not it. I want details, RK, information. I think it is very important that I know."

"It is forbidden," mourned RK, "forbidden. It is forbidden that I should even have said the word to you, and I could not help it, and I am as great a traitor as she is now, I have betrayed my people and am accursed forever. . . ."

He fell into a hopeless, heartbroken sobbing, and Coyote could push him no farther. This was much worse than he had meant it to be, but he had not realized the barrier was so great.

"RK," he said finally, "one thing . . . since it is forbidden for your people to tell me about this, could I find out from the Furthester edcomputers?"

RK sat straight up in the bed, the sobs choked off, his face white with terror.

"If you do that," he breathed, "if you use your offworld credit disc and do that, the police will come and we are all dead as of that moment, my sister and I for traitors and you for a dirty spy. Are you going to do it?"

"Of course not," Coyote reassured him. "I wouldn't harm you or Bess for anything in the universe, not to mention the affection I have for my own hide. But—"

No. He decided at once that further talk would be ridiculous. After the strongarm mental tactics he had already used, a little more was not going to hurt RK and would scarcely be noticed. He turned a single thought toward the bed . . . SLEEP NOW . . . and RK was lost at once, as deeply asleep as if he had been drugged.

Poor young one. Coyote covered him carefully and stood over him a moment, apologizing in advance for what he must do, trying to think if there could be any reason why it would not work.

The comsystems of Furthest were primitive, manually operated by keyboard instead of voice-sensitive like those of the Inner Galaxies. He was reasonably sure that so

long as he did not insert an offworld credit disc he would
be safe. Why not? On a planet where offworlders were
rare as green swans, why take elaborate precautions
against them?

Knowing RK would not wake up for hours, he went
to the table that stood by the bed, and where lay the
small synthovelvet pouch, purple striped with deep blue,
that held RK's personal things. He opened it and took
out the boy's credit disc, closed it and laid it carefully
back on the table. He didn't like doing this, but he dis-
liked it a good deal less than what he had already done to
his young friend, and it would at least be painless. Unless
there was some safeguard mechanism about which he did
not yet know anything, no one would suffer from what
he was about to do.

What could a mindwife be?

Whatever it was, it was mighty nice. He could still
feel her in his mind, that sensation of almost unendurable
pleasure that was a sort of constant, whole, and total
orgasm, of the body and mind and spirit. That was a
mindwife, eh?

He smiled, thinking of his previous conception of Bess
as a cold, sexless Scenic Wonder. It showed how little he
knew . . . but who would ever have thought of such a
thing as this?

He had too many questions, and they wouldn't wait.
But he was going to have to phrase them carefully. Even
with the Furthester credit disc, if he came on bluntly at
three-thirty in the morning with a straight "What is a
mindwife?" the computers were likely to think something
curious was going on and send the police to check him
out. He couldn't risk that. He would have to sacrifice
some time, in spite of his raging curiosity, to the devising
of a suitably subtle phrasing, one that would not bring
tragedy down upon them all. Probably the most casual
possible approach would be the best, but he must be very
careful.

Thinking again how goddam *good* he felt, all over, he
folded his hand around the little credit disc and went
back to his room.

Mindwife, eh? Roses and waves and golden spirals and
an unending continuum of pleasure?

# CHAPTER·NINE

"Frustration is a wholesome part of education, and a necessary one, but it must be the frustration of not knowing what one is eager to know. The child for whom all the answers are always PROVIDED may well develop the ability to memorize, but unless he is very unusual he will never learn how to think. Education by spoon-feeding is less trouble for the adults involved, but useless and destructive for the learning child. Teaching must be a matter of ALLOWING—not of forcing—a child to learn."

(from the Devotional Book of Tham O'Kent)

*Handbook for the Elders of the Holy Path:
On the Training of Mindwives*

THE TRAINING of a mindwife is a sacred office. It is not to be taken lightly. With the exception of the mindwife herself, there is no higher status to be attained among our people. If at any time you should find yourself looking upon this holy work as tedious, as a tiresome and ordinary task, you are to go at once to your chambers and pray for illumination. If the feeling does not pass in three days, you are to surrender your post irrevocably. For one who has failed in the nurture of a mindwife charged to his care, or caused harm to any mindwife in the care of any Elder of the Ahl Khres'sah, the penalty is death. Beware that you do not neglect any aspect of the training set out in this manual because you feel that it is trivial or because you personally dislike it;

the training of mindwives is a part of our sacred history, and no smallest portion of it may be changed or eliminated. You are to follow the dictates of this manual as you would follow the Book of the Holy Path, from which its instructions are taken.

The mindwives will reach you no younger than two and no older than four years. A child whose training is not begun by the age of four can never achieve full mindwife status.

These children will be of a uniform personality type— they will be headstrong, willful, brave to the point of folly, selfish, opinionated, and completely undisciplined. This last is the case because, from the moment the potential for mindwifery is discovered in the child, the parents are forbidden to attempt any sort of discipline, however mild, except in those cases where it is necessary to prevent actual physical injury. If a girl is brought to you gentle and docile she is spoiled for mindwifery; she is to be sent home, and her parents must be brought before the Elders of their city for judgment and discipline.

Before beginning the detailed instruction in the training of these sacred children, it would be well to review in a general way the basic stages through which they go, as follows:

FIRST STAGE (Be'naq'qal)

The first thing done is to administer, by hypodermic syringe through the front of the throat, a chemical which inhibits the activity of the vocal chords to such an extent that no speech is possible. In order that the child may not move her hands in an attempt to communicate by gesture, her hands are manacled behind her back. In order that she may not vent her fury physically upon the other little girls in the room, she is strapped into a chair and restrained. This is done, by groups of six to ten girls, day after day, for the full length of the day. It is continued until the child either goes mad or discovers the telepathic channels of the mind. (The madness rate, we are proud to say, is exceedingly low, less than eight percent.) This may take no more than a week; it has taken as long as six months on some occasions. No sympathy is shown the children, and no tenderness—lest this seem cruel, it should be understood that anything which lessens their frustration and rage will only lengthen the time that must be spent in this state by the child. It is therefore the seeming kindness that is really cruel. You will find complete instructions for the heightening of this frustration at a later point in the manual.

It is of course possible to hasten this stage and the breakthrough as well, by administering a number of drugs, in particular the juice of the waterweed known popularly as Heaven's Ladder. However, such a technique is resorted to only in those cases in which it has become apparent that the child is not going to achieve breakthrough by herself; it is to be considered a last resort. Maximum mindwife strength can be achieved only when the child accomplishes the communications goal without artificial aids; mindwives trained by use of drugs are inevitably less strong and thus less effective.

The inevitable question is, of course, what disposition is made of that eight percent of the children for whom the end of our training is with total madness, in this first stage. It is right that you should ask this question, and its answer should be further indication to you of the grave responsibility which you bear. Since we know that it is the Most High, and not ourselves, who chooses the mindwives, and since it is not possible for the Allknowing to err in His choice, it follows that a girl who goes mad is our failure and ours alone. Thus, when everything has been tried and madness is its result, the child is secluded in the Temple of Tiba Ness, there to be cared for to the ultimate limits of our ability until the natural end of her life. These are the Holy Madwomen of Tiba Ness; they are to be treated with tenderness and with our deepest love, for we have failed them. Because of our inadequacy they have been denied the opportunity to fulfill their destiny as the chosen of the Most High, as sacred mindwives.

SECOND STAGE (Tazh Hari)

At this second stage we attempt to make up to the little girls to some extent for the seeming brutality of the first stage. We introduce discipline, slowly but surely. We begin the training in all of those arts and skills which are expected of an accomplished woman of the Ahl Kres'sah. The little girls are now taught to play the paliss, the harp, and the flute. They are taught to read and to write, to practice the Five Sciences and the Seven Disciplines. They are given the education that would be given any wealthy young girl of our people, with the difference that it is even more intensive, that these girls always and without exception have the very best teachers and facilities that are at our command.

We have learned that the skill of telepathic communication is basically different from most skills in one respect; i.e., that enforced practice during the period of learning and unfamiliarity is not required. We have learned that once the non-vocal channels are established the individual will always prefer them. It is therefore no longer necessary at this stage to continue the vocal inhibitor medication. We have never seen a girl revert to vocal communication as the preferred medium once the mental channels were opened to her. The factor of frustration is therefore much less at this time.

It is of course the case that the children hate us to the very depths of their beings by this time. That is quite all right; it is in fact desirable. It is of great help to them in learning that love is not a necessary ingredient for social functioning, and that the three qualities of respect: compassion, and patience—plus good manners—will do very nicely as a basis for most relationships. It does happen that occasionally a little girl of an affectionate nature will attempt to *show* that affection by such manifestations as climbing into your lap, patting your hand, calling you by pet-names, and the like. It cannot be too strongly emphasized that all such manifestations are to be met with THE MOST TOTAL REJECTION AND COLDNESS YOU CAN MUSTER. These are appealing children, and it will be a temptation for you to respond to their overtures in kind, but you absolutely must not do so. You must remember that their successful functioning as mindwives will be wholly dependent upon their being forced to find a mental channel for their sexual needs just as they did for their speech needs; this can only be achieved if they are met with complete frustration of their every attempt to employ normal sexual channels. As was true in the case of speech, seeming kindness on your part can only lengthen the time of their frustration. Therefore, the children are met at all times with coldness, in order that they may be broken of any tendency to normal sexual activity.

During this second stage the children are exposed to the most intensive training in color, pattern, and form perception that we can offer them. They are surrounded by beauty, in order that as mindwives they will have at their mental disposal the greatest possible variety of images. It is at this time that the use of drugs is begun as a standard measure for all the girls in order to increase their ability at mental imagery; there is no hazard now, so far as we can determine, that any girl will develop that dependence upon the drugs in every situation of stress that is so unfortunate a tendency when they are begun too soon.

No formal training in the use of their unusual mental capacities is practiced at this stage. This is first of all because of the extemely heavy curriculum of other materials which they must learn. Secondly, much of what they must know cannot be taught them properly until they have reached puberty. Psi training is therefore confined to our hearty encouragement of their use of telepathic communication and to a large number of games which are made available to them and which are designed to strengthen their psibilities without formal instruction.

And finally, of course, the children are given intensive religious instruction just as are all our children. We must never forget that these sacred children are as much in need of the Holy Path as any of the rest of us, and that it is our responsibility to insure that their spiritual development is not neglected. Any failure here will be sure to cause us trouble at a later date.

THIRD STAGE (Kehl Be'aff)

The third stage begins at the time of puberty, whenever that may be for each girl. (In any case in which puberty has not been attained by the twelfth year it is artificially induced by injection of hormones.) By this time each girl should have the basic elements of her education, in the general sense, and it should have become evident what sort of talents each one has. At this point it should be possible for you to decide what would constitute a suitable specialty for each girl under your tutelage, and further education should be in the specialty rather than the broad spectrum training which has been given up to this point. The most common specialties for mindwives are Instrumental Music, Water Dancing, Poetry, and Theology, although others are possible.

There is a very great danger at this point, a matter of balance and proportion, that requires fine judgments on the part of the Elders. It must be remembered that the mindwives are expected to function as the most intimate companions of our greatest men. Such men are not going to be satisfied with a merely charming woman, no matter how beautiful she may be; therefore, it is necessary that the mindwives should be educated far in excess of the amount generally provided for the women of the Ahl Khres'sah. However, since normal channels of affection have been totally cut off in these girls, there is a tendency for them to substitute for such affection an all-encompassing dedication to their specialty. This must be precluded, since a mindwife must be devoted to mindwifery first and above all; she cannot place her sacred functions beneath her absorption in one of the arts or sciences. However valuable might be her contributions to our people otherwise (we refer you to the case of Mindwife Beness T'al Qylthr'a, whose work in the isolation of sensory areas in the brain, although the source of major medical breakthroughs on this planet, was a great handicap to her in the exercise of mindwifery) it must be emphasized that no value may be set above that of mindwifery itself.

This creates an elemental dichotomy, very naturally, since we are in a manner creating what we must destroy. Therefore we take upon us the unpleasant task of furthering in these girls a tendency that we would discourage in our women under any other circumstances. That is to say, at this stage, along with training in the specialty, the girls are exposed in heavy saturation to every sort of CENSORED stimulation we are able to provide, UNDER CONDITIONS WHICH INSURE THAT THEY WILL BE ABLE TO FIND NO CHANNEL OF EXPRESSION FOR THAT STIMULATION. This means that they must sleep in a room kept fully lighted at all times, a room so warmed that no bedcoverings are required, and a room that is under guard. This guard is provided by servomechanisms which are of course themselves immune to CENSORED and are therefore not the hazard to the girls that would be the case with any other arrangement. (We can only look with admiration upon the holy asceticism of those Elders who were charged with the task of guarding the mindwives in those primitive days before efficient servomechanisms were available.) This condition of constant frustration without possible outlet has as its primary function the preparation of the mindwives for telepathic sexual communion. The analogy with the earlier forcing of telepathic speech should be apparent. The frustration which is induced in the mindwives at this point is so severe, however, that we now find an additional three percent of the girls succumbing to madness, and this a madness of so repulsive an aspect that total Erasure is the only measure possible for dealing with it. (This is of course therapeutic rather than punitive Erasure.)

We suspect that the reason the madness rate is so low at this stage, in view of the intensity of the frustration, is that the girls, who now are in total control of telepathic communication, are able to combine their efforts in discovering a solution. We also suspect that an unfortunate byproduct of this combined effort is telepathic homosexual relationships among the mindwives. Unfortunately there is no surface evidence of any such relationships, and we have no way of checking on our suspicions. We must rely, therefore, upon their religious training and the principles which have previously been instilled in these girls to prevent any such unnatural developments.

At this point, once the frustration level of any given girl gives us reason to believe that she has discovered the proper channel for telepathic sexual communion, it is necessary that she be removed from the other girls and prepared as rapidly as is possible for her final status as mindwife. She must be provided at once with an Elder who will serve as husband-surrogate for the exercise of her abilities during this final stage of training, in order that she learn to prefer a male partner. (Reference to the previous paragraph should make this more clear.)

FOURTH STAGE (Leth)

It is our suggestion that you very carefully consider the following paragraph. At this time you will be associated as training Elder with perhaps as many as four girls at a time. Although you are sworn to celibacy, both physical and mental, it will be your sacred duty to serve as object of the mental attentions of these four girls. WE WARN YOU SOLEMNLY: You will be subjected to the most intense ecstasy that it is possible to produce in a human being—direct mental stimulation, and exceedingly skilled stimulation, of the pleasure centers of the brain. You are to look upon yourself as no more than a training mechanism, a physical object, upon which the novice mindwives may practice their holy skill. IT IS FORBIDDEN FOR YOU TO DERIVE SEXUAL ENJOYMENT

FROM THIS FUNCTION OF YOUR OFFICE AS TRAINING ELDER. Should you find that CENSORED, should you find that constant prayer is not enough to prevent you from perverting this sacred function for personal pleasure, you are to go at once to your Chief Elder and request that you be relieved of your duties, as unfit. The penalty for ignoring this rule is death.

Assuming, as we do assume, that you will be able to fulfill your role in an appropriate manner, your work now consists in helping the mindwives in your care to further refine their techniques. You must discuss with each of them the particular characteristics of their performance. You must tell them if you find their attentions sterile, devoid of imagery, unsatisfactory in any way. You must help them polish and perfect themselves in the exercise of mindwifery to the utmost limits of your ability. At the end of this fourth stage each girl will be formally wed to a man of our people who is of sufficient value to the Ahl Khres'sah to merit such a reward, the highest reward that we can give. She will have no further opportunity for training, and she must not disgrace us. It is our proud record that in all the history of our people only two mindwives have ever been returned to us by their husbands as unsatisfactory. You must use this last period of training to perfect, to polish, to intensify, to instruct. The specific techniques which are to be employed are described in detail in the later chapters of this text.

We have now come to the end of our brief summary of the nature of your duties. We caution you, AS YOU VALUE YOUR ETERNAL SOUL, if you now feel that your nature is such that you will find it difficult or impossible to carry out the procedures described, it is time NOW to request release from your post. We remind you that telepathic sexual communion is experienced only by those of our men who are the rare beneficiaries of this honor on the part of the nation. That you should yourself experience it, through the attention of not one but many of the holy mindwives, when it is otherwise denied to all but our finest men, even though you serve only as a training mechanism, is evidence of the high esteem in which you are held. We repeat what was said at the beginning of this discussion—with the exception of the mindwives themselves, there is no higher or more sacred office than that of Training Elder. And with *no exception,* there is no office more dangerous spiritually. Think well, before you continue; if you are not strong enough, you must say so at once and before you put yourself in a position of eternal damnation.

We close this introductory chapter with a brief poem from the personal works of Dekh Habid'dah, revered Training Elder of the Third Cycle:

> Let it be, Most High,
> that in the midst of flame
> I feel only the quenching wave;
> that in the midst of scarlet
> I see only the purest white;
> that in the midst of bliss
> I feel only serenity....

Swim well, Elder.

NOTE: THE BALANCE OF THIS MANUAL IS AUTHORIZED FOR RELEASE ONLY TO THE TRAINING ELDERS OF THE HOLY PATH. IF YOU ARE A TRAINING ELDER THE COMSYSTEM WILL RELEASE THE REST OF THIS MATERIAL TO YOU UPON PRESENTATION OF YOUR CREDENTIALS.

NOTE: THE MATERIAL ABOVE IS AUTHORIZED FOR RELEASE ONLY TO MALES ABOVE THE AGE OF FOURTEEN. IT IS YOUR RESPONSIBILITY, IF YOU NUMBER IN YOUR HOUSEHOLD WOMEN, AND CHILDREN OF EITHER SEX BELOW THE PRESCRIBED AGE, TO SEE THAT THIS TEXT DOES NOT FALL INTO THEIR HANDS. SHOULD ANY SUCH ACCIDENT OCCUR IT IS TO BE REPORTED AT ONCE, IN ORDER THAT IT MAY BE DEALT WITH.

# CHAPTER TEN

"To have proved yourself able to defend your property is to have proved not that you are a man, but that you are a slave."

(from the Devotional Book of Tham O'Kent)

COYOTE PUT the MF viewer down and slowly pulled out the film cassette. His head was aching from the succession of shocks he'd gone through this night, pleasant as well as unpleasant, and from lack of sleep, and from a state of overwhelmedness unparalleled in his memory. And now, instead of his former condition—an almost total lack of data—he found himself with too much of it, and not sure what to do next. The revelation about the mindwife system on Furthest raised a number of interesting questions when an attempt was made to integrate it with known facts.

He pulled a stylus and a senslate from the shelf by his bed and sat down to attempt just that sort of integration. Perhaps then he would be able to decide if not what to do, at least where to look, next.

FACT ONE: The communications system of the Three Galaxies is dependent upon the Communipaths, a select class of state-trained, highly skilled telepaths to whom the interstellar distances are irrelevant.

FACT TWO: Every child born throughout the Three Galaxies is tested at birth for the mutant blood characteristic called Factor Q, which is the unfailing mark of an unusual potential for psi activity, and for telepathy and telekinesis in particular. There are no exceptions to this rule.

FACT THREE: The children who grow up on Furthest to become mindwives are obviously possessed of extremely high telepathic abilities.

PUZZLE ONE: Given the first three facts, then, how does it happen that the potential mindwives are not taken from their parents at birth for raising and training in the Communipath Creche at Mars Central?

FACT FOUR: At the end of the introductory chapter of the manual on the training of mindwives is the phrase, "Swim well, Elder."

FACT FIVE: There is only one illustration in the introductory chapter of the training manual, and that single illustration is completely unlike anything previously noted in Furthester culture. There are no curiously antique houses with cumbersome furnishings; there are no elaborate costumes swathing hidden bodies till nothing shows but faces and hands. Instead the picture shows a naked group, both males and females, without even the ever-present ear coverings. And their surroundings appear to be an underwater cave—full to the top with water and growing water plants.

PUZZLE TWO: Facts Four and Five.

Coyote stared at the list, weighing the combination of all these things with the fake citydome that covered nothing at all, with the strange over-structured secretive behavior of the Furthesters he had met, with all the little bewildering pieces of data that he had accumulated. He willed his mind to achieve some synthesis, some breakthrough that would show him at least the proper direction for his further investigation.

But he didn't know enough, obviously. It was still just a collection of unintegrated motley facts. What else could he add to his information?

He could add the fact that these Furthester religious were a pack of bastards so sadistic that his stomach was threatening him with rebellion. Tying gagged little girls to chairs for days at a time . . . rebuffing their every touch or word . . . arousing them to a sexual fever pitch and putting them under twenty-four hour guard by servo-mechanisms. . . . He was going to be sick if he didn't keep busy.

It was beginning to get light outside; he could tell from the crack of pale white that streaked the bottom of the heavy door to his room. Soon RK would be awake and calling him to breakfast. Whatever he was going to do had to be done rapidly.

He went back to the comsystem console and requested the Book of the Holy Path, hoping that it would contain some facts and not just theological claptrap, and knowing how very unlikely that was. The comsystem delivered the MF with a minimum of delay, the cassette emerging within a minute or two from the duplicator slot.

It was obviously a sacred book like any other sacred book, he saw, divided into sections which themselves were divided into "verses" like the ancient Holy Bible of Old Earth and the inner planets. The dialect was not the same as that currently spoken on Furthest, and he was going to have trouble translating it into Panglish.

He was flicking through the pages in his viewer, nervously trying to decide where to begin, when the knock came at his door and sent him into a panic. He left the MF viewer loaded, but attached it again to the chain around his neck, grabbed a robe almost as voluminous as Furthester garb, and called out, "Yes, RK? What is it?"

"It's not RK," said a voice coolly. "It's Bess. I suggest you let me in."

Bess! His stock of wonder was too depleted to allow him to be surprised, and he went straight to the door and let her in as if he were accustomed to having her come to his room at dawn and demand entrance. She was wearing her usual costume—head to foot total enshroudment, fancy earmuffs—even at this hour.

"Come in, lady," he said wearily. "Come in, and astonish me some more."

"Were you astonished, then?"

She sat down facing him on a low bench against the wall, folded her hands in her lap, and looked at him with merry eyes, and he hadn't the remotest idea what to say to her. Confronting him in the flesh, she was his Scenic Wonder, cool and remote and cynical; but he had his memories of the past night, when she had danced an ecstatic mind-dance with him in his bed and in a world that he had not known existed.

"Didn't you enjoy my skilled services?" she asked him. "Wasn't it satisfactory, Citizen? You could complain to the Elders, you know."

"Bess—"

"Oh, you could, Citizen. It is your right. We mind-wives are supposed to be good at what we do. A great deal of time and money and rather perverted energy goes into ensuring that we are."

"Oh, Bess," he said weakly, "there's no question about it. You are superb at what you do. It's just that I can't, somehow, tie what you do together with what you appear to be."

"Ah," she said softly, "I see. Well, I suppose that depends somewhat upon your preconceptions about the way a government whore should look, doesn't it?"

"Bess!"

"Oh, it's quite true," she said, her voice flat as the floor. "What we mindwives do, after we get through prattling about our sacred duty and our holy office and our service to the faith, what we do is whore for the state. I should not want you to misunderstand me—I'm a very high-class whore, but a whore all the same."

"You weren't whoring with me, Bess," he said firmly. "What you may do for the Furthester government is between you and them, but what you did for me was absolutely beautiful."

"You were in need," she said. "I might say you were in need to the most incredible degree—it reminded me of my old fun days back at the Training Temples. . . . I used to be in need like that, a great deal of the time. And I couldn't leave you like that, not when I was able to do something about it."

Coyote smiled at her. "I thank you, Bess," he said seriously. "With all my outworld heart, I thank you."

"And now you have questions, I suppose?"

He reached over and retrieved the MF on mindwife training, and tossed it to her.

"I thought I was going to get some answers from this," he said, "but all I got was more questions."

Bess whistled under her breath.

"How did you manage to get this?" she asked tensely. "The police should be here by now."

Coyote held up her brother's credit disc and said, "This, first of all. And as for finding that specific item, I just kept requesting general bibliographies until I found a listing that was pertinent. Clever?"

Bess put her hands to her face and let her breath out slowly.

"Oh, my," she said, her voice shaking, "yes, that was clever. But isn't it funny? Wouldn't you think that by now I would be a little less impressed by the dangers of being a criminal?"

"I wouldn't have risked your safety, Bess," he said. "You should know that."

She shrugged, strong slender shoulders eloquent in dark brown velvet under the flowing silken hair.

"It was I who risked my safety," she said, "not you, Citizen." Her voice turned bitter. "I have betrayed my people once again . . . this time perhaps I really have. Except—except that I could not have left you so in pain, Citizen. And I trust you. For some strange reason, I trust you."

"I've got something else," Coyote told her gently, fighting the urge to draw her close and try to comfort her in her all too obvious misery. He had no idea how she would react to physical contact after the mindwife conditioning regime. "Look here, Bess."

He handed her the MF of the Book of the Holy Path, hoping that he was not defiling it in some way by the way he handled it.

"You can't read this," she said at once. "How did you know to ask for it?"

"It's mentioned in the other one," he said. "How do you know I can't read it?"

"Well, can you?"

"Probably not."

"I thought not. What good will it do you, then?"

"I suppose none. Unless you care to tell me something more about it. You *can* trust me, you know."

"Would you like to duel, Citizen?"

The barbed mockery in her voice startled him, and he stared at her, astonished.

"Well, would you?" she said.

"I don't know what you mean," he said.

"Nonsense. Let us have no games of lies between us, Citizen. I am sick to death of lying and hiding. What I mean is that if you would like to test your full projective strength at convincing me that you are to be trusted, I am willing to try my *own* strength at distracting you from that goal."

"I see."

"I'm sure you do."

"I would lose, I think," Coyote chuckled. "I'm sure I couldn't concentrate."

"For shame, Citizen. Where's your devotion to your work?"

"Where's yours?"

She smiled, acknowledging the point, and then turned the full sweetness of her eyes upon him, empty of all the sardonic goading they usually held, and he felt blinded and naked before her."

"I do trust you," she said. "I don't know what it is that you are here to do, but I believe that I could safely tell you what you want to know. At least I can make a beginning."

"Tell me, then!"

"Ask me, then!"

"How does it happen that the children who become mindwives are not sent to the Communipath Creche, Bess? They're obviously telepaths, they must bear the Q Factor—how is it that they are excepted from service?"

"They aren't excepted, Citizen. They don't have Factor Q in their blood."

"You're not serious."

She nodded. "Indeed I am. Factor Q does not appear in the blood of the Ahl Kres'sah."

"But that is very, very strange."

"No. It is fortunate. If that were not the case, and if someone were to try to take away the mindwife novices from Furthest, there would be war—our men would die, to the last one, before they would surrender them."

"I understand that," said Coyote. "That is, I understand why they don't wish to surrender the mindwives. What I do not understand is why there's no Factor Q in your blood."

Bess sat silent, looking at him and waiting.

"Wait a minute. . . ." He had a sudden thought. "Bess, this is going to sound foolish. No, it's too foolish. Tell me something else, first. Why are the mindwives kept secret?"

"I'll quote for you," she said, "from that book you cannot read. And put it in good Panglish, too."

"Please do, Bess."

" 'And it shall come about, that the day will dawn at

last, when the mindwives shall be laid naked before the Three Galaxies by reason of the loose tongue of a wicked man; and beware, then, ye people, O Ahl Kres'sah, for the holy women of the mind shall be taken from you and sold throughout the Galaxies and shall serve as the slaves of evil men forevermore.' "

"That's in the Holy Book, Bess, just like that?"

"Word for word, Citizen."

"And your people believe it?"

"Of course they do."

Coyote nodded. "I begin to see," he said slowly. "Bess?"

"Yes?"

"What does it mean—Ahl Kres'sah? Can you put that in Panglish for me, love?"

"Are you that wicked man," she mused, "the one named in the Book, the one who shall make me whore for the galaxies instead of just for my own world?"

"Bess, I would not—I would not ever harm you. It is just really necessary that you believe that."

He went over to her then, slowly, to allow her time to pull away if she wanted to, and put one hand on her arm, feeling her shiver at his touch as if she had been burned.

"Tell me, lady," he said casually, "what does Ahl Kres'sah mean?"

"It means," she said, "I'm not sure . . . yes. The closest thing would be 'Children of the Dolphin.' "

"What!" Coyote stared at her. "Bess, I just don't understand."

" 'In the first days,' " she said, and he realized that she was quoting again, " 'when the ancient ones went out from their mother world under sentence of death, it came about that they met the dolphin and that they drew near them and bore children by them, as they were instructed by the Most High. And He blessed their union, and bid them hide from all the universe, for all men would curse them and turn upon them and kill them, and He spoke and said that they should be known thereafter forever as the Ahl Kres'sah, Children of the Dolphin. And they praised His name, and they swam for joy.' "

There it was, at last. Coyote sat down again and tried to ignore the whirling of his head, and she watched him without speaking.

"That's why there is no Factor Q among your people," he said finally. "The mutation doesn't show up in your blood because it is of very different composition, that's all."

"That must be right, Citizen," she agreed. "I wouldn't know."

"Let me see if I have this straight, Bess," he said. "Your people came here originally, a thousand years ago, fleeing religious persecution. And there was a race already here—an amphibious race, with which you intermarried, something like the dolphin. Is that right, lady?"

"Yes." She smiled sadly. "I think 'dolphin' is the nearest Panglish equivalent. And now, if I have made a mistake in trusting you, the armies of the Three Galaxies will come, with rockets and bombs and lasers, and they will exterminate us, from the smallest baby to the oldest man, as an abomination in the sight of all humankind."

"And your people have kept this secret, all these hundreds of years? And the earmuffs you wear—of course, they cover gills of some kind!"

Bess leaned back against the wall, arms behind her head.

"And what are you going to do now, Citizen?" she asked quietly. "Have I given up my people into slavery and death? It is said, in our Holy Book, that you others will kill us, one and all . . . will you give us up to be destroyed, Citizen Jones, owner of a failing MESH? Is that what you are about to do?"

Coyote stood up.

"What I am about to do," he said, "is clear up some thousand-year-old misunderstandings. Come along, though, Bess, and let's get RK. I want him to hear this, too, and I see no reason for doing it all twice."

# CHAPTER ELEVEN

"to have lain with you, beloved,
is to have known
how the sun feels, rising. . . ."

(Anonymous)

COYOTE FOUND RK already awake and dressed and busy with breakfast. The boy showed the strain of the previous night. His hands trembled and his lips were tight with the effort he was making not to show his distress. He looked up at Bess and Coyote, one swift bitter glance, and then dropped his eyes at once and refused to look at them again.

"RK?"

"Yes, Citizen Jones?"

"I want you to bring all that stuff over here—that's right, man, just bring it along. Fruit, bread, cheese, coffee, that's plenty for breakfast. No elaborate carryings-on with paté of waterweed or anything like that are necessary, okay?"

"It's no trouble," RK said. "I'd rather do it."

"And I'd rather you didn't," said Coyote firmly. He went over and gathered the food up on a round blue tray, took RK by the arm, and moved both to the table.

RK sat down, sullen and grim, and stared at his plate, and Coyote really didn't blame him. Last night's antics had been a little much for one young over-disciplined uptight kid. Things weren't going to get any better for a while, either.

"RK," he said, "I'm not going to say I'm sorry about

what happened last night, because it would be a bloody lie. What I *am* sorry about is that I had to be so rough."

"It's all right."

"It's not all right," said Bess, "and you know quite well it's not. You must quit posing, Ahr, and learn the virtues of honesty."

"You dare to talk to me of virtue!"

Coyote took RK's credit disc and held it up.

"Look here, RK," he said. "I've got something of yours. I'm sorry I had to take it without asking you, but you wouldn't have given it to me, you know."

RK stared at the disc and then snatched it from Coyote's hand, his face flaming, and pushed his chair back from the table and stood up.

"Now that's too much," he said, fairly spitting his words at them. "You've gone too far, Citizen!"

"And so? Are you going to call the police, RK, and complain to them that you've been robbed?"

"You know I can't! Because of her!"

"Then you might just as well sit down and listen to what I have to say. I did what had to be done. I didn't like doing it, but I did it. I've read the introductory portion of the Manual for the Training of Mindwives. I've seen your Book of the Holy Path. I know what Ahl Kres'sah means. And you have your property back once again. There are accomplished facts, the situation is as it is, irrevocably, and there is nothing to be gained by your stamping out of here."

"I won't listen to you, Citizen," RK hissed. "You are a common criminal, a thief and a fraud and a bully—and worse. I'm leaving this place, right now, and I'm not coming back."

"I can make you stay," said Coyote calmly.

"You would do that?"

"I would because I must," Coyote said. "I would and I will. Either you sit down and listen, as contemptuously as you like, but willingly, or I force you to sit down and listen. That's all the choices you have."

"You are—"

"That's enough, Ahr," said Bess. "You will hear him out before you spew any more of that sort of thing. Sit down and hold your tongue."

RK sank down, beaten and seething, in his chair. Coyote took bread and cheese from the tray and waited a moment, giving the boy a little time to recover before he began to talk. The cheese was revolting, having been made from the milk of some mysterious animal on a planet that went by the charming name of Wall-Hole, but it was all there was out here in the fringes, and if you wanted cheese you ate it, and that's all there was to it. He cut a wedge of it, tore off a chunk of bread, and chewed a generous bite of both, feeling the bubbling of RK's mind and astonished at the viciousness of it. The boy was really furious, and it was not all pride.

"Well, get on with it," RK said. "Enjoy yourself."

"I don't know how to begin," Coyote said.

"I can believe that easily enough."

"Not for the reason you mean," said Coyote. "I'm not at all embarrassed, I don't feel guilty, and like I told you already, I'm not even sorry. So I hurt your feelings and dented my image—that's tough, RK. Now I want to explain, and I want you to listen, voluntarily, if possible, under force if it isn't."

"Go ahead, then!"

"It seems," said Coyote with care, "that your people are suffering from two very large and serious misconceptions. I want to take them up one at a time, okay?"

"I have a choice?"

Coyote ignored him and went on. "The first one is this bit about having to hide the mindwives because they will be kidnapped if their existence is known, RK. That just isn't true."

"It is written—"

"I know. I know very well. It's written in the Book of the Holy Path. RK, who wrote that book? Think a little. Men did, you know. Men, who were fallible and who did not know everything."

"They were holy men, divinely inspired."

"Divinely inspired, shit."

"Shit?"

"Never mind. Term of opprobrium. Look, RK—at the time that that book was written, hundreds of years ago, your people were fleeing from religious persecution. The universe was full of barbarisms, then; people had to live in terror of idiocies from other people. Things have changed since then."

"You think so?" asked Bess. "Have you taken a good look at the culture of my people, Citizen?"

"Wait a minute, Bess," Coyote objected. "I'm not talking about behavior within the Ahl Kres'sah society —I'm talking about this Big Bogeyman from the Inner Galaxies that's supposed to descend out of the sky and steal all your pretty ladies. That's something else—and it's just not a real danger anymore."

"You can't know that," said RK.

"I can, because I do," said Coyote. "In the first place, since the mindwives are part of your *religious* tradition, it really isn't necessary that anyone know very much about them. Through all the Three Galaxies the right to secrecy in religion, the respect for cultural taboos, is accepted. Only a few people, people in positions of trust, need even know that the mindwives exist. That's point one. In the second place, there are exotic sexual delights beyond imagining or description in the Three Galaxies today. A new one no longer causes riots—it's just not that important. Even if the worst were to happen, even if the full details about the mindwives had to be splashed in living color across the Galaxies, it still wouldn't matter."

"You're wrong," said RK.

"No, RK," said Coyote. "I'm right. Listen, let me give you an analogy. In the ancient Bible of Old Earth, right alongside the commandments like 'Thou shalt not kill,' in the early books, there were all sorts of dietary restrictions, given exactly the same commandment status. They were *necessary*, at the time that they were written down, because there was no satisfactory method then for preserving food properly, for preventing food poisoning, for doing all the things necessary for dietary hygiene. But thousands of year later, long after none of that was needed at all, long after refrigeration was developed, people were still practicing this long list of ridiculous 'commandments' because they had turned up originally in a sacred context. This is exactly the same kind of thing, RK. The law about secrecy for the mindwives was absolutely necessary in the days when religious persecution still existed, when kidnapping was a reality, but such crimes have been unknown in the Three Galaxies for hundreds and hundreds of years."

"Oh, Citizen," said Bess softly, "if only you are right —and I'm sure that you are."

"I am," said Coyote, and he poured himself another cup of coffee.

"Now," he said, "that's the first misconception. And that's the smaller of the two."

"The smaller!"

"Yes, RK, the smaller. The really big one you people are lugging around with you is the one about this dolphin-human mating, and how all of you will be destroyed by the rest of the human race for it, and blah-blah-blah."

"Ah, Citizen," Bess objected, "there I can't go along with you. I feel that you are right about the other point, I know what the chances of the mindwives being kidnapped are and just how silly that all is. But about this other matter—since you talk of the Bible, I remind you of the laws on just this subject that are to be found there."

"I know, Bess," said Coyote. "But look—nobody cares any longer. In the first place, the merging of your people and the dolphin-people is so complete that no one would ever notice the difference between you and ordinary human beings, whatever an 'ordinary human being' might be. Those tiny gill-slits you hide so carefully are not only not the spectacular mutation you consider them to be, they are just short of invisible. And whatever made you people think that this was the only planet where there existed humanoid—different, but humanoid—native races with which mating took place? Not to mention the incredible changes brought about by adaptation to various kinds of planetary conditions. Lord, you should see some of the so-called 'humans' that are to be found in the peopled universe today! If the Ahl Kres'sah had not deliberately shut themselves up like pariahs—although I do agree that it was probably necessary early in your history—if they had not done that, and if tourists could come to Furthest as they go everywhere else, you would long ago have seen that your fears were ridiculous."

"Is that true, Citizen? You are not lying, it's not a trick?"

Coyote breathed a sigh of relief. That was the first

sign that RK was beginning to listen instead of just sitting there in a state of blind rage. He was encouraged.

"No, RK," he said. "I'm not lying. There are 'humans' who are almost indistinguishable from birds. There are 'humans' who have manes like lions, and tails, and claws. There are 'humans' that are not even describable —you have to see them to believe them. No one pays the slightest attention."

The silence around the table was so thick that it was almost visible. Coyote waited, wondering if anything more was going to be necessary.

"Citizen Jones," said the boy, "if what you say is true, then my people are undergoing a cruel hardship that is totally unnecessary and stupid."

"Exactly," said Coyote, pleased. "That is exactly right. And that is why I said I was neither ashamed nor embarrassed or sorry about what I'd done. Your people must be told the truth, RK. They must not be allowed to continue in this isolated purdah state because they feel they have to do so—if they just *prefer* it, of course, that's different. But otherwise, it's all superfluous. They can move as freely and as openly about the Three Galaxies as any other members of the Federation. There's just no need, none, for all these restrictions, and there hasn't been any need for them for centuries."

Tears pouring down her face, Bess fought to speak, but RK grabbed her hands and held them tight.

"Do you understand what this means?" he cried. "Do you know, do you see what it means?"

"It means freedom," said Bess. "It means that we are no longer to be hidden and caged, Ahr."

RK stood up. "Now," he said, "now I am so strong that you couldn't possibly stop me from leaving the table! Now I am going to go up to the roof and I am going to sit and think about all of this until I can stand being so happy."

Coyote laughed. "I wouldn't try to keep you now, RK," he said. "I've said what I had to say and succeeded in what I wanted to do. Later I'll tell you why I wanted to do it."

"Don't bother about it, Citizen," said Bess. "I'll go with him and tell him the whole thing."

"Bless you Bess," said Coyote promptly. "That's good of you, because I think I'm talked out," and he watched them go off together, very pleased with his morning's work.

When he went to his bed that night he found he had one task left to do, but this a pleasant one. Bess lay in his bed, free of her trappings of velvet and silk, in her own spare strong beauty of skin and bone, waiting for him.

Because he could not believe it he reached out and touched her, and found her trembling.

"I'm so frightened," she said. "I can't believe how frightened I am . . . for a hardened criminal I don't do very well."

He sat down beside her on the bed and stroked her hair.

"What can I do for you, love?" he asked gently.

"I want something."

"Can you tell me?"

In a very small voice, she said, "Citizen, I would like you to show me what the other kind of love is like. I don't have any idea, you know—would you teach me?"

Coyote held his breath, and thought about a lot of things he could have said, about how it probably wouldn't be very nice for her the first time, especially with her conditioning against physical release, about how she might well be disappointed by comparison with the ecstasy she was accustomed to, about how it might very well actually hurt her.

And then he decided that he really had talked enough for one day, and he pulled his robe off over his head and lay down beside her.

"Yes," he said. "I'd be delighted."

And he was.

# CHAPTER TWELVE

"No matter how inconvenient or unpleasant an illusion may be, if a man has chosen it himself and held it long enough, if he has built it up in sufficient detail and become accustomed to taking it into account upon every occasion, it will become precious to him and he will fight to maintain it in preference to even a pleasant truth. This is because it will have become one of the anchoring points of his mind, like the points which anchor the web of a spider, and to displace it will cause a shift in equilibrium for which painful compensation must be made. This is only a form of self-defense; nonetheless it inhibits growth."

(from the Devotional Book of Tham O'Kent)

BESS SAT beside him in the dark room, running the antiquated projector that he could not have managed without her, prepared to offer explanations when explanations were required, and otherwise simply pleasing him by her presence at his side. She had made a choice of several films which she thought would give him a generally accurate conception of the Ahl Kres'sah culture and customs, the last customer had left the MESH for the night, and all was almost right. Coyote forgot sometimes that the girl who pleased him so was a condemned criminal, under sentence of Erasure; try as he would he could not make it seem real.

"This first one, now," she was saying, "is one of our classic films. It's a love story . . . the couple fall in love, and then they are separated when the boy's family is called for Surface Duty."

Surface Duty? The capital letters had been unmistakable. Coyote wondered, but becided to wait.

"It's a bit trite and dated," said Bess, "but it's one of those things that everyone sees several times as he is growing up, and that becomes really part of you. That's the kind of thing you need, isn't it?"

"Exactly."

"This should make a good beginning, then. It starts in a little village, called Saad Tebet; there's no Panglish equivalent for that, I don't think. You won't be able to understand it at all, I'm afraid. I'm sorry about that."

"Why not? My Furthester isn't fluent, but it should handle film dialog, Bess; at least for the most part it should."

Bess chuckled. "Did you ever try to talk underwater, Citizen?"

For a moment he was puzzled, and then he saw it.

"My god," he said, "that should have been obvious even to me, but I never thought of it. How do you communicate then? Telepathy?"

"No," she said, shaking her head. "Telepathy among our people is confined almost entirely to mindwives. We use a finger alphabet, and a set of gestures, when we are at home—a sign language."

"When you're at home. I see."

"The easiest thing, of course, would be for me to just translate it for your mind, but you don't do *that* very well either; you'd miss most of it. I'll just try to interpret it as it goes along."

"Good enough, Bess."

"Now—there's the beginning. That's an ordinary street, on an ordinary day. The ordinariest of the ordinary."

On the pale stone wall the colors suddenly leaped to life, in old-fashioned two-dimensional projection. There was water, and a sort of stone corridor through which it flowed, and people, both men and women, swimming along as easily as any fish. They were naked, except for the broad bands that tied back the long hair of the women. Some carried net bags as they swam, others had small satchels on their backs. Several children swam by, darting in and out among the adults, obviously playing a game of some kind.

"What are the colored circles on the corridor walls, Bess?" he asked.

"Those are doors. You see the little disc at the side of each? That is like a doorknob—you push it and the circle swings round on a central pivot to let you in. All the homes of the Ahl Kres-sah have that sort of door, and the colors are traditional, very bright so that they can be seen in the water."

"Those are Ahl Kres'sah homes? But what about the houses here in the city?"

"Oh, those aren't real, Citizen!"

"Bess, that doesn't make sense."

"What I mean is, those houses were built by the ancient Elders who first settled this planet. When the requests first began to come out from the Inner Galaxies for statistics and information about our people, we built more of those—exactly enough. One city, one town, and one village. No one would ever live in them by choice."

"But—"

"There, Coyote, there comes the heroine. You see, she is looking for the boy she loves . . . and there he is. Now, they are just going to talk together for a little while, it isn't anything important. They talk about loving each other, about their plans to marry. None of the speech is really important for a while."

Coyote watched the girl swim up to her lover, saw them embrace—a rather chaste embrace, but more than he'd thought would be usual with these people. The girl's eyes shone, the boy set a tender kiss on her forehead, and their fingers flashed in the water. The girl wore narrow enameled rings on the fingers of her left hand, he noticed, a different color for each finger.

"Why does she wear the rings, Bess?"

"To make it easier to use the finger alphabet. There is a 'letter' on each fingertip, each fingerjoint, the tip and joints of the thumb, and the palm of the hand, twenty in all. We touch the 'letter' with the right hand to spell out the words."

"I see."

"This next scene is all local color, Citizen. These two are going through the market; he's helping her shop."

"Your markets are under water?"

"Everything is under water."

"But what about the city, then? What's its function?"

"You're going to miss the film, Citizen."

"No. I can watch while you talk."

"The surface cities are simply a kind of cover, so that if any high government official should wreck a starship here, for example, and have to be admitted to the planet, there would be someplace to admit him to without giving away our secrets. People are chosen to live in the cities, chosen by lottery; anyone who is so chosen must take his whole family and serve three years, and one term of service exempts you for life. There is almost nothing more hated, Citizen, than Surface Duty, but we all must take our turn."

"So that explains the empty citydomes?"

"That's right. We have a dome for each hypothetical 'city' that we show on the faked atlas that is in the libraries on other planets. They're all empty; having to staff three of them is burden enough."

"And all the statistics about population, education, taxes, and all the rest?"

"All fake. There—they're coming out of the market now."

"What does she have in the net bag, Bess?"

Bess shrugged. "I can't really tell; salad vegetables, I think. Watch this, now—here comes the boy's younger brother with the bad news."

On the wall a younger boy, his face distraught, swam up to the young people and began the rapid hand speech. He, too, wore the rings on his left hand.

"Do you have rings like those, Bess?" Coyote asked.

"Yes, of course, when I am at home and not on Surface."

"What is he saying now?"

"It's very sad. He's telling his brother that their family has just been chosen in the lottery. Just as I was telling you, it's a tragic occasion."

"Why is it hated so?"

"Wouldn't you hate it?" she demanded. "Away from everything that is dear to you, forced to breathe air that hurts your lungs and burns your skin, having to be wrapped up like a mummy all the time when you are accustomed to wearing nothing but a hairband, isolated from your people and everything that is going on —surely you can't think you'd like that?"

"The girl is crying."

"Yes. Yes, of course she is. Her family was not chosen; that means she will be separated from her lover for three years, and no hope of any change."

"What will she do?"

"Watch."

Coyote watched as the story progressed. He saw the hurried, tearful packing done by the boy's mother in their home, a home which appeared to be a series of rooms cut in the solid rock and connected by halls through which the people swam. He could not see what the light source was, but there was a soft glow every-where in the rooms. There was no furniture, as such; anyone wanting to rest curled into one of the colored nets that were slung in groups in the corners of the rooms.

Now the chosen family was leaving for the surface, pulling behind them on a sort of powered sled a large trunk that Bess told him held their personal belongings and their "uniforms." Everything else they needed would already be in the surface house assigned to them for their term of duty. They emerged onto the familiar gray waste that Coyote knew so well, in the brilliant glare of noon when it was its ugliest, and stood looking around them in seeming resignation, except for the boy, who was taut with despair.

"Bess, do your people ever come out on the surface to watch the water—the colors in it, I mean?"

"No, Citizen. There are many places on our planet where most of the surface rock has been worn away; we watch the night colors from below, in such places."

"I see."

"Watch, now!"

There was a scene where the family struggled into their heavy surface clothing, fighting with hooks and but-tons and belts that were obviously totally unfamiliar to them. And then there was the weary trek into the town and into their house.

Then it flashed back to the girl under the water. She was going about various tasks inside her house, he sup-posed; her movements meant nothing to him, but seemed purposeful.

"What is she doing, Bess?"

"That is one of the classic Water Dances, Coyote. Lis-ten, you will hear the drums and shells; they are the traditional accompaniment for Water Dancing. That dance she is doing—see how graceful she is?—is called the Dance of Unbearable Sorrow. The actress is famous for this sequence."

"She should be; it's beautiful."

They watched in silence for a while, and then Bess speeded up the film.

"I've got to skip some of these things," she said, "or we will never get through. Now, here is the important part. See what she's doing?"

It was dark now on the surface of Furthest, except for the rainbows of water. As Coyote watched, the girl, painted black from head to foot, slipped out onto the surface of the planet and headed for the city, crawling in the open, running where she was sheltered.

Bess turned off the projector.

"I think that's enough of that one," she said. "Most of the rest of it is trivial, and predictable. She is trying to join the boy on the surface, and that is strictly forbidden."

"No volunteer service, eh?"

"No. They tried it and found it didn't work; it meant a city staffed entirely by all the wrong sorts of people. Desperate people, sets of lovers like the two in this film, people running away from domestic crises, any thing but the cross-section of normal, ordinary families that is supposed to meet the eye."

"Does she make it?"

"She gets to the steps of the boy's home, but the family has gone away for the night to visit friends that were called to the Surface earlier. She doesn't know this, and she is forced to spend the entire night in the open, waiting for them to return. The boy finds her in the morning when the family finally comes back, but of course she is dead."

"Why should she be dead?"

Bess glanced at him, surprised. "Surely you have guessed that by now? Our skin is incredibly delicate, it requires a great deal of moisture. If it is exposed to the open air, to sun and wind and dust, we die in a very few hours. Even covered as we are, we suffer."

"I understand, Bess. And that's a sad film."

"Very sad. And it's reasonably true to life. People

*are* separated in tragic ways by Surface Duty, someone does occasionally find himself trapped in the open and die of exposure."

"The girl couldn't have knocked at some other house and saved herself?"

"This is an old-fashioned film, Citizen. Technically, she cannot do that because anyone whom she appealed to for help would be duty bound to turn her in to the police. I don't think anyone would really do that, frankly, but that's what the film is intended to convey."

"All right, Bess. What else have we got?"

"Let me see. This is the best for your purposes, I think."

She slipped another clip into the projector, explaining, "It's the biography of one of our heroes, a man called —well, you couldn't pronounce it. In Panglish his first name would be Andrew, I believe. It should show you what constitutes the Furthester ideal for the male."

Coyote nodded approvingly.

"That should be useful," he agreed. "Go ahead, love, run it."

He was frankly astonished by the film as he watched it. The hero was a scientist, a man who was offered a great deal of money to put aside research that would lead to medical benefits for the people but that would eliminate the need for a drug brought out by a powerful chemical monopoly. This was heroic in any culture, especially when the man continued with his work despite threats on his life, threats to his family, and the usual bag of tricks trotted out in such situations.

What was surprising was the profile of character that emerged from the film. It was nothing like what Coyote had expected. The difference was so great that it made him half sick; his error could have been very dangerous.

He had based his conception of an ideal Furthester man upon the men he had seen in the city and in the MESH, men he had not for a moment suspected were literally "on duty." He had assumed that such a man, the very epitome of male Furthester, would be proud, cold, totally devoid of any display of emotion except conceivably a display of anger, given to abrupt arrivals and departures, interested in nobody and nothing except himself and his possessions. This was the estimate he had made and would have reported, based upon months of the closest observation he could muster.

And he had been wrong, deeply wrong. The man he saw on the screen was not like that at all. He was gentle, warm, affectionate, patient, compassionate, loving. He was not given to open exhibitions of affection of the exuberant sort, but strong male affection, reserved but obviously tender, displayed frequently and willingly.

The personality that Coyote had been seeing had been entirely the pattern shown by a man conscripted into a life he despised, suffering the irritations of an environment literally poisonous to his body, encumbered by the unfamiliar trappings of a vanished culture, knowing that his wife and children were at that moment suffering the same indignities and miseries that he was. No wonder they appeared cold and unapproachable!

At the idea of the immensity of the mistake that he had been making Coyote felt like the embodiment of an elderly cliché—his blood "ran cold." Never mind that it was trite, it was exact. If he had not learned the truth there would have been some very grave difficulties when a Furthester man became President of the Tri-Galactic Congress. No doubt he would appear even more cold, even more distant and miserable, in the alien environment of the Inner Galaxies, and yet his normal personality profile was totally unlike the picture he would present.

"Bess, he asked suddenly, "didn't you tell me that your people are forbidden by law to leave this planet?"

"That's correct," she said. "No one may leave."

"Then how does it happen that you have a delegate to the Tri-Galactic Council?"

"I'm sorry," she said, "I had forgotten about him. But he is the one and only exception to the law. And even for him, it requires a special dispensation from the Chief Elder, and a long period of cleansing when he returns."

"Is it a religious prohibition?" Coyote asked in amazement.

"Yes, of course; what other reason could there be?"

"I'm afraid I don't see how it fits into the religious pattern."

"Well, Citizen, if you've based an entire theology upon the necessity for total secrecy, you are almost certain to find your goings and comings restricted by religious law."

"You're right, of course. Again, that should have been obvious to me."

"Why is it that all these things that should be so obvious to you are so opaque, Citizen? Perhaps it is the strain of worry about your financial situation?"

He tugged at a lock of her hair until she yelped.

"Be serious, Bess," he said severely. "Everything is supposed to be serious. After all, I'm a spy and you're a heretic."

She sighed and said, "Well, then, what else do you want to see from these?"

"What else do you have?"

"Some travelogs. An example of our humor. A film of a musical program. And something very special."

"The others could wait until later. What's the 'very special' one about?"

"It should really interest you."

"Don't tease, Bess."

"I'm not teasing——I'm simply embarrassed."

"Embarrassed? Why?"

"The other one is all about me. I'm the plot, the star, the suspense, the whole bit. All me."

Coyote raised his eyebrows. "I had no idea you were that important, Citizenness."

"I'm a mindwife," she reminded him, "one of the best, potentially perhaps the very best."

"So RK told me."

"And it's unheard of for a mindwife not to glory in her role, not to revel in her so-called sacred functions. They made a whole film about it. Full of dire moral pronnouncements and urgent calls to prayer. It has my trial ... and my wedding."

"Oh, Bess. You're married?"

"Nope. I went to the wedding, though."

"Bess," he moaned, "will you stop, please?"

She chuckled. "You want to see it, Citizen? It's just full of cultural foibles. Not to mention the fact that it's an excellent portrayal of how a mindwife is *not* supposed to behave."

"Of course I want to see it," Coyote said. "But not now. It's almost three o'clock in the morning. I couldn't do you justice in my present condition, I'm falling down tired. Let's see it tomorrow night, love."

"How much longer are you staying, Citizen?" she asked him.

It was a question he was accustomed to hearing from women, and one to which he had learned the only possible answer.

"Long enough, Bess," he said easily, smiling at her. "Just long enough."

# CHAPTER THIRTEEN

"The vast majority of activities which take upon themselves the name 'revolution' are not revolution at all; they're just foreplay."

(from an old commercial)

BESS TOUCHED his hand and leaned over to speak to him.

"This will be a lot easier," she said.

"In what way?"

"Because in this one you get vocal speech. It's a news documentary, a weekly 'Story of the Week' kind of thing, and they're all done in vocal only."

"Where do they film them, then?"

Bess laughed. "Even our primitive society is up to the construction of a watertight underground chamber, Citizen."

"Sorry, love."

"The reason for it is that many people collect these documentaries. You must realize that, as isolated as we are out here, what happens on our own planet takes on an immense importance to us. And many people who could not afford to buy the films are able to buy tapes of the sound track; so they put them together with that in mind."

"Good old profit motive," said Coyote with satisfaction. "I'm tired of getting everything secondhand."

"Here it goes—they're pretty. . . . Wait a minute. I don't have a word for it, I don't think, not one that you would understand. It's a slang word. 'Cheq'thah.' "

"Does it paraphrase?"

She frowned. "Let's see. Something aimed at the lowest common denominator. Full of bad jokes, with all the meanings underlined twice and everything pointed out to you with red pencil. You're lucky; your Furthester speech isn't good enough for you to see the puns. The language is completely behind the times, my parents' generation, but salted with current slang in what they think are appropriate places. Home, mother, and waterweed loaf. Have you a word for it?"

"Corny."

"Corny?"

"Ancient Earth word, but it's survived because it's needed. The sort of thing you described is called 'corny.' "

"Good enough. All right, the narration, the transition, all that stuff, is going to be corny. The actual events were all filmed as they happened, though, so they haven't been able to foul those up, they're authentic. Try to ignore the fillers. Ready?"

NARRATOR: Citizens! Once again we are proud to bring you—the NEWS—in DEPTH! DEPTH, BREADTH, AND LIVING COLOR . . . brought straight to you!

"You see?" said Bess.

"Pretty bad."

NARRATOR: This week's story concerns the recent scandalous tragedy of Mindwife Kh'llwythenna Be'essahred Q'ue, who as you know is now a fugitive attempting to evade the execution of her sentence—TOTAL ERASURE! Citizens, this is one of the most vital, one of the most gripping, one of the greatest stories of our times, a story with deep import for all of us—and now, Citizens —NEWS . . . IN . . . DEPTH! We take you first to Mind-wife Q'ue's wedding in the Grand Hall . . .

FADE TO VAST UNDERWATER GROTTO. A CROWD OF PEOPLE IS GATHERED IN NETS ALONG BOTH SIDES OF THE ROOM. GLOBES CONTAINING FOODS ARE TIED TO THE NETS. SERVOMECHANISMS SWIM SLOWLY ABOUT THE ROOM OFFERING TUBES OF DRINKS. AT THE FAR END

OF THE GROTTO A SORT OF ALTAR IS CARVED
IN THE ROCK . . .

"Bess?"

"What?"

"How did you get away?"

She chuckled in the darkness.

"We're supposed to be so bloody law-abiding. It never
occurred to them I wouldn't sit docilely waiting for them
to get around to Erasing me. I just walked out when the
guards weren't looking."

"Clever of you."

"No. Stupid of them. Ah . . . here come the Marrying
Elder."

AN OLD MAN SWIMS DOWN THE AISLE BE-
TWEEN THE NETS, FOLLOWED BY A LINE OF
FOUR YOUNGER MEN. THE OLDEST IS CARRY-
ING A NET BAG CONTAINING A BOOK AND
THREE CARVED SHAPES OF WOOD. ALL FOUR
WEAR NARROW COLLARS OF GOLD AROUND
THEIR NECKS AND BANDS OF GOLD ON THEIR
ANKLES, SET WITH TINY DOLPHIN-LIKE CREA-
TURES DIVING MADE OF A PALE GREEN
STONE.

"What are the dolphins, Bess? Just decoration?"

"No. A sacred symbol. Only officials of the church
may wear those bands. Some of the devout wear a dolphin on a chain around their neck, but only one, and
not on a band."

"What are they made of? Is it jade?"

"What's jade?"

"A jewel stone, about that color."

"I don't know, Coyote—we call it 'atk.' "

"Well, it doesn't matter."

THE ELDERS FORM A ROW, THE OLDEST HOLD-
ING A LOOP ATTACHED TO THE WALL BESIDE
THE ALTAR, THE OTHER FOUR IN A GOLDEN
NET SLUNG TO THE LEFT. MUSIC BEGINS.

"Wait a minute . . . Bess, this is under water. How are
they going to do vocals?"

"It's just for the wedding. The speech—exactly as it was made in hand speech—is dubbed in later, like the music. The actress who does my speech is very good. Everything else, then, took place in the watertight rooms."

"I see."

"You'll see their fingers moving, but you'll hear vocal speech from the film."

"Got it."

"Here I come now . . . followed respectfully by my intended. He's a Senator in our Planetary Council, owns a monopoly on half a dozen products essential to our people, is a very powerful man."

"And you were *awarded* to him."

"Exactly. Like a medal."

BESS SWIMS INTO VIEW AND THE CAMERA MOVES IN FOR A CLOSEUP. SHE IS WEARING A SORT OF NECKLACE OF GOLD NET WITH THE GREEN STONES, A NECKLACE THAT EXTENDS DOWN OVER HER BREASTS AND SHOULDERS AND IS ALMOST A JEWELED CAPE, WITH LONG FRINGES OF GOLD THAT EXTEND DOWN HER ARMS. THE MAN WHO SWIMS BEHIND HER IS WEARING A SIMILAR CAPE, BUT WITHOUT JEWELS.

"Those are wedding costumes, I suppose?"

"Yes, indeed. Very high class wedding costumes they are, too. There now, you see, we've taken our places at the altar, holding those rings set in the rock. All traditional."

"Is the ceremony the same for mindwives as for—what do you call them—body wives?"

"Just the same. Now it's beginning."

ELDER: In the eyes of the Most High, under the blessed auspices given and ordained by Him Who knows all, I come to you this afternoon as Marrying Elder of the Ahl Kres'sah. I greet you; may you swim well.

ALL: May you swim well, Holy Elder.

ELDER: Upon this solemn occasion it is my joy to name as husband Tri T'tha Hahlw-Obe'an, who comes not as Senator, not as a man of power, but as a simple man,

like any other man, to claim his wife. I call upon you,
T'tha Hahlw-Obe'an, is it your will that I should proceed?

TRI: That is my will, Holy Elder.

ELDER: Upon this solemn occasion it is my joy to
name as wife Kh'llwythenna Be'essahred Q'ue, who comes
not as sacred mindwife, not as a woman blessed and
chosen by the Most High, but as a simple woman, like
any other woman, to be claimed by her husband. I call
upon you, Kh'llwythenna Be'essahred Q'ue, is it your
will that I should proceed?

BESS: It is not. I'll swear fidelity to no man and take
no oath meant to make me a sacred whore for the government of this . . .

PANDEMONIUM BREAKS OUT, THE NOISE OF
THE HORRIFIED ONLOOKERS DROWNING OUT
THE WORDS OF THE SOUNDTRACK. THE CAMERA
FADES OUT.

"That was a mighty short wedding Bess."

"Wasn't it?"

"Why didn't you just refuse to go in the first place?"

"And miss an opportunity like that?"

NARRATOR: Citizens, this was a first. Never before, in
the history of the Ahl Kres'sah, has any woman so dis-
rupted and despoiled a sacred ceremony, much less her
own wedding! And this was no ordinary woman, Citizens, this was a mindwife, a mindwife who—of course
I know nothing of these things, but I quote her Training
Elders—a mindwife who would have been one of the
greatest mindwives we have ever had. . . . Citizens, this
was a sad occasion. But it didn't begin here, no, it began
long, long before. . . .

"Really?"

"Really. Watch."

NARRATOR: Citizens, the man whom you now see on
your screens is the Senior Training Elder of the Temple
of Mindwives. He has graciously consented to speak to
us today of this unfortunate woman. Good afternoon,
Holy Elder.

ELDER: Greetings, may you swim well.

NARRATOR: Thank you, Elder. Now, you know of this sad incident—

ELDER: The wedding that was so abruptly cut off? Yes, I know of it. I could hardly avoid knowing of it.

NARRATOR: Of course, of course. Now, could you tell us something of this woman? You had her training, did you not?

ELDER: Yes. A heavy burden, a very heavy burden.

NARRATOR: I'm sure it must have been.

ELDER: She was so obviously superior, from the very first week that we had her in our care, that it was felt best for me to take over supervision of her training personally.

NARRATOR: What was she like, as a child?

ELDER: Like any mindwife. Rebellious, angry, undisciplined, wild. That is normal and to be expected.

NARRATOR: Was she unusual in any way?

ELDER: In the degree of her abilities, yes; she was very unusual. The power of her mind has not been met with before or since, so far as I am able to determine.

NARRATOR: But she did submit to discipline, when she was a young girl at the Temple?

ELDER: Well. . . . You must remember, she was a very unusual case. Because of her brilliance, which is to a great extent a function of her *lack* of discipline in the sense you mean, we tolerated a greater degree of deviance from her than we would normally have done. That was our mistake, of course, as we can see now. But at the time it seemed justified.

NARRATOR: I see, I see. Then this . . . performance . . . of hers was not unexpected?

ELDER: The business at the wedding ceremony? Good heavens, man, of course it was unexpected! She fooled us very neatly . . . there had been an initial resistance on her part, but we thought that she had gotten over that when she saw that we were not going to give in to her nonsense.

NARRATOR: Well, what sort of 'nonsense' was it that she advocated?

ELDER: I don't know quite how to put it. This is, after all, a family program, is it not?

NARRATOR: Well, perhaps we can come back to that.

Can you tell us, had she been a source of difficulty to you before?

ELDER: Oh, yes. Yes, she had. She had been a source of havoc, if you really want to know. It had been necessary for us to keep her in total isolation . . . solitary confinement . . . off and on for the past six years, because of her influence on the other mindwives.

NARRATOR: But isn't that rather futile? I mean, isn't she able to communicate with them all the same? Mentally?

ELDER: Mmmh. Hmhmm. It isn't . . . uh, it isn't generally known, but we do have a sort of cell from which it is not possible for the mindwives to project their thoughts or receive the thoughts of others. It's heavily shielded against any sort of electrical activity—or any other sort of activity. In fact, if she had been returned to our care after her arrest instead of to the civil authorities, she would not be at large now.

"Is he right about that, Bess?"

"I don't know. I had never before really tried to get out of that cell of theirs, so I just don't know. But I think I would have gotten away."

NARRATOR: When you say she had been a source of havoc, what exactly do you mean?

ELDER: Well, she had a lot of radical ideas, which, as I said, I can't possibly express to you here and now, when children might be listening. She communicated these ideas to the other mindwives, and although she wasn't too successful, there was always the possibility that they might spread. As I say, it was for that reason that we isolated her.

NARRATOR: You didn't feel she would remain a danger after her wedding?

ELDER: She fooled us, I told you. She seemed chastened, docile, very repentant. She had just spent an uninterrupted period of eleven months in the shielded cell. We felt that she had learned her lesson and would welcome, rather than abuse, her freedom.

NARRATOR: Ha, ha, ha. She really pulled the gills over your ears, didn't she?

ELDER: I don't find it particularly amusing.

NARRATOR: Well, Citizens, you can see why the Elder's becoming a little upset. He has been under a severe strain, of course, we must all remember that. . . .

"Bess?"

"Yes, Citizen?"

"How bad was it . . . the solitary confinement?"

"Would you like to try it some time?"

Coyote pulled her into his arms, conditioning be damned, and rocked her gently.

"Hush," he said. "I'm an utter ass sometimes. Too damn often. What's left in the film?"

"My trial."

"They let you talk then?"

"After a fashion."

"Let's see it."

"You're seeing it. That's what he was doing while you were gabbling, going through the 'now we take you to the sensational trial etc., etc.' bit."

"Oh."

NARRATOR: . . . speaking in her own defense.

THE TRIAL IS BEING HELD IN A CLOSED CHAMBER, BEFORE THREE JUDGES. THERE IS NO JURY, AND NO AUDIENCE. THE JUDGES WEAR NARROW COLLARS OF SILVER, OTHERWISE THEY ARE NAKED. BUT BESS IS COMPLETELY CLOTHED, IN A LONG ROBE OF WHITE CLOTH, A PRISONER'S GARMENT, OBVIOUSLY INTENDED TO BE A TORMENT UNDER WATER BECAUSE IT CLINGS AND TWISTS ABOUT THE BODY AND MAKES SWIMMING AN AWKWARD, NEARLY IMPOSSIBLE PROCEDURE.

JUDGE: What have you to say for yourself, Mindwife? Are you repentant? Do you regret your disgusting behavior?

BESS: I regret nothing.

JUDGE: How do you expect mercy from us, if you insist upon taking that position?

BESS: CENSORED.

"What did you say, Bess?"

"I said 'kluth your mercy.'"

"'Kluth'? What does that mean?"

"In Panglish? It's a pejorative term for non-mental sexual intercourse, if I may be so formal. I don't know the word."

"Oh, I see. 'Fuck' your mercy is what you said."

"Is that the word?"

"That's the one, love."

JUDGE: Obscenities will be of no use to you here, Mindwife. We are accustomed to such things and you waste
your time and ours. If you have anything to say in your
defense I suggest you say it.

BESS: My defense is composed entirely of the fact
that I am guilty of nothing.

JUDGE: And how did you arrive at that interesting
conclusion? Your crime was public, woman, how are
you to deny it?

BESS: I deny that it was a crime.

JUDGE: I allow you to continue with this nonsense only
because I am indulgent; I warn you that my indulgence
has limits.

BESS: I am guilty of protesting agasint a system that
is called holy, but is infamous. I am guilty of trying to
bring the truth into the open. I am guilty of trying to
cleanse our Holy Path of a festering dungheap.

JUDGE: You speak in riddles.

BESS: Judge, you know perfectly well what we mindwives are. Holy! We are filth. We are a special, very
highly trained, very expensive sort of filth, reserved for
the secret pleasures of those who teach us to perform our
"duties" and for the men of our society who are powerful
enough to buy one of us. You know this as well as I do. I
refused, and I do still refuse, to take part in such a per-
version, and that is not a crime.

JUDGE: You would put an end to mindwifery?

BESS: Either it should be stopped, irrevocably and
forever, or it should be made free, for the benefit of everyone. Every Ahl Kres'sah, man, woman, and child, must
pay for the training and the maintenance of the mindwives, either directly through taxation or indirectly in that
he is deprived of what that money could purchase for our
people if it were not so used. If all must pay for it then
all should enjoy it—and you know quite well, Judge, that
any one of us, any capable mindwife, could bring ecstasy
to fifty men a day instead of one.

"Bess, I don't understand."

"What?"

"Surely . . . I thought this was for general viewing . . ."

"It was never released to the public, Citizen. I have a stolen copy."

"I see."

THE JUDGES ARE ON THEIR FEET, LIVID WITH RAGE. ONE RAISES A FIST AND SHAKES IT AT BESS, ENTIRELY FORGETTING HIS DIGNITY.
JUDGE: Enough! You cannot expect me to believe that this filth, this blasphemy, this unspeakable obscenity, is to be seen and heard by the people of this planet! I order that the cameras and the other equipment for duplication be turned off as of this instant—

There was a quiet click as the projector came to the end of the film.

"He got rather upset," Bess observed. "He never let me say another word."

"You weren't allowed to speak again?"

"Not once."

"That's incredible."

"I was summarily sentenced and taken away to prison —the state prison, fortunately, not the Temple one."

"But you had no lawyer, Bess—don't you people have specialists in the defense of criminals, people who act on their behalf and have special knowledge of the law?"

"For civil crimes, yes. Not for religious ones. For a religious crime it is a foregone conclusion that you will be sentenced, and the only purpose of the trial is for the accused to plead for mercy. No one is ever acquitted under such circumstances."

"That's barbaric, Bess."

"Agreed. Many things are barbaric."

She got up and began putting away the viewing equipment.

"You know, Citizen, that judge who was shaking his fist had a very good reason to be angry?"

"Oh? Why is that?"

Bess laughed, tucking the cassettes into the shelves under the projector.

"Because, he has a mindwife of his own."

# CHAPTER FOURTEEN

"Up above the world so high
Like a windbag in the sky."

(from an old nursery rhyme)

TO BE BACK on Mars Central again was a strain on his already abused powers of readjustment. Twice before he had done this switch, from a primitive mode of existence to the advanced technological style that was characteristic of the Inner Galaxy, and each time he found it more of a wrench. The cities seemed vast and noisy and swarming with people, the machines that had been an unnoticed part of the background like the walls and the floor suddenly seemed ugly and obtrusive, and everything looked foreign. He knew it would wear off in a day or two, but it bothered him now. And of course he missed Bess. The two months it had taken him to get here had been only two days for him—the first day, while he was processed for the hibernation tanks, and the last, while they readied him for landing. But he missed her already. She was good company.

He turned into the offices of the Tri-Galactic Intelligence Service, stepped into an anti-grav chute and drifted up to the seventh floor, where he found the Fish still attended by the Amanuensis Mark IV.

"Drop dead," he told it in chill tones, and it began blinking and clicking frantically, finally producing, "That activity is not one for which I am programmed, sir."

"Stop monkeying around with my equipment, Mr. Jones," ordered the Fish.

"You know something?"

"What?"

Coyote regarded him stonily. "It seems to me that a man who employs a servomechanism for a secretary should be advanced enough to give up the use of an ancient form of address like 'Mister.'"

"The reason," said the Fish, "that I am reduced to employing such a servomechanism, is that I am no longer able to find the ancient form of human being known as a secretary. Everyone is a lunasthetist or a biosylthesist or a starship stewardess or some such idiocy these days. I do not see that this misfortune, over which I have no control, should constitute a reason for an alteration in my personal habits."

Coyote shrugged. "All right," he said. "Be an odd old pansy. I don't care."

"Pansy?"

"Archaic term for homosexual."

"I'm not a homosexual. I'm not a heterosexual. I have no use for either alternative, and I'm sure you'd be more use to the Service if you'd follow my example."

"Mmm. Nonetheless, in this day and age, to call people 'Mister' or 'Miss' is very pansy."

"Irrelevant. Please get to the point, Mr. Jones."

"Have you read the reports I sent ahead?"

"I have. I found them singularly uninformative. Not one word in them that the computers didn't already have in their databanks. What have you been *doing* all this time?"

"The reason the reports are uninformative is because they are faked. I am quite sure that three-fourths of the personnel on Mars Central read the reports that come in from the agents of TGIS and I wanted them to be sure they had the full story, so there'd be no problem in accomplishing what I really want."

"I see. Then that's not really the situation?"

"No, no. Actually it couldn't be less like the stuff you have in your files."

"Tell me about it."

"No."

"What do you mean, no?"

"I mean, no. Period. I won't report to you, alone. I want to report to the full Board, plus a representative from the Tri-Galactic Council who's one of us and has some influence."

"Look, Mr. Jones—"

"Or I won't talk at all."

"Nonsense, Mr. Jones. We'll put you on hypnodrugs and you will tell us everything."

"You try that and I'll kill every member of your staff cheerfully. Would you like to refer to your files and see just what sort of damage it's possible for a mass projective telepath to do if he really puts his head into it?"

The Fish leaned his cheek on his hand and sighed.

"You are so difficult," he said solemnly. "Is it really necessary for you to be so difficult?"

"Yes," said Coyote. "Otherwise nothing would get done. Ever."

"All right," said the Fish. "Who do you want in the meeting?"

"I told you. The full Board of TGIS plus a Council member with influence and sympathy for us. That shouldn't be hard to arrange—especially since none of the Board does anything but sit around on their butts and think of new regulations for the agents to break."

The Fish ignored him and began to dictate to the Amanuensis Mark IV, which then went to the comset by his desk and punched out the proper buttons to call the meeting. Coyote watched, unbelieving.

"You're even more of an idiot than you were when I was here last time!" he said finally. "Do you mean to tell me that the taxpayers of these three galaxies are paying for the maintenance of this Amanuensis that does things for you like punch the buttons on your comset? Do you mean to tell me—"

"I don't mean to tell you anything, Mr. Jones. You want your meeting, I'm getting it for you. You don't need to concern yourself with anything else—especially my office furniture."

"Especially my office furniture," Coyote mimicked, in a high falsetto voice. He pulled his hair, which was longer and redder by half a year, up onto the top of his head into a raggedy knot, and went swishing around the room with one hand on his hip. "My goodness deary me, I do think that next year I'll get one of those automatic chair cushions that wipes my ass for me . . . perhaps with the TGIS insignia embroidered on it in pearls—"

"That reminds me," said the Fish, "where precisely do you wear *your* TGIS insignia?"

"Look," Coyote said, in his normal voice, "I'm supposed to be a folksinger, remember? I'm not *supposed* to be a TGIS man. It's called a cover, right?"

"In this office," said the Fish in icy tones, "you are a TGIS man. I am not interested in this trivial musical drivel you mouth about the galaxies at the expense of those taxpayers for whom you are otherwise so concerned. While you are here you will wear your insignia. Where is it?"

"I have no idea."

"One moment."

The Fish went through a complicated succession of servomechanisms, both human and plastic, and then he said into the receiver, "Miss Kai? Who? No—I am calling Miss Tzana Kai, will you put her on, please?"

"You're calling Tzana?" asked Coyote. "What for?"

The Fish ignored him, speaking into the receiver again.

"Miss Kai?" he said. "This is the Fish, at Mars Central. Would you please tell me whether, last time he visited your quarters, Coyote Jones left his TGIS insignia somewhere around?"

There was a lengthy pause and then he went on.

"I rather thought so," he said. "In that case would you / please send it along by the next mail rocket? Mr. Jones finds that he is uncomfortable here on Mars Central without his insignia."

Another pause went by, during which the Fish grinned with gleeful satisfaction and Coyote prayed for him to be electrocuted by his comsystem.

"Thank you, Miss Kai, we'll appreciate that," he said at last, and hung up.

"I just plain and purely can't stand you," Coyote said to him.

"I know that," said the Fish. "Come along then; I'm sure everyone is here by now."

Coyote stood at the end of the table beside the screen where his photographs were being projected, along with the classic boy-meets-girl film which Bess had let him bring along. When he had explained it all, he waited, and got the expected reaction. My goodness. Heavenly days. Who'd have thought it. That sort of thing.

"Yes," he said, "I agree with you. It's hard to imagine that a hoax of this scope could have been perpetrated on all of us for hundreds of years. But it's really a long, long way out there. There's not another inhabited planet or asteroid or anything else within nineteen million miles. If they'd been closer, of course, we would have gotten to the bottom of it long ago; but out there at the end of nowhere they've managed very nicely to fool us all. It's hard on the pride, but it's true."

A member of the Board observed that it was very interesting, and Coyote agreed. Another marveled at the cunning of the Furthesters and at the dedication that had maintained the Surface Duty construct for so long, and he agreed some more. A third asked him for a few more details about the mindwives, and he refused.

"They're a sort of state geisha," he said. "Awarded like prizes to men who have done unusual public service. That's all I know."

"That is your full report, then?" asked the Fish.

"That's it."

"In that case, may we have the outrageous request?"

"I beg your pardon?"

"In that case," said the Fish firmly, "may we now hear the totally outrageous request that is the *reason* you insisted upon reporting to this body instead of just sending in a report in a normal fashion?"

"Well, there *is* something I want. Two somethings, as a matter of fact."

"I thought so. What?"

"I want a total blackout on the mindwife custom. On the grounds that it is an intrinsic part of the religious taboo complex of the Ahl Kres'sah."

"Done, of course," said the Fish. "That's quite routine. Now the other one—the outrageous one."

"I want an arbitrary one hundred year quarantine for Furthest," said Coyote, and then he sat down and let it all go on over his head.

Impossible. The scientists would want to go at once and observe these people. The anthropologists would want a chance at observation of a culture which still actually maintained the worship of an anthropomorphic god. The phonologist . . . such an interesting system of consonant clusters. The eugenicists . . . no other instance known of man/amphibian interbreeding. The dolphin experts, for that matter! My goodness. Oh deary me.

"Look," he said when it all began to die down a bit, "I appreciate all of these things you're saying. I realize that the observation of a planet like Furthest, with an artifact culture that's been isolated for a thousand years, would be a matter of intense interest to science. And I don't really care. These are people, not pieces of data. The scientists will just have to wait."

"On what grounds?" demanded the Fish.

"On the grounds that if you go in right now you'll break their culture to bits and destroy them, that's on what grounds."

"How can you maintain that?"

"Their whole lives," he said patiently, "their entire belief system, their religion, their conscription to Surface Duty, everything they do, is based upon the maintaining of these two big hairy secrets. Secrecy is the absolute foundation of their every move. And now they must be told that neither secret is of the slightest importance—"

"And how are they going to learn that?"

"I am going back and tell them about it," said Coyote. "At government expense. And when they learn that, when they learn that they have devoted their lives, and their parents and grandparents have devoted their lives, to the service of something that is entirely meaningless and stupid, it's going to be a profound cultural shock. It's not going to be a small thing for them. You're going to have to give them time to readjust—time uninterrupted by a flood of prying poking scientists and tourists. I'm sorry if that's inconvenient, but it has to be like that."

"But look here, man," cried a member of the board, "if they are told that and given one hundred years to rearrange things, it will no longer *be* an artifact culture! You'll have destroyed the very things that would be most valuable to science!"

"That's tough," said Coyote.

"You can't do it like that!"

"If you don't do it that way," he told them, "you'll have destroyed a people. I think that's more important than the data the scientists want to look at. Even this way, even my way, the Furthesters may not make it, it may be more of a shock than they can bear. But at least they'll have a chance."

"But—"

Coyote cut off the protester with a wave of his hand. "No," he said firmly. "Just no. It would be all wrong. I've been there, okay? I am the expert on this subject, and I tell you it would be all wrong. Submit it to the computers, give them the data I brought you, and ask them—they'll back me up."

The Fish was nodding his head at the opposite end of the table. "He's right," he told the others. "Unfortunately. I don't like it, but he's right. He usually is."

"Give me whatever you want in the way of equipment," Coyote said, by way of comfort. "I'll take films, record measurements, do threedies, anything you like. I'll bring back enough data on the state of the culture right now, before it begins to change, to make a tremendous contribution to all the sciences that would be interested. Just guarantee me the century quarantine."

There was a good deal of sighing and moaning and regretting.

"Do I have it?" Coyote insisted.

"You have it," said the Fish with decision. "Nasty. But you have the quarantine. We'll send the directive down to the Council—computer-supported, of course."

Coyote let out his breath in a long sigh of relief. He had been a little scared he wouldn't be able to bring it off.

"I'll go back and tell them, then," he said softly. "I want to leave in twenty-four hours; you've got that long to get me a list of the experiments, pictures, tapes, all that stuff that you want, and the equipment to do it with. Then I'm leaving."

"Twenty-four hours?" asked the Fish sarcastically. "I suppose that's so you can go see Miss Tzana Kai?"

It hadn't been, but it sounded good. He could always do with seeing Tzana.

"That's right," he said. "Don't you wish you could?"

# CHAPTER FIFTEEN

"There is only one sort of love that has any value,
and that is the love that leaves the beloved free.
All the rest is sickness."

(from the Devotional Book of Tham O'Kent)

IT SEEMED TO COYOTE that he had spent the
majority of his time since he arrived on Furthest in two
activities—bewildered waiting, and astonished staring. It
was the latter of the two that was occupying him now.

He had arrived just after dawn and had all but run
back to the MESH, his eagerness to see Bess and to pass
on his good news so great that it was not even dampened
by the monstrous list of scientific crap that he was supposed to do in the few months that remained to him here.
And now he was faced with something that had done
more than just dampen his enthusiasm; it had totally destroyed it.

The sign on the front of the MESH, dim in the early
light, was most explicit: CLOSED BY ORDER OF THE GOV-
ERNMENT—TRESPASSERS WILL BE SEVERELY PUNISHED.
And underneath, a comsystem number for emergencies.
It wasn't something he had expected to have to deal with.

There was a public comset at the corner, and at this
hour he would not have to wait to use it. He headed for
the intersection at a fast walk that turned into a run, inserted his credit disc in the slot, punched out the number
from the sign, and got a servomechanism which, after
hearing that he had neither fire nor burglary to report,

refused to discuss anything else with him. Now what?

He sat down on the stone curb with his head in his hands and tried to think, fighting a sense that something was more than just casually wrong. A jeebie chimed, close by his ear, and he didn't move a muscle; a cold wind whined all around him. He wondered if Furthest was about to enter its equivalent of a winter season, and supposed it must be; he didn't remember ever feeling cold here before.

Obviously, if the MESH had been closed by the government, something had happened to Bess, and perhaps something had also happened to RK, and neither of those somethings was likely to be anything nice. In addition, it was perfectly possible that he himself was under some sort of sentence, although it was unlikely that he would have been allowed to land if that had been the case. He hoped. What with the damned starship having had to be repaired, and the bloody scientists having talked him into giving them extra time to get their lists together, and the ship having to go around a meteor storm, one damned delay after another, it had been seven months since he'd left Furthest. One hell of a lot of things could have happened, in seven long months.

"Are you ill, Citizen?"

"Ill?"

He looked up into the face of a tall Furthester male, seemingly ten feet tall, in a costume of purple and black with high black boots. He hadn't seen those before either; they must be something that came out for this season.

"No, thank you, Citizen," said Coyote. "I'm just thinking."

"On a curb?"

"I was just leaving," Coyote told him. "Relax. I haven't defaced your kluthatz curb."

He left the outraged man staring after him and walked away. He knew where to go because there was only one possible choice. That was the home of RK's parents. If they didn't know what had happened to their children then he would have to tear the planet apart. In scuba gear. But he could try the Qu'e's first.

He took two wrong turnings before he found the right

house, and as he looked his tension grew, and the conviction that he was too late.

Tzana Kai had asked him what he was going to do.

"What am I going to do about what?"

"About Bess, Coyote," she had said. "You can't just leave her there—sooner or later she would be caught."

"I know."

"So what are you going to do?"

"Tzana, damn it to hell—"

"Never mind damning it to hell," she had said firmly, nudging him over onto his stomach so she could rub his back. "Damning it to hell won't help her. You know what I want you to do?"

"Tell me."

"Bring her to me, Coyote. I can easily make one of these rooms watertight and keep it filled with water for her. And no one would dare touch her if I had her with me."

"It's a good idea, Tzana."

"Of course it is."

It was, too. Tzana's home, like the offices of the translation bureau that was her cover, was entirely made of inflatable plastic bubble chambers. It would be no problem to convert one for Bess, and Tzana was right; as a TGIS agent she could claim virtual immunity to any sort of harassment for herself and her household.

"I don't know that she'd be willing to come, Tzana," he said.

"You could ask her. That's more useful than damning it to hell."

"I'll ask her, all right?"

"All right."

The major problem then had seemed to him to be getting Bess off Furthest to begin with, without her being taken away from him by the Furthester police. He hadn't been sure it could be done. Now that problem seemed relatively minor—all he wanted to do was find her.

He knocked on the Qu'e's' door, seething, and shuffled his feet impatiently, while minutes went by and no one answered. And then at last the door opened and there stood RK.

"Citizen Jones!" the boy shouted. "Mother. . . . Father. . . . It's Citizen Jones! He's back!"

There was the sound of running feet on the stairs, and both of the parents appeared, arms and hands held out to greet him. He couldn't imagine what was the source of this sudden informality, but he returned their greetings with all the warmth he could muster through his worry, until he could contain his impatience no longer.

"Please. . . ." he said at last. "Please tell me what's happened to Bess."

RK opened his mouth and his father put a firm hand across it.

"She's all right," said Citizen Qu'e. "We want to tell you all that has happened, and what has happened to her. But not here in the doorway. Not like this."

"Could we take him down into the water?" his wife asked breathlessly. "It would be so much better. . . . He could wear diving equipment . . . it—"

"You know that's not allowed."

"But Father, Surface Duty is a farce now, a completely unnecessary farce. So there's a regulation forbidding anyone on Surface Duty from going below the surface—it's meaningless!"

Citizen Qu'e shook his head at his son. "RK, I wish you were right. Unfortunately, the laws have not been repealed, pending the report your friend here is bringing back from the galactic government."

"But everyone knows already!" RK protested.

"How could they know?" Coyote asked, bewildered. "Would someone please explain all this to me?"

RK's father nodded. "Come with us," he said. "We'll go up to the water garden, and we can tell you there. But first we have something to show you. Will you follow me, please?"

Coyote was sick with impatience, but it was obvious to him that he was going to accomplish nothing by objecting. He would be told as it suited them to tell him, and in no other way, and there was nothing he could do about it. The Fish would have been pleased to see that tactic used against him for a change.

He followed them up the steps and down the corridor, and then into a small stone chamber on the right of the hall.

"Look there," said RK's mother gently. "See what we have for you?"

"What is it?" he asked, staring around him at the

usual set of bare walls, stone tables, chairs of warm loving nutwood.

"There," RK said. "Look there in the corner, Citizen. Go see what Bess left for you."

What do you say? He looked and looked and waited for appropriate words to come, something suitable for the occasion, but all he managed, finally, was, "Can I hold it?"

"It's your own baby," said Citizen Qu'e. "Of course you may hold it."

He picked up the warm little body and held it close, expecting to be awkward, but finding that he wasn't awkward at all; the child fit into the curve of his arm and lay confident against his chest, as if he had always held it there.

"Bring the baby along," said Citizen Qu'e. "Bring her with you and we'll go up to the garden."

"Her? It's a little girl, then?"

"Her name is Ratha. Bess chose that especially because it is one of the few names in our speech that you would be able to pronounce easily. And it's a good name, as well; the Ratha is a kind of high grass, pale green and very lovely."

And when they were seated beside the running water on the upper floor, the baby close in his arms, he asked them.

"Where is Bess?"

"I think you already know," said her father, his voice harsh with his own grief.

"I know that something is deeply wrong. That's all I really do know."

RK's mother spoke then, biting off her words like stones, "You are being cruel, husband. There is no excuse for putting it off just because you find it difficult to say, not when you are tormenting him like that. Citizen Jones, Bess has undergone her sentence. She was taken away and she has undergone Erasure, and there it is."

The pain of it might well be bearable later. Now what was important was not to drop the child that Bess had borne him. He took a deep breath and waited until he could control his voice, and said, "How did it happen?"

"I will tell you," said RK. "In a way it was my fault."

"No, son," said his mother. "There was nothing else you could have done."

"We were alone, you see," RK went on, "and no one except Bess and I knew about the child, and her time came early. And I was afraid. She was unconscious, and the pain had been so terrible, there was so much blood —Citizen Jones, forgive me, I did not know what to do. I went for a doctor because I was afraid that Bess would die."

"And he turned her in?"

RK nodded. "We thought perhaps he would not, because he waited a week. But then they came. The police, I mean. And they took her away, and closed the MESH, as you saw it, and I took the child and came here to my parents."

"He should have come to us sooner," said Citizen Qu'e. "If he had, perhaps something could have been done before the time came for the child to be born. But he was afraid we would not understand."

"And Bess forbid it absolutely," added RK. "She would not have it that I should involve our father and mother as well."

Erasure. There was a final sort of punishment for you. It meant that somewhere, depending on just how long it had been, there was a tall strong woman who had been Bess but was no longer. Her mind would be empty as a cave. They would have changed her face, made sure that no one would recognize her and punish her for a crime she no longer even remembered. Someone, patiently, would be teaching her once again all those things she needed to know to function as a citizen of the galaxies. How to walk. How to dress herself. How to talk. How to read and write. How to fill some useful slot.

How do you bear what you cannot bear?

"I didn't know," he said wonderingly. "I didn't know how much I loved her. And now I can't tell her."

How could it be that he had not realized until she was irrevocably gone from him how much she had meant to him? Why had he not taken her with him when he left the first time? Because he was a foolish arrogant man for whom treasures had been thrown down with no payment asked in return, and he had walked away and left them without even thinking.

RK's mother reached over and touched his hand, a

gesture he appreciated because he knew its rarity among these people.

"Bess knew," she said.

"Nevertheless," said Coyote, "I wish I had told her. It was one thing to know, and it was another to hear me say it. Perhaps she felt a need to hear those words from me, and I was too stupid to know."

"Enough," said Citizen Qu'e firmly. "Enough and too much. It is a thing that has been done and is over. We cannot forget, but we must go on now, for ourselves and for this child. When I told you Bess was all right, Citizen, I meant it—she has no burden to bear, she remembers nothing. It is we who have the grief of it. And now we must put that grief aside and think of what there is to do."

"You are quite right," said Coyote. "We will do as you say, as far as it is possible. And I have some questions."

"Shall I take the child?" asked RK's mother.

"No." He shook his head. "No, I want to hold her, it comforts me. Tell me what the situation is now. Is there a sentence on RK, for instance? Was he charged with complicity?"

"Oh, no," said Citizen Qu'e. "He's far too young. They simply assumed that Bess had used her mental abilities, which they knew to be strong beyond their comprehension, to force him to hide her and do what she wanted. He was reproved, scolded a bit. That's all. And as for us, since we knew nothing of it at all, there was no question of our being held responsible in any way."

"That's all good," said Coyote with satisfaction. "And what about me? Am I a fugitive?"

"Bess took good care of that," her father laughed. "She was a very clever woman."

"What did she do?"

"Well, like any other society, my friend, we have unfortunate newsmedia that capitalize on the scandalous and the sensational. Bess had prepared a full 'confession' of her so-called crimes long before they came for her, in anticipation of something like what did actually happen. When she heard the knock at the door and they knew it was the police, she had RK delay them long enough for her to send the full text she had prepared, by comsystem, to one of our scandal sheets. And they printed it, of course."

"But what did she say?"

"That she was a wicked, wicked woman. That she had fallen in love with an offworlder. That she had used her vicious mental wiles to ensnare you and force you to do as she wanted, and that you had been helpless against her. That she had manipulated her brother as she had you, for the sake of her hopeless passion."

"I'm going to be sick," said Coyote.

"No!" said Citizen Qu'e. "Listen, it was genuinely clever. It cleared you completely of any complicity, it made it impossible that anyone should persecute this child, it cleared Ahr, it left the guilt wholly upon Bess, who was under final sentence in any event."

"Not only that," said RK's mother, "but it gave her a motive that the Ahl Kres'sah could understand. Guilty passion, irresistible love that drives one to unspeakable crimes, all that has a long tradition for our people. In a certain sense, it cleared her of guilt, too. Not in the eyes of the government, or of our church, of course, but the majority of people will forget the crimes that she committed against the state and concentrate on her 'betrayal' of our people to an offworlder for the sake of an overpowering love."

Coyote frowned. "You are telling me," he said, "that they will forget that she was a revolutionary, and remember her as a lovestruck fool?"

"Yes, yes. That's just what I mean," said the woman, beaming at him, apparently pleased that he understood. And surprised? Possibly.

"I see," he said.

He did see. He saw very well. That she should have done that for him was amazing, and if she'd been around he'd have told her precisely what he thought of it. He wasn't about to let her get away with it, either, clever or not, but there was no point in upsetting her parents in advance by telling them what he planned to do, so he let it go by.

"Citizen Qu'e? Citizenness?"

They looked at him expectantly.

"I want to take the child with me," he said.

"We expected that you would."

"There are arrangements that I must make, though," he went on. "I will be here perhaps two weeks, tying up details with your government and carrying out some commissions given me by the scientists of the Inner Galaxies. I must find out if Ratha can safely travel in hibernation, and arrange for her passage, or for both of us to take a slowship if she cannot. May I leave her with you during that time?"

"You may," said Citizen Qu'e. "And you will stay here with us. In that way you will not have to be separated from the child and she will learn to know you before she leaves with you. Will that be satisfactory?"

"That is very satisfactory," said Coyote. "I thank you with all my heart."

"And what will you do first?" asked RK's mother, still smiling at him.

"I am going to go for a walk," he said.

"On the surface?"

"On the surface."

He had to have privacy. He had to think. Tomorrow he was to make a public telecast to the entire population of this planet, and he had a few changes to make in his planned speech. A hysterical lovesick woman swept by passion, indeed! *That* he could do something about.

# CHAPTER SIXTEEN

"... AND SO YOU SEE, people of Ahl Kres'sah," he said, "you see that she was something more than just a woman who had the misfortune to be overfond of me. She was something a great deal more important than that.

"She was a woman who saw, before anyone else did, that you were a people enslaved by a myth. She was a woman who saw that you were being held back, as surely as if you had been shut away behind impenetrable doors, from the freedom that it really is to be a citizen of the Tri-Galactic Federation today.

"For the sake of all of you, in order that you might enjoy that freedom, in order that the undignified and miserable burden of an ancient conscription that had turned into a meaningless masquerade might be lifted from your shoulders, Bess gave me the information that I had to have. She saw past the meaningless restrictions and the ludicrous secrecy that was imposed upon you, saw far enough and clear enough to know where her duty lay, and she sacrificed herself for you, for every last one of you.

"She knew that she would not be believed if she tried to explain what she had done, and she knew that I could not return in time to save her. Nonetheless, knowing full well what lay ahead of her, she gave me the information that I set before the government of these galaxies, the information that will allow you people to go where you will, to move freely, to learn, to share the multitude of advances that are truly your right as galactic citizens, and that have been denied you.

221

"She has set you free from slavery, and for that she has had her mind taken from her and Erased. If you remember her only for the crime of passion to which she confessed—to protect me, and to protect her family—you are unworthy of the sacrifice that she has made. You are to remember her as she should be remembered, as a heroine, as one who has brought you out of a slavery of centuries, as one who ignored the danger that she knew was certain, in order that all of you might at last take your rightful place among the people of the Tri-Galactic Federation. . . ."

That he was laying it on a bit thick, he knew perfectly well. He was quite sure that Bess could not have listened to it with a straight face. It served her right.

# BOOK III

## At the Seventh Level

## Prologue

# FOR THE SAKE OF GRACE

The Khadilh ban-harihn frowned at the disk he held in his hand, annoyed and apprehensive. There was always, of course, the chance of malfunction in the com-system. He reached forward and punched the transmit button again with one thumb, and the machine clicked to itself fitfully and delivered another disk in the message tray. He picked it up, looked at it and swore a round assortment of colorful oaths, since no women were present.

There on the left was the matrix-mark that identified his family, the ban-harihn symbol quite clear; no possibility of error there. And from it curled the suitable number of small lines, yellow for the females, green for the males, one for each member of his household, all decorously in order. Except for one.

The yellow line that represented at all times the state of being of his wife, the Khadilha Althea, was definitely not as it should have been. It was interrupted at quarter-inch intervals by a small black dot, indicating that all was not well with the Khadilha. And the symbol at the end of the line was not the blue cross that would have classified the difficulty as purely physical; it was the indeterminate red star indicating only that the problem, whatever it was, could be looked upon as serious or about to become serious.

The Khadilh sighed. That could mean anything, from his wife's misuse of their credit cards through a security leak by one of her servants to an unsuitable love affair—although his own knowledge of the Khadilha's chilly nature made him consider the last highly unlikely. The only possible course for him was to ask for an immediate full report.

And just what, he wondered, would he do, if the report were to make it clear that he was needed at home at once? One did not simply pick up one's gear and tootle off home from the outposts of the Federation. It would take him at the very least nine months to arrive in his home city-cluster, even if he were able to command a priority flight with suspended-animation berths and warp facilities. Damn the woman anyway, what could she be up to?

He punched the button for voice transmittal, and the com-system began to hum at him, indicating readiness for dialing. He dialed, carefully selecting the planet code, since his last attempt to contact his home, on his wife's birthday, had resulted in a most embarrassing conversation with a squirmy-tentacled creature that he had gotten out of its (presumed) bed in the middle of its (presumed) sleep. And he'd had to pay in full for the call, too, all intergalactic communication being on a buyer-risk basis.

". . . three-three-two-three-two . . ." he finished, very cautiously, and waited. The tiny screen lit up, and the words "STAND BY" appeared, to be replaced in a few seconds by "SCRIBE (FEMALE) OF THE HOUSEHOLD BAN-HARIHN," which meant he had at least dialed correctly. The screen cleared and the words were replaced by the face of his household Scribe, so distorted by distance as to be only by courtesy a face, but with the ban-harihn matrix-mark superimposed in green and yellow across the screen as security.

He spoke quickly, mindful of the com-rates at this distance.

"Scribe ban-harihn, this morning the state-of-being disk indicated some difficulty in the condition of the Kha-dilha Althea. Please advise if this condition could be described as an emergency."

After the usual brief lag for conversion to symbols, the reply was superimposed over the matrix-mark, and the Khadilh thought as usual that these tiny intergalactic screens became so cluttered before a conversation was terminated that one could hardly make out the messages involved.

The message in this case was "Negative," and the Khadilh smiled; the Scribe was even more mindful than he of the cost of this transmittal.

He pushed the ERASE button and finished with, "Thank you, Scribe ban-harihn. You will then prepare at once a written report, in detail, and forward it to me by the fastest available means. Should the problem intensify to emergency point, I now authorize a com-system transmittal to that effect, to be initiated by any one of my sons. Terminate."

The screen went blank and the Khadilh, just for curiosity, punched one more time the state-of-being control. The machine delivered another disk, and sure enough, there it was again, black dots, red star and all. He threw it into the disposal, shrugged his shoulders helplessly and ordered coffee. There was nothing whatever that he could do until he received the Scribe's report.

However, if it should turn out that he had wasted the cost of an intergalactic transmittal on some petty household dispute, there was going to be hell to pay, he promised himself, and a suitable punishment administered to the Khadilha by the nearest official of the Women's Discipline Unit. There certainly ought to be some way to make the state-of-being codes a bit more detailed so that everything from war to an argument with a servingwoman didn't come across on the same symbol.

The report arrived by Tele-Bounce in four days. Very wise choice, he thought approvingly, since the Bounce machinery was totally automatic and impersonal. It was somewhat difficult to read, since the Scribe had specified that it was to be delivered to him without transcription other than into verbal symbols, and it was therefore necessary for him to scan a roll of yellow paper with a message eight symbols wide and seemingly miles long. He read only enough to convince him that no problem of discretion could possibly be involved, and then he ran the thing through the transcribe slot, receiving a standard letter on white paper in return.

"To the Khadilh ban-harihn," it read, "as requested, the following report from the Scribe of his household:

Three days ago, as the Khadilh is no doubt aware, the festival of the Spring Rains was celebrated here. The entire household, with the exception of the Khadilh himself, was present at a very large and elaborate procession held to mark the opening of the Alaharibahn-Khalida Trance Hours. A suitable spot for watching the procession, entirely in accordance with decorum, had been chosen by the Khadilha Althea, and the women of the household were standing in the second row along the edge of the street set aside for the women.

There had been a number of dancers, bands, and so on, followed by thirteen of the Poets of this city-cluster. The Poets had almost passed, along with the usual complement of exotic animals and mobile flowers and the like, and no untoward incident of any kind had occurred, when quite suddenly the Khadilh's daughter Jacinth was approached by (pardon my liberty of speech) the Poet Anna-Mary, who is, as the Khadilh knows, a female. The Poet leaned from her mount, indicating with her staff of bells that it was her wish to speak to the Khadilh's daughter, and halting the procession to do so. It was at this point that the incident occurred which has no doubt given rise to the variant marking in the state-of-being disk line for the Khadilha Althea. Quite unaccountably, the Khadilha, rather than sending the child forward to speak with the Poet (as would have been proper), grabbed the child Jacinth by the shoulders, whirling her around and covering her completely with her heavy robes so that she could neither speak nor see.

The Poet Anna-Mary merely bowed from her horse and signaled for the procession to continue, but she was quite white and obviously offended. The family made a show of participating in the rest of the day's observances, but the Khadilh's sons took the entire household home by mid-afternoon, thereby preventing the Khadilha from participating in the Trance Hours. This was no doubt a wise course.

What sequel there may have been to this, the Scribe does not know, as no announcement has been made to the household. The Scribe here indicates her respect and subservience to the Khadilh.

Terminate with thanks.

"Well!" said the Khadilh. He laid the letter down on the top of his desk, thinking hard, rubbing his beard with one hand.

What could reasonably be expected in the way of repercussions from a public insult to an elderly—and touchy —Poet? It was hard to say.

As the only female Poet on the planet, the Poet Anna-Mary was much alone; as her duties were not arduous, she had much time to brood. And though she was a Poet, she remained only a female, with the female's inferior reasoning powers. She was accustomed to reverent homage, to women holding up their children to touch the hem of her robe. She could hardly be expected to react with pleasure to an insult in public, and from a female.

It was at his sons that she would be most likely to strike, through the University, he decided, and he could not chance that. He had worked too hard, and they had worked too hard, to allow a vindictive female, no matter how lofty her status, to destroy what they had built up. He had better go home and leave the orchards to take care of themselves; important as the lush peaches of Earth were to the economy of his home planet, his sons were of even greater importance.

It was not every family that could boast of five sons in the University, all five selected by competitive examinations for the Major in Poetry. Sometimes a family might have two sons chosen, but the rest would be refused, as the Khadilh himself had been refused, and would then have to be satisfied with the selection of Law or Medicine or Government or some other of the Majors. He smiled proudly, remembering the respectful glances of his friends when each of his sons in turn had placed high in the examinations and had been awarded the Poet Major, his oldest son entering at the Fourth Level. And when the youngest had been chosen, thus releasing the oldest from the customary vow of celibacy—since to impose it would have meant the end of the family line, an impossible situation—the Khadilh had had difficulty in maintaining even a pretense of modesty. The meaning, of course, was that he would have as grandson the direct offspring of a Poet, something that had not happened within his memory or his father's memory. He had been given to understand, in fact, that it had been more than three hundred years since all sons of any one family had entered the Poetry courses. (A family having only one son was prohibited by law from entering the Poetry Examinations.)

Yes, he must go home, and to hell with the peaches of

Earth. Let them rot, if the garden-robots could not manage them.

He went to the com-system and punched through a curt transmittal of his intention, and then set to pulling the necessary strings to obtain a priority flight.

When the Khadilh arrived at his home, his sons were lined up in his study, waiting for him, each in the coarse brown student's tunic that was compulsory, but with the scarlet Poet's stripe around the hem to delight his eyes. He smiled at them, saying, "It is a pleasure to see you once more, my sons; you give rest to my eyes and joy to my heart."

Michael, the oldest, answered in kind.

"It is our pleasure to see you, Father."

"Let us all sit down," said the Khadilh, motioning them to their places about the study table that stood in the center of the room. When they were seated, he struck the table with his knuckles, in the old ritual, three times slowly.

"No doubt you know why I have chosen to abandon my orchards to the attention of the agrirobots and return home so suddenly," he said. "Unfortunately, it has taken me almost ten months to reach you. There was no more rapid way to get home to you, much as I wished for one."

"We understand, Father," said his oldest son.

"Then, Michael," went on the Khadilh, "would you please bring me up to date on the developments here since the incident at the procession of the Spring Rains."

His son seemed hesitant to speak, his black brows drawn together over his eyes, and the Khadilh smiled at him encouragingly.

"Come, Michael," he said, "surely it is not courteous to make your father wait in this fashion!"

"You will realize, Father," said the young man slowly, "that it has not been possible to communicate with you since the time of your last transmittal. You will also realize that this matter has not been one about which advice could easily be requested. I have had no choice but to make decisions as best I could."

"I realize that. Of course."

"Very well, then. I hope you will not be angry, Father."

"I shall indeed be angry if I am not told at once exactly what has occurred this past ten months. You make me uneasy, my son."

Michael took a deep breath and nodded. "All right, Father," he said. "I will be brief."

"And quick."

"Yes, Father. I took our household away from the festival as soon as I decently could without creating talk; and when we arrived at home, I sent the Khadilha at once to her quarters, with orders to stay there until you should advise me to the contrary."

"Quite right," said the Khadilh. "Then what?"

"The Khadilha disobeyed me, Father."

"Disobeyed you? In what way?"

"The Khadilha Althea disregarded my orders entirely, and she took our sister into the Small Corridor, and there she allowed her to look into the cell where our aunt is kept, Father."

"What!" shouted the Khadilh. "And you made no move to stop her?"

"Father," said Michael ban-harihn, "you must realize that no one could have anticipated the actions of the Khadilha Althea. We would certainly have stopped her had we known, but who would have thought that the Khadilha would disobey the order of an adult male? It was assumed that she would go to her quarters and remain there."

"I see."

"I did not contact the Women's Discipline Unit," Michael continued. "I preferred that such an order should come from you, Father. However, orders were given that the Khadilha should be restricted to her quarters, and no one has been allowed to see her except the servingwomen. The wires to her com-system were disconnected, and provision was made for suitable medication to be added to her diet. You will find her very docile, Father."

The Khadilh was trembling with indignation.

"Discipline will be provided at once, my son," he said. "I apologize for the disgusting behavior of the Khadilha. But please go on—what of my daughter?"

"That is perhaps the most distressing thing of all."

"In what way?"

Michael looked thoroughly miserable.

"Answer me at once," snapped the Khadilh, "and in full."

"Our sister Jacinth," said his second son, Nicolas, "was already twelve years of age at the time of the festival. When she returned from the Small Corridor, without notice to any one of us, she announced her intention by letter to the Poet Anna-Mary—her intention to compete in the examinations for the Major of Poetry."

"And the Poet Anna-Mary—"

"Turned the announcement immediately over to the authorities at the Poetry Unit," finished Michael. "Certainly she made no attempt to dissuade our sister."

"She is amply revenged then for the insult of the Khadilha," said the Khadilh bitterly. "Were there any other acts on the part of the Poet Anna-Mary?"

"None, Father. Our sister has been cloistered by government order since that time, of course, to prevent contamination of the other females."

"How," breathed the Khadilh, "*how* could such a thing have touched my household—for the second time?"

He thought a moment. "When are the examinations, then? I've lost all track of time."

"It has been ten months, Father."

"In about a month, then?"

"In three weeks."

"Will they let me see Jacinth?"

"No, Father," said Michael. "And, Father—"

"Yes, Michael?"

"It is my shame and my sorrow that this should have been the result of your leaving your household in my care."

The Khadilh reached over and grasped his hand firmly.

"You are very young, my son," he said, "and you have nothing to be ashamed of. When the females of a household take it upon themselves to upset the natural order of things and to violate the rules of decency, there is very little anyone can do."

"Thank you, Father."

"Now," said the Khadilh, turning to face them all, "I suggest that the next thing to do would be to initiate action by the Women's Discipline Unit. Do you wish me to have the Khadilha placed on Permanent Medication, my sons?"

He hoped they would not insist upon it, and was pleased to see that they did not.

"Let us wait, Father," said Michael, "until we know the outcome of the examinations."

"Surely the outcome is something about which there can be no question!"

"Could we wait, Father, all the same?"

It was the youngest of the boys. As was natural, he was still overly squeamish, still a bit tender. The Khadilh would not have had him be otherwise.

"A wise decision," he said. "In that case, once I have bathed and had my dinner, I will send for the Lawyer an-ahda. And you may go, my sons."

The boys filed out, led by the solemn Michael, leaving him with no company but the slow dance of a mobile flower from one of the tropical stars. It whirled gently in the middle of the corner hearth, humming to itself and giving off showers of silver sparks from time to time. He watched it suspiciously for a moment, and then pushed the com-system buttons for his Housekeeper. When the face appeared on the screen he snapped at it.

"Housekeeper, are you familiar with the nature of the mobile plant that someone has put in my study?"

The Housekeeper's voice, frightened, came back at once. "The Khadilh may have the plant removed—should I call the Gardener?"

"All I wanted to know is the sex of the blasted thing," he bellowed at her. "Is it male or female?"

"Male, Khadilh, of the genus——"

He cut off the message while she was still telling him of the plant's pedigree. It was male; therefore it could stay. He would talk to it, while he ate his dinner, about the incredible behavior of his Khadilha.

The Lawyer an-ahda leaned back in the chair provided for him and smiled at his client.

"Yes, ban-harihn," he said amiably, having known the Khadilh since they were young men at the University, "what can I do to help the sun shine more brightly through your window?"

"This is a serious matter," said the Khadilh.

"Ah."

"You heard—never mind being polite and denying it —of my wife's behavior at the procession of the Spring Rains. I see that you did."

"Very impulsive," observed the Lawyer. "Most unwise. Undisciplined."

"Indeed it was. However, worse followed."

"Oh? The Poet Anna-Mary has tried for revenge, then?"

"Not in the sense that you mean, no. But worse has happened, my old friend, far worse."

"Tell me." The Lawyer leaned forward attentively, listening, and when the Khadilh had finished, he cleared his throat.

"There isn't anything to be done, you know," he said, "You might as well know it at once."

"Nothing at all?"

"Nothing. The law provides that any woman may challenge and claim her right to compete in the Poetry Examinations, provided she is twelve years of age and a citizen of this planet. If she is not accepted, however, the penalty for having challenged and failed is solitary confinement for life, in the household of her family. And once she has announced to the Faculty by signed communication that she intends to compete, she is cloistered until the day of the examinations, and she may not change her mind. The law is very clear on this point."

"She is very young."

"She is twelve. That is all the law requires."

"It's a cruel law."

"Not at all! Can you imagine, ban-harihn, the chaos that would result if every emotional young female, bored with awaiting marriage in the women's quarters, should decide that she had a vocation and claim her right to challenge? The purpose of the law is to discourage foolish young girls from creating difficulties for their households, and for the state. Can you just imagine, if there were only a token penalty, and chaperons had to be provided by the Faculty, and separate quarters provided, and——"

"Yes, I suppose I see! But why should women be allowed to compete at all? No such idiocy is allowed in the other Professions."

"The law provides that since the Profession of Poetry is a religious office, there must be a channel provided for the rare occasion when the Light might see fit to call a female to Its service."

"What nonsense!"

"There is the Poet Anna-Mary, ban-harihn."

"And how many others?"

"She is the third."

"In nearly ten thousand years! Only three in so many centuries, and yet no exception can be made for one little twelve-year-old girl?"

"I am truly sorry, my friend," said the Lawyer. "You could try a petition to the Council, of course, but I am quite sure—*quite* sure—that it would be of no use. There is too much public reaction to a female's even attempting the examinations, because it seems blasphemous even to many very broad-minded people. The Council would not dare to make an exception."

"I could make a galactic appeal."

"You could."

"There would be quite a scandal, you know, among the peoples of the galaxies, if they knew of this penalty being enforced on a child."

"My friend, my dear ban-harihn—think of what you are saying. You would create an international incident, an intergalactic international incident, with all that implies, bring down criticism upon our heads, most surely incur an investigation of our religious customs by the intergalactic police, which would in turn call for a protest from our government, which in its turn——"

"You know I would not do it."

"I hope not. It would parallel the Trojan War for folly, my friend—all that for the sake of one female child!"

"We are a barbaric people."

The Lawyer nodded. "After ten thousand years, you know, if barbarism remains it becomes very firmly entrenched."

The Lawyer rose to go, throwing his heavy blue cloak around him. "After all," he said, "it is only one female child."

It was all very well, thought the Khadilh when his friend was gone, all very well to say that. The Lawyer no doubt never had had the opportunity to see the result of a lifetime of solitary confinement in total silence, or he would have been less willing to see a child condemned to such a fate.

The Khadilh's sister had been nearly thirty, and yet unmarried, when she had chosen to compete, and she was forty-six now. It had been an impulse of folly, born of thirty years of boredom, and the Khadilh blamed his parents. Enough dowry should have been provided to make even Grace, ugly as she was, an acceptable bride for someone, somewhere.

The room in the Small Corridor, where she had been confined since her failure, had no window, no comset, nothing. Her food was passed through a slot in one wall, as were the few books and papers which she was allowed —all these things being very rigidly regulated by the Women's Discipline Unit.

It was the duty of the Khadilha Althea to go each morning to the narrow grate that enclosed a one-way window into the cell and to observe the prisoner inside. On the two occasions when that observation had disclosed physical illness, a dart containing an anesthetic had been fired through the food slot, and Grace had been rendered unconscious for the amount of time necessary to let a Doctor enter the cell and attend to her. She had had sixteen years of this, and it was the Khadilha who had had to watch her, through the first years when she alternately lay stuporous for days and then screamed and begged for release for days . . . now she was quite mad. The Khadilh had observed her on two occasions when his wife had been too ill to go, and he had found it difficult to believe that the creature who crawled on all fours from one end of the room to the other, its matted hair thick with filth in spite of the servomechanisms that hurried from the walls to retrieve all waste and dirt, was his sister. It gibbered and whined and clawed at its flesh—it was hard to believe that it was human. And it had been only sixteen years. Jacinth was twelve!

The Khadilh called his wife's quarters and announced to her servingwomen that they were all to leave her. He went rapidly through the corridors of his house, over the delicate arched bridge that spanned the tea gardens around the women's quarters, and into the rooms where she stayed. He found her sitting in a small chair before her fireplace, watching the mobile plants that danced there to be near the warmth of the fire. As his sons had said, she was quite docile, and in very poor contact with reality.

He took a capsule from the pocket of his tunic and gave it to her to swallow, and when her eyes were clear of the mist of her drugged dreams, he spoke to her.

"You see that I have returned, Althea," he said. "I

wish to know why my daughter has brought this ill fortune upon our household."

"It is her own idea," said the Khadilha in a bitter voice. "Since the last of her brothers was chosen, she has been thus determined, saying that it would be a great honor for our house should all of the children of ban-harihn be accepted for the faith."

It was as if a light had been turned on.

"This was not an impulse, then!" exclaimed the Khadilh.

"No. Since she was nine years old she has had this intention."

"But why was I not told? Why was I given no opportunity——" He stopped abruptly, knowing that he was being absurd. No women would bother her husband with the problems of rearing a female child. But now he began to understand.

"She did not even know," his wife was saying, "that there was a living female Poet, although she had heard from someone that such a possibility existed. It was, she insisted, a matter of knowledge of the heart. When the Poet Anna-Mary singled her out at the procession . . . why, then, she was sure. Then she knew, she said, that she had been chosen."

Of course. That in itself, being marked out for notice before the crowd, would have convinced the child that her selection was ordained by Divine choice. He could see it all now. And the Khadilha had taken the child to see her aunt in her cell in a last desperate attempt to dissuade her.

"The child is strong willed for a female," he mused, "if the sight of poor Grace did not shake her."

His wife did not answer, and he sat there, almost too tired to move. He was trying to place the child Jacinth in his mind's eye, but it was useless. It had been at least four years since he had seen her, dressed in a brief white shift that all little girls wore: he remembered a slender child, he remembered dark hair—but then all little girls among his people were slender and dark-haired.

"You don't even remember her," said his wife, and he jumped, irritated at her shrewdness.

"You are quite right," he said. "I don't. Is she pretty?"

"She is beautiful. Not that it matters now."

The Khadilh thought for a moment, watching his wife's

stoic face, and then, choosing his words with care, he said, "It had been my intention to register a complaint with the Women's Discipline Unit for your behavior, Khadilha Althea."

"I expected you to do so."

"You have a good deal of experience with the agents of the WDU—the prospect does not upset you?"

"I am indifferent to it."

He believed her. He remembered very well the behavior of his wife at her last impregnation, for it had required four agents from the Unit to subdue her and fasten her to their marriage bed. And yet he knew that many women went willingly, even eagerly, to their appointments with their husbands. It was at times difficult for him to understand why he had not had Althea put on Permanent Medication from the very beginning; certainly, it would not have been difficult to secure permission to take a second, more womanly wife. Unfortunately he was soft-hearted, and she had been the mother of his eldest son, and so he had put up with her, relying upon his concubines for feminine softness and ardor. Certainly Althea had hardened with the years, not softened.

"I have decided," he finished abruptly, "that your behavior is not so scandalous as I had thought. I am not sure I would not have reacted just as you did under the circumstances, if I had known the girl's plans. I will make no complaint, therefore."

"You are indulgent."

He scanned her face, still lovely for all her years, for signs of impertinence, but there were none, and he went on: "However, you understand our eldest son must decide for himself if he wishes to forego his own complaint. Your disobedience to him was your first, you know. *I* have become accustomed to it."

He turned on his heel and left her, amused at his own weakness, but he canceled the medication order when he went past the entrance to her quarters. She was a woman, she had meant to keep her daughter from becoming what Grace had become; it was not so hard to understand, after all.

The family did not go to the University on the day of the examinations. They waited at home, prepared for the inevitable as well as they could prepare.

Another room, near the room where Grace was kept, had been made ready by the weeping servingwomen, and it stood open now, waiting.

The Khadilh had had his wife released from her quarters for the day, since she would have only the brief moment with her daughter, and thereafter would have only the duty of observing her each morning as she did her sister-in-law. She sat at his feet in their common room, making no sound, her face bleached white, wondering, he supposed, what she would do now. She had no other daughter; there were no other sisters. She would be alone in the household except for her servingwoman, until such a time as Michael should, perhaps, provide her with a granddaughter. His heart ached for her, alone in a household of men, and five of them, before very long, to be allowed to speak only in the rhymed couplets of the Poets.

"Father?"

The Khadilh looked up, surprised. It was his youngest son, the boy James.

"Father," said the boy, "could she pass? I mean, is it possible that she could pass?"

Michael answered for him. "James, she is only twelve, and a female. She has had no education; she can only just barely read. Don't ask foolish questions. Don't you remember the examinations?"

"I remember," said James firmly. "Still, I wondered. There is the Poet Anna-Mary."

"The third in who knows how many hundreds of years, James," Michael said. "I shouldn't count on it if I were you."

"But is it possible?" the boy insisted. "Is it possible, Father?"

"I don't think so, son," said the Khadilh gently. "It would be a very curious thing if an untrained twelve-year-old female could pass the examinations that I could not pass myself, when I was sixteen, don't you think?"

"And then," said the boy, "she may never see anyone again, as long as she lives, never speak to anyone, never look out a window, never leave that little room?"

"Never."

"That is a cruel law!" said the boy. "Why has it not been changed?"

"My son," said the Khadilh. "it is not something that happens often, and the Council has many, many other things to do. It is an ancient law, and the knowledge that it exists offers to bored young females something exciting to think about. It is intended to frighten them, my son."

"One day, when I have power enough, I shall have it changed."

The Khadilh raised his hand to hush the laughter of the older boys. "Let him alone," he snapped. "He is young, and she is his sister. Let us have a spirit of compassion in this house, if we must have tragedy."

A thought occurred to him, then. "James," he said, "you take a great deal of interest in this matter. Is it possible that you were somehow involved in this idiocy of your sister's?"

At once he knew he had struck a sensitive spot; tears sprang to the boy's eyes and he bit his lip fiercely.

"James—in what way were you involved? What do you know of this affair?"

"You will be angry, my father," said James, "but that is not the worst. What is worse is that I will have condemned my sister to——"

"James," said the Khadilh, "I have no interest in your self-accusations. Explain at once, simply and without dramatics."

"Well, we used to practice, she and I," said the boy hastily, his eyes on the floor. "I did not think I would pass, you know. I could see it—all the others would pass, and I would not, and there I would be, the only one. People would say, 'There he goes, the only one of the sons of the ban-harihn who could not pass the Poetry exam.'"

"And?"

"And so we practiced together, she and I," he said. "I would set the subject and the form and do the first stanza, and then she would write the reply."

"When did you do this? Where?"

"In the gardens, Father, ever since she was little. She's very good at it, she really is, Father."

"She can rhyme? She knows the forms?"

"Yes, Father! And she is good, she has a gift for it— Father, she's much better than I am. I am ashamed to say that, of a female, but it would be a lie to say anything else."

The things that went on in one's household! The Khadilh was amazed and dismayed, and he was annoyed besides. Not that it was unusual for brothers and sisters,

while still young, to spend time together, but surely one of
the servants, or one of the family, ought to have noticed
that the two little ones were playing at Poetry?

"What else goes on in my house beneath the blind eyes
and deaf ears of those I entrust with its welfare?" he demanded furiously, and no one hazarded an answer. He
made a sound of disgust and went to the window to look
out over the gardens that stretched down to the narrow
river behind the house. It had begun to rain, a soft green
rain not much more than a mist, and the river was blurred
velvet through the veil of water. Another time he would
have enjoyed the view; indeed, he might well have sent for
his pencils and his sketching pad to record its beauty.
But this was not a day for pleasure.

Unless, of course, Jacinth did pass.

It was, on the face of it, an absurdity. The examinations
for Poetry were far different than those for the other
Professions. In the others it was a straightforward matter:
one went to the examining room, an examination was dis-
tributed, one spent perhaps six hours in such exams, and
they were then scored by computer. Then, in a few
days, there would come the little notice by comset, stating
that one had or had not passed the fitness exams for
Law or Business or whatever.

Poetry was a different matter. There were many de-
grees of fitness, all the way from the First Level, which
fitted a man for the lower offices of the faith, through
five more subordinate levels, to the Seventh Level. Very
rarely did anyone enter the Seventh Level. Since there
was no question of being promoted from one level to another, a man being placed at his appropriate rank by the
examinations at the very beginning, there were times
when the Seventh Level remained vacant for as long as a
year. Michael had been placed at the Fourth Level instead of the First, like the others of his sons, and the Khadilh had been awed at the implications.

For Poetry there was first an examination of the usual
kind, marked by hand and scored by machine, just as in
the other Professions. But then, if that exam was passed,
there was something unique to do. The Khadilh had not
passed the exam and he had no knowledge of what came
next, except that it involved the computers.

"Michael," he said, musing, "how does it go exactly,
the Poetry exam by the computer?"

Michael came over to stand beside him. "You mean, should Jacinth pass the written examination, even if just by chance, then what happens?"

"Yes. Tell me."

"It's simple enough. You go into the booths where the computer panels are and push a READY button. Then the computer gives you your instructions."

"For example?"

"Let's see. For example, it might say—SUBJECT: LOVE OF COUNTRY . . . FORM: SONNET. UNRESTRICTED BUT RHYMED . . . STYLE: FORMAL, SUITABLE FOR AN OFFICIAL BANQUET. And then you would begin."

"Are you allowed to use paper and pen, my son?"

"Oh, no, Father." Michael was smiling, no doubt, thought the Khadilh, at his father's innocence. "No paper or pencil. And you begin at once."

"No time to think?"

"No, Father, none."

"Then what?"

"Then, sometimes, you are sent to another computer, one that gives more difficult subjects. I suppose it must be the same all the way to the Seventh Level, except that the subject would grow more difficult."

The Khadilh thought it over. For his own office of Khadilh, which meant little more than "Administrator of Large Estates and Households," he had had to take one oral examination, and that had been in ordinary, straightforward prose, and the examiner had been a man, not a computer, and he still remembered the incredible stupidity of his answers. He had sat flabbergasted at the things that issued from his mouth, and he had been convinced that he could not possibly have passed the examination. And Jacinth was only twelve years old, with none of the training that boys received in prosody, none of the summer work-shops in the different forms, scarcely even an acquaintance with the history of the classics. Surely she would be too terrified to speak? Why, the simple modesty of her femaleness ought to be enough to keep her mute, and then she would fail, even if she should somehow be lucky enough to pass the written exam. Damn the girl!

"Michael," he asked, "what is the level of the Poet Anna-Mary?"

"Second Level, Father."

"Thank you, my son. You have been very helpful—you may sit down now, if you like."

He stood a moment more, watching the rain, and then went back and sat down again by his wife. Her hands flew, busy with the little needles used to make the complicated hoods the Poets wore. She was determined that her sons should, in accordance with the ancient tradition, have every stitch of their installation garments made by her hands, although no one would have criticized her if she had had the work done by others, since she had so many sons needing the garments. He was pleased with her, for once, and he made a mental note to have a gift sent to her later.

The bells rang in the city, signaling the four o'clock Hour of Meditation, and the Khadilh's sons looked at one another, hesitating. By the rules of their Major that hour was to be spent in their rooms, but their father had specifically asked that they stay with him.

The Khadilh sighed, making another mental note, that he must sigh less. It was an unattractive habit.

"My sons," he said, "you must conform to the rules of your Major. Please consider that my first wish."

They thanked him and left the room, and there he sat, watching first the darting fingers of the Khadilha and then the dancing of the mobile flowers, until shadows began to streak across the tiled floor of the room. Six o'clock came, and then seven, and still no word. When his sons returned, he sent them away crossly, seeing no reason why they should share in his misery.

By the time the double suns had set over the river he had lost the compassion he had counseled for the others and become furious with Jacinth as well as the system. That one insignificant female child could create such havoc for him and for his household amazed him. He began to understand the significance of the rule; the law began to seem less harsh. He had missed his dinner and he had spent his day in unutterable tedium. His orchards were doubtless covered with insects and dying of thirst and neglect, his bank account was depleted by the expense of the trip home, the cost of extra agrirobots on Earth, the cost of the useless visit from the Lawyer. And his nervous system was shattered, and the peace of his household destroyed. All this from the antics of one twelve-year-old female child! And when she had to be shut up, there would be the necessity of living with her mother as she watched the child deteriorate into a crawling mass of filth and madness as Grace had done. Was his family cursed, that its females should bring down the wrath of the universe at large in this manner?

He struck his fists together in rage and frustration, and the Khadilha jumped, startled.

"Shall I send for music, my husband?" she asked. "Or perhaps you would like to have your dinner served here? Perhaps you would like a good wine?"

"Perhaps a dozen dancing girls!" he shouted. "Perhaps a Venusian flame-tiger! Perhaps a parade of Earth elephants and a tentacle bird from the Extreme Moons! May all the suffering gods take pity upon me!"

"I beg your pardon," said the Khadilha. "I have angered you."

"It is not you who have angered me," he retorted; "it is that miserable female of a daughter that you bore me, who has caused me untold sorrow and expense, that has angered me!"

"Very soon now," pointed out the Khadilha softly, "she will be out of your sight and hearing forever; perhaps then she will anger you less."

The Khadilha's wit, sometimes put to uncomfortable uses, had been one of the reasons he had kept her all these years. At this moment, however, he wished her stupider and timider and a thousand light-years away.

"Must you be right, at a time like this?" he demanded. "It is unbecoming in a woman."

"Yes, my husband."

"It grows late."

"Yes, indeed."

"What could they be doing over there?"

He reached over to the comset and instructed the Housekeeper to send someone with a videocolor console. It was just possible that somewhere in the galaxy something was happening that would distract him from his misery.

He skimmed the videobands rapidly, muttering. There was a new drama by some unknown avant-garde playwright, depicting a liaison between the daughter of a Council member and a servomechanism. There was a game of jidra, both teams apparently from the Extreme Moons, if their size could be taken as any indication. There were half a dozen variety programs, each worse than the last. Finally he found a newsband and leaned forward, his ear caught by the words of the improbably sleek young man reading the announcements.

Had he said—yes! He had. He was announcing the results of the examinations in Poetry. "—ended at four o'clock this afternoon, with only eighty-three candidates accepted out of almost three thousand who—"

"Of course!" he shouted. How stupid he had been not to have realized, sooner, that since all members of Poetry were bound by oath to observe the four o'clock Hour of Meditation, the examinations would have had to end by four o'clock! But why, then, had no one come to notify them or to return their daughter? It was very near nine o'clock.

The smallest whisper of hope touched him. It was possible, just possible, that the delay was because even the callous members of the Poetry Unit were finding it difficult to condemn a little girl to a life of solitary confinement. Perhaps they were meeting to discuss it, perbers of the Poetry Unit on the comset. At once the law being found that could be used to prevent such a travesty of justice.

He switched off the video and punched the call numbers of the Poetry Unit on the comset. At once the screen was filled by the embroidered hood and bearded face of a Poet, First Level, smiling helpfully through the superimposed matrix-mark of his household.

The Khadilh explained his problem, and the Poet smiled and nodded.

"Messengers are on their way to your household at this moment, Khadilh ban-harihn," he said. "We regret the delay, but it takes time, you know. All these things take time."

"What things?" demanded the Khadilh. "And why are you speaking to me in prose? Are you not a Poet?"

"The Khadilh seems upset," said the Poet in a soothing voice. "He should know that those Poets who serve the Poetry Unit as communicators are excused from the laws of verse-speaking while on duty."

"Someone is coming now?"

"Messengers are on their way."

"On foot? By Earth-style robot-mule? Why not a message by comset?"

The Poet shook his head. "We are a very old profession, Khadilh ban-harihn. There are many traditions to be observed. Speed, I fear, is not among those traditions."

"What message are they bringing?"

"I am not at liberty to tell you that," said the Poet patiently.

Such control! thought the Khadilh. Such unending saintlike tolerance! It was maddening.

"Terminate with thanks," said the Khadilh, and turned off the bland face of the Poet. At his feet the Khadilha had set aside her work and sat trembling. He reached over and patted her hand, wishing there were some comfort he could offer.

Had they better go ahead and call for dinner? He wondered if either of them would be able to eat.

"Althea," he began, and at that moment the serving-woman showed in the messengers of the Poetry Unit, and the Khadilh rose to his feet.

"Well?" he demanded abruptly. He would be damned if he was going to engage in the usual interminable preliminaries. "Where is my daughter?"

"We have brought your daughter with us, Khadilh ban-harihn."

"Well, where is she?"

"If the Khadilh will only calm himself."

"I am calm! Now where is my daughter?"

The senior messenger raised one hand, formally, for silence, and in an irritating singsong he began to speak.

"The daughter of the Khadilh ban-harihn will be permitted to approach and to speak to her parents for one minute only, by the clock which I hold, giving to her parents whatever message of farewell she should choose. Once she has given her message, the daughter of the Khadilh will be taken away and it will not be possible for the Khadilh or his household to communicate with her again except by special petition from the Council."

The Khadilh was dumbfounded. He could feel his wife shaking uncontrollably beside him—was she about to cause a second scandal?

"Leave the room if you cannot control your emotion, Khadilha," he ordered her softly, and she responded with an immediate and icy calm of bearing. Much better.

"What do you mean," he asked the messenger, "by stating that you are about to take my daughter away again?

Surely it is not the desire of the Council that she be punished outside the confines of my house!"

"Punished?" asked the messenger. "There is no punishment in question, Khadilh. It is merely that the course of study which she must follow henceforth cannot be provided for her except at the Temple of the University."

It was the Khadilh's turn to tremble now. She had passed!

"Please," he said hoarsely, "would you make yourself clear? Am I to understand that my daughter has passed the examination?"

"Certainly," said the messenger. "This is indeed a day of great honor for the household of the ban-harihn. You can be most proud, Khadilh, for your daughter has only just completed the final examination and has been placed in Seventh Level. A festival will be declared, and an official announcement will be made. A day of holiday will be ordered for all citizens of the planet Abba, in all cities and city-clusters and throughout the countryside. It is a time of great rejoicing!"

The man went on and on, his curiously contrived-sounding remarks unwinding amid punctuating sighs and nods from the other messengers, but the Khadilh did not hear any more. He sank back in his chair, deaf to the list of the multitude of honors and happenings that would come to pass as a result of this extraordinary thing. Seventh Level! How could such a thing be?

Dimly he was aware that the Khadilha was weeping quite openly, and he used one numb hand to draw her veils across her face.

"Only one minute, by the clock," the messenger was saying. "You do understand? You are not to touch the Poet-Candidate, nor are you to interfere with her in any way. She is allowed one message of farewell, nothing more."

And then they let his daughter, this stranger who had performed a miracle, whom he would not even have recognized in a crowd, come forward into the room and approach him. She looked very young and tired, and he held his breath to hear what she would say to him.

However, it was no message of farewell that she had to give them. Said the Poet-Candidate, Seventh Level, Jacinth ban-harihn: "You will send someone at once to inform my Aunt Grace that I have been appointed to the Seventh

Level of the Profession of Poetry; permission has been granted by the Council for the breaking of her solitary confinement for so long as it may take to make my aunt understand just what has happened."

And then she was gone, followed by the messengers, leaving only the muted, tinkling showers of sparks from the dancing flowers and the soft drumming of the rain on the roof to punctuate the silence.

## Interlude

# THE ROLL OF IAMBS AND
# THE CLANG OF SPENDEES

"Father?"

"Yes, my son?" The eminent Doctor ban-Claryk spoke abstractedly, his mind not at all on the boy who sat at his side. He was watching the threedy projection that filled the corner of the room, spreading across the white wall of the living semblance of the hills outside the capital city of Abba. Alsabaid, the Jewel City, lay in the arm of the deep green river, and about it curved the even greener mountains, little more than hills now with their advanced age. The threedy moved in, outlining less sharply the panorama of summer day and sky, centering on the narrow gray bridge that spanned one loop of the river. The battle bridge.

"Father?" the boy said again, and ban-Claryk turned to face him, sorry for his discourtesy. To be discourteous to a child was only to ensure his future discourtesy to others.

"I'm sorry, Nilder," he said, "my mind was not here but out there, on that bridge. What is it?"

"Well," said the boy, "it seems to me that nothing's happening. How can it be a war—and nothing be happening?"

Doctor ban-Claryk shook his head at his son, smiling, but he spoke sternly.

"A war is not intended to 'be an entertainment for children," he said. "I told you, don't you remember, that there will be very little to see."

"But in my books, Father——"

"In your books, my son, you read of the ridiculous excesses of primitive civilizations! This is the thirty-first century, not the Dark Ages. It has been many thousands of years since any violence was allowed among our people, any sort of *spectacle* of battle."

The boy drew a sharp breath and leaned forward, staring in disbelief at the projection where figures were now moving in solemn procession onto the narrow bridge.

"Father!" he said, his voice thin with shock. "Father, that is a female at the head of the column!"

"It is indeed, Nilder."

"But how can a female fight in a war? Only the Poets are allowed to do battle!"

"And the Servicemen, who bear the pain."

"But the actual battle—that is for the Poets, Father!" Doctor ban-Claryk nodded sadly.

"Yes, my son," he said. "Precisely. And that is exactly what the war is about, you see."

On the bridge, alone in the whipping wind from the river, the Poet Jacinth ban-harihn stood in a battle robe of rough scarlet linen and waited for the challenger, her heart sick and heavy, her sorrow too deep even for tears. She had wept all the night before; now her eyes were dry and she felt her whole being dry too, a husk standing there for the wind to rattle.

At the crest of a low hill she saw a figure marching along at the head of an army identical in number and in dress to the one that stood in ranks on the banks of the river behind her. The battle bridge apparently noted his appearance as well, for the War Computer rose at once from the center of the bridge and stood, stolid and square, a barrier between the two Poets.

The Poet Avhador approached rapidly, took the bridge in three strides, and faced Jacinth across the War Computer's black back.

"Greetings, Poet Jacinth, on this day
    When you shall see your title torn away!"
said Avhador, inclining his head the ritual quarter of an inch due a female of high birth, but not the deep bow due a Poet.

Jacinth gathered her mind carefully, placing the rule of tranquillity upon herself without haste, her face blank of any reaction to his rudeness. She was determined not to allow his deliberate provocations to upset her in any way. The one hundred men who stood now at attention on the riverbank, five lines of twenty in black robes of war, wearing the ritual battle masks, were totally dependent upon her clearness of mind.

She smiled, when she was ready, and bowed deeply, the full ritual obeisance to a Poet, but she made no answer.

The War Computer waited, humming to itself, all its little buttons blinking their readiness. It was very sleek, and very black, and deadly in its efficiency. Jacinth loathed the sight of it.

"Father?"

"Yes?"

"What is going to happen now? What are they going to do?"

The Doctor shrugged. "It's quite simple. They are going to compose sixteen lines of poetry, in four sets of four lines—four quatrains. The pattern of rhyme must be abba, the subject must be the subject of the war. Since the Poet Avhador is the challenger he must give the first line. The Poet Jacinth will give the second, and Avhador must then give the third, which must rhyme with hers. The Poet Jacinth must then finish the quatrain with a fourth line, which must rhyme with the first one given by Avhador. The order then changes, with the Poet Jacinth giving the first line of the second quatrain."

"That's all?" the boy demanded.

"Yes. It's not difficult. It's the sort of form you do in school."

The boy considered for a moment.

"They should do something harder than that," he said scornfully, "if they're going to call it a war! That's only baby Poetry—I could do that!"

"Ah, but there's a difference," said his father.

"And what is that?"

"When small children compose a line of Poetry, no one else has to suffer if the line is not a good one."

"Oh. Oh, I see."

The boy was quiet for a moment, watching, and then he asked, "Father? What are they doing now?"

"Praying. I hope."

The Poet Jacinth was very much aware of her responsibility to the men who were her army. She shivered in the wind, damp and chill even now in early summer, and waited for the challenge.

Avhador raised his hands above his head. He was ready.

She held her breath; if she missed a word it would not be repeated.

"NO FEMALE MAY STAND IN THE PLACE OF A MAN!" Avhador flung at her, and dropped his arms to his sides.

She weighed the line rapidly, noting the trochaic meter, the subtle internal rhyme, the fact that he had challenged by stating the thesis of the war.

"YET THE LIGHT CAN CHOOSE ONLY THE RIGHT," she replied.

"AND A TAMPERING BROTHER MAY TRAVEL BY NIGHT!" shouted Avhador, not pausing even for a second.

Jacinth recoiled, her indrawn breath hissing through her teeth. The other was mad, to accuse her brothers of having tampered with the computers in the examinations that had named her a Poet! If he were to win the war he would be very fortunate indeed if he did not have to do battle again for the insult to her family.

"AND A FOOL MAKES THE NOISES HE CAN," she said with contempt, the line dropping from her tongue almost unconsciously.

And then she turned pale. She might well have sacrificed this quatrain for the sake of a flippant insult, badly stated, empty of internal rhyme. What *had* it had to recommend it? A minor hissing assonance, perhaps. She would have to be more careful, much more careful, of her temper.

The Poet Avhador ignored her, standing rigid and staring fixedly ahead. To be called a fool by a female, before all the watching citizenry of the planet, was very probably a possibility that had never occurred to him. And since he was bound by the rules of war he could neither insult her in return, nor call for a Women's Discipline Unit, nor even formally chastise her. The frustration of it showed in his face, which was alternately white with rage and flushed with humiliation.

The War Computer was making satisfied noises, humming and chuckling to itself, rapidly reviewing the four lines of the first quatrain.

"Now, Father, now what happens? What happens next?"

"Now comes the price of war," said ban-Claryk. "The Computer will judge the lines of the quatrain by rhyming pairs, and of each pair ít will choose that line which is superior. And then the pain centers will be activated."

"Father—is it a terrible pain?"

"It is direct stimulation of the pain centers of the brain, my son. There is no more dreadful agony known—and those men must stay on their feet as long as they are still alive."

"Some die, Father?"

"Some. The weaker ones."

"And the Poets feel no pain?"

"No, of course not."

"But that's not fair, Father!"

"My son," chided the man, "you are thinking like a woman. The lives of the armies depend upon the clarity of the Poets' minds, and the Poets can do battle only if they are at the peak of their attention. How could they function if they bore the pain of the War Computers? How could they compose? And you must realize, Nilder, what an unspeakable punishment it must be to hear the screams of agony from one hundred men standing behind you who have counted on you to see that they were spared that agony."

As he spoke a small panel on the front of the War Computer lit up, and the screams rose, screams more like the howling of maddened animals than the cries of men. The howling seemed to last forever, although each administration of pain was limited to forty seconds, with a respite of twenty seconds before the next one. What, ban-Claryk wondered, must it be like during that respite, knowing that the second dose of punishment was almost upon you? He shuddered.

"Father?"

"Yes?"

"I don't want to see any more, Father."

"But you must," said ban-Claryk grimly. "You must see what war is like—perhaps then when you are grown you will not be a party to such folly."

"But why are they doing it, Father? How can they do such things?"

"Well," said the man, biting off the words as if they tasted foul to him, "although the Holy Light Itself chose to make of the female Jacinth a Poet of the Seventh Level,

our Poet Avhador has taken it upon himself to deny the
Light that privilege. He has declared himself in a holy
war, declared himself a purifier of Poetry, claiming that it
is his duty to purge the holy profession of this female . . .
and as you can see, my son, he is being roundly punished
for his blasphemy. It was his men who took both rounds
of the Pain for the first quatrain."

The army of the Poet Avhador had at last ceased to
scream, and the lighted panel of the War Computer had
gone dark again. Jacinth fought a rising gorge. She could
not afford the luxury of sickness; she was more determined than ever that no round of that agony was to touch
her men, and yet sick that by sparing her own troops she
must inflict it upon the others.

Her hatred for Avhador so suffused her that she felt she
must be ablaze with it . . . she fought to master herself,
lest she speak too quickly. It was by passion and hasty
action that wars were lost, and that men died, as two men
of the army of Avhador lay dead now, their agony-twisted
faces hidden behind the ritual war masks.

She raised her hands high, waited a courteous second to
be sure of her opponent's attention, and threw the first
line of the second quatrain at him with what she hoped
was calm precision. She must be a dart of light, a spear of
fire, a laser's cobweb tongue; this was no place for clubs
and cudgels and the swung mace.

"LET HIM WHO WOULD QUESTION THE
LIGHT BEAR THE SMITING!"

"LET HER WHO DEBASES THE LIGHT BEAR
THE SHAME!"

"LET HIM WHO CRIES LIES BEAR THE PAIN
OF THE FLAME!"

"FOR A BLASPHEMOUS WRONG THERE IS
ONLY ONE RIGHTING!"

"That was a bad line, Father!" cried the boy, watching
the rows of tiny lights flickering on the War Computer.
"He's lost again, he's lost again!"

"If even you can recognize that, my son," said his

father sadly, "then he is lost indeed. Nonetheless, a boy of nine does not refer to a Poet of the Sixth Level as 'he.' "

"I beg your pardon, Father."

There was a silence, and then the boy said, "That can't be right!"

"What can't be right?"

"One round went to the Poet Jacinth, and the other to the Poet Avhador! How could that be?"

"Well . . . that is difficult for me to say. I am a Doctor and the rules of Poetry are not my strongest suit. However, I would venture to say that the War Computer felt that the Poet Jacinth gave a poor challenge in her first line. Do you remember it, Nilder?"

"Yes . . . 'Let him who would question the Light bear the smiting.' "

"That's it. Now consider it. What an ugly sound it has . . . it's very bad, Nilder. Very hard to say, and unpleasant to the ear."

"Perhaps that was the reason, then, Father."

"I think so, yes. But later, when it's all over, there will be an analysis on the comset, and we can see what the War Computer actually did."

"Oh, I didn't know that! That's good."

Jacinth had known at once how bad the line was. Despite her mental self-admonishment, she had flung that first line in passion and hatred, and it had been worthless. For that moment's indulgence of her own emotions, she had lost one of her men and who knew how many others had had their minds destroyed forever! No one bore much of the pain administered by the War Computer without permanent damage, and it was for that reason that no man might be required to serve twice in the armies of Abba.

She knew, too, and it was a bitter knowledge, that had she not been a woman the Council would never have permitted a war for such a petty cause. There were those in the Council yet, after all these years, who would have rejoiced to see Avhador win and herself exposed as a fraud, curse them for the blackness of their souls!

It was Avhador's turn to challenge. The score stood now at three to one. She intended to hold the pain rounds her men bore to that figure, and might the Light forgive her that even one had gone past her guard. She held herself in readiness, and the Poet Avhador raised his hands.

"Is it over, Father? Is that the end?"

"Yes, my son. The Light be praised, it is over."

"And the Poet Jacinth has won the war! A female!"

The Doctor did not answer. He went to his comset and pushed the stud that would inactivate the threedy projection.

"Father?"

"Yes, Nilder?"

"What will the Poet Avhador do now? His men took seven of the eight rounds, and eleven died, because he could not even do battle with a *female!* What will he do now?"

The Doctor made a sound of utter contempt.

"If he has any worth at all," he said, "he will request a ritual death of the Doctors. And that speedily."

"Perhaps it will be you who sends him into the Light, Father!"

"I, kill a Poet? Let us hope, my son, that it will not be my misfortune to be chosen for so repugnant a duty."

"I am sorry, Father."

"And let us also hope . . ."

"Yes, Father?"

"And let us also hope that there will be no more of this folly of war and battle and pain upon our world. See to it that you grow to be a man who knows that the job of a man is to give life and to maintain it, and to cherish it, not to destroy it."

"Yes, my father."

"And now we will watch the analysis by the War Computer. You will please be very attentive."

"Yes, my father."

And then the boy sighed happily.

"That was quite a war!" he said.

# ABBA

## CHAPTER ONE

SHE STOOD before him, the skin that was normally the color of coffee with lots of cream flushed almost rose with her anger, and stamped her foot.

"I know what will happen!" she said, spitting the words at him. "You will say you are going away for just a little while, but you will be gone for ever and ever."

"It's only because you are so young, Ratha, that it seems that way," Coyote said patiently. "Even if this assignment took longer than any of us expect, even at the very worst it couldn't keep me away more than three months."

"How many days is that?"

"Ninety. Almost a hundred."

"If I cry for a hundred days," she said, raising both hands in front of her face, spreading her fingers wide and peering at him through them, "I will be ugly before you come back. No one will ever want to look at me again, and it will be your fault."

"Oh, Ratha," Coyote sighed, "what am I going to do with you?"

How many times, since she was born, had he asked himself that question?

"If you keep on like this," he said carefully, "you will have to be punished."

"Ha!" She tossed her head at him, flipping the long silky mane of red-brown hair. "You can't do it—you never can!"

Coyote stared at her, angry now himself, and she stared back, not giving an inch. He felt ridiculous. Here he was, the most powerful mass projective telepath in Three Galaxies, able to control huge crowds at distances of miles, and he could not manage one small, furious five-year-old girl.

He turned to the woman who sat beside him and asked, "Do you suppose her mother could have managed her?"

Tzana Kai smiled at him, a very sarcastic smile. "I'm quite sure she could have," said Tzana, "and so could you, if you had any guts at all."

"I won't stay with you, Tzana," said the child. "I already said I won't."

"Go, then," said Tzana crisply. "That might be the best thing of all, since your father is a total eunuch where you're concerned."

"What's a eunuch?"

"No balls, my dear."

"Are there such things?"

"There used to be, long ago."

Ratha shook her head in amazement. "What use would they be?" she demanded.

"Tzana," Coyote began, but she hushed him immediately.

"Wait," she said.

"Why?"

"Well, look at her!"

"So?"

"She's thinking it over. Now—here it comes."

"If you are saying that I can go," said the child carefully, "but you were on Coyote's side before, then you are playing a trick on me."

"Not at all," said Tzana. "In fact, it was you who convinced me that you should go."

"How?" asked Ratha and Coyote together.

"When you said that your father was never able to punish you. I realized then that it would be very simple for him to punish you on Abba, because he won't have to do it himself."

Coyote opened his mouth and Tzana kicked him brutally on the ankle and he closed it again.

"Why?" asked Ratha. "Explain, please."

"On the planet Abba they have a very useful thing," said Tzana, "called the 'Women's Discipline Unit.' Any man who is having any sort of difficulty with a female of his household doesn't have to do any punishing. In fact, it would be beneath him to do so. He just goes to his com-set, punches out a call to the Women's Discipline Unit, and one of their men comes and gets the woman and takes her away and does the punishing for him."

"I would never——" began Coyote, and Tzana kicked him again.

"Wait!" she said.

Ratha clasped her hands behind her back and glared at the floor, thinking the whole thing through.

"It's a very good thing," observed Tzana softly, "that she's not psi-kinetic."

"Why?"

"Because she would keep making holes in the floor."

Ratha looked up at them.

"All right," she said, "I will stay with Tzana."

"Good," said Tzana Kai. "That's very sensible."

"But see here," protested Coyote, "I don't want her to agree to do something because of fear! I don't care to be obeyed because she's afraid of me."

Ratha's clear laugh cut across his words and Tzana nodded grimly.

"Don't be ridiculous," she said. "That child is not afraid of anything in this universe."

"Then why did she give in?"

"Because," said Tzana patiently, "she now believes what you told her before. That if you were accompanied by a female, even a very small female, your whole life would be impossibly complicated and the assignment would take twice as long. That's all."

Coyote sighed. "She couldn't have just taken my word for it?"

"I thought," said Ratha solemnly, "that you were making it worse than it really was."

"Exaggerating?"

"Yes."

"And now you don't any more?"

The child shook her head. "Not any more," she said. "Tzana doesn't do that."

"But I do?"

"Yes, you do. You do it all the time."

Coyote gritted his teeth, and Tzana grinned at him.

"You see what an insufferable little beast you've made of her?" she said. "Good thing you're going; perhaps I can teach her some manners while you're gone."

"Now, Tzana," Coyote said hastily, "I don't want you doing anything——"

And then he stopped. Far from being intimidated by Tzana, Ratha stood, hands on her hips, laughing at the two of them. He threw up his hands in despair.

"I give up!" he said. "I don't understand any of this."

Tzana reached over and touched his cheek. "Just go on to Abba, love, and take care of whatever it is that needs taking care of. Ratha and I will manage, won't we, Ratha?"

"We always do, you know," said the child. "We just always do."

Even the Fish was appalled by Abba, and he didn't appall easy. He had explained the assignment to Coyote with a faint air of distaste, like a Martian Orthodox Flannist discussing poultry farming.

"The whole system is ridiculous," Coyote told him. "How can such a thing be allowed to go on?"

The Fish shrugged. "It's a vast improvement over what they had before," he said.

"That's a matter of opinion."

"Let me review the basic facts for you," said the Fish. "And don't, for the Light's sake, go tramping about Abba suggesting improvements in their social system. In the first place it's none of our business. In the second place, they have ten thousand years of *recorded* history, and evidence of thirty thousand before that, and they look upon the rest of us as kindergarteners at the business of being civilizations."

"Which effectively disproves the idea that the progress of a culture through time is necessarily a progress from worse to better."

"Quite so," said the Fish. "But you must admit that what they've done shows a high degree of practical expertise at social manipulation."

"I've forgotten the details."

The Fish rubbed his hands together and smiled. He was always pleased when Coyote had to listen to him.

"I could just go check out a microfilm on it," said Coyote at once, noting the pleasure.

The Fish raised his hand.

"That won't be necessary," he said smoothly. "I have it all on the tip of my tongue."

Coyote said nothing.

"When our space colonists worked their way out to the

middle of the Second Galaxy," the old man went on, "they found Abba already settled, as I said before. The people were humanoid, indistinguishable from Earth-type humans except for the presence of three extra ribs and some sort of difference in the liver that escapes me."

"Not important," said Coyote.

"At that time the Galactic Council was already well established, the Federation was a firm entity, and there were many very obvious advantages to Federation membership. It was almost unknown for a planet to refuse membership—however, in this case the Federation wasn't offering."

He pressed a stud on his desk and a threedy flashed on the wall behind him. Coyote stared at it and shuddered.

"Exactly," said the Fish. "The colonists reacted as you did, with total repulsion. They found a civilization at a high degree of technological advancement, the male citizens living in luxury, and all the females in breeding pens, with stables for inclement weather, treated *precisely* as we treat domestic animals."

"Sick," said Coyote. "Just plain sick."

"It seemed perfectly reasonable to the Abbans," the Fish went on, "that being the way they had always done things, and so far as they knew the only way there *was* to do things. But it was most definitely not acceptable to the members of the Galactic Federation. The impasse was solved by a gentleman named David Rutherford Williams, who went out to Abba with a proposal and managed to produce the ingenious compromise they have today."

"The harem. The Women's Discipline Unit."

"Well, I agree with you that it doesn't seem very enlightened, Mr. Jones, but it was at least a form of society that was tolerable to the members of the Federation at the time. And you must admit that it shows a high degree of organization for a society so totally unEarth-like to be able to superimpose a sort of amalgamation of ancient Egypt, Arabia, and the French diplomatic service over its own culture. Practically overnight."

"How long did it take?"

"Less than six months, as I recall. Williams showed them a stack of threedies, they went 'Ah, yes' at him, their carpenters and masons trotted off and built women's quarters to specifications, and it all worked. Amazing."

"Does it really work?"

The Fish shrugged again. "Who can tell? It seems to. At least, since the Abban conversion to the religion of the Holy Light, they believe that women have souls."

Coyote made a sound of disgust, and the Fish raised a warning hand.

"I think you'll be surprised," he said. "I really do, Mr. Jones. If you expect primitive barbarians lurching about whipping their concubines you are going to be very surprised. Why don't you wait and see? And since no interference is allowed in any case, you might just as well relax."

"Oh, all right," said Coyote. "I'll try not to be so damned provincial. For the moment. Now let me see if I have the details of this assignment straight."

"Good."

"The Abbans have a lady whose profession is Poetry—is that right? It sounds odd."

"No, that's right. The Professions on Abba are like religions elsewhere. One joins for life, wears a special costume, and so on. Women are admitted only to Poetry. Poetry is a religious office, even in *their* culture, and someone managed to convince them that it was possible that a female might have a religious vocation."

"Okay. Now this lady is of very high status."

"Poet of the Seventh Level. There is no higher status on Abba."

"How the hell can that be? If women are barely tolerated——"

"Wait and see."

"All right—but I don't like it. Now, this woman is being poisoned."

"Correct."

"And because of her status, her death would be a planet-wide scandal."

"Correct again."

"And you're sending out a member of the Tri-Galactic Intelligence Service, a TGIS agent, to catch a bloody *poisoner?*"

"Abba pays very heavy taxes to the Federation, Mr. Jones," said the Fish. "They are an influential planet, with great power. They inform us that the taboo structure on Abba makes it impossible to deal with the situation as they would if the victim of the poisoning were not both

female and a Poet, and they have asked us—politely—
for an agent to help. We are glad to oblige."

"We are, eh?"

"We are. And you should be delighted, Mr. Jones. For
once you have an assignment that a child could handle.
No danger. No messy counter-espionage. Just an ordinary
garden-variety poisoner. You will have luxurious quarters,
your every wish granted, and you should be back here in
about ten weeks, give or take a week or two. Why are you
bitching? Perhaps you cannot bear to be separated from
your charming Tzana Kai even so briefly?"

Coyote snorted into his beard, and the Fish smiled.

"Is it an ego problem then, Mr. Jones?" he cooed.
"Perhaps you feel that an agent of your stature should not
have to stoop to dealing with such a minute problem?"

That was it, of course. Coyote rather fancied himself
beyond routine bogeyman-chasing assignments. But he
wasn't about to answer. He shut his mouth tight and let
the Fish giggle.

"Look on it as a kind of vacation," said the old man.
"Like a summer by the sea, all expenses paid."

Coyote left as abruptly as he could, leaving the Fish
snickering at his desk. He could have turned the assignment down, of course; since it was not a matter of intergalactic security he was not obligated to take it.

But he had a reason. He had never, not once in his
entire life, seen a subjugated woman.

Curiosity took Coyote lots of places.

# CHAPTER TWO

COYOTE ARRIVED at the rocketport of Abba's capital city at dawn, an arrangement not wholly to his liking. Cities tended to be gray and ghastly and deserted in the early morning hours; he had dismal memories of at least half a dozen where he had waited, too awake to sleep, for the city to wake up with him and begin its day.

He stepped off the rocket into an embarking-tube, and stood restlessly while its moving belt carried him into the station. He had only two fellow-travelers, a pair of Abbans in dark blue robes with a broad stripe of purple at hem and wrist. He looked at the chart in his tourist's manual, running his finger down the list. There it was: Dark blue robe, purple stripe—Profession, Law. That meant that they were lawyers, or judges, or politicians, or diplomats, or possibly policemen, all these being subsumed under the single heading, Law. They rode quietly behind him, murmuring in soft, well-bred voices, and he smiled. No whips yet. No litters carried by concubines.

At the end of the embarking-tube there were two waiting gentlemen, in robes vertically striped in light blue and tan, alternating. He checked the list quickly. Profession—Service. That could mean almost anything. Whatever it meant, they were apparently here to serve *him*. One stepped forward and took his kit, the other murmured, "Citizen Jones? We are honored; this way, please," and they went off with him in tow. Just as the Fish had promised him. Lots of service.

He had no time to catch more than a jumbled, hasty impression of the enormous rocketport before he was outside again, half out of breath, and then to his amazement he stood before a light four-wheeled vehicle, pulled by a pair of—what? He didn't have any idea.

"What is it? Are they?" he asked bluntly. "The animals, I mean?"

"They are *thaans*," said one of the gentlemen, flawless Panglish dropping from his lips like sweet oil flowing. "A fine animal, Citizen Jones. Almost like the ancient Earth animal that was called a mule, but rather more elegant. Won't you get in, Citizen?"

A mule? Even an elegant mule! To come here by government rocket, in hibernation, and then board a mule-drawn carriage? Coyote chuckled.

"You are amused, Citizen?" asked one of the men. "Perhaps you would share your joke with us?"

He told them and they smiled.

"We have whatever you might require in the way of transport," said the one who had asked him why he laughed. "Personal fliers, ground-cars, moving belts, hover-buses, whatever you prefer. But this is your first visit to our city, Citizen, and you will see it far better by thaan-carriage, if you will allow us to show you."

"Oh, certainly, certainly!" Coyote agreed hastily, afraid that he had been rude already. It always happened, but usually he managed to get through the first half hour on a planet without putting his foot in his mouth. This might well turn out to be a new record. He stepped into the carriage, hoping he looked eager, and sat down. The two men followed him, one took the reins, both smiled reassuringly, and they were off.

"My name is ban-Ness," said the driver. "Joel ban-Ness. It will require most of my attention to take us to our destination, and so my assistant will tell you of our city as we go along. He is of the household of Halfa, and is called Nikolas. Nikolas ban-Halfa. You may trust him implicitly; he is one of the most able guides in all of the capitol."

Nikolas ban-Halfa took up the conversation without so much as a pause. "Look around you, my friend," he said. "Look around you and know that I envy you. To come for the first time to Alsabaid is indeed a happiness to be treasured. This, Citizen Jones, is Alsabaid, the jewel of Abba."

The name "Alsabaid" meant just that, Coyote knew from the tourist manual. "Sabaid" was Abban for "jewel," and the place was well named. Coyote stared at it, half-hearing the guide's steady murmur of information beside him. The city glowed in the morning light, every street running under a deep green arch of ancient trees that met and mingled their leaves above the men's heads. The buildings were white, and of a curious shape, square at the bottom but with tapering walls; some were topped with pointed domes; about all of them ran balconies and verandahs of metal lace. Down from the balconies poured flowering vines, scarlet and amber and pale yellow, deep purple and brilliant blue. The morning sun stained the white walls in yellow and rose. At every intersection Coyote caught glimpses of the beauty the arching trees hid from him. Graceful bridges, flights of red-brick steps that wound up low hills, great buildings that must have been temples or cathedrals, small parks filled with fountains and flowers. The people were already up and moving in the streets, even at this hour, and they formed a patchwork in the colored robes that marked the Professions, blending and changing, sounding the same ten notes, a mobile tapestry for the pleasure of the eye.

Ban-Halfa's lecture went on without a break, and Coyote let it flow and gawked shamelessly about him like the most rank of tourists. He had never seen a city like this before, nor was he likely to do so again. No one had time these days to put loving thought and care into the building of cities, except to be sure that their power plants and sewage systems worked properly, that the re-cycling mains were adequate, and that the connections to the central computers were correctly set up. Alsabaid was an ancient city, a city laid out thousands and thousands of years ago by men who had the time and the inclination to do it properly. He would have to take some threedies home to Ratha, especially now since she admitted to suspecting him of chronic exaggeration.

"Citizen Jones?"

"Yes?" he said quickly, hoping he had missed nothing of importance. "I'm sorry. I'm a little stunned by your jewel city."

"I understand," said ban-Ness. "I wanted you to know that we are taking you to breakfast at the Palace of Law. His Excellency, Chief of Legislators, Ruler of all Abba, awaits you there."

"At this hour?" Coyote was amazed.

"Oh, certainly," said the Abban. "No man of Abba would lie in bed after the sun has risen, and waste the best portion of the day."

"But surely," said Coyote, "I don't really need to see the Chief of Legislators himself. Wouldn't just one of your heads of police be sufficient?"

"No, no," said ban-Ness firmly. "This is a matter of the very gravest importance to all of us. The Chief of Legislators holds the safety and happiness of the Poet Jacinth as dear as does any one of us. He would not think of turning over to some lesser person the task of informing you of our difficulty."

"I am honored," said Coyote at once. This, he had been told, was the all-purpose phrase of Abba. In any emergency one need only decide between "I am honored" and "I am ashamed" and everything else would take care of itself.

The carriage was nearing the heart of the city now, and he saw the Palace of Law ahead of them, recognizing it from the tourist threedies he had hurried through at Mars-Central before leaving. It was surrounded by gardens, and every one of them was choked with young men in the brown tunics of students, every tunic bordered with the dark blue and purple stripes that marked them as Majors in Law. They seemed happy; he wondered if their wives were. Or their concubines, or whatever they had.

"May students marry?" he asked suddenly, pointing at a group of tunic-clad young men.

"Not usually, no," said ban-Halfa, as the other man drew the carriage up to the front of the Palace of Law. "When they have finished their training in their Major, then their fathers arrange marriages for them, but not generally before. It would be very foolish to do otherwise; they have no time for females."

They stepped out of the carriage and the thaans' reins were taken by another man in the tan-and-blue robes. Coyote followed the others up the marble steps, down a corridor, and through an arched door into a huge room with walls of dark blue, bordered in intricate patterns of deep purple tile. At the far end of the room windows taller than he was looked out over the gardens and the streets. The room was empty, but as they entered, another member of the Profession of Service came forward to greet them from a niche in the far wall.

"Citizen Jones," he murmured. "Citizen ban-Ness. Citizen ban-Halfa. You are welcome here. Citizen Jones, our city is your city."

There was a rapid flow of phrases in Abban, and then the greeter—Coyote assumed that must be his function—stepped to the niche in the wall from which he had come and struck a silver bell with a hammer of the same metal.

"You may go on in now," he said then, bowing slightly. "His Excellency is expecting you."

Coyote followed the two Abbans to the door, and then, to his surprise, they fell back and motioned to him that he was to go on. What were they called, he wondered—servants? Servitors? And then he remembered. The list in the handbook had told him; they were called Servicemen. Apparently an agent of TGIS might eat with His Excellency, Chief of Legislators, but a Serviceman might not. He went with what he hoped was a confident step into the smaller room, and held out his hands to clasp those of the tall, white-haired man who waited for him there. He too wore a dark blue robe; the purple stripes were perhaps a bit wider, the fabric perhaps a bit more luxurious; otherwise there was no indication that this was the chief official of an entire planet.

"Your Excellency," said Coyote, and then added for good measure, "I am honored."

"Nonsense," snapped His Excellency, "how could you be honored? It's too early in the morning to be honored, and at my age a man would like to sleep. Damn this thrice-damned code that drags us out before the sun itself!"

Coyote didn't know what to say, and therefore he kept still. It was something you learned early in his business; better to offend vaguely by saying nothing than to offend specifically by saying the wrong thing.

"In only three more years I will be retired, however," went on the Abban. "And then I shall sleep until nine every morning and let the females of my household cluck about my senility all they want."

Coyote murmured the pleasantest murmur he had at his command, and the other man smiled, a smile of amazing elegance.

"Enough," said the Chief Legislator. "You have not come all the way from Mars-Central to listen to an old man complain. If you will come with me, they have set us breakfast on the balcony overlooking the river. I think you may find the view worth having risen early for."

They went out into the balcony and Coyote found himself in complete agreement with the Abban. The river sparkled in the morning light below them, not more than ten inches deep perhaps, foaming and frothing around boulders and pouring over low falls of rock. Occasionally a fish jumped, a pure arc of silver in the golden air. The balcony was alive with the flowers he had seen everywhere as they drove into the capital, the air filled with their scent.

"It's very beautiful," Coyote said, sitting down across from the other man. "I am only sorry that I am here for business rather than pleasure."

His Excellency smiled. "Perhaps the pleasure will be more than you had expected," he said. "You have been given quarters here in the Palace, and you will not find it a dull place to live. A thaan-carriage has been put at your disposal, as well as a small flier. And there are, of course, the women; you will have to tell your valet when you go to your rooms just how many you will require, whether it is necessary that they be virgins, what your tastes are as to hair and eyes, and so on. I think you will find your business trip rather enjoyable."

Coyote sat speechless. How many women, eh? On wheat or on rye? With pickles or without? He shook his head, aware that the Abban was amused at his reaction.

"If I am not honored," he said finally, "I am at least overwhelmed."

The Chief Legislator laughed.

"Then let us get at once to business," he said briskly, "so that you may recover your equilibrium. You know our problem here?"

"Only in a broad, general way, Your Excellency. I counted on people here to explain it all to me in more detail."

"Well, then. The problem is the Poet Jacinth. She is the third female Poet, only the third, in ten thousand years. That should tell you how rare such a creature is."

"How does a woman get to be a Poet?"

"It's relatively simple. She has only to send a message to someone at the University, on the Faculty of Poetry, signifying her intention to compete in the yearly Poetry Examinations."

"I see. And only three women have done so, in ten thousand years?"

"The examinations are given by computer, and they are extremely difficult. Of perhaps five thousand men who take them each year only a handful are accepted. For a woman even to compete—much less to do well—is a rare thing. I remember very few cases."

"And why is that? Since it is the only profession open to them I should think there would be many trying."

"Well," said His Excellency, "they are perhaps deterred by the penalty for failure."

"Penalty?"

"It's solitary confinement for life, Citizen Jones. A woman does not take such a prospect lightly. Very few compete."

Coyote concentrated, with some difficulty, on a bunch of pale pink grapes that reminded him of giant pearls. It would not do to lose his temper.

"Why such an incredible penalty?" he asked carefully. "It seems a little extreme."

"Perhaps it does," said the Abban, "until you consider it in context. No woman should attempt such a thing unless it is the will of the Holy Light, you see. If that is the case, of course she will pass, she cannot fail; if it is not, she is guilty of blasphemy, not to mention conduct unbecoming a female. And the disgrace is not just her own, she will have brought shame to her entire household, which may well number several hundred people. A severe penalty is unfortunately necessary, in order to prevent just the situation you describe—large numbers of bored females competing for Poetry just because they are allowed to do so."

"And the Poet Jacinth?" Coyote said. "She did pass?"

"At the Seventh Level. That is the most remarkable thing of all, you see. Perhaps one percent of the men who attain the Major in Poetry reach this level. We have no higher position in our society than Poet of the Seventh Level . . . there is even a sense in which, repugnant though it may be, the Poet Jacinth outranks me also."

"And you hate her for it?"

The Abban looked at him with an expression that could not have been faked. Total, utter astonishment.

"Hate her?" he said. "Why?"

"Because she is a woman. And she outranks you."

"Oh, good heavens, Citizen Jones, of course I don't hate her. Nor does anyone else. She is not a woman like other women, she is holy, chosen of the Holy Light. As such she is very precious to us."

"To everyone?"

"With the exception of a few fanatics who either claim that she rigged the exams—a total impossibility—or prattle nonsense about purifying Poetry by removing her, she is universally beloved."

"Are these fanatics dangerous?"

"Not at all. They are idiots. They have parades, carry banners, that sort of thing. They're a nuisance, but harmless."

"I see." Coyote paused for a moment. "But someone, Your Excellency, someone is poisoning her."

"Yes. Why, we cannot imagine. Even the poor benighted fools I mentioned would not want to harm her, only to banish her to her father's household. It's unthinkable that anyone should hurt her."

Coyote peeled a peach carefully and cut it into precise sections.

"You could explain to me, perhaps, why your own police could not handle this matter?"

"It is difficult to explain."

"Perhaps Your Excellency would try."

After a moment the Abban cleared his throat and spoke.

"As you say, I must try. You see, it is very difficult for us to deal with the Poet Jacinth in any way at all."

"Why?"

"It is a matter of rituals and taboos, my friend. The appropriate attitude to be taken by anyone, male or female, toward a Poet—especially at one of the high levels —is one of reverence, almost of subservience."

"Yes. Go on."

"The proper attitude to be taken toward a woman is very different indeed."

Coyote remembered the threedies of the women in their pens, lined up at the feeding troughs, with the brands livid on their hips and the heavy collars around their throats, and he could well believe that His Excellency spoke the truth. Things had changed, time had passed, since those threedies were taken, but nonetheless the situation was awkward. The mental habits of thousands of years cannot be discarded overnight, whatever the surface evidence.

"It must make for a certain conflict," he said.

"It does. It certainly does. There is no precedent for such a relationship, that of policeman and female Poet. And in our culture there is precedent, ritual, approved behavior, for every other situation. You see, Citizen, it is difficult for us. Our policemen simply cannot manage this particular case."

"Very well," said Coyote, "I will do the best I can."

"We are told that you are the finest agent the Tri-Galactic Intelligence Service has ever had."

Coyote dropped his eyes to his plate.

"I am honored," he murmured.

# CHAPTER THREE

IT WAS INCREDIBLE how much time one could waste on a planet with ten thousand years of recorded civilization. Coyote felt it might take five of the ten thousand just to develop the damned etiquette. The breakfast with the Chief of Law took a couple of hours, and then there was a brief interlude in the chapel of the Palace—obligatory—and then there was a tour, also obligatory, of of the gardens. There was a discourse on the history of His Excellency's favorite mobile flowers, and another on the Earth-roses he had managed, at enormous expense, to develop here where it was alleged they could not be grown. By that time it was the hour for lunch, and there were plans already made for Coyote for that, and then there was the siesta—obligatory—that followed lunch, and by the time *that* was over it was halfway into the afternoon. Coyote was seething with frustration.

And even then it was to get worse before it got better. Every office he tried to reach by comset was either closed or in the charge of a congenital idiot. Every call was a series of near-burlesque delays that he knew perfectly well were only the result of his not knowing the appropriate words to say to get him past the secretaries and lower officials, all of whom were human on Abba.

At last, completely defeated, he called the Serviceman in charge of his living quarters, explained that he was having difficulties, and requested that he be issued an interpreter.

"But the Citizen's command of Abban is superb! Not native, perhaps, but fluent, eloquent, nuanced! One would almost think the Citizen had learned Abban as a child!"

The Citizen's command of the how-dee-do's and the curtseys and the thankee-ma'am's is abominable," said Coyote grimly.

"Ah!" said the Abban. "Ah, yes! I see! Most wise, Citizen, most wise! If the Citizen would simply sit back and relax, make himself comfortable, it would be seen to. And at the same time, would the Citizen specify the women he wished sent to him?"

"Women?" For a moment Coyote was puzzled, and then he remembered. "Oh, yes, the women. Go ahead, send them, just get me an interpreter."

"How many women, Citizen?"

"Two."

"The Citizen's needs are modest," said the Abban admiringly.

"The Citizen is a very busy man," Coyote said.

"Of course, of course. And the physical characteristics, Citizen?"

"Characteristics?"

"Of the women. Tall? Short? Plump? Blue eyes?"

"Light's beard, I don't care! Pick me out whatever seems suitable and send them along. *And* the interpreter."

The Abban left, bowing and scraping, and Coyote spent what seemed to be interminable hours while nothing at all happened. The women arrived, which seemed a hopeful sign; at least there was now reason to believe that the Serviceman had not simply gone home to take a second siesta.

At last the com-set sounded two soft tones, and Coyote went to answer it.

It seemed that there would be a very slight delay—but only so very slight, surely the Citizen would be patient? Appointments were being made with all the people the Citizen wished to see, for the following day, beginning very early in the morning. An interpreter would be sent in plenty of time, suitably instructed, and the Citizen would find that everything would go smoothly.

Coyote cut it short.

"All right," he said wearily, "all right. This man will be here first thing in the morning—you promise me that?"

"We promise you."

"And if the Poet Jacinth should die of the poison tonight, or strangle in red tape—"

"I beg the Citizen's pardon?"

Coyote stared at the face in the comset screen. It was a round fat face with a flourishing moustache and empty eyes. He decided he was wasting his time.

"Never mind," he told it. "Thank you for your help."

"Perhaps this evening the Citizen will take advantage of his unexpected leisure to explore our beloved city?"

"I doubt it," Coyote snapped. "I will probably go to bed early. I am exhausted with courtesy."

He mumbled his way through the requisite six lines of farewells and thumbed the TERMINATE button.

One of the women appeared with a tray of steaming food, her face—undoubtedly a beautiful face, Coyote had to give his Serviceman credit for that, at least—showing concern. She dropped to her knees before him with the tray, and waited, still with that silent frown troubling her eyes.

"What is your name, Citizeness?" Coyote asked.

"I am called Aletha," she said softly.

"Aletha. A pleasant name."

He reached over and took the tray from her, assuming that she would get to her feet, but she remained kneeling.

"Aletha?"

"Yes, Citizen?"

"Is something wrong?"

She looked at him for just a moment, long enough to give him a glimpse of lovely dark eyes, heavy-lashed and shaped like almonds, and then dropped her glance again.

"The Citizen is angry," she murmured.

"The Citizen is that. Yes."

"May I ask why?"

He tried to explain, eating the food as he went along. Aletha was joined by the other woman, also kneeling, and he tried explaining to her, too. So far as he could tell he got nowhere at all. Apparently they could not conceive of a life that was not punctuated with endless ritualized delays, even when another woman's life was endangered. The second woman, whose name was Josepha, even went so far as to hint that she was appalled by the idea of a life that was not circumscribed by a kind of court etiquette.

"How," she asked gently, "does one know what to do?"

Coyote gave it up, reminding himself that social reform not only was not his task but was forbidden to him, thanked them for the excellent dinner, and told them he was going out.

He took a map of Alsabaid and inserted it in the display slot of his comset, pushing the PROJECT button. The map flashed onto the wall behind the set. He looked at it carefully. Let's see. He was in the Palace, facing out on the Kef Dibad, the Street of Law. Directly across the street was a small area of exotic shops offering wares from all over the Three Galaxies, running down to the banks of the river that surrounded the Jewel City. It was not the shop area that interested him, however.

He went to the window to look out, orienting himself again, and then turned back to the map to be sure.

Yes. It was dead ahead of him. He had only to go down into the Street of Law, cross it and follow the Kef banfeliz for perhaps three blocks, and he would come to the Vice Quarter, a small triangle that was bounded on one side by the shops, on the second by the wharves of Alsabaid's harbor, and on the third by the great river Lara, the River of Gold. Although why it should be called that was difficult to imagine, since all water on Abba was pale green.

The Vice Quarter of Abba had a certain noxious fame, even at the heart of the First Galaxy. He had not mentioned to the gentleman on the comset that he intended to go there, because he knew there would have been protests, and probably a companion forced upon him to prevent any ticklish intergalactic incidents. But it was in Vice Quarters, on planets which would tolerate them, that one learned things—if there was anything to learn.

He turned off the projection, pulled a light gray cloak from his gear and slipped it over his head, and went out into the corridors of the Palace of Law. The gray cloak was enough like the garments worn by the members of the Profession of Business that he felt it might very well get him by; certainly in the darkness of the Vice Quarter there would at least be a chance that he would draw little attention. And if he was challenged, of course, he had only to show his off-world credit disk, and everyone would at once begin to carry on about how honored they were.

He waved away the Serviceman who came forward at the end of each corridor to greet him, as well as the one who leaped up at the outside door. There could not, he thought, possibly be any unemployment on Abba. A place for everyone and everyone in his place.

"A walk," he told the man at the door. "Air, to clear my head after my long trip."

The Serviceman smiled and bowed. "You would not perhaps prefer the thaan-carriage which has been set aside for you, Citizen? You might lose your way in these streets at night."

"No, thank you," said Coyote. "If I lose my way I'll ask someone for directions. I prefer to walk."

"That pleasure rush to meet you, then, Citizen," said the Serviceman respectfully. "It is a beautiful night. The *halfa* are in bloom."

The Serviceman pointed. "See there, Citizen? On the balcony across the street?"

Coyote followed the pointing finger with his eyes. Down from the Balcony hung a thick tangle of vines, swaying gently in the soft wind off the river. The flowers spread great yellow disks the size of saucers, flecked subtly at the heart with deepest purple.

"Very lovely," said Coyote approvingly.

"Thank you, Citizen," the Serviceman answered. "They bloom only during this month; the Citizen is fortunate."

Coyote moved out into the night, crossed the street, and to distract the Serviceman, who he knew was watching, he wandered down the street of shops, pausing to peer into the windows like any tourist, waiting for an opportunity to slip out of the man's line of vision. He found it at the fourth storefront, where a narrow arcade of pale rose tile ran back into the heart of the block, with display windows down both sides and a tiny garden down the middle.

He turned into this and went quickly down the arcade, coming out on the other side of the block safely beyond the Serviceman's eyes, on the Kef ban-feliz.

He smelled the Vice Quarter before he saw it. Perfumes, incense buring in braziers, fountains with scented water spraying the night, cheap restaurants cooking the Light only knew what. And then he saw it and stopped to stare. It was something to see. Not just the shops and buildings; they were odd, to be sure, since no planet that Coyote knew of in the inner two galaxies had had open display windows for over five hundred years. To buy something from a store on Mars-Central you dialed its number on your comset, requested a goods display, watched the photographs of things to buy until you saw what you wanted, placed the order, and in perhaps fifteen

minutes the selected items arrived at your door by ro-
boconveyer.

But what held Coyote's interest was an enormous tree
of some crystal plastic, rising perhaps three stories into the
air and spreading its limbs out over an entire block. From
every branch there hung the opaque spheres of camping-
bubbles, in every conceivable color, so that the whole
effect was something like a giant Christmas tree flung up
by someone with abominable taste. The bubbles were
not to look at, though; as Coyote watched, a private flier
pulled up at one of them and a man leaned out and
tapped gently upon its side. At once the opacity became
translucence and Coyote saw the slender woman within,
arranged for maximum sales appeal upon a bed that filled
the small, round room. The man looked, also, apparently
was not satisfied with what he saw, and shook his head;
immediately the bubble went opaque again.

Coyote chuckled. What a way to run a whorehouse,
after all! This arrangement must be for the benefit of
tourists, travelers in from the excursion rockets, students,
men too poor to have households of their own, and the
like.

There was a soft sound beside him; it turned into the
usual train of remarks about what the Citizen might desire
and how our humble planet was honored to have the
Citizen aboard, and Coyote gritted his teeth and pulled a
smile out of his intergalactidiplomatic hat.

"I, too, am honored, Citizen," he said to the man who
had moved to walk beside him. "I am immeasurably
honored. The significance of all previous experiences
pales beside——"

The Abban chuckled and raised his hand in a cutting-
off gesture that was pangalactic.

"Careful, Citizen," he said with amusement. "If you get
too good at that no one will believe you are an off-worlder,
and without the robes of a Criminal it would go hard with
you to be carrying a faked off-world credit disk.

"The *smile* didn't even convince me. You come from a
more rough-and-ready planet, a place where business
comes before pleasure, if pleasure ever comes at all.
You find it difficult to be patient with all our manners'
claptrap. Fine. I am an adaptable man. We will dispense
with all of that. What brings you to the Ruby Ring,
Citizen? What can I do for you?"

The Ruby Ring, eh? Coyote smiled, a real smile this time. The name was apt. He looked at the man who strode easily at his side. The Abban wore the lavender robe of the professional criminal, and although he was a very tall man, even taller than Coyote, and skeletally thin, with the stooped bearing of one who is accustomed to having to continually bend over to hear and to be heard, he walked with grace. About his forehead were looped strands of beads, braided in fours, and in his nostrils he wore a ring of ivory. He was an imposing man, obviously a man secure in his position and that position one of power.

"Well, Citizen? Can I help you in any way? Is it a woman that you need?"

"Oh, no," said Coyote, "not a woman."

"A man, then?"

"I prefer women."

"Perhaps you have a wife at home, my friend, very fresh and new, still preferred above all others—that doesn't last, of course, but it's nice while it's going on."

"No. I've no wife. No wife and no women."

The Abban made a soft, sympathetic noise.

"And you don't want one. You must have been sadly mistreated by some female, Citizen."

"Mmm . . . not exactly," Coyote said, rather taken with the man and his talk, especially since he himself was being expertly guided, seemingly without any deliberate intent, straight toward the heart of the quarter. What sort of establishment might the fellow have there, he wondered?

"No," Coyote went on, "I haven't been mistreated. I'm afraid I'm one of the stupid ones where women are concerned. There was a woman I should have appreciated. Unfortunately she asked for nothing, and so that was exactly what I gave her. I talked a lot of garbage about having no ties, not that she had tried to create any. And then one day she was gone and I realized that being without her was unpleasant."

"It had never occurred to you before?"

"Not once."

"Like the air," said the Abban. "You certainly don't appreciate the stuff, but if the supply is cut off, the discomfort is striking."

"Exactly like that," said Coyote.

"I see. And by the way I am not—I repeat, I am not —leading you to my personal place of business as you think I am."

A small warning bell rang in Coyote's head.

"You are a telepath, then?" he asked.

"Well, of course," said the Abban. "How could one be a Criminal without being telepathic?"

Coyote immediately activated his own shields and the Abban smiled acknowledgment.

"I see," he said, and inclined his head on its long bony stem of neck. "You, too."

"You specialize in what?" asked Coyote. "Murder? Rape? Arson? Forgery?"

"None of those."

"What, then?"

"Poison, of course."

"Ah, Coyote said. "That's why you came to me!"

"Precisely."

"And where are we going?"

"To a man who knows everything there is to know about poisons."

They had turned a corner and were in an open square filled with transparent bubbles where legitimate goods were on display, and Coyote assumed anything at all, legal or illegal, could probably be purchased. The Abban took Coyote's elbow and led him a winding way among the bubbles. The smell of spice and flowers was choking; Coyote ducked his head in a futile attempt to escape the overpowering burden of perfume borne by the air. On his left he saw a threedie house, advertising incredibly ingenious combinations—of salaciousness. What would a Mars-turtle be doing as a sexual act with a Venusian flame-tiger, for the Light's sake?

Ahead of them was a sort of labyrinth of arcades, dim archways leading down past doors through which he could glimpse people moving, a whirl of many-colored robes in the dimness. They entered one of these paths along with a pack of shoving tourists and Abbans; through a triangular window in a wall beside him Coyote saw a circle of people crouched with their foreheads touching while a single light flashed blinding silver again and again in their center.

"What are they doing?" he asked his guide.

The man shrugged. "A cult," he said. "We have cults

for every taste here. Jehovans. Satan-worshippers. Hi-feedists. Deep Night Dancers. Mescalists. Swordswallow-ing Fundamentalists. You name it, we've got it. Ah, here we are!"

"Here" was a dark and narrow doorway, in which both Coyote and the Abban had to stoop.

"Sorry, my friend," said the Abban. "This part of the city is eight thousand years old, and we were a shorter people when it was built. Duck—there you are."

Coyote looked around him, blinking even in the dimness, the entry had been so very dark. It was a kind of café, apparently; at least there were small, low tables surrounded by piled cushions. The Abban took him over to a table set in a niche in the brick wall of the place. Two more Abbans sat there, relaxed on the cushions, both in the lavender robes of Crime.

"Marcus? White-Eyes?" said the Abban, addressing them, Coyote noted happily, without the usual pre-liminary formulas. "Here he is, Coyote Jones, come all the way from Mars-Central to learn about the poisoners of Abba."

"How much did he know? Coyote wondered behind his shields, and then had to laugh at himself. He was not accustomed to being sent on missions that were a matter of public knowledge; the cloak-and-dagger response was automatic.

"Well done, Neo," said the one he had called Marcus. "Sit down, Citizen Jones; we have already ordered for you. Now tell us, since Neo has brought you to experts, what we can tell *you* about the poison and poisoners. Is there a specific question?"

Marcus smiled, White-Eyes—whose eyes were very brown—smiled, Neo smiled, Coyote smiled. Coyote was amazed. He could hardly wait to get back and tell Tzana about the whole thing. The ingenuity of it all . . . a planet where crime was legal! Then what would real crime be? Or could there be a real crime?

"The Citizen is shielded," murmured White-Eyes, and the others nodded, and they all smiled some more.

"Your questions, Citizen?" Marcus prodded gently.

A Serviceman came and set their drinks in front of them, steaming pale blue liquid in little crystal cups.

"I am here to investigate the poisoning of the Poet

Jacinth," said Coyote, sipping his drink. It was excellent. And then the thought hit him, a little too late.

"Is this drink poisoned?" he asked stupidly, watching the room whirl around him, watching White-Eyes double and merge, flow into Marcus, watching Neo elongate and spread across the cushions, watching the dark become a tunnel in front of his eyes, and then he knew nothing more.

# CHAPTER FOUR

THE TASTE IN his mouth was beyond belief. If he had been psi-kinetic he could have at least removed the slime that coated his teeth; as it was, he gulped air, hoping that would help. It didn't.

He was in a tiny room, he lay on a pile of straw on the floor, and he was expertly bound. Cords circled his ankles and wrists and throat, intricately knotted so that any attempt at movement forced him to choke himself. Very nice.

He was disgusted with himself; after all, what would be the business of professional poisoners on Abba? To posion, naturally. He would have been wiser to have stayed on Mars-Central and sent Ratha on the assignment. *She* would have been too smart to fall for that cup-of-tea-in-a-cozy-nook bit.

He tried to roll over, and the building, whatever it was, swayed alarmingly beneath him. His stomach lurched and he fought back the bile that threatened to foul his already stinking nest. In such close quarters the last thing he needed was a puddle of his own vomit. Although if he had to stay here long there were bound to be puddles of one kind or another.

He lay still and studied his surroundings. The floor seemed to be rough synthowood beneath the straw. There was no door, as far as he could tell, only a single window high in the wall. They must have chucked him through it already trussed like a bird for roasting. The walls slanted up to a near-point . . . the building would have to have roughly the shape of a beehive. For a large and very stupid bee who had come straight to the nectar laid out for him. The place was very dirty, it could not have been used recently, but where was it? The swaying bit bothered him. For all he knew he was suspended by a thread over a precipice, or floating around in an ocean full of the Abban equivalent of sharks. Anything was possible. He was going to have to get to that window and look out, somehow, if he could keep from strangling in the process.

He ignored the sickening movement of the structure, rolled as carefully as he dared until he lay directly beneath the widow, and then took a long breath and held it. The air in his lungs held him just long enough for the single lunge to his feet, and then he fell with a bone-shattering crash to the floor again. It was fortunate that he had been able to get a glimpse of the situation in that one try, because he could not have made a second one. The muscles of his neck felt as if they had been crushed, and everything else—legs, back, arms, chest— was in agony.

He rested without moving until the building ceased to sway and the room stopped exploding with circles of red and black before his eyes, and then considered the situation. He had had only a glimpse, but the glimpse had been sufficient. There was no precipice involved, no sharks, no ocean. This structure he was in, whatever it was, was perched on slender poles in the middle of a river. Muddy green water stretched in all directions around it, and in the distance, almost out of sight, was the city of Alsabaid.

Damn. He was going to miss all those interviews. They would probably cancel the interpreter and it would turn out that there was some regulation limiting him to one application-for-interpreter per Abban year. The Poet Jacinth would be dead before he ever got started investigating. This was where curiosity got you. Tzana Kai had pointed that out to him once.

"Curiosity," she had said flatly, "is useful only when it is an intellectual vice. When it becomes a matter of the passions, as it is with you, it ceases to be simply a tool of the mind and becomes a way of getting oneself killed."

She had pointed it out to him only once; Tzana never pointed anything out twice.

And he had had no chance whatsoever, in all the

time he'd spent here in this hyperorganized pseudo-Arabian-Nights, to find out anything at all about the thing his curiosity had lured him here to investigate—that is, what a docile, subordinate, underdog woman was like. If he had stayed home last night—he hoped it was only last night, and assumed it to be, since he had no puddles of any variety to deal with as yet—if he *had* stayed home and satisfied his curiosity on *that* particular matter, he wouldn't be in this mess now. That was where devotion to bloody *duty* got you!

He wasn't in any danger, of course. Unless the poles broke and threw him into the water, where he would no doubt drown, tied up as he was. But that wasn't likely. The problems that faced him at this moment were protocol-type problems.

Mass projective telepathy, his only talent, was just the thing for a situation like this. He had only to shape a thought—GET THE BLINKING HELL OUT TO THE RIVER AND GET ME OUT OF THIS STUPID HUT—and head it Alsabaid-ward. Inside of ten minutes there would have been a hundred people knocking each other down to rescue him and a thousand behind them trying to help. But that would be very bad form indeed. If it became known to all of Alsabaid that he was not just a rather bumbling TGIS agent with a long red beard and a minor talent for shielding against other people's telepathic probing, if it became known that he could handle hundreds of people at a time just by thinking at them, it would be a ninety days' wonder, all Three Galaxies would know about it in a week's time, and he'd be no more use to the Tri-Galactic Intelligence Service.

For a moment that certain result almost tempted him, particularly when he thought of the helpless rage of the Fish in such a situation. But there were also personal consequences of being a Tri-Galactic marvel. He'd have no privacy ever again. Everywhere he went people would get out of his way, fast, and hide behind things and point and go "There-goes-the-famous-mass-projective-telepath." He didn't want that to happen.

No, it wouldn't do. He would just have to wait until some person or some group of no more than two or three persons came by. He could manage to get one or two people to come out here, rescue him, get him to shore, and then convince them that they hadn't done anything of the kind, without any troublesome results.

Although of course it might be a couple of weeks before anybody came out this way.

Coyote sighed. It was all very inconvenient. Perhaps on the next assignment he could convince them to send someone along to take care of him, since he apparently couldn't manage for himself.

In the meantime, what could he do?

He couldn't review the problem, because until he could get to the interviews with the police and the officials at the Temple of Poetry he didn't have anything to review.

He could think about Bess, but that would be embarrassing. Ratha's mother had been a revolutionary, a guerilla fighter—and she had always gotten away, until the day she was turned in for reasons entirely beyond her control. She would never have found herself in a situation like this.

He could sleep. That seemed the most sensible course, if he didn't die of the taste in his mouth before he woke up. Whatever the poison had been, its basic ingredient must have been rotted fish.

He relaxed as much as he could, closed his eyes, sighed again, and waited. A blank mind in a blank body, he told himself. Sure sign of health.

What was that thing the Maklunites had taught him that would put you to sleep? He stirred around in his memory a bit, wishing he had a few of those gentle, loving people to keep him company while he waited—although he wouldn't have breathed at them, in his condition—and it came back to him. Fifteen syllables, carefully chosen for harmony, euphony, rhythm. Imagine them on a string, each syllable a small, serene sphere unto itself. Fasten the two ends of the string together and go round and round and round and round. . . .

It was almost dark when he woke up again, miserable, aching, half-starved, and with a bursting bladder. The sound of a movement on the river below had wakened him, as he had known it would; now it was time.

He gathered his thought carefully and headed it out in the general direction of the sound, not too powerfully, and not for long. This was harder, actually, than blasting a crowd of people into doing what he wanted, because he had to be so careful. Just enough and not too much, and unless they had set a constant telepathic watch on him, someone good to whom distance was irrelevant, he could be reasonably sure of getting away with it.

THERE IS SOMEONE IN THE BUILDING WHO NEEDS HELP, he projected carefully. THERE IS SOMEONE IN THE BUILDING WHO NEEDS HELP.

The sound outside, the sound that had been a steady, rhythmic interruption of the water, suddenly stopped.

THERE IS SOMEONE IN THE BUILDING. WHO NEEDS HELP, Coyote repeated, adding to himself, "You thick-headed ass." How long was it going to take him?

He felt the hut shudder violently, and then the failing light from the window was cut off altogether as someone peered through the opening at him.

"Hello, there?" said a voice uncertainly. "May the Light shine upon you? Is someone there?"

"Only me," said Coyote, amazed at how tired he was. "Only me and the ropes I'm tied up with."

"What can I do?" asked Someone. "There's no door to this thing . . . you're tied up . . . I don't know how to get you out."

"Do you have a knife with you? Something to cut with?"

"I have a fishing knife."

"Then throw it over to me—no, wait. If you throw too hard it may go somewhere where I can't get to it. Tie something to it, a piece of string, your sash, whatever, a piece of fishing-line. Then throw it."

Almost at once there was the clatter of metal on the bare floor of the hut, and Coyote swore.

"I meant," he said carefully, "for you to hold the other end of the line you tied it to, friend. The point was that you could then pull it back and throw it again, if necessary."

"I'm sorry. I'm very sorry," said the Someone. "I didn't think. I am a plain man. I have never done anything like before."

"Never mind," said Coyote. "You did fine, actually. The knife landed an inch from my throat and I can reach it easily."

"Oh. I am sorry."

"And I," said Coyote, cutting the last cord, "am honored."

"You are honored?" The voice was full of wonder, and Coyote left it that way.

"How are you staying at the window like that? he asked. "Can you fly?"

"No. no. There's a ladder here. Awfully shaky, but a ladder. It goes right up to the window."

"And below? Do you have a boat down there?"

"Yes, Citizen.| A small boat, but it will bear our weight."

Coyote let out his breath slowly. This was going to be easy after all. Only one man, and a small boat.

"Look here," he said as he tested his cramped muscles, "your boat may be able to take both our weights but that ladder won't. You climb down and get your boat to the foot of the ladder and I'll follow you, all right?"

His legs were full of needles and the situation in his shoulder muscles didn't bear thinking of. He would probably fall off the ladder, hit his head on the boat, and kill himself. Like the ancient folk-hero, Big Guthrie, who had hit himself over the head with a toilet seat and knocked himself unconscious.

"Are you coming? Are you all right?"

"I'm fine," Coyote shouted back to the voice from below. It was a flat-out lie, but he had a certain amount of professional pride. He staggered over to the window on legs he could not feel and looked out to make sure about the ladder. There it was; old, rickety, and likely to pull the hut down when he put his weight on it. Nevertheless . . .

"Be careful, Citizen," said the man with the boat, superfluously.

Coyote went down the ladder in one rush, feeling that if he was going to simply fall off it into the boat, which was the most likely thing, he might just as well look as if he wasn't worried about that possibility. If he did fall it would look as if he'd overestimated his abilities, but if he didn't he'd look peaches and roses.

And he made it. The boat rocked alarmingly, and the poor man, who wore the robes of Service, kept looking at him with unhealthy suspicion, but they made it to shore and stepped out on the banks just a hundred yards from the outskirts of Alsabaid.

THERE WAS NOBODY IN THE BUILDING. EV-

ERYTHING HAS BEEN PERFECTLY ORDINARY TODAY, Coyote projected very carefully as the man pulled away. NOBODY WAS IN THE BUILDING, NOTHING HAPPENED. YOU HAVE BEEN FISHING, NOTHING UNUSUAL HAPPENED.

He watched the man's back get smaller, satisfied that that would do it. And then a bony hand clapped him on the shoulder and a voice said enthusiastically. "Well done, Citizen Jones! Well done!"

He whirled around, doing more violence to his bruised body, and there stood Neo, like an El Greco fanatic in lavender, and a smaller flier beside him.

"Well done?" he asked. It sounded feeble, but it was all he could say.

"Yes, indeed," said Neo. "It's been a pleasure dealing with you, I must say. But enough of this shop talk. I know you're tired and miserable—let me give you a ride back to the old Law shack, all right?"

When they were in the flier and headed toward the Palace of Law, at a satisfying speed for once, Coyote asked Neo a question.

"My friend," he said, with no sarcasm intended—after all, it had only been a man doing his job—"would you answer a question about Abban poisons now? Without poisoning me again, that is?"

"Gladly," said Neo. "One question, free of charge. What is it?"

"Is there a poison on Abba, as far as you know, that can be introduced into food or drink, leave no trace whatsoever, but cause violent pain about thirty minutes after ingestion? Without being fatal, that is?"

"Certainly," said Neo. "I can think of a dozen that would do that. However, they would all be fatal eventually; that is, the effects are cumulative."

"No trouble for someone to find such a thing, though?"

"None at all," said Neo cheerfully.

He set the flier down expertly at the curb in front of the Palace and let Coyote out.

"It's been a genuine pleasure dealing with you, Citizen," he said again, as he took off. "A very genuine pleasure. A lot of people die from that stuff we gave you."

"They don't die from the poison," Coyote told him

with great relish. "You're flattering yourself. What they die from is the lack of a toothbrush afterwards."

He turned on his heel and left the poisoner laughing at the curb, swept, with what he hoped was dignity, past the Servicemen posted in door and niches, and made it to his rooms.

Just in time.

# CHAPTER FIVE

WHEN HE HAD made himself respectable once again, Coyote went through the rooms looking for the two women who had been sent to him. He was hungry and assumed they might well be hungry, too, and for all he knew they could not eat unless he ordered the food for them.

"Aletha?" he called. "Josepha? Citizenesses? Where are you?"

A figure rose from his couch and bowed. He wore the insignia of the Women's Discipline Unit.

"Good evening, Citizen Jones," he said. "We have been wondering where you were. I am Kidj ban-Kidj, at your service."

"I was unavoidably detained," said Coyote curtly.

"Well," said ban-Kidj, "you would insist on going to the Ruby Ring, Citizen. I'm afraid your unpleasant experience in the river hut is entirely due to your own lack of wisdom."

"Oh, you know all about it, then? The poisoning, the dumping in that miserable hut, all that stuff?"

"Of course, Citizen. Neo ban-Valdeverl is a respectable man; the crime was registered with the Palace of Law immediately upon its completion."

Coyote stopped dead in his tracks.

"You mean to tell me," he shouted, "that you people *knew* what had happened to me, and you didn't send anyone to help me?"

Ban-Kidj raised his eyebrows.

"Citizen Jones," he said, "if the result of registration of crimes were immediate interference by the Law, the profession of Crime would die out in a year. Criminals have certain rights, too, you know, and they are respected."

"But in that case," Coyote demanded, "what are the police *for?*"

"They are very busy men," said ban-Kidj. "They have to keep track of the crimes, everything must be accounted for. It is necessary to be certain that all forms have been filled out, all fees paid, all regulations conformed with. And then they protect us, of course, from crimes committed by scum who are not members of the criminal profession."

Coyote sat down wearily. There was absolutely nothing he could think of to say or to do. The whole thing was mad. The Fish had told him not to expect barbarians, and he had been quite right; the thing to expect on Abba was raving lunatics.

"Where," he asked finally, in the weariest voice he'd heard in many a day, "are my good friends Aletha and Josepha? I would like them to join me for dinner. And incidentally, where is my interpreter?"

Ban-kidj bowed again. "The interpeter was provided, as agreed, and he kept your appointments for you. The transcripts of the interviews, very complete in their details, very satisfactory, I am sure, are in the red folder on your desk there. Verbatim. The interpreter was accompanied by a secretary."

"Good," said Coyote. "I'll read them right after dinner. Have I appointments for tomorrow?"

"You are to see the Poet Jacinth herself, Citizen. At nine o'clock."

"Good, good. If she lives through the night. And the women?"

"Women, Citizen?"

"Aletha and Josepha. Where are they, do you know?"

"Why, they have been taken away, Citizen."

Coyote sat up straight. Something in the tone of the fellow's voice didn't strike him as quite what it should be. For the perhaps two millionth time he regretted the fact that he was only a projective telepath and not a receptive as well.

"What do you mean, exactly?" he asked cautiously. "Taken away where? And why?"

"They have been taken to the nearest Women's Discipline Unit for punishment, Citizen. We certainly have no intention of neglecting your rights in any way, however. Nothing has been done to them, pending your notification as to what sort of punishment you wish inflicted."

Coyote took a deep breath. He felt as if he were under water.

"Ban-Kidj," he said softly, "please explain. Please grope around in the depths of your bureaucratic brain and explain to me why those two women are to be punished."

Ban-Kidj regarded him with bland, wondering eyes.

"Why, for the usual reasons, Citizen," he said.

"Explain!" Coyote thundered.

"They did not please you, Citizen; therefore they must be punished."

"How do you know that they did not please me? Did I complain?"

"They reported in this morning, as it was their duty to do," said ban-Kidj. "They are excellent females, well trained and eager to do what they are told. They were honored to be chosen to serve a person as important as yourself. I am amazed, myself, that you found them unsatisfactory—however, that is your right."

"But, look, Citizen," said Coyote, straining for comprehension, "how can they know or you know if I was or wasn't pleased with them? I haven't had a chance to find *out* if I was pleased, for the Light's sake!"

"Exactly," said ban-Kidj, as though that settled it. "Exactly."

Coyote sat and thought a minute. The idea that came to him was intolerable.

"What did these two criminals report to you this morning?" he asked carefully. "What, exactly?"

"They are not criminals, Citizen, they are females. Females have no sense of right or wrong and therefore cannot commit crimes. They simply called in, as they are required to do, and told us that you had not so much as touched either one of them."

"But I haven't even been here!"

"Citizen Jones," said ban-Kidj, "if you had been pleased with them you would not have gone out into the Vice Quarter."

Coyote buried his head in his hands until he was able to talk once again.

"Do I have this straight," he asked finally, "do I have this exactly right? Neo and Marcus and what's-his-name —White-Eyes—can poison me, tie me up, and abandon me to die in a hut in the middle of the river. That's all right with everyone, that's their Profession, and we must concern ourselves with their due rights and privileges. But those two poor women, just because I—who am here to find a poisoner, I remind you, not to take part in orgies—just because I did not leap on those two women and take advantage of the facilities, so to speak, they are to be punished?"

"A very good analysis of the situation, Citizen Jones," said ban-Kidj with approval. "You see things very clearly. And if you will just give me instructions I will go at once to the comset and let the Unit know what punishment you have ordered for the women. And then, of course, I will see that you are sent two replacements at once."

Coyote came out of the chair with a single movement and took ban-Kidj by the collar of his robe, lifting the elegant official right off the floor and into the air.

"You will not!" he bellowed. "You will do nothing of the kind! You will take me—at once—this instant— to wherever you have shut up Aletha and Josepha, who please me, very much, do you hear? And you will release them to me and I will bring them back here, where I will damn well just sit and *look* at them if that happens to be what I want to do! Do you understand me? Either you will do that or I will tear down your accursed Women's Discipline Unit, synthobrick by synthobrick, until I find them!"

He set the man down on the floor with a thud and hit his right between his eyes with a thought that turned ban-Kidj as green as the River of Gold.

"Yes, Citizen," said ban-Kidj in a hasty gargle. "At once, Citizen. If you will just come with me, Citizen. We are honored, of course, to carry out the Citizen's wishes."

"You are accursed!" shouted Coyote. "Honored bem-dung! Hurry up!"

"The Citizen does not wish to eat first?"

Coyote fixed him with a glance that froze him to the spot.

"All right," said ban-Kidj, raising his hands imploringly. "If the Citizen will follow me."

The Women's Discipline Unit was a circular building, cut up into sections like a pie, with a central business office at the hub of the circle full of computers and robots and men in dark blue robes. Ban-Kidj and Coyote went through it like a whirlwind, gathering astonished looks as they passed, Coyote driving the Abban before him like a terrified steer.

Ban-Kidj took him to a round door with a number of studs set into it. Then he began punching out various combinations of the studs, which lit up in different colors, red, yellow, and green, as he touched them.

"What are you doing?" Coyote demanded.

"I am sending a message through," said ban-Kidj with a quaver. "I am having Three-oh-nine-one and One-four-four-four sent down here to us at once."

"Three-oh-nine-one and One-four-four-four? What is that?"

"The two women, Citizen. They are numbered, of course, for the convenience of the Unit. You realize, surely, that there are hundreds of Alethas and Josephas in this district, you realize——"

He was interrupted by the sounding of a small bell, and the door slid open. Behind it was another door, equally massive, and in the space between the two doors stood Aletha and Josepha. Apparently, whatever horrors lay behind the door, he was not going to get a glimpse of them.

The two women were white and trembling, it hurt him just to look at them. He counted to ten, reminding himself that he must not offend the citizens of this very powerful planet that paid so large a sum of taxes, may they all—the males, anyway—boil in eternal oil, and spoke to the women.

"Are you all right?" he asked them.

They dropped at once to the floor and hid their faces on their knees.

"What the devil have they done to them?" Coyote demanded. "I have given no instructions as to the type of punishment and you had no right to take action without such instructions!"

"Nothing has been done to them," said ban-Kidj,

who had become a great deal more virile now that he
had two females watching him. "Don't be ridiculous,
Citizen, we know the law. They are simply ashamed."

"Ashamed of what?"

"Of having displeased you, of course."

With hearty contempt in his voice, he added, "As they
certainly should be."

The two women winced and caught their breath, and
Coyote longed for the freedom to kill the WDU man.

"Aletha?" he said instead. "Josepha? I have come to
take you back with me. Ban-Kidj here is anxious to go
make arrangements for transportation. We are going to
have a pleasant dinner together, just the three of us."

He pulled the two of them, unbelieving and protesting
that such things could not happen on Abba, to their feet,
and he took them to the front entrance as rapidly as he
had brought ban-Kidj to the door behind which they
were being kept. A small flier waited for them there,
fitted out with heavy black curtains to hide the women
from view as they flew. Coyote gave it a vicious kick
with the toe of his sandal.

"Get in, please," he told the women.

They stared at him and he opened the flier door and
repeated, "Get in. Please. I would be honored if you
would go back with me to the Palace of Law."

He had about as much sexual interest in these two poor
cowed creatures as he had in the flier, probably less, but
nobody was going to get punished because he hadn't laid
them, not as long as he was conscious and in full possession of his private parts. They would have dinner, and
perhaps an hour's sleep, and then, sore muscles or no
sore muscles, he would get to the business of providing
Aletha and Josepha with proper references for *their*
next assignment.


Aletha and Josepha lay sleeping, finally, with their
various emotional injuries as satisfactorily repaired as
he had been able to manage. Coyote gave them a glance
of inspection and ticked it off—two females, one bru-
nette, one blond, both asleep, breathing deep and slow,
cheeks charmingly flushed, no sign of tension on either
face. Check.

He went out into the main room of the suite, trying
not to stagger, and picked up the folder of transcribed

interviews from the desk. He sat up to read them, since he knew he could not possibly stay awake if he lay down, and at that the print kept swimming out of focus before his eyes. He went to the bath and put his head under a stream of cold water until he felt capable of keeping his eyes open, wondering if he wasn't perhaps getting too old for this work, then went back and settled down with what looked to be the most informative report, the one from the police.

Q: You are Helix, of the Household of Min, member at the Fifth Level of the Profession of Law, police division. Is that correct?

A: That is correct.

Q: And you have been handling the investigation of the attempted poisoning of the Poet Jacinth?

A: Yes. At least, I have been trying to do so. It is rather complicated by the problems of procedure.

Q: I understand. Very well. What is the usual location of these poison attempts?

A: Well, the Poet Jacinth, of course, lives in the Trance Cloister of the Temple of Poetry. She usually takes her evening meal in her own rooms, on the second floor of the Cloister. She then goes into a small garden, which is her favorite place for meditation, and spends perhaps two or three hours there, and that's when it happens.

Q: Is she attended during her meal?

A: She has a servingwoman with her.

Q: When do the effects of the poison first appear, usually?

A: Generally from thirty minutes to an hour after the Poet Jacinth has completed her meal.

Q: At that time she would be in the garden?

A: That is correct, yes.

Q: And what are the usual effects? Vomiting, or convulsions, or————

A: There has never been any vomiting. It is always exactly the same. The Poet Jacinth will be kneeling in deep meditation, perfectly tranquil. Suddenly she will gasp and fall to the ground as if she had been struck. She describes the pain as being primarily confined to her head and says that if it were not that it is of such brief duration it would certainly kill her, so intense is it.

Q: I see. How long does this go on?

A: Apparently what it amounts to is repeated impulses of this pain, each impulse extremely brief, but with only short intervals of relief in between. At first it generally continued for no more than five minutes or so, but recently the length of the attacks has been increasing. Last night the Poet had to endure almost an hour of the pain, and this morning she is very ill and despondent as a result. She feels that she cannot possibly stand very much more of it.

Q: Does this occur every night, without exception?

A: No. At one time, three nights passed without any such occurrence.

Q: And how long has this been going on?

A: About four weeks, Citizen.

Q: What measures have you taken for the protection of the Poet? What investigations have been made?

A: The things you would expect. Routine. We have changed the persons who prepare her food. We have changed the location of that preparation and had it all prepared under the uninterrupted surveillance of other Poets and our own men. Still, somehow, the poison is put into the food. Whoever is responsible is unbelievably clever.

Q: Perhaps it is the Poet's servingwoman? Have you considered that?

A: Of course. We're not fools here, you know, Citizen. We've changed servingwomen—much against the Poet Jacinth's will, since she was deeply attached to the old one. We've set every conceivable guard, set watches everywhere throughout the Temple, tried every combination of safeguards our best men could devise. It makes no difference, still the poisoning goes on. The doctors are seriously alarmed . . .

Q: No one else has been affected?

A: No one. Only the Poet herself.

Q: Do you know of any reason why anyone would want to harm her?

A: None whatsoever.

Q: Very strange. The food has been analyzed, I suppose?

A: Of course. Numerous times.

Q. And the results?

A: There were no results.

Q: I don't understand.

A: There has never been any detectable poison in the food or drink. This is not surprising, however, since the poisoners are extremely clever at devising new combinations with which our chemists are not familiar. It is, of course, an unregistered crime, you must remember, or we would know what poison was involved—not that any respectable Criminal would harm a Poet, female or not.

Q: I understand. Well, then, perhaps we had best leave the next step to Citizen Jones. He has had a great deal more experience in dealing with this sort of thing than I have.

A: So we have heard. And you will be assisting Citizen Jones in the future?

Q: I expect to do so, although at the moment the Citizen is having some minor difficulties.

A: I hope that he is able to resolve them satisfactorily. We can't afford to have this sort of thing going on, it leads to a lack of confidence in the police.

Q: I wouldn't worry.

They wouldn't worry, eh? The agent they had requested stuffed full of drugs, tied up and abandoned to die, but not to worry. It being a registered crime.

Coyote glanced through the other transcripts, which did little more than recapitulate the one he had already read, and then flung the folder across the room in disgust and went to sleep where he lay.

# CHAPTER SIX

COYOTE STOOD uncomfortably in the room where the student had brought him and waited. For this interview the interpreter had refused to help him.

"I would have far more difficulty in dealing with the Poet Jacinth than you would, Citizen," the Abban had insisted. "You have no taboos to hamper you. And as for ritual and precedent, in this case there *is* none. You will handle it better without me there, nervous and confused, hampering you."

They had dressed him in a blue tunic and sandals, his hair was caught back with a clasp of hammered silver set with amethysts, and over the tunic in an elaborate drape he wore a robe of deepest purple, made of the silken fur of the hela-foxes of Abba. He carried a silver staff bearing the insignia of the Palace of Law, it having been decided that this was closest to his professional status, and around his neck swung an ankh of a rare lavender metal from the Extreme Moons. This extraordinary costume had been produced from somewhere in the depths of the Palace of Law, and he was assured that some such garb—and usually more elaborate than this—was expected of anyone speaking directly to the lady Poet Jacinth. The intent was, of course, that his splendor should convey a compliment to the Poet; he only wished that his inner confidence matched his outer magnificence.

Another student appeared in the door, smiling, and indicated that Coyote should follow him. They went down a long hall, turned left and went down yet another, and stopped in a smaller room, octagonal, paneled in wood and smelling of subtle incense. At each of the eight sides there was an oval window, and the student indicated to Coyote that he should go look out.

"Are you allowed to speak to me, Citizen?" Coyote

asked the boy abruptly, and was answered by a polite negative shake of the head. He looked at the narrow "student" stripes on the boy's brown tunic; there were three. Apparently this young man was of too high a level to be excused from the rule of speaking only in verse, and not skillful enough to convert the Abban verse to Panglish.

"I thank you, then," said Coyote. "This is the Trance Cloister?"

Another nod.

"I will wait until the Poet has finished her meditation, since she is expecting me. She will come through here afterwards, I take it?"

Another nod, and he was gone. Coyote snorted. Good riddance. How the hell was the business of a Profession, even a religious Profession, to be carried on when people were forbidden to speak except in rhymed couplets?

He went to one of the windows and looked out into the garden of the Trance Cloister. It was oval, like the windows, densely green, set with pools and fountains; at the far end there was a circle of great boulders and set within the circle a triangle of gaza trees. Their slender branches were borne almost to the ground with the weight of the huge green star-shaped blooms they carried at this season. In the middle of the triangle he could see the Poet Jacinth, kneeling in a plain robe of scarlet, with her black hair flowing loose down her back. She was motionless, her arms spread to the heavens and her head thrown back, and Coyote fought the impulse to turn and bolt. He felt like a perfumed monkey sent to profane a temple service by a gang of adolescent humorists.

He sent a thought her way, gently, SOMEONE IS HERE, and she turned her head and rose from her knees, looking at him with wide eyes. She hesitated, and then began walking toward him, the scarlet cloth clinging to her in the wind, and he saw that she was very beautiful. Her hair was absolutely straight and fell to her waist like a scarf of black silk, caught back at each temple with a silver clasp. She was deeply tanned, and no wonder, if she spent—as he had been informed—six hours of each day in meditation in that garden. It was a classical face, with high, abruptly slanted cheekbones, a perfect oval shape, an aristocratic nose, black eyebrows like wings, and a slender mouth with a flawless curve. Almost too perfect a face, for his taste; he liked a bit of difference, some flaw to break the mask. But her eyes, as she came nearer, made him frown with interest. He reminded himself to find out if she was on any sort of medication; perhaps the famous Permanent Medication so beloved as a punishment from the Women's Discipline Unit? The eyes were black and enormous, the almond shape praised in old poems, with a violet line around the pupil, and they were so wide open that she looked like a startled animal ready for flight.

She came in through a door at the side of the room and reached out her hands in a gesture that he supposed must be a traditional greeting, though he had not seen it before. He did not touch her, but waited, and when she sank gracefully to the bare floor, her hands folded inside her long, full sleeves, he followed suit and sat facing her. Whatever code of etiquette might apply here, she would not expect him to be flawless at it; he would do the best he could.

She smiled at him, and then spoke slowly, in heavily accented but charming Panglish.

"It is my pleasure that you visit me; so few distractions come to fill my days. And days and nights alike are long when one is all alone."

Coyote considered the speech carefully. Probably, if she had confined herself to the prescribed couplets, he could have followed her, although he did not know the special vocabularies of Poetry. But he was glad no one had told her, because she must be translating the rhymed Abban into English blank verse, a sort of virtuoso performance that he could take pleasure in. There was a pause, a hesitation with closed eyes, before she spoke, but so brief as to be almost unnoticeable. It must take considerable skill.

"Thank you, Citizeness," he said. "If I can offer you welcome distraction I will be honored. But even more important, I come to attempt to insure your safety."

The wide eyes opened wider. The effect was almost frightening.

"Can you tell me, please, my lady Poet, about this poison that they are tormenting you with?"

She closed her eyes for a moment and then looked at him again, solemnly.

"Each morning when I go into the garden, and always when the moon has touched the trees, the poison comes —like knives within my skull—and drives me to the earth, and pins me there. The pain comes again and again, till I feel no more . . . each stab no more than seconds long, but deathly deep."

"Where is the pain?" he asked her. "Can you tell me *exactly* where you feel it?"

"But I have told you once—inside my head!"

"Never cramps in your muscles, or stomach pain— always just stabs of pain in the head?"

She nodded, still smiling, watching him like a child, waiting for miracles.

He thought for a moment. He knew no poison that could behave as this one was supposed to, but then he knew very little about poisons.

"Citizeness?" he asked tentatively. "Is it forbidden for a man to enter the garden where all this happens, once you are there?"

"If you are a man, the keys unlock all doors," she said. "Be at my side, if you will, and welcome there."

She had understood at once, and he was pleased with her.

"That's exactly what's needed," he said with approval. "I need to be near you when the poison takes effect, then perhaps I will be better able to judge. At the moment I'm mystified."

She lowered the disturbing eyes, looking down at her knees.

"If you fail, my friend, I go joyously to death," she said. "If not, I will carry this burden yet a while."

He wanted to reach out, touch her, reassure her, but the memory of the staring eyes kept him back where the rigid, foolish etiquette could not have. The more he sat near her the more he felt that what he saw in her eyes was perhaps not the effect of drugs alone but of some subtle warping of the mind as well, some trace of the ancient sickness they called "madness." He would have to ask if a doctor could be brought to her; in this day and age it was barbaric to find a woman suffering a plague out of the Dark Ages of the twentieth century.

He took leave of the Poet, asking that she arrange for his return visit that night, and waited while she summoned another student to lead him back out to his

waiting flier. There was just time for him to have his dinner, make sure that the two women who shared his
quarters would not be punished for his neglect in the
morning, and then it would be time to come back.

When he lay between Aletha and Josepha, his duties
suitably discharged, he asked them about the Poet Jacinth's condition.

"Could she have a doctor?" he asked.

The girls looked at him, amazed, and Josepha spoke
to him wonderingly. "Is she sick, Citizen?"

"I think so; I am afraid so. Could she have one?"

"Of course," said Josepha. "She is given the tenderest
of care, always. She is beloved of all of us. You must tell
them at the Trance Cloister that she is not well, and they
will send a specialist at once."

Coyote sighed. "Well that at least is a relief. I thought
it might be difficult . . . and she's pathetic."

Josepha leaned on one elbow and turned to him the
inevitable face of one woman hearing of another's physical
ruin.

"You are not speaking now of the effect of the poison?" she asked.

"No . . . there is something else."

"What is the matter with her, then, Citizen? Could
you tell?"

"I think she is mad," he said flatly. "I'm no expert,
but it seems to me there is madness in her eyes."

"Madness?"

Aletha spoke then, in Abban, too rapidly for him to
understand, and both women laughed softly, turning
their heads away. In order not to offend him with
their noise, he supposed.

"What's so funny?" he demanded. "Madness isn't funny
at all, it's a disease, and a damned unpleasant one. Do
you know what it is?"

"Yes, Citizen," they answered respectfully.

"Then why is it funny? Just because the mad don't
bleed or break out in spots doesn't mean they aren't
suffering."

"Citizen—"

"Yes. Aletha?"

"We would not contradict the Citizen, lowly women
that we are."

"Contradict me. I don't find you lowly at all. I find you highly."

"Highly?"

"Highly attractive. Highly pleasant. Highly intelligent. Highly to be recommended."

It was a lie, but he had an obligation to these two helpless hunks of flesh entrusted to his whims.

"Highly lovable," he added, for good measure. He *could* have loved them, too, in exactly the same way Ratha loved her dog. Not one iota's difference.

They were still hesitant, so he coaxed them. When he got back home he was going to say something so outrageous to Tzana Kai that she would hit him for it, just to get the bad taste out of his mouth.

"Please," he said gently. "Tell me. I really want to know why you reacted that way."

Aletha, the braver of the two, sat up and crossed her legs neatly and folded her hands in what he now knew to be the standard posture for respectful discourse.

"Her madness is known, Citizen," he said. "The Poet Jacinth would, of course, be mad. And you must not wish to take her madness from her. That would be very cruel."

"I don't understand."

"Perhaps the Citizen has not taken thought," murmured Josepha.

"Perhaps the Citizen is stupid," said Coyote. "Please explain."

"Think of the way she lives," said Aletha. "She rises each morning at four, and for two hours she must meditate in the Cloister. Then she receives the sick; because she is holy, she can heal where doctors have failed."

"How does she heal?"

"With poetry, of course, how else?"

"Go on."

"That takes her morning, usually. Then she must spend several hours more in meditation. Then two hours at her official duties—preparing poems for state occasions, for officials who have need of sacred lines to ease the burden of their work, many things of that kind."

"When does she eat, for the Light's sake?"

"Once a day, at the evening dinner hour. Then into the garden for more meditation."

Coyote made a sound of disgust. "And her friends? When does she see them? When———"

"She has no friends," said Aletha. "She is a holy woman, thus she cannot have females for friends. And of course no woman can be the friend of a man; the female brain is not fit for such a role."

"That is not true," said Coyote, raising a mental finger at the Fish and his warnings.

"But it is," said Aletha serenely. "I would not contradict the Citizen, of course, but things are as I describe them."

"As you describe them?"

"The Poet Jacinth cannot have friends; it is forbidden."

"That's not what I meant," said Coyote, but she looked at him blankly and went on, and he gave it up.

"Her madness, under the circumstances, is a necessity."

"Part of her professional qualifications, in short," said Coyote.

"Yes, Citizen. You have understood in spite of the inadequacy of our explanations."

"May she read? Look at threedies? Play a musical instrument? Pick flowers? Swim? What is she allowed to do? When does she have time off for herself"

Aletha looked shocked and Josepha made distressed noises.

"A holy Poet of the Seventh Level," said Aletha, "even if by the will of the Light that Poet should be a female, has no need of such things, Citizen."

"She summons madness instead."

"Yes, Citizen. It is expected."

"Tell me," said Coyote, "if she were a man, instead of a woman, would she still need madness to support her?"

Aletha laughed and lay down beside him once again, while Josepha went to prepare his bath.

"Of course not," said Aletha. "If a man is Poet of the Seventh Level, his concubines see to it that he is happy. It's not the same thing at all."

"And why has she no male concubines?" Coyote demanded.

At the very mention of such heresy, Aletha leaped from the bed and scuttled after Josepha, leaving him to fume alone.

# CHAPTER SEVEN

COYOTE SAT in the darkness of the gaza trees, where a low chair had been placed for his comfort, and waited for something to happen. Abba's twin moons had just risen and were flooding the garden with their pale green light so that everything seemed edged and stippled with silver-green. The trees stood out in the moonlight like silhouettes cut from paper, no depth to them, like scenery trees for children's plays. The air was thick with the smell of flowers and the wind off the river. From inside the cloister he could hear the sounds of thumb-pianos and small bells, ringing under the tireless hands of the meditating students.

The Poet went to her accustomed place within the circle of great stones, and raised her face to the skies, lifting her arms and spreadng them wide. He had watched her the night before; she had stood motionless there for hours, sometimes moving her lips in words he could not hear, sometimes silent. And nothing had happened. No poison. No pain. He was here again tonight to see if it would be different.

He was sure that no one could possibly have come over the walls or down from any of the trees to do her harm, even if it were possible to do so without her noticing—which was not unthinkable in view of the depth of her trance. The moonlight was bright, though, so bright that no smallest movement could go unnoticed. And he was in no trance, except that of boredom.

The minutes crept, one after another. Coyote was tired, as well as bored. He caught himself wishing there would be another attack on the Poet so that he could get on with this, and was mildly astonished at his own callousness. However, it was possible that his presence here was sufficient to keep whoever was out to harm Jacinth from trying it again, and in that case what would he do? He could not sit here every night from now on, like the guardian angels of prehistory. Eventually he would have to go back to Mars-Central, heavy taxes or no heavy taxes.

The moons rose higher, their brillance almost blinding. He could easily have read by their light, if he had dared bring anything to read. The poet still yearned toward the sky, not the smallest fraction of her body moving except the ends of her hair streaming in the wind from time to time, and her lips that murmured mysteries. The eyes were always wide; he was sure she had not blinked them once, and he marveled that she could stare into the face of those burning moons . . .

When it happened at last it was so sudden that he was caught by surprise. She dropped without a sound to the grass and lay there, eyes finally closed, mouth wide in a silent scream, her back arched like a bow in her torment. For an instant she relaxed, moaned softly, and then as the pain struck her again she was once more twisted into an arch of agony.

Coyote ran toward her, caught her up in his arms, feeling the spasms of the muscles reacting against the pain, and carried her toward the trees to lay her down. At once, when he passed the border of the circle of stones, she relaxed, and he realized that she had lost consciousness.

He laid her down under the trees, examined her briefly to be sure that she was in no immediate danger, and went quickly back to the spot where he had seen her fall. There might be something there, some clue, something that would give him at least an indication of where to look. Poisons did not simply come out of the air and strike their victims to the earth, not even on a planet where crime was an honorable profession—although, come to think of it, perhaps that was a thought. A dart? A hypodermic from a gun? Both were certainly more plausible than the undetectable poison in the food! He hurried, pleased with this new idea.

He stood where Jacinth had stood and looked around him, then knelt to examine the grass under his feet, and when the pain lanced through his skull he cried out in astonishment. Caught off guard, he almost activated the shields that would have protected him against the attack, but he recovered enough of his balance to realize that shielding would at once give away to the attacker the fact that someone else was standing in Jacinth's spot, and someone who knew a bit more about what was going on than she did. Instead of shielding he stepped out of the circle; as he had suspected, there was no repetition of the pain. He went back to Jacinth's usual place; immediately the hot knife slashed through his mind, and he moved away again. Again it stopped as he left the circle of stones.

Poison, indeed! He was breathing hard, as much in rage as from the effects of the pain. He went to where he had laid the woman and found her resting, but conscious, smiling up at him, her smile tired but aware, and free of pain.

"My lady Poet," he said softly, "I think we have found the answer to your problem."

She opened her mouth to speak, but he laid his fingers across her lips.

"Don't try to talk," he said. "I am going to carry you into the Cloister and send for your servingwoman to stay with you. When you feel entirely yourself again, we will talk. In the meantime, there is no problem about protecting you against the animal that's after you—just stay out of the circle of stones. You're not required by your office to meditate only in that spot, are you?"

She shook her head, and he nodded approvingly.

"Good," he said. "Stay away from those stones and nothing will happen to you, at least not until it is discovered that you have changed your place of meditation. It would be best if you moved to a different spot each night until we have settled this ugly thing."

He lifted her in his arms and carried her across the garden, indifferent to whether or not such contact was forbidden to her. The extent to which she had been neglected sickened him; obviously no one had bothered to stand close to her at the time of the attacks, but had simply watched from the comfort of the Cloister. If anyone had been with her, any one of the members of the Profession of Law—surely they were at least minimally trained?—any one of them should have known at once that it was not poison but a psi-weapon that was being used against their Poet.

He saw her safely resting in comfort, with a steaming drink beside her and a servingwoman to watch her in case she should need anything, before he left her. He made sure that his instructions about her nightly change of place for meditation were known to someone who would not forget, even if she did, and then he set out to walk back to his rooms, refusing the offer of transport the Poets made him and sending his own flier back empty.

"I'm too angry to ride," he said to them bluntly. "If I walk all the way back to the Palace of Law I may be fit to face another human being by the time I get there."

"And the Poet Jacinth——"

"Take care of her!" he bellowed at them, his patience exhausted. "She has suffered only because you have not prevented it, you versifying fools! Keep her away from that spot in the garden that I showed you, see that she does not always go to the same spot and present herself as a target, and I will see what I can do! Naturally nothing can be done tonight; the Citizen realizes that the hour of accomplishing anything has passed!"

They made no further effort to interfere with him, and he went out into the night to walk off his rage.

When he explained the situation to the proper official the next day he got the response he expected.

"But that is impossible," said the Abban.

"Citizen ban-Drakl," said Coyote wearily, "I'm sorry. Impossible or not, it is so. There is no poison involved in this case at all, as you would have found out for yourself if you had gone to the, pardon the expression, scene of the crime. The Poet Jacinth is being subjected to psi-probe of an impressive intensity, projected at considerable distance."

"How can this be?"

"What do you mean, how can it be? It simply *is*."

"But it is against the law!"

Coyote regarded him carefully and thought for a moment, then shook his head.

"How?" he said finally. "You tell me what that means to you—it is against the law. I see no evidence of any law here on Abba, Citizen ban-Drakl, unless perhaps as applied to the status of your women."

Ban-Drakl made an astonished face. "Perhaps the Citizen has suffered a slip of the tongue?" he wondered. "Is this not the Palace of Law itself?"

"This," said Coyote, "is the Palace of Rules and Regulations. There can be no law—and no justice, my friend—in a society where any law may be broken as long as the proper form has been filled out first. That system prevailed on Old Earth for centuries, and came very near bringing about the destruction of the human race on that planet. It works no better now than it ever did."

"The Citizen is overwrought," murmured the Abban politely, and Coyote shrugged.

"I am not here to argue philosophies with you," he said. "Let us drop this discussion, Lawyer ban-Drakl, and take up the problem of locating the individual who wants to destroy the Poet Jacinth. I am as aware as you that the use of psi-probe as a weapon is against the law. It is against intergalactic law as well as Abban, my friend. Nonetheless, someone is doing it, and doing it well. Your Poet could not survive many more such attacks."

To Coyote's amazement the Abban proceeded to pull out a heavy file marked "Current Registered Crimes" and look painstakingly through it.

"No such crime is registered," he said at last. "Shocking. Just shocking."

"The crime or its unregistered status?"

"What, Citizen?"

"Our shock will not help the Poet Jacinth," Coyote went on, ignoring the question. "Have you any idea who might be doing this thing?"

"The Citizen must allow me a moment to think," said the Abban, and Coyote sat back to wait.

"Citizen Jones?"

"Yes?"

"You say this attack is of great intensity, great force?"

"Correct."

"Then it is not something that could be done by just anyone?"

"Oh, no. It would require a real expert, someone of unusual ability and strength, a psi-adept with extensive training."

"All such persons are registered, throughout the Three Galaxies," mused ban-Drakl.

"Right," said Coyote. "And do you know how many of them there are, by any chance?"

"No—do you?"

"Exactly four hundred and thirty-six. Each one was registered with Mars-Central at birth and is employed in some official function for which his abilities specifically fit him. Some are Communipaths, some are in Multiversities . . ."

And some, he thought but carefully did not say, some are TGIS agents.

"You know that all our Criminals on Abba are psitrained," said ban-Drakl. "Is there any chance that it might be one of them?"

"You mean someone with ordinary psi-talent and a year or two of training?" asked Coyote, thinking of Neo. "Is that the extent of it?"

"Yes," said ban-Drakl. "Could one of them do it— that is, assuming one of them would be so depraved as to commit such a crime, and unregistered, too?"

Coyote shook his head.

"No," he answered, "this isn't on that scale at all. One of your criminals might be able to cause a moderate headache at ten paces, nothing more."

"I see," said the Abban. "I see."

"Good. I am pleased to hear it."

"The Citizen is angry."

"The Citizen bloody well is. This is inexcusable, you know."

"Mmmm. The publicity will not do Abba any good."

"That's right, my friend. It may cut into your tourist trade quite a bit. Psi-probers are not exactly the favored culture-heroes of the citizens of the Tri-Galactic Federation."

"Oh, dear," sighed Lawyer ban-Drakl.

"Oh, dear," mimicked Coyote. "What do you expect to accomplish by sighing and dear-dearing, Citizen?"

"Nothing at all," said the Abban with sudden briskness. "We must do something specific. What would you suggest?"

"First of all, we notify Mars-Central of the situation and have them check the location and activities of the four hundred and thirty-six people we mentioned.

Second, we have one of the Communipaths check those same four hundred and thirty-six to see if one of them is lying."

"They will permit that?"

"If a psi-adept refuses to allow examination by a Communipath, then he has something to hide," said Coyote. "His refusal is as revealing as an admission of guilt."

"I see."

"Then," Coyote went on, "when we find—as I'm sure we will—that none of our known adepts is involved in this filthy business, we set all the Communipaths scanning the galaxies in search of a rogue."

"Rogue?"

"A rogue telepath," said Coyote, "someone who has by some freak managed to keep secret the psi-powers that he has, and is misusing them against others."

"This can happen?"

"It has, on at least one previous occasion; that time it was a baby. But babies don't go around psi-probing people."

"What if they don't find anyone?"

"There has to be a source," Coyote chided. "Psi-probes don't grow like flowers, or fall like rain, Citizen. They come from human minds. And any source of sufficient power to do what this one is doing will be detectable by the Communipaths."

"What if he's shielded?"

"It could be a woman, you know," Coyote said, watching ban-Drakl. The Abban recoiled, as he had known he would, and Coyote scored one point for his side.

"He—or she—" he went on, "cannot simultaneously maintain shields and initiate an attack. The instant the shields are dropped to allow projection of the probe, the Communipaths will be able to locate the source."

"That means the Poet Jacinth must undergo more of this pain? But that is very unfortunate!"

"What is unfortunate," said Coyote carefully, "is that I am prohibited by law—a *real* law this time, from a planet where crime is not conducted like a business— from wringing your unfortunate neck."

"Perhaps the Citizen will explain?"

"There is no necessity whatsoever for the Poet Jacinth undergoing anything at all, can't you see that? Whoever this psi-criminal is, he or she is not sufficiently skilled to select an individual as a target. The projection is being done by visualization of the particular place where the Poet is known to go each night to meditate, and whether there is anyone there in that spot to undergo the attack is not something the criminal knows, probably. Certainly, anyone at all could stand there in her place and provide the proper feedback of pain."

"The attack is simply blind projection, then?"

"Exactly. It will probably be some time—if no one shoots off his big mouth—before it becomes known that the Poet Jacinth no longer goes each evening to that ring of stones in the garden of the Trance Cloister. For as long as that is the case the attacks will probably continue, just as if the Poet were there. It would be a good idea to issue daily reports of her sufferings . . . no, I take that back. Since we can't be sure it will be every night, we mustn't do that, we might give the whole thing away. We need vague rumors, only. And the Poet will be quite safe, but the Communipaths will be able to scan for the source of the probe."

"I see," said the Abban again. He saw a great deal, once it had been clearly pointed out to him; it would have been more useful if he had been able to see something by himself.

"Can you take care of the details of all this?" asked Coyote.

"Notifying Mars-Central, asking for Communipath scanning, all of that? Of course, Citizen Jones. It will be done at once. You need not concern yourself further about it."

Coyote stood up. "Very good, then," he said. "I'll go back to my rooms and make my report to Mars-Central."

# CHAPTER EIGHT

FILE 1143.01.b, Segment 2
TOPIC: Rogue Telepath (presumed)
FROM: Office of the Director
      Communipath Data, and Detail
      GALCENTRAL, STATION 7
TO: Lawyer ban-Drakl
    Palace of Law
    Alsabaid, the planet Abba
DATE: Octoberninth 3028

1. Thorough checking of the 436 known psi-adepts within the area of the Three Galaxies reveals that each is engaged in the performance of activities known to the Communipath Bureau and fully approved. In those cases where deviancies were found they were personal matters and in no way connected with this situation; therefore no report will be made on them.

2. Extensive scanning of the Tri-Galactic area to its farthest perimeters has as yet revealed no evidence whatever, REPEAT NO EVIDENCE WHATEVER, of any rogue psi-activity emanating from any single source. It is felt that this alternative can safely be eliminated from consideration.

3. Communipaths scanning in the area of the planet Abba itself, however, have located the probable source of the psi-activity directed toward

the Poet Jacinth ban-harihn. The coordinates of said source indicate that it is to be found in that section of the city of Alsabaid known as the "Ruby Ring"—that is, in the Vice Quarter. It was not possible for the Communipaths to locate the source more precisely because of the difficulties with the signal (see below for explanation), but the Vice Quarter is small enough that further investigation by the agent on the spot should not be difficult. Another agent could of course be sent out to assist Citizen Jones in this investigation; however, since intergalactic distance is irrelevant to the Communipaths' efficiency, it is felt unlikely that there is anything that could be done there in the way of psi-scanning that has not already been done by them. (Coordinates will be found below.)

4. It should be noted that the Communipaths report that the signal itself coming from the psi-source in the Ruby Ring is aberrant in some way that they are not able to specify. As is well known, the psi-voice of any given individual, rather than being recognizable by sound as is the overt voice, is usually identified by such factors as a specific taste, smell, appearance, and the like, which is perceived by the individual receiving the telepathic projection of the voice. The Communipaths state that this particular signal is so muddy and distorted and full of static that they find it impossible to describe in any significant way. They feel that this fact may be of the utmost significance for the investigating agent, since it indicates that the source is not one of the usual ones with which we are accustomed to deal.

5. If the difficulty in handling this situation persists, Communipath Bureau (Data and Detail Division) should be notified in order that further action may be discussed. In writing, please refer to above file number.

END OF REPORT

PS: This signal is really weird, friends . . . it tastes like chocolate/peanut butter/fish/cactus-fruit/seaweed/lake-spice/casserole, and it smells like everything it doesn't taste like. We wish you luck and would like to know what the character putting it out is like.

Andy Maryn

Coyote read the report through carefully, then handed it back to the Lawyer.

"That's clear," he said. "I'll go down to the Ruby Ring this evening at the proper time for the attack to take place, and see what I can find."

Ban-Drakl cleared his throat. "I seem to recall, Citizen, that the last time you went to the Ruby Ring there was some sort of unpleasantness."

"Oh, that," said Coyote blandly, "that was quite all right. Just some of your honorable Criminals playing their little registered games, no?"

"The Citizen would make us very unhappy if he fell once again into participation in these games to which we are referring."

"Don't worry," said Coyote. "I'll have my interpreter along with me this time. He'll be careful—he wouldn't dare let me get into trouble."

"That will be a load off our minds," said ban-Drakl. "We have grown fond of you, Citizen."

Coyote refused to answer that. He left with dispatch and went to brief his interpreter, who seemed perfectly calm about the whole thing.

"See here, ban-Dell," Coyote asked him, "are you sure we can get through the evening without my ending up maimed in some way? Otherwise I'm going to demand a police force to go with us."

Citizen ban-Dell was a small man and a chubby one, but he had great dignity. "There is no occasion for alarm," he assured Coyote. "I am not to be tricked so easily as all that."

"Good," said Coyote. "Very good. Because I am. I am to be tricked more easily than you can imagine."

If ban-Dell felt that that was a strange thing for an intergalactic agent to say he carefully suppressed his opinion.

They arrived at the Ruby Ring just as the moons were rising, since all the known attacks had occurred shortly after moonrise. Coyote wore the gray robe that almost let him pass as a man of Business; his interpreter scuttled protectively beside him.

"Where shall we begin?" ban-Dell asked, putting one hand on Coyote's arm. "We can't just prowl the Ring at random."

Coyote shrugged. "You're the expert, you know, a native of this society. What would be *your* suggestion?"

"Well . . . there are two possibilities. Since this crime is unregistered it is being committed either by an amateur or by a real expert. That is, our criminal is going to be at one of the extreme ends of the scale, not some average person in the middle."

"Not Citizen Joe Criminal, you mean."

"I beg your pardon?"

"Where would we look for one of these extreme ends, Citizen ban-Dell?"

"That's hard to say."

"You must have some ideas."

It was, of course, the case that if Coyote could get within fifteen feet, roughly, of the attacker, he would be aware of him. His psi-bilities were adequate for that. But the Ruby Ring covered a very large area compared with the fifteen feet that represented his maximum receptive range.

The little man bit his lip and frowned.

"I think," he said, "that we might save some time if we went first to the Kalif."

Coyote raised his eyebrows.

"The term," said ban-Dell, "is borrowed from old Earth culture, I believe. Some kind of an official. When our culture was . . . er . . . adjusted to suit the requirements of the Tri-Galactic Federation, the gentleman from Mars-Central who helped us with the adjustments made us quite a list of such terms. The Criminals took a fancy to 'Kalif.'"

"What is his function, exactly?"

"He's a sort of administrator, coordinates all the activities . . . you could accurately say that he does the same thing for the Criminals that our Chief of Legislators does for the members of Law, except that of course the Kalif's authority does not extend beyond the limits of his own profession."

"By all means, let's go see him. Where do we find him?"

The Abban pointed to a street sign above their heads. It was shield-shaped and made of a scintillant lavender material, and it bore a plain legend. The Panglish equivalent was "Street of the Kalif."

"Follow me," said ban-Dell.

They crossed the street, brushing off, as they went, the Criminals who stepped up to them with an extraordinary variety of propositions, and headed down the Street of the Kalif. Half a block, and Coyote was standing in a state of total awestruck delight before the Palace of Crime.

He was simply going to have to get over this culture-bind that kept him associating crime with the furtive, the secret, and the squalid, he thought. If anything, the Palace of Crime was even more magnificent than the Palace of Law; it was a full city block of archways, and balconies, and gardens, and hanging vines, and winding staircases. The architects had apparently, must have, worked directly and with meticulous fidelity from the illustrations of an expensive edition of the *Arabian Nights*.

"Are those real woods and real tiles?" Coyote marveled.

"Oh, no," said ban-Dell. "That would have been rather ostentatious, don't you think? The construction materials are synthetics. But I find them extremely convincing, don't you?"

"Indeed I do," said Coyote. "I would have taken them for the real thing."

They were ushered into the offices of the Kalif of Crime after a number of subordinates had expressed their great pleasure at seeing with their own eyes a high-ranking agent of a Tri-Galactic anticrime organization. Some of the Criminals ran down corridors and brought back little groups of others to marvel at him, and Coyote tried unsuccessfully to ignore the wondering murmur of Abban that seemed to follow and surround him.

"Why, exactly," he demanded under his breath, "are they so amazed at the sight of a TGIS agent?"

"Well . . . we are, a practical people, you know."

"So I've heard."

"What strikes them as so incredible is that governments would go to the expense of an organization like TGIS instead of simply incorporating crime into their own political structure. As we do here. They find you an example of off-world extravagance, unheard-of luxury, and decadent waste."

"They don't realize that their taxes help pay for TGIS?"

"Of course not. Why should they?"

When you are as accustomed as Coyote was to being considered an unfortunate and regrettable necessity, the idea that you are instead the priceless toy of a society that can afford to spare no expense is something of a shock. Coyote followed ban-Dell into the Kalif's office without another word.

The Kalif greeted them expansively, listened to their description of their problem with attentive nods, and then stretched out his delicate long hands to express his surprise.

"Such a terrible thing," he mourned, "such a dreadful thing. And within my own territory! I can hardly bring myself to believe it—are you quite sure?"

"Your Excellency," said Coyote, hoping that was the right title, "if I were to ask you where your comset is, would you have any difficulty in telling me?"

"Of course not, Citizen. I see it right here, at the left side of my desk."

"Well, for a Communipath the location of a psi-source is just as simple. They perceive its location just as surely as you do your belongings. It can't be a mistake."

"Citizen ban-Dell?" said the Kalif. "Do you verify all this?"

"I do, Your Excellency," said ban-Dell. "I know very little about the Communipath system, except to be greatful that they are able to serve as a communications network for the galaxies and spare us waiting centuries between the question sent and its answer. But Citizen Jones is an expert on this subject; he remembers, for example, when the life expectancy of a Communipath was only eighteen years."

"There was such a deplorable condition as that?"

"Until very recently," said Coyote, feeling ancient, "and reform is only just beginning."

The Kalif clucked his tongue in distaste. "And I hear you Inner Galaxy people criticize *our* political system! Amazing!"

Coyote stared at his feet, determined not to rise to this sort of baiting. All he needed to thoroughly foul up this evening's work was to become involved in a political debate with the chief Criminal of Abba.

The interpreter put in a tactful word. "Can you help us in any way, Citizen Kalif?"

Citizen Kalif! thought Coyote. He hadn't expected that.

"Hmmmm . . ." said the Kalif. "Let me think . . . certainly I know of no one who would do a thing like this. On the other hand, I know everyone who is within the area of the Ruby Ring, I know what each one of them will and will not do, and I have assistants who are experts on each and every activity carried on in the Ring. If I call them all in and we all put our heads together, I see no reason why we should not come up with some answers."

IF WE ALL PUT OUR HEADS TOGETHER!

It was like an electric shock. Coyote sat there, stunned. He was remembering, as a child, the training in the Communipath Creche on Mars-Central. The matrons had had them all sit on the floor in a circle, with their foreheads touching, and they had played games, trying to guess which one was thinking, trying to touch each other's thoughts. That was it. It had to be.

He stood up abruptly and both Abbans looked at him with polite surprise.

"I know who's doing it," he said wearily. "I should have known the first night I was here, if I hadn't been so wrapped up in that red herring about poison. Damn it all! I must be getting old."

"Well, tell us, Citizen!" the Kalif exclaimed.

"It's very simple, and it was you that gave me the information."

"I did."

"You did. We should all put our heads together, you said. And then I remembered. The first night I was here, when I was wandering around the Ring in the clutches of your estimable poisoner, Neo what's-his-name . . ."

"Ban-Valdevere," murmured the Kalif.

"Ban-Valdevere? Really?"

Coyote blinked and went on.

"Anyway, we went down a kind of alley, and through a window I saw this circle of people, sitting on the floor with their heads touching, all of them chanting . . . Neo said it was a religious cult. I haven't thought of it since."

"Of course!" The Kalif struck his desk with his fist.

"You say the Communipaths complained that the signal was muddled!"

"Exactly. And that's what you would expect, under the circumstances. None of those people could project across a dining table by themselves, but by all sitting close together and concentrating on a single image, night after night, they are able to amplify their individual weak signals into a single strong one."

"Amazing," marveled the Kalif. "I will have to be very stern with them."

"You know who they are, then?"

"Certainly. The cult of the Holy United Mind. I'm as bad as you are, Citizen Jones; I should have known at once, if only from the stupid name they chose to give themselves."

"Well, then!" said the interpreter, standing up to join Coyote. "Let's go deal with this matter at once. It should be a matter of routine, now that we know what's going on."

Coyote shook his head. "No," he said. "I know exactly what should be done about this, and I'll handle it myself. And it can't be done tonight, it's too late. Tomorrow night I'll come back and put a stop to their dangerous little game for good. In my own way."

"You realize that we cannot allow you to do them harm, Citizen?" the Kalif put in. "TGIS or no TGIS——"

Coyote stopped him with a gesture.

"Don't worry," he said. "Not only won't I harm them, I'll provide them with the peak religious experience of their lives. I'll come get you both and take you with me to watch, and if at any moment you feel some of their precious rights are being violated, you can interfere, okay? Fair enough?"

"Fair enough," said the Kalif. "I look forward to the demonstration."

Then he clapped his hands and a subordinate entered.

"I want to show our friends around the Ruby Ring personally," the Kalif said cheerfully. "Summon a thaan-carriage at once and call ahead to all my favorite places —tell them to expect us and to make ready."

He looked at Coyote and winked, a long, slow, experienced, evil wink.

"I think you're really going to like this," he beamed.

# CHAPTER NINE

COYOTE WAS IMPATIENT the next day, as well as suffering slightly from the effects of the previous night's tour with the head man from Crime. He told the women good-bye, effusively enough so that they would not jump to the conclusion that he was in some mysterious way displeased with them, and went out to walk through the streets of Alsabaid.

There were women on the street, moving along in twos and threes, heavily veiled and covered by shapeless, full, flowing robes in colorful patterns. Thaan-carriages were everywhere, and mobs of students on their way to their classes. The city was beautiful; Coyote felt better just from looking around him.

He went into a park where a display of mobile flowers was whirling solemnly around a fountain, and sat down on a bench to watch the flowers and the pale green water leaping in the sunshine. The flower leading the dance was an enormous specimen, almost five feet tall, with diamond-shaped petals of a gold so pure it hurt the eyes, and great sawtoothed leaves perhaps six inches in length. He wondered where it came from, and then saw the tag on one of its leaves—Alepha 238. Coyote whistled softly . . . that was a long way from Abba.

A small bell rang at his ear, and he jumped. In the air beside his head there hung a small star-shaped bauble, repeating the same bell sound at intervals of ten seconds or so and evidently a constructed, rather than a natural, phenomenon. He looked around him at the other citizens enjoying the fountains, and noted that none of them seemed at all alarmed by this pretty toy that had appeared so suddenly in their midst.

"Citizen," he said to the man closest to him, a burly gentleman in the white robe with dark blue stripe that marked him for a Scientist, "can you tell me what that thing is?"

"That thing?"

Coyote pointed.

"Oh, yes," said the Scientist, "you mean the Memo Star?"

"Memo Star . . . I am an off-worlder, Citizen. Could you explain?"

"Assuredly, Citizen. I would be honored. The Memo Star is attuned to any given citizen's registration number—"

"What registration number?"

"On your Federation credit disc, Citizen."

"Oh yes. I'm sorry."

"Quite all right. As I was saying, the Memo Star is attuned to your personal number and can be sent after you to convey messages. Yours must have something rather private to say to you."

"Why do you say that, Citizen?"

"Because it hasn't given you your message. If it were only some business appointment, or a message that one of your sons wished to speak to you, something of that kind, it would simply make that announcement by your ear and return to the sender."

"Ah," said Coyote, pulling his beard. "Interesting. Well, then, how do I go about getting it to divulge this private message it has for me?"

The Abban pointed toward a small egg-shaped structure down one of the paths in the park where the fountains were.

"That is a privacy booth, Citizen," he said courteously. "Take the Memo Star with you and go into the booth. There you will find a star-shaped projection on the wall. Touch the Memo Star to the projection and it will deliver your message."

"Thank you, Citizen," said Coyote, "you are most kind."

"Not at all," smiled the Citizen. "I am honored."

Coyote reached out cautiously and plucked the star out of the air, still chiming at him. It did not burn him or shock him or sting him, and he made his way to the privacy booth. Presumably, since the Abban had not worn the robes of a Criminal, he was safe in following his instructions; he went into the booth, located the star-shaped stud on its wall, touched the Memo Star to it, and waited.

At once the little bell rang again, and then the Star spoke to him in a tinny, mechanical voice.

"The Poet Jacinth sends you her best wishes," it said, "and asks that you come to her tonight at the seventh hour. She will send her servingwoman to the west entrance of the Trance Cloister to guide you. End of message."

Not sure that he had heard properly, Coyote touched the little gadget to the wall stud again and listened to the message a second time. There was no mistake. But what could the lady Poet want? He was willing to go, but he was *not* going to get dressed up in the monkey suit again. She would see him in his own clothing or she would not see him at all.

He went back out, carrying the Star, which promptly took off and disappeared from sight. He nodded at the questioning look of the Abban Scientist, to indicate that he and the trinket had managed without difficulty, and began to walk.

Could the Poet Jacinth perhaps have some information on the psi-attacker that they did not have? It seemed very unlikely. Or was she simply requesting a report from him on the progress of the investigation? Her days were so fully occupied with her duties that the evening meeting she had specified was not surprising, and if she did not keep him long he would still be able to reach the Ruby Ring soon after moonrise.

His curiosity was aroused. He went to find a ship where he could buy her some little gift to take along with him. Finding something suitable would help to pass the time.

When he finally sat before her, not in the anteroom this time, but in another, smaller room that he supposed must be her own, he handed her the gift that he had chosen. It was a small scroll of synthosilk, bearing a delicate drawing of gaza trees blowing in the breeze. He saw that she was pleased, and accepted her thanks, glad that he had chosen something she could enjoy.

"Now," he said, "what can I do for you, my lady Poet? I will be happy to do anything I can."

She hesitated for a moment, and then spoke, slowly, in her oddly accented Panglish.

"I would dispense with the speech of Poetry for this one evening," she said carefully, "if you would not find it offensive."

"Why should I?" asked Coyote, surprised and touched. "You must speak however you want to speak."

"Then I will speak as any woman to any man," she said. "The fashion of poetry alone in my speech is only of meaning if you are a man of Abba . . . I ask your patience, I am clumsy."

Coyote waited, and when he saw that she was also waiting he spoke again.

"What is it, Citizeness? Did you want me for some particular purpose? The investigation is going well, you should be safe from the psi-attack after tonight, if that is worrying you."

She shook her head.

"There is another burden, Citizen, of which you might ease me, if you were willing."

"You have only to tell me," said Coyote. "If it is within my power, I will do it gladly."

"It is difficult."

"Try," he coaxed, gently.

"At the age of twelve," she said slowly, "I was brought here from my father's house. Since then, to the limits of my poor ability, I have served the Holy Light. Through all that time I have written poems of every kind, the poems of love as well, but I have never known love, Citizen. No man of Abba dares touch a woman who is a Poet."

Coyote was silent, unable to think of a single suitable thing to say.

"Citizen Jones," she said, "I am weary of my condition. Will you help a poor woman of Abba?"

Coyote stared at her, not quite certain that he understood, but very much afraid that he did. She looked back at him, unwaveringly.

"I have never seen such huge eyes as you have, Citizeness," he said softly, playing for time.

"That is because each day a liquid is dropped in them —so that I am able to look at the twin moons without harm.

"Will you help me, Citizen?" she asked him again. "They say that I am mad, but I would not hurt you."

Coyote considered the matter. Even allowing for the difference in cultures, there didn't seem to be any way he could misinterpret what she was saying. The lady desired to be deflowered and felt he was the proper agent of that defloration.

Just what, he wondered, might be the diplomatic repercussions if he complied? Would he find himself legally her husband, for example, by Abban law? Or would he be guilty of an "unregistered" crime? He was reasonably sure he had too much diplomatic immunity to be in any serious danger, but it could get very unpleasant, and the Fish would get a kick out of letting him stew in an Abban jail.

"Would you give me a moment?" he asked, finally. "I'll come back at once." He bolted from the room with as much haste as seemed possible when he took into consideration Jacinth's feelings. He found a student and demanded a Memo Star, with instructions for its use.

When it came back to him ten minutes later, and he took it into a cubicle meant for other functions, to listen to it, he was satisfied. The interpreter had made the answer quite clear.

"By all means take the Poet to bed," the return message said. "We've always wished someone would, because it would be certain to improve her poetry, but none of us could possibly have managed it, not with her being Poet and woman at one and the same. We would be honored, Citizen Jones."

There was no getting out of it, then. Coyote went back to Jacinth's room, whistling softly under his breath, and went to find her still sitting as he had left her, waiting for his answer.

She looked up as he came in, and smiled sadly.

"I have offended you, Citizen," she said. "I ask your forgiveness; a woman does not always know what is best to do."

"Hush," said Coyote. "I can think of nothing I would rather do than love you. I just had some business that had to be settled first."

He reached out and gathered her up, carried her over to her narrow bed, and laid her down.

"You are always carrying me," she laughed.

Coyote chuckled. "The Citizen is honored," he said.

"I am very frightened."

He touched her hair gently. "Don't be," he said. "I have never had any complaints yet."

Tenderly he removed the scarlet tunic that covered her small, perfect breasts, the breasts of a young girl, and the untouched flaring curve of her loins. He was so involved with her beauty, and with the rush of desire that he felt at the sight of her, naked but for the black hair that flowed about her like silk, that he thought of nothing else. Certainly not of the Palace of Crime, and the men who waited for him there.

She cried out once, softly, as he entered her, and he gentled her tenderly with his hand.

"That's all the pain that there will be, love," he said to her. "That's all there is; from now on it should be only joy."

He hoped so. It mattered deeply to him that this first—and possibly last, for her—lovemaking should be something she could look back upon with happiness rather than regret. He settled to the grateful task of pleasing her, to making all things one for her, knowing that the chances of bringing her to climax were very slim but determined that she should at least find pleasure, and was rewarded finally by the high cry of perfect ecstasy that he would not have dared promise her.

Afterward she fell asleep in his arms, and the moons were high in the sky before he could bring himself to lay her aside, put on his gray cloak, and make his way to the Palace of Law.

# CHAPTER TEN

"You're sure," said the head of the Criminal Profession as the three of them made their way to the meeting place of the cult called Holy United Mind, "you're absolutely sure that there's nothing in your plan that will harm any of these people?"

"You have my word," said Coyote. "Am I to understand that you don't consider that a sufficient guarantee?"

"The Citizen is justifiably annoyed," murmured the Abban. "I withdraw my question."

Coyote looked as offended as possible, glaring straight ahead of him and pulling at his beard.

"We are almost there," put in the interpreter hastily. "What do you want us to do?"

"Just stay by the windows so you can see the fun," Coyote said, "and don't interfere."

"Where will you be?"

"I'm going around the other side and come in through that little door there on the right. All you have to do is wait here and watch."

He left them there and slipped around to the other side of the room where the cultists were crouched uncomfortably with their heads pressed together. Beside the door he shucked his long robe and gave his costume a last look to be sure it was satisfactory.

It was certainly unusual. He wore a skin-tight suit of brilliant scarlet and a hood of synthetic golden feathers with silver tips and flecks. Wings of the same splendor trailed from his shoulders almost to the ground, looped up and fastened to his wrists so that when he raised his arms he looked amazingly birdlike. Giant birdlike. Carefully scattered all over the scarlet skin-stocking were small pinhead-size mirrors; they were of no use now, but later they would be indispensable to the effect he intended to create. Lightning bolts were going to issue from them, for example, and some very fancy rainbows. Whatever his inspiration dictated.

He'd used this costume twice before and it always did the job. He rarely went on an assignment without it, taking it along as a matter of course, along with a couple of others of slightly different design but equal magnificence. This one had been carefully prepared by the TGIS psychologists to combine half a dozen ancient archetype figures, with a heavy saturation of Angel/Devil. Coyote rather fancied himself in it, and regretted the fact that he was unable to see it in its full splendor, since he was immune to his own illusions.

He prepared a careful image, also prescribed by the psychology staff. Clouds of smoke, booming thunder, tongues of flame, and all the little mirrors activated. He imagined himself surrounded by a seething maelstrom of noise and turmoil and tumultuous color, and when he had the whole thing visualized he projected it at sufficient strength to blanket the room ahead of him, and walked in, straight into the center of the chanting circle.

The effect was all that he had hoped it would be. The cultists were paralyzed with fear and with the "DO NOT MOVE FROM YOUR PLACE, YOU SINFUL SCUM" instructions that they were getting from Coyote along with the fancy stage props. As one man, they prostrated themselves before him and peered at him through trembling fingers from flat on their bellies on the floor.

"Shame!" he thundered, projecting each word as he uttered it, although that was probably not necessary. He believed in being absolutely sure.

"A POX UPON YOUR HOUSES! MAY YOUR WINDOWS CAVE IN AND YOUR DOORS CRUMBLE ABOUT YOU! MAY YOUR BEDS CATCH FIRE AND BE CONSUMED IN FLAME! MAY ALL YOUR SONS BE IMPOTENT AND YOUR DAUGHTERS INCURABLY CROSS-EYED! MAY YOUR LIVESTOCK DIE, MAY YOUR FLIERS ALWAYS BE BROKEN DOWN! MAY YOUR WOMEN RISE UP AND REBEL AGAINST YOU AND SHAME YOUR HOUSEHOLDS! MAY YOUR CHILDREN CURSE

YOU TO YOUR FACE AND YOUR SERVANTS THROW THEMSELVES INTO THE RIVERS RATHER THAN REMAIN WITH YOU IN DIS- GRACE! MAY YOUR HOMES FALL IN ABOUT YOU AND SUFOCATE YOU IN THEIR RUBBLE! MAY THE VERY HILLS OF ABBA MOVE TO COVER YOUR SHAME!"

The men began to wail, begging for mercy, pleading their innocence. Coyote knew what they were seeing. A giant creature, far larger than a man, garbed in lightning and rainbows, winged like a bird, around whom swirled colored mists and jets of flame. No wonder they were scared. He would have been, too.

"I AM OFFENDED!" he bellowed. "GRIEVOUSLY HAVE YOU OFFENDED THE HOLY LIGHT AND ME, ITS SACRED MESSENGER! HOW DARE YOU MOVE TO HARM THE HOLY WOMAN JACINTH, CHOSEN POET, CHOSEN VOICE OF THE HOLY AND ALMIGHTY LIGHT? SCUM! SWINE!"

He took a deep breath and upped the output of light- ning, putting it out now not only in the standard natural yellow but in poisonous greens and purples as well. He wreathed his golden head with a whirling circle of hissing snakes.

"ONLY IN ONE WAY CAN YOU SAVE YOUR SHAMEFUL SOULS! I AM COME TO SPARE YOU ETERNAL DAMNATION, SENT BY THE HOLY LIGHT, IN INFINITE MERCY, TO OFFER YOU AN OPPORTUNITY TO ESCAPE THE JUST PUNISH- MENT THAT YOU SO HEARTILY DESERVE! DOGS! PIGS!" And he added the ultimate insult . . . "WOMEN!"

. They were utterly destroyed, he noted with satisfac- tion. It wasn't even a challenge, it was so easy. But then he should have expected that; if they hadn't been pretty piss-poor they wouldn't have been in this idiot cult any- way.

He let them grovel and beg a while, stepping up to the local color that filled the three-foot area in the center of which he stood, and then he told them.

"YOU ARE TO CEASE YOUR PERSECUTION OF THE POET JACINTH."

They would.

"YOU ARE TO KNOW THAT SHE IS HOLY,

THAT SHE IS BELOVED OF THE HOLY LIGHT, THAT NOT ONE OF YOU HERE IS FIT TO KISS HER SLENDER FEET."

Yes, yes. They knew that now.

"HENCEFORTH IT IS YOUR SOLEMN TRUST TO DEVOTE YOURSELF TO THE GLORIFICA-TION OF THE POET JACINTH, AS BEFITS HER HIGH STATION. YOU WILL MEDITATE UPON HER BEAUTY. YOU WILL COMPOSE HYMNS TO HER MAGNIFICENCE, TO HER TOTAL PERFEC-TION, TO HER UNSPOTTED SUPERBNESS."

They would do that, they assured him in unison. They would, they would! If he only would go away and allow them to begin.

"NOT UNTIL I AM CERTAIN THAT YOU HAVE UNDERSTOOD WHAT YOUR FUNCTION IS TO BE HENCEFORTH, MISERABLE DOGS!" he shouted at them. "NOT UNTIL EVERY LAST ONE OF YOU HAS CONVINCED ME THAT HIS LIFE, FROM THIS MOMENT ON, WILL BE DEVOTED TO THE GLORIFICATION AND THE WORSHIP OF THE LADY POET JACINTH, BELOVED OF THE HOLY LIGHT, WILL I LEAVE THIS ROOM OR REMIT THE CURSE THAT HANGS OVER YOU!"

He did quite a lot of that stuff. The more he did of it the more he enjoyed it, as a matter of fact. He threw in some restrictions and some ritual and half a dozen em-bryo prayers based upon careful review of half a dozen assorted guaranteed "holy" books from a number of plan-ets. He told them what kind of flowers they were to put in the bouquets they sent the lady Poet, what kind of in-cense to burn. He even added a sacred day of feasting and celebration, to be held in Jacinth's honor each and every year. He saw no reason why she should not get all the mileage possible out of this, after the suffering these idiots had caused her.

It was so satisfying that he hated to quit, particularly since he was only just beginning to really hit his stride. But he knew what would happen if he didn't stop. He'd get carried away and overdo it. There'd be a great reli-gious revolution sweeping Abba, with no foundation what-soever except the visions he'd laid on these poor groveling specimens. There'd be protests from the Abban govern-ment, hysteria from the officials of the already extant churches, offended heavy taxpayers, the Light knew what else. Generalized hell to pay.

He settled for a last threat of what would happen to them if they did not obey this holy vision they'd been so fortunate as to share, the threat involving their foreskins, their testicles, and their pubic hair, and then disappeared in a cloud of purple and orange smoke.

He made it out the door, collapsed the wings, pulled his gray cloak on over the rest of it—just remembering to pull off the golden feathered hood as he started outside—and then hurried to where the Abbans were waiting for him. He was anxious to have their reactions to all this. They should have been pleased, he felt. After all, no one had been hurt, the story of the punishing messenger would spread and serve as a significant deterrent to any like misuse of psi-power, and the new cult of Jacinth-Glorification should keep a lot of otherwise bored misfits happy, busy, and out of trouble.

It was not until he had almost fallen over them, where they knelt on the sidewalk moaning and shivering, that he remembered. He shouldn't have let them watch. And not just them. There were two other converts to the new sub-religion, citizens who had just happened to wander by during his performance.

He leaned against the building and ticked off a list on his fingers. First. Convince the two innocent bystanders that nothing had happened. Second. Convince the Chief of Crime, and the interpreter, that nothing had happened. Third. *Tell* the last two what had happened, once they were free of the mystical experience he'd just shoved down their heads.

It took him a while.

He had in fact been away only nine weeks, and apparently Tzana had not missed him at all. He noted that fact with great pleasure, and sat down and watched her at her work. As he sat he amused himself by sending a series of elaborate projected insults her way.

"What's the matter with you, Coyote, have you lost your not overly impressive mind?" she demanded finally, her hands on her hips and her words fairly spitting sparks. "May I suggest that you go play Super-Telepath somewhere people don't have any work to do? There are some children down there in the park, I noticed them as I came in; why don't you go down and play with them? They'll probably let you be It!"

Coyote grinned at her.

"Well? Did you come all the way over here just to pick a fight?"

"No, blessing," he said cheerfully, "I'm just trying to get the nasty taste out of my mouth and head."

"What nasty taste?"

"The nasty taste of subservient women!" he crooned. "Nasty, foolish, docile, subjugated, subservient women, with no minds of their own, and no thoughts to put in them if they had any! The Light be praised, I'm back here once again with you, just as you are—obnoxious, arrogant, pigheaded, overbearing——"

Tzana was a telepath of no mean projective power herself, and she almost tore his head off before he could get his shields into action. A little stunned, he reached out and took her in his arms.

"Thank you, love," he murmured, holding her tight, "I really needed that. . . ."

## Epilogue

# MODULATION IN ALL THINGS

## I

THE YOUNG MAN in the student tunic motioned the emissary to be seated on a low wooden bench against the wall. The bench was the only furnishing the room contained except an altar in the center and a high case of ancient books.

"Please be seated," he said, "and when the Poet Jacinth has ended her meditation I will come and take you to her."

"You are allowed to speak to me in prose?" marveled the emissary.

"Certain Poets serving in the function of communicators between the Temple of Poetry and the people are excused from the vow of verse-speaking while on duty, Citizen," murmured the student.

"Very good. And you'll go with me to see this . . . this Poet?"

"Yes, Citizen."

"The Light be praised," said the emissary with satisfaction. "I wasn't happy about going by myself."

The student nodded to show his understanding. "One's first interview with the Poet Jacinth is not an experience to be taken lightly."

"Do you know her well?"

"I? Certainly not! She is female, and not of my household."

The emissary stared at the floor. "I see," he said. "I am sorry to have offended you, young Citizen."

"It's perfectly understandable," said the student gravely. "There are no traditions available to our people for dealing with a Poet of the Seventh Level who happens, the Light alone knows why, to be female."

"It hardly seems possible, even after all these years."

"And yet," said the student, "she has given our Temple the finest poems of this age. The Light does not err, you see."

"She is expecting me, of course?" asked the emissary.

The student frowned and studied his fingernails. "There was a messenger from the Council this morning," he said. "However, the Poet Jacinth has been in meditation since before dawn; there has been no opportunity for the messenger to communicate with her."

"What! You mean to tell me, man, that I must see her without any advance preparation whatsoever? Surely *she* is allowed to speak only verse?"

"Correct, Citizen ban-Dan."

"Then how am I—how are we to communicate?"

"I would suggest that you instruct the Poet Jacinth merely to listen, Citizen. That would be less complicated."

"What," breathed the emissary, "are they trying to do to me? What are they trying to *do?*"

The student chuckled softly. "Apparently," he said with a sly casualness, "the Council acted rather hastily on this question."

He was gone before the hot words that leaped to the emissary's lips could be spoken, and it was thoroughly apparent that Citizen ban-Dan's elaborate costume and impressive title had not impressed the student in the least. It was, of course, quite possible that the youth was the son of a wealthy family and accustomed to elaborate dress and ceremony. One could not tell with students, since they must all dress alike until graduation, regardless of their rank or the circumstances of their households.

There was therefore nothing left to do but wait and hope that he would do and say the right thing, and that the Poet Jacinth would see him soon, before he died of the heat.

The student erred, though, mused Citizen Arafiel ban-Dan, Emissary Extraordinary of the Legislative Council of the Planet of Abba. The Council had not acted hastily. The formal carrying out of the decision had perhaps been rather abrupt, but it had required three days of angry debate in the Council Hall before all the members had been convinced that it was really necessary—or for that matter, seemly—to disturb the Poet Jacinth with this problem.

Some of the Elder Members had been almost apoplectic with rage at the very idea. Indeed, the Member from the Sector of the Lion, a conservative and wealthy sector inhabited mostly by the old and sedate families of Abba's very rich, had threatened to retire from the Council if the others persisted in their intention.

"I say it is blasphemous!" he had shouted, his old voice trembling but still powerful. "Never in the history of Abba, never once in ten thousand years, has a female been involved in matters of government—that is the first thing! And even if the Poet Jacinth were not a female, even if that did not enter into this, the very idea, the very concept, of approaching a Poet of the Seventh Level, a holy being dedicated to a life of meditation and sacred composition, and asking that Poet to assist in a . . . a translation! Gentlemen, my gorge rises at the thought! On two counts, this whole plan is both blasphemous and obscene, and I will take the Sector of the Lion out of Abba if necessary before I will see it implemented by this Council!"

The emissary chuckled, remembering the old man's thunder and fire, ringing through the hall and all being duly noted by the robosecs on their aluminum pedestals. Nothing bothered *them*, of course, except noises that interfered with the performance of their duty.

It had been far from easy to persuade the old man—and many others who, though perhaps less dramatically vocal, sided with him on the question. It *was* a tricky problem, an unheard-of problem, with no precedent to follow, and a planet with ten thousand years of recorded history is accustomed to a heavy backlog of precedent.

Fortunately, they had had a powerful weapon on their side. The Elder Member from the Sector of the Lion was a wealthy man, and it was his credit disc that was being hurt by the situation that they wanted the Poet Jacinth to solve for them. Had it been anything else he would never have given in.

They had shown him the figures, patiently repeating, until he at last grasped the size of the sum that it was costing the planet of Abba—and the taxpayers of Abba, including himself as one of the heaviest-paying of those taxpayers—to provide the ten planet-colonies of Abba with enough edible protein to maintain their populations. They had reminded him, also, of the inevitable tragedy that faced Abba if the planet-colonies could not be made more economical to operate, to provide living-space for the ever-growing population that threatened to swamp the home-planet. They had shown him the bill that resulted from attempting to ship food out from Earth, the agricultural planet two galaxies away. And they had waved under his nose, finally, all the incredible advantages of that ubiquitous plant from the distant world X513, the *ithu* plant that was 93 percent edible protein, and that would grow anywhere, anywhere at all.

The old man had gasped and stuttered and spluttered, but in the end he had given in and the rest with him.

And now here *he* sat, Emissary of the August Council, all decked out in title and finery to cover the trembling man beneath, all alone with the task of justifying all this to the holy woman.

The Emissary sighed a mighty sigh. He was not a devout man. Religion, he felt, was a necessity, since it kept the females busy and out of trouble, and since it provided the Three Galaxies with those very useful people, the Maklunites, with their insane dedication to service and self-sacrifice. It was not for men, however, particularly busy men like himself. It was only at moments like this that he felt its lack. He gave the altar across from him an uneasy look, wondering, and then put the unworthy thought from his mind. After all, this was but a female he was to deal with.

When at last he was allowed to enter the garden of the Trance Cloister he found the Poet Jacinth sitting on a boulder underneath a small waterfall, waiting for him to speak. He stood before her, miserable, torn between his proper knowledge of the proper attitude to take when speaking with a female and the proper attitude to take when speaking with a Poet—never mind a Poet of the Seventh Level!—and she had smiled at him and nodded pleasantly and put him at ease with a casual couplet on the weather, and he had simply thrown tradition to the winds, since it failed him here, and began to speak.

"I come to you today on a strange errand, my lady Poet," he began. "It would perhaps be easier for both of us if you would hear me out before you speak."

She nodded, her lovely face solemn and attentive, leaning forward slightly to hear him better. It was most flattering. She reminded him of one of the youngest and most delightful of his concubines, and he warmed slightly to his task.

"You will know, of course," he said, "of the ten planet-colonies maintained by Abba. They are planet-surrogates, of course, artificial asteroids except for three that were once this planet's moons. On all of these ten planets, Poet Jacinth, there is a very serious problem, and it is the opinion of the Council that only you can help us find its solution."

She frowned, the perfect brows drawing together charmingly over her dark eyes, but she had remained silent as he had asked her to do. It crossed his mind that she was after all only as a young female, and that it was not going so badly.

The Emissary relaxed, and if he had been watching Jacinth he would have seen a smile tug at the corners of her mouth; but he was staring at the blossoms of the gaza trees and trying to keep his mind on the seriousness of his mission, and he did not notice the Poet's lack of respect.

"You see," he went on, "the living-space on these ten colony planets is desperately needed by our people. The crowding in our cities in such that, given the culture of our people, we cannot continue to support our population. You understand, of course, that the extended household of the family, with women's quarters and parks and garden, could not lend itself to blocks of buildings hundreds of stories high?"

She nodded charmingly.

"We must then send colonists, pioneers, to the new planets. And it is quite true that people, particularly the young people, and most particularly those young people who have not managed to win a place in any of the Professions except that of Service, are eager and willing to go as colonists.

"Unfortunately, most unfortunately, however, the colonies are not succeeding." A gaza blossom, a great green star covered with white pollen, fell onto his robe, and he brushed it off impatiently.

"Where was I?"

To his great pleasure, the Poet clapped her hands

softly, and immediately a student appeared with a tray of teas and wine, giving him a moment to recollect himself.

"Ah, yes," he said, as the student poured their drinks, "the colonies are failing. They are failing because on not one of the ten planets within the practical reach of our starships can any of the protein plants which we know of be successfully cultivated. This leaves us with three choices. One, we can send edible protein, grown on Abba, to the colonies; this we are now doing, but we are no longer able to bear the drain on our own resources. Two, we can send protein from Earth, at an incredible and unendurable cost; this would not help much longer even if we could afford it, since almost all of Earth is now given over to fruits and vegetables. Third, protein synthesis can be instituted by the colonists themselves. This, too, is being done; but with the best facilities available to our scientists, it has been impossible to devise any sort of synthetic protein that can be eaten with pleasure over any long period of time. The colonists rebel against the diet, they find it tasteless and boring, and the eventual result, if they force themselves to eat it for the sake of the colony, is an epidemic of psychosomatic stomach difficulties— all in their heads, certainly, but quite as destructive to their health as genuine organic disease. We have been at our wit's end, my lady Poet—until we learned, two years ago, of the existence of a protein plant which is both good to eat and economical to grow, and which can be grown on the ten colonies . . . or anywhere else, for that matter."

He glanced at his ring, saw with horror that there was little time left before the compulsory Hour of Meditation. He would have to get through the rest of it in a rush.

"This plant," he said, "comes from the world X513, whose inhabitants are known as the Serpent People. We need only establish communication with them, only learn how trade may be discussed! It is that simple—and this we have not been able to do. The greatest linguists of Abba have put two years of work into the attempt to learn this language, and they have failed. In every conversational attempt made so far, the Serpent People have left after only a few sentences, obviously deeply offended in some way, and it has only been with great difficulty that we have managed to obtain their consent to one more meeting, two months away, at the Intergalactic

Trade Fair. They do not come to the Trade Fair ordinarily . . . they are a curious, proud people, apparently quite self-sufficient on their world, not at all anxious to engage in any social or business activity. We do not understand them, and they either do not understand us or do not care to try."

She was nodding gravely, her eyes lowered, one hand idly playing in the falling water behind her.

"Poet Jacinth," he said earnestly, "the future of the colonies, and therefore the future of this planet, depends upon you. You are the greatest expert in language and the use of language that we have. There is no one else we can turn to now to determine how the language of the Serpent People can be used successfully. It is for this reason alone that we have interrupted your solitude and your meditation. We hope that you will appreciate the gravity of the situation. We hope you will forgive us."

He had come to an end at last, and he realized, ashamed, that he was trembling and covered with perspiration. There he stood in his almost-royal garments, he, a male of the Profession of Government, trembling like a frightened child before a slender little female in a red linen shift. It had been too much for him; never in his lifetime had he so exposed himself before a female, not even before his mother. He *had* bolted then, as he had wanted to do at the beginning, thrusting into her hands the packet of language tapes and the translations of the experts, and had almost run for the exit gate. There had been no time for her to speak, nor would he have waited to hear her if there had. His only concern was to escape, to get out of his borrowed finery and into his own clothing, and to spend at least half an evening in the company of his most humble and unintelligent concubine. He did not even know if he had succeeded or failed in his mission, nor did he care; he had done all that he could do.

## II

Jacinth went over the data for the third time, wonderingly. The linguists, all Poets of the Fourth Level, had done what appeared to her to be an excellent job. They had taken standard tapes beamed from X513, submitted them to computer analysis in the ordinary way, and seemingly had produced all the needed information. And yet it had not sufficed for communication.

Methodically she went over it again, one infopacket at a time. The answer had to be in there somewhere.

They had isolated and catalogued the consonant phonemes first. M, B, V, TH, Z, L, R, NG. Only eight? Two nasals, two liquids, three fricatives, and one stop. That wasn't much to make a language of, eight consonant phonemes. And only eight vowels as well, three nasals plus the standard five, A, E, I, O, U. A sixteen-phoneme system did not offer much complexity of sound, unless it was a tonal system, and the computer had ruled that out. It was a non-tonal.

Morphemes appeared to be all of one syllable, all simple in construction. It looked like a language constructed by a child, or an extremely language-naïve adult. It was curious that it should have offered difficulty at all, much less that it had stumped the best of their linguists for two years.

The Poet Jacinth wished, not for the first time, that she had someone to talk to. As a fully invested Poet, however, she was required to speak only in verse, and it did very badly for general discussion. Plus, she was not allowed to speak to females, lest she give them unseemly ideas of aspiring to the Profession themselves. And males did not care to talk to her because of the conflict between the attitude of paternal tolerance due her as a female and the attitude of humble reverence due her as a Poet.

She sighed and went to the corner of the room where her comset console stood, and punched the key for a servorobot. When it appeared she requested a small computer and a linguistics program tape.

She attached the computer hook-up to her comset, folded her slim legs under her, and sank down at the keyboard to work.

REVIEW LINGUISTICS PROGRAM, she tapped out.

In a moment the computer clicked and its side panel flashed the single word COMPLETED.

She then inserted the tapes prepared by the linguists for the language of X513, instructing the computer to indicate deviations from the basic information on the first tape. While the computer hummed its way through the task she examined once again the threedy image of a citizen of X513 that had been included with the data, marveling at the beauty of the being whose picture glowed in her hand.

She inserted the threedy slide in her comset and punched the PROJECT button, and at once the image was projected lifesize in the center of the room for her examination.

These were a very beautiful people, if the specimen whose image she saw before her was any example. It stood perhaps eight feet high, if "stood" was the proper word to use, since the Serpent People resembled a serpent more than any other creature with which Jacinth was familiar, and their manner of "standing" was much that of the King Cobra of Earth. How much length might be involved in the coiled body she could not judge, but eight feet was held upright. The entire body was transparent, except for what she assumed was the head, and appeared to be made of strung beads of translucent crystal, caught together at the top and twisted into a rope. Alternate strands of the "beads" were in shades of deep green and blue, the others were without color, and the whole meshed at the top in a sphere of opaque beads which must house the being's brain and whatever structures it might use for speech.

She studied it silently, knowing very well how deeply she might be in error in her analysis even of its physical structure. Perhaps the seeming "head" was really the creature's foot, or its stomach, or its sexual organs. Perhaps it was not one being but a colony, each strand representing a unique individual, all joined in some communal life-system. There was as yet no way of knowing, since no citizen of X513 had ever been examined by the Doctors of Abba, or of any other planet so far as was known.

Behind her the computer clicked again to signal completion of the review. She turned off the slide and went to examine the side panel. It said NO DEVIATIONS.

Very well, then. Her instinct had found no flaws in the analysis. Her computer agreed with her instinct. Therefore there *were* no flaws in the analysis, the translations of the language were as correct as could be asked, the representations of the sounds on the tapes were adequate, and no portion of the system violated the base theory of universal linguistics. Nonetheless, it had not been possible to speak to the Serpent People.

The Poet Jacinth smiled; it was a stimulating problem.

Somewhere in all of this there had to be the reason, the single explanatory factor that was being overlooked.

She left everything as it was so that she might return to it when she chose, deactivating the servorobots that would otherwise have put everything away for her, and went out into the garden.

Sitting on her favorite stone, the soft sound of falling water on her back, she closed her eyes and performed the ritual seventeen breaths, allowing all consciousness of her surroundings to leave her. When her relaxation of consciousness was complete, all that was left to her of physical awareness was the sensation that both the light and the water flowed through her being as freely as through the air, and she waited, patient and poised. Somewhere, there was something that she almost knew, something that she almost realized, something that was familiar about the language and about the problem, something that she remembered, almost. . . . She let the time pass, unaware, and waited.

And then she had it. She allowed her consciousness to return to her gently, becoming aware of the garden about her, noticing that it had grown almost dark and the air in the garden had turned cold and heavy with pale green dew. There would be people upset about her.

She rose quickly and went into her room, gathered up the materials and reactivated the servorobots, and then she began to dictate, ignoring the soft bell that called her to eat. She would eat when she had finished with this, after she was sure that she had captured all that she must say, before she became in any way confused. She began to dictate to the comset, watching with pleasure the intricate pattern of its dancing lights as it wrote down her words:

## TO THE COUNCIL OF ABBA:

When first I read the letters that you sent me
(and I am honored that you asked my help,
for in the service of this spinning world
lies my whole happiness and my satisfaction)
there came to me a sense that I had known,
somewhere before, a problem of this kind,
a feeling that I once solved such a problem,
as a child, perhaps? Certainly long ago.

And so I went at once into my garden
and let the Light direct me to your aid.

Then I remembered what I had forgotten.
I was a child, a small and noisy female,
spending my days in the courts of my lady mother,
and there had been summoned to the household ban-
harihn
a student of Poetry, ranking at Third Level,
whose single function was to teach us all to sing,
and some were to learn to play the singing strings.
And so . . .

The members of the Council were hushed as it came
to an end. It was, somehow, blasphemous that a female
should write so well; it was humiliating that she should
solve a problem that had baffled the greatest of their linguists; it was embarrassing that the solution should have
been so—once pointed out—overpoweringly obvious.

Emissary ban-Dan stepped to the center of the Council
Chamber and cleared his throat.

"Is it clear to all the Members," he asked, "just what
the Poet Jacinth is telling us? I should like to add that
her conclusions have, of course, already been checked
by the linguists and she is quite correct. There should be
no further problem in our communicating—after a fashion
—with the people of X513."

"But how is it possible," demanded a Member, "how
is it possible to speak such a language?"

The Emissary tried to think of some tactful way to
put his answer, but there didn't seem to be one.

"You are familiar with the colorful birds of Old Earth.
. . . the parrots?" he asked courteously.

"Yes," snapped the Member, "not that I see how that
is relevant."

"It is quite, quite relevant. You see, actually we *cannot* speak the language of X513. As members of the human
race, our human capacity for language does not allow
us to do so, any more than the parrots can speak Abban
or Panglish or any other human language. However—
again, like the parrots—we can learn to mimic, and, after
a fashion, to communicate. At least to the extent of trade,
which is all that we really need, you know."

Several Members were on their feet now, demanding

the floor. The Chairman recognized one, who demanded, his voice shaking, if Citizen ban-Dan was insinuating that these people of X513 were superior in intelligence to humans and that we were in effect too *stupid* to speak their language?

"Citizens," said ban-Dan worriedly, hoping the information the linguists had given him would get him through this without disaster, "I have said nothing of the kind. I said to you that their language equipment was *different*. Superiority has nothing to do with it. What reason has there been to believe that an alien race, totally nonhuman, would share the language equipment of humans? What sort of pompous, insular idea is that?"

The Council was silent, and the Emissary drew a deep breath and went on.

"I cannot imagine it, myself," he admitted. "But it is nonetheless true that the people of X513—who, by the way, resent being called 'Serpent People' since they are neither serpents nor people—the people of X513 speak their language with no difficulty whatsoever. Their infants speak it flawlessly by the age of three or so, just as do your Abban children. Certainly we of Abba shall not be able to speak it, however, without the aid of some sort of mechanical device."

There was still no comment, and he smiled to himself and went on. "I have here a set of threedies for projection prepared by the linguists. They have been hastily put together and are somewhat rough; I think, though, that they will make everything clear. In fact, I probably need show only the first."

He lifted his hand and on all sides of the Council Chamber a single image was projected. It was a huge circle, divided into eight equal segments, like the ancient dessert called a pie. At the center point of each segment there was a single vowel symbol; at the boundary between each segment, on the outside rim, there was a single consonant; and each segment was numbered.

"This is the whole solution, gentlemen," said the Emissary quietly. "There are, as you can see, only sixteen sound segments in the entire language.

"What the Poet Jacinth remembered was an incident from her childhood. A music teacher had been brought to instruct the women of her household. He had explained to them the manner of playing and singing a simple folksong in the key of A. Then he showed them how to play the same song in the key of E, and again in the key of C. The Poet Jacinth remembered her amazement and her disbelief; it seemed to her at that time that it could not be true that the same song, with the same words and tune, could be played in two different keys. And what struck her even more forcibly was that the same song, played in two different keys at the same time, created an unholy discord. She was so concerned about all this that it was necessary for the music teacher to explain to her the theory of keys and modulations, something that bored the other females of the household to such an extent that the child was punished for her curiosity.

"Citizens, this is a language that modulates; the analogy with music is exact and precise."

The Emissary glanced at his notes, hoping that he would not become as confused in reading aloud the example given him by the linguists as he had become in reading it to himself.

"Refer to the projected chart, if you please," he said. "Now, a given segment, say the syllable represented by the letters MEB—see them there, E at the point of the segment, and M and B at the boundaries—this syllable "meb" meaning roughly "table for eating," will transpose in another environment. For instance, if one says to a servant, 'Set the table for dinner,' the syllable must be rendered VITH, using the letters of the third segment of the circle, the one reserved for speaking to someone of lower status. If, on the other hand, one calls a beloved friend to join one at the table, the word must be pronounced MEB, using segment one of the wheel of letters. In an emergency, if the table was on fire, for example, the word would become THUZ, using segment four. If the table were a work of art, it would be referred to as a LER, using segment six, which is reserved for art and ritual.

"And so it goes, you see—there was nothing wrong with the translations of the words as prepared by our linguists, it's just that the 'word,' for the people of X513, is not a stable unit. It changes constantly, depending upon the social situation, the status of the speakers, and the like."

"Ah, yes," said the senior Member from the Sector of the Fish. "Now I begin to see. Let us say that one of our linguists heard a citizen of X513 referring to a necklace as a BLUB when speaking to an assistant. That would be the proper term for addressing someone of inferior position. Then when our linguist attempted to compliment the X513 person on the fine workmanship of the BLUB he would have addressed *him* as an inferior! No wonder they were offended."

"But surely," commented the Member from the Sector of the Panther-Ram, his beard quivering with indignation, "surely they should have been aware that one could make unintentional errors in a language of such incredible intricacy!"

"Why?" asked the Emissary. "They have no difficulty with their language, nor do they see it as one of incredible intricacy. They had no difficulty avoiding making errors in *our* language, apparently, either—why should they expect us to make errors in theirs?"

"It's utterly incredible," said the president of the Council, wearily. "You realize, I am sure, that the only way we will be able to speak this language is with the help of a computer; certainly we could not follow the modulations quickly enough without such help."

There was an embarrassed murmur through the Council Chamber and, to his horror, the Emissary heard mutterings in the back about the feasibility of applying the same principle to Abban in order to allow a modulation of the language that would be suitable for speech with females. As if life were not complicated enough!

"What we *can* do," the president went on, oblivious to the absurdities in the back of the room, "is have the linguists and computers compose for us an opening speech to be addressed to the people of X513 at the Intergalactic Trade Fair. This must be a speech which will unambiguously explain our linguistic situation to them. This is most important, since presumably once they understand what the problem is they will be more tolerant of our subsequent errors. And," he concluded, "we will have our protein source for the colonies. This is a great day for Abba, Citizens, and one to be long remembered."

Emissary ban-Dan raised his staff of office, requesting permission to speak, and the president nodded gravely.

"Citizen President," said ban-Dan, "what about the Poet Jacinth?"

"What about her? What do you mean?"

"Well, you realize what she has done—she has single-handedly solved the major problem of the future existence of ten planets. It is not as if the people of X513 would have been willing to discuss matters in the intergalactic gesture language, you know. The situation was *really* desperate, and it was the Poet Jacinth who came to our rescue. It seems to me that she should have some sort of reward, some recognition."

"She is a female, Citizen."

"But—"

"She has been signally honored, after all, in being allowed to participate in an activity of our government, something no female has ever done before."

"But—"

"No doubt our own linguists, had they had sufficient time, would have reached the solution without her assistance."

"But, Eminent Citizen, I still feel——"

The president leaned from his chair and shook a warning finger at the Emissary.

"Modulation—that is, *moderation*—in all things, young man! Moderation in all things!"

And he rang the gong to dismiss the Council.